John Henry Cliffe

Notes and Recollections of an Angler

rambles among the mountains, valleys, and solitudes of Wales

John Henry Cliffe

Notes and Recollections of an Angler
rambles among the mountains, valleys, and solitudes of Wales

ISBN/EAN: 9783337316341

Printed in Europe, USA, Canada, Australia, Japan

Cover: Foto ©Andreas Hilbeck / pixelio.de

More available books at **www.hansebooks.com**

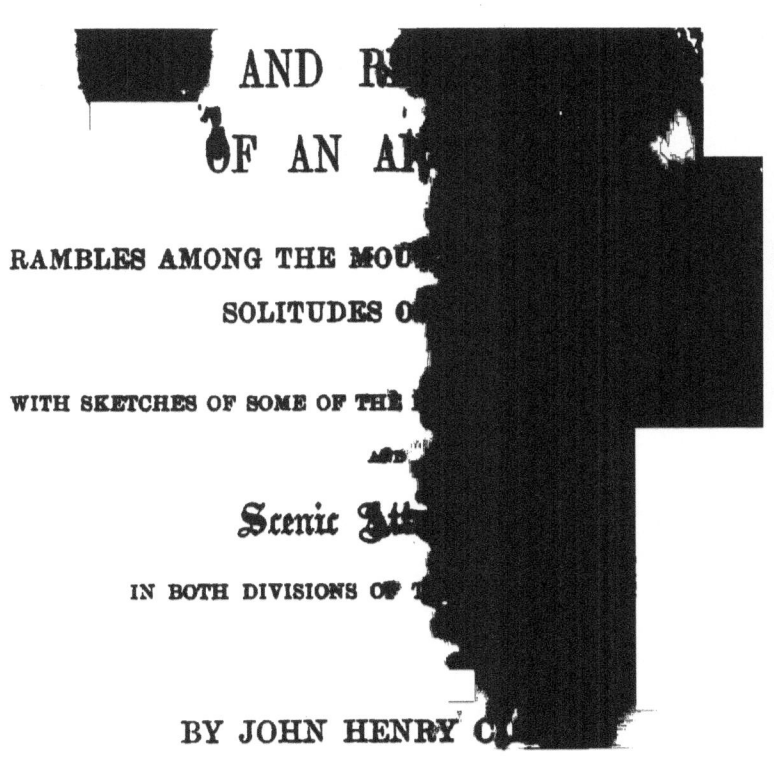

AND R...

OF AN A...

RAMBLES AMONG THE MOU...

SOLITUDES O...

WITH SKETCHES OF SOME OF THE...

Scenic At...

IN BOTH DIVISIONS OF...

BY JOHN HENRY C...

" LLYGAD A ALL WELED NATUR;
CALON A ALL DEIMLO NATUR;
A PHINDERFYNIAD A FEIDDIA
DDYLYN NATUR."

" AN EYE THAT CAN SEE NATURE; A HEART THAT CAN FEEL NATURE;
AND A RESOLUTION THAT DARES FOLLOW NATURE."

Old Welsh Triad.

LONDON:

HAMILTON, ADAMS AND CO. PATERNOSTER ROW.

BRISTOL: OLDLAND AND MAY. GLOUCESTER: E. NEST.

1860.

Preface.

THE following pages are the result of excursions into WALES, extending over a period of more than twenty years. Some of the wild solitudes described are entirely out of the beaten track; and, as far as I am aware, are either not mentioned, or only slightly alluded to in the various "Tours" and Guide Books.

In consequence of the increased facilities for travelling afforded by the railways, which have been constructed within the last few years, the influx of tourists and anglers into Wales has very greatly increased; and my object has been to point out, not only the *hidden* scenery of the country—if I may so term it—seldom explored, the wild mountain tops, the lonely *Llyns*, and the secluded *cwms*, but to afford the lovers of angling more minute particulars of some of the principal Fishing Stations than have hitherto ever been published. In short, I have endeavoured to set before the reader a truthful description of the several localities I have visited, and have described, with one or two exceptions, only what has actually come under my own observation. How far I have succeeded in my humble attempt, it will remain for the public to judge. I have also glanced at some of the antiquities of the country—"those silent memorials of a by-gone age"—more especially, the CELTIC and DRUIDICAL remains which have fallen in my way during my rambles amongst the wilds.

I may here be permitted to express my warmest thanks to the subscribers whose names are appended to this book, and more particularly, the obligations I am under to several kind friends for their zealous exertions to promote its success.

J. H. C.

Contents.

CHAPTER VII.

CHAPTER VIII.

CHAPTER IX.

CHAPTER X.

CHAPTER XI.

CHAPTER XII.

CHAPTER XIII.

CHAPTER XIV.

List of Subscribers.

Ackers, James, Esq. *Prinknash Park, Gloucestershire.* 2 COPIES.

Abbot, Henry, Esq. *Bristol.*

Addison, Thomas, F. Esq. *Gloucester.*

Allcroft, J. M. Esq. *Lower Wick*, near *Worcester.* 2 COPIES.

Allcroft, John, D. Esq. *55, Porchester Terrace, London.*

Allen, John, Esq. *Swansea, Glamorgan.*

Andrews, J. Esq. *Alderman, Gloucester.*

Ashbee, J. Esq. *Hillfield, Gloucester.*

Browne, Rev. Canon Murray, *Standish Vicarage, Gloucestershire.*

Bayly, Rev. F. T. J. *Brookthorpe, Gloucestershire.*

Barber, Rev. F. H. *Sedgborough*, near *Evesham.*

Brown, Rev. J. J. *Harlech, Merionethshire, North Wales.* 4 COPIES.

Burrup, J. Esq. *Gloucester.* 2 COPIES.

Boughton, Edmund, Sen. Esq. *Gloucester.* 4 COPIES.

Boughton, Mrs. Ann, *Kingsholm, Glo.*

Boughton, John, Esq. *Gloucester.*

Boughton, Mr. E. *Westgate Street, Glo.*

Bravender, J. Esq. *Cirences.* 2 COPIES.

Bravender, Miss, *Cirencester.* 2 COPIES.

Bravender, Thomas B. Esq. *Pembroke, South Wales.*

Brown, J. H. Esq. *College Green, Glou.*

Brown, H. Esq. *Weston-super-Mare.*

Brunsdon, Mr. Henry, *Swindon, Wilts.*

Brookes, S. P. Esq. *Tewkesbury.*

Billett, Mr. J. H. *Gloucester.*

Bundy, Mr. W. *Upton-on-Severn, Worcs.*

Codrington, Sir C. W. Bart. *Doddington Park, Gloucestershire* 2 COPIES.

Colt, Rev. Sir E. V. Bart. *Hill Vicarage*, near *Berkeley, Gloucestershire.*

Covey, Rev. Charles, *Alderton Rectory*, near *Cheltenham.*

Crawley, Rev. Charles Y. *Minor Canon, Gloucester Cathedral.*

Clarke, J. A. Graham, Jun. Esq. *Frocester, Gloucestershire.*

Castree, Josiah, Esq. *Alderman, Gloucester.* 2 COPIES.

Castree, Mr. Josiah, Jun. *Sandhurst*, near *Gloucester.* 2 COPIES.

Castree, Mr. Edward James, *Uckington*, near *Cheltenham.*

Clarke, J. Esq. *Gloucester.* 2 COPIES.

Coles, Robert, Esq. *Clifton, Bristol.*

Cooke, W. H. Esq. *4, Elm Court, Temple, London.*

Commeline, Samuel, Esq. *Gloucester.*

Calton, Mr. John, *Gloucester.* 2 COPIES.

Churchill, Mr. William, *Gloucester.*

Curtis, Mr. William, *Gloucester.*

Carrington, Mr. G. F. *Gloucester.*

Clift, Mr. Thomas, *Chacely Lodge*, near *Tewkesbury.* 2 COPIES.

Davies, Rev. James, *Moor Court, Kington, Herefordshire.* 2 COPIES.

Dupre, Rev. Edward, *Temple Guiting, Gloucestershire.*

Dent, John Coucher, Esq. *Sudeley Castle, Gloucestershire.* 2 COPIES.

Dowling, James Henry, Esq. *Barnwood*, near *Gloucester.*

Davies, Mr. Rees, *Chepstow, Monmouthshire.*

Davies and Son, Messrs. *Gloucester.*

Evans, Thomas, Esq. M.D. *Gloucester.*

Elliott, John, Esq. *Gloucester.*

Francillon, James, Esq. *Ryeworth House, Cheltenham.*

Fulljames, Thomas, Esq. *Hasfield Court*, near *Gloucester.*

Fryer, K. H. Esq. *Gloucester.* 4 COPIES.

Fletcher, George, Esq. *Shipton, Andoversford*, near *Cheltenham.*

Fowler, W. Jun. Esq. *Birmingham.*

Gist, H. W. Esq. *Temple Guiting, Glos.*

Goodyar, George A. Dinely, Esq. *Weston-super-Mare.*

Gwinnett, W. H. Esq. *Cheltenham.*

Green, Miss, *Gloucester.*

Green, W. H. Esq. *Gloucester.*

Houlditch, Rev. E. *Matson*, near *Glou.*

Hale, Colonel, *Wotton-under-Edge, Gloucestershire.*

Hopkinson, Edmund, Esq. *Edgeworth Manor*, near *Cirencester.*

Hunt, C. Brooke, Esq. *Bowden Hall*, near *Gloucester.*

Helps, Richard, Esq. *Alderman, Gloucester.* 2 COPIES.

Holt, Thomas, Esq. *Registrar, Glo.*

Heane, Captain Robert, *Saintsbridge*, near *Gloucester.*

Home, John, Esq. *Tewkesbury, Glo.*

Hughes, W. H. Esq. *Alderman, Glo.*

Hepworth, George, Esq. *Gloucester.*

Hanvey, J. Esq. *Gloucester.* 2 COPIES.

Heffill, Henry, Esq. *Diss, Norfolk.*

Hawkins, Mr. J. *Staunton Court, Worcestershire.*

Innell, C. F. Esq. *Gloucester.*

Jenkins, Arthur H. Esq. *Gloucester.*

Jew, Thomas, Esq. *Gloucester.*

Jenner, Mr. Daniel, *Gloucester.*

Knollys, Rev. Erskine, *Rectory, Quedgley, Gloucestershire.*

Knowles, Mr. William, *Gloucester.*
    2 COPIES.
Lechmere, Sir Edmund A. H. Bart. *The Rhydd Court, Worcestershire.*
Lechmere, Rev. A. B. *Hanley Vicarage, Worcestershire.*
Luscombe, Rev. E. K. *Minor Canon, Gloucester.*
Lovegrove, J. Esq. *Glouc.* 10 COPIES.
Lovegrove, G. H. Esq. *Gloucester.*
Lovegrove, H. J. Esq. *Glouc.* 2 COPIES.
Lovesy, R. W. Esq. *Cheltenham.*
Lord, John P. Esq. *Gloucester.*
Lucy, W. C. Esq. *Gloucester.*
Lloyd, William, Esq. *Gloucester.*
Lloyd, Mr. Charles J. *Machynlleth, Montgomeryshire.*   2 COPIES.
Lewis, L. W. Esq. *Tewkesbury.*
Lambley, Mr. C. *Bushley, near Tewkesbury.*
Monk, Charles James, Esq. *Eversleigh House, Cricklade, Wilts.*
Mutlow, Rev. W. W. *Rudford, near Gloucester.*
Marsh, R. Esq. *Cloisters, Westminster.*
Moore, C. W. Esq. *Tewkesbury.*
    2 COPIES.
Morris, J. C. Esq. *Swansea, Glamorgan.*
Manley, John, Esq. M.D. *County Asylum, Fareham, Hants.*
Maberly, A. W. Esq. *Gloucester.*
Meyler, W. Morgan, Esq. *Gloucester.*
Meyler, Thomas, Esq. *Taunton, Somersetshire.*
Mills, W. M. Esq. *Woolstone, near Cheltenham.*
MacDougall, P. Sheridan, Esq. *The Old Bank, Ross, Herefordshire.*
Matthews, William R. A. *Gloucester.*
Mann, Thomas, Esq. *Gloucester.*
Mann, Mr. William, *Gloucester.*
Nicks, William, Esq. Mayor of *Glo.*
Price, William Philip, Esq. *Tibberton Court, near Gloucester.*
Price, William, Esq. *Benhall, near Ross, Herefordshire.*
Price, Rev. H. T. *Gloucester.* 2 COPIES.
Pope, Rev. J. N. *Longdon, Worces.*
Powell, John P. Esq. *Pump Court, Temple, London.*
Phillpotts, A. H. Esq. *Severn Bank, Minsterworth, Gloucestershire.*
Prior, F. J. Esq. *Tewkesbury.*
Pigott, R. Esq. *Stoke Ferry, Norfolk.*
Page, E. Esq. *Smethwick, Birmingham.*
Pike, Mr. T. H. *Gloucester.*
Power and Son, Messrs. *Gloucester.*
Roberts, Rev. George, *Cheltenham,*   2 COPIES.
Rowlatt, Rev. J. C. *Gloucester.*
Reece, W. H. Esq. *Birmingham.*
Rees, William, Esq. *Llandovery, South Wales.*
Seymour, Rev. Canon Sir John Hobart C. Bart. *North Church, Herts.*
    2 COPIES.
Salter Rev. J. *Iron Acton, Gloucesters.*
Sevier, Rev. J. *Hasfield, near Gloucester.*

Sevier, J. Ford, Esq. *Maisemore, near Gloucester.*
Stone, Edward Gresley, Esq. *Chambers' Court, Longdon, Worcestershire.*
Stone, Guy, Esq. *Comber, County Down, Ireland.*
Smart, Mrs. 12, *Warwick Road, Maida Hill West, London.*
Smith, J. K. Esq. *Newnham, Glos.*
Smith, John P. Esq. *Gloucester.*
Smith, R. T. Esq. *Gloucester.*
Spier, Mrs. *Islington, Lond.* 2 COPIES.
Stafford, Mr. W. *Gloucester.* 2 COPIES.
Taylor, Rev. H. J. *Upton-on-Severn, Worcestershire.*   2 COPIES.
Taylor, Samuel, Esq. *Gloucester.*
Taylor, Thomas L. Esq. *Harleston, Norfolk.*
Tunstall, W. C. Esq. *Glouc.* 2 COPIES.
Trinder, E. N. Esq. *Cirencester.*
Thomas, W. Esq. *Swansea, Glamorgan.*
Thomas, J. Esq. *Bredon, Worcestershire.*
Trenfield, John, Esq. *Chipping Sodbury, Gloucestershire.*
Trenfield, William, Esq. *Gloucester.*
Timbrill, Miss, *Tewkesbury.*
Tooby, Mrs. *Gloucester.*
Vernon, T. G. Esq. *Tewkes.* 2 COPIES.
Worsley, Rev. P. W. *Canon of Ripon Cathedral.*
White, Rev. Robert Meadows, D.D. *Slimbridge Rectory, Gloucestershire.*
Watkin, Rev. Edward, *Cogenhoe Rectory, near Northampton.* 4 COPIES.
Witts, Rev. R. *Upper Slaughter, Glos.*
Whalley, G. H. Esq. M.P. *Plas Madoc, Rhuabon, Denbighshire, N. Wales.*
Weaver, T. Esq. *Mayor of Tewkesbury.*
Whithorn, Henry Kear, Esq. Alderman, *Gloucester.* 4 COPIES.
Washbourn, Buchanan, Esq. M.D. Alderman, *Gloucester.*
Whitcombe, John, A. Esq. *Gloucester.*   2 COPIES.
Williams, G. E. Esq. *Cheltenham.*
Whitehead, R. W. Esq. *Amberley Park, near Stroud, Gloucestershire.*
Wood, A. J. Esq. M.D. *Barnwood, near Gloucester.*
Wilton, Henry Hooper, Esq. *Whitminster House, Gloucestershire.*
Wilton, John W. Esq. *Gloucester.*
White, Joseph, Esq. *Nottingham.*
Waller, F. S. Esq. *Sandywell Park, near Cheltenham.*
Wilkins, W. Esq. *County of Gloucester Bank, Gloucester.*
Washbourn, Edward, Esq. *Gloucester.*
Walker, Charles, Esq. *Matson House, near Gloucester.*
Weatherhead, Mr. Robert, 15, *Old Jewry, London.*
Wheeler, Mr. A. C. *Gloucester.*
Williams, Mr. W. R. *Gloucester.*
Williams, Mr. James, *Hasfield, near Gloucester.*
Young, George, Esq. *Glamorgan Bank, Swansea.*

NOTES AND RECOLLECTIONS
OF AN ANGLER:

RAMBLES AMONG THE MOUNTAINS, VALLEYS, AND SOLITUDES OF WALES.

———•———

CHAPTER I.

TAL-Y-LLYN— SCENERY —ANGLING—LLYN MWYNGIL—LLYN-Y-CAE
—SUBLIME SCENERY—CADER IDRIS—ASCENTS TO SUMMIT.

> "There is a sweet accordant harmony
> In this fair scene—
> These pure waters, where the sky
> In its deep blueness shines so peacefully,
> A spot it is for far off music made,
> Stillness and rest."

NOTHING in landscape can exceed the soft beauty of the Vale of Tal-y-Llyn, nor is there a "nook" in Cambria more fascinating in its aspects, than this valley and its beautiful lake. It will not bear comparison in sublimity with some of the more profound and secluded recesses in Snowdonia, although it is not deficient in grandeur when viewed under the dark lowering clouds which frequently hover over the summits of the surrounding heights. Under peculiar lights—especially after rain, or in lowering weather —the exquisite colouring of the mountains on either side is perfectly magical; and the intimate intermixture of mountain and lake scenery—the contrast from the sublime to the beautiful— leave an impression upon the mind which time cannot erase. The finest view of the vale is unquestionably from Minffordd,

B

about one mile from the head of the lake. At this point the eye
embraces the waters of the Llyn, glistening perchance in the rays
of the sun, with the picturesque village and church at the lower
extremity embosomed amidst trees; whilst on the right the
"grey, tempest-worn, blasted steeps," of the lofty Cader Idris,
disrobing himself in the early morning of the heavy clouds which
have gathered over his brow, entrance the beholder and lift him
from "this world's turmoil into some planetary paradise."

> "I looked on the mountains—a vapour lay
> Folding their heights in its dark array;
> Thou breakest forth—and the mist became
> A crown and a mantle of living flame."
>
> HEMANS.

Sweet romantic Llyn Mwyngil! "lake of the charming retreat—"
how often in other days have we passed hours on thy placid
bosom in a summer's morn, when scarcely the lightest zephyr
ruffled the surface of thy limpid waters, surveying the tranquil
scene around us! Or with eyes uplifted to "that sun-glorified
beautiful blue arch of heaven above all." Who is there that
cannot find a place in his heart—if not preoccupied by worldly
feelings—for such a scene as this? or, after a lapse of years—
hallowed, perhaps, by the recollection of better and happier days
—refer to the tablets of his memory, and refresh the mind's eye,
by tracing anew the weather-stained and lichened rocks on the
sides of Cader Idris, or some picturesque group of wild homes,
nestling in one of the frowning cwms under his majestic heights.

Since the days of Captain Medwin, who gave to the world an
account of Tal-y-Llyn, some twenty-five years ago, in his very
clever and amusing work, "The Angler in Wales," this "angler's
paradise" has undergone a great change. From being a place
comparatively little known, it is now annually resorted to by
swarms of anglers, artists, and tourists; so that the "air of tranquillity" it formerly enjoyed is now frequently interrupted by
joyous troops of visitors, whose boisterous merriment clashes on
the ear of such as used formerly to delight in the quiet seclusion
of this "charming retreat."

Tal-y-Llyn has been described by various topographers, but by
none so truthfully or graphically as by the late lamented author

of "The Book of North Wales." As we have not, however, met with any very recent or accurate accounts of sport obtained in this romantic locality, we shall present the results of many years' angling experience on the lake and neighbouring localities, and such useful information to the sportsman as we may deem requisite.

In Captain Medwin's time, A.D. 1832, as we have already observed, Tal-y-Llyn, as an angling-station, was little known. A few gentlemen—several of them clergymen, and occasionally an artist or two—were the chief visitors.[1] The rude old-fashioned inn at Pen-y-bont—where the waters of the lake find an outlet, and form one of the sources of the river Dysynni—was the only accommodation the place afforded. This consisted of a parlour, somewhat dark and homely, but quiet and comfortable, and two or three small sleeping apartments. Anglers in those days were content to "rough it;" they were, in short, satisfied with humble fare and lodging. Some years afterwards, in the year 1844, the late Colonel Vaughan, of Hengwrt, the proprietor of the lake, built a neat and more commodious inn on the shore, at the southwest corner, near the village, and under the picturesque mountains Mynydd Rhinog and Craig-Goch. This was called Ty'n-y-Cornel inn. He also most liberally provided two boats for the use of visitors, and the inn was exceedingly well conducted by the landlord, the late Edward Corbet Owen. In former years we used to take up our quarters at the "Blue Lion," Minffordd, about one mile from the pool, where there was a comfortable parlour and bedroom, but of course we could not command the use of a boat. This "aunciente hostelrie" is mentioned by Warner in his first "Walk through Wales," in 1797. He also alludes to an eccentric character named David Pughe, who acted as guide to the "sublime mountain Cader Idris," and seems to have been highly diverted with "his pompous manner and affected dignity." The excellent accommodation and attention to "creature comforts" at Ty'n-y-Cornel, added to the flourishing accounts of the sport afforded there in the various guide-books and local prints, began

---

[1] "It is but a few years since this lake was first known, and was, I believe, first discovered by a descendant of the celebrated C——."—*Medwin's "Angler in Wales."*

to draw the attention of professors of the "gentle art" from Liverpool, Birmingham, Shrewsbury, and other more distant places; so that since that time (1844) Ty'n-y-Cornel has become a place of general resort by anglers of all shades; and since the introduction of the "iron road" to Shrewsbury and other places, they have been annually on the increase. Edward Corbet Owen, a most obliging, intelligent man, unfortunately for his widow and family, died in 1847; in 1852, Mrs. Owen, from poverty and inability to manage the house, was obliged to retire; and the present tenants, Mr. and Mrs. Evans,—who had been in the service of the late Sir Robert W. Vaughan, Bart.—succeeded her. The same year the inn was considerably enlarged and improved: several more bed and sitting rooms were added, and every comfort and convenience belonging to a good inn are now to be found there. Of course, a large increase of visitors brought with it a corresponding demand for boats, and there are now at least five or six boats on the pool. Such is a brief history of the rise and progress of the fishing-station of Tal-y-Llyn.

· Llyn Mwyngil—which signifies in English the "Lake of the Charming Retreat"—is nearly one mile and a quarter long, and in no part much exceeds a quarter of a mile in breadth; the average being about two furlongs and a half. It is, in fact, an expansion of the narrow vale; the waters from the surrounding mountains being confined and dammed up at the lower extremity, where they run off in a rapid stream at Pen-y-bont, under an excellent new bridge erected a few years ago. The tributaries to the lake are several small rivulets, the chief of which flows from a wild alpine Llyn high up under Cader Idris, called Llyn-y-Cae, the "Pool of the Chasm," supposed by some, from its profound depth, to be the crater of an extinct volcano. We shall have occasion hereafter to more fully describe this lake. These brooks absolutely swarm with small trout; and in summer, when these waters are clear and low, you may see legions of tiny fish, not larger than minnows, disporting themselves on the surface of the water. Indeed, the fecundity of the trout which spawn in these brooks is really wonderful. Were it not so, the lake would speedily be despoiled of its finny inhabitants by the numerous anglers who daily frequent it. Many trout and eels also fall a prey to black cormorants which haunt the lake. It is very amusing sometimes to watch these great birds sitting on the top of a rail or post by the edge of the pool, to dry their wings after their immersion. They put one in mind of a "spread eagle," their wings being extended to the full stretch. These birds cannot fly well until their wings are dry, and being disabled from this cause and a full meal, they not unfrequently fall victims to the gun.[1] The trout in Tal-y-Llyn, though of rapid growth, are rarely caught of great size; few, if any, during the season being taken much larger than one pound. The lake is *said* to contain two distinct species—the common brook trout, the average weight of which does not exceed three to the pound, although on some occasions fish are taken from half a pound to one pound and upwards; and the great lake trout (*salmo ferox*), which at rare intervals have been caught in the net, of seven or ten pounds weight. We cannot, however, aver to the truth of this; indeed, we doubt whether the true *salmo ferox* is to be found in any Welsh lake. They are plentiful in some of the lakes in Ireland and Scotland. We also find it mentioned in one of the guide-books, that a "trout weighing more than twelve pounds was found a few winters ago frozen under the ice." A few instances are recorded of large trout being taken with the fly, one of which occurred a few years since to the present worthy incumbent of the parish, the Rev. J. Pring, who informed us that he had caught at the head of the lake a fish weighing about four pounds; but it apparently was dying of old age, as it made very little resistance when he captured it. After a few hours it was found to be totally unfit for the table. We have lately read of another instance of a trout weighing three pounds and three-quarters being taken with the artificial fly. These captures are, however, extremely rare. There is little doubt that if Tal-y-Llyn was strictly preserved, instead of being

[1] It is a singular fact, but you never observe more than two of these birds on the lake at a time. Should one happen to be killed or disabled, another will immediately supply its place. They come from Craig Aderyn, the "Bird Rock," a striking scene on the banks of the Dysynni, a few miles from Tal-y-Llyn, where they breed, and at certain seasons it is thronged with them. Their appetites are insatiable. "Their craws are full of worms, that are continually gnawing for food."

free to the public, trout of much larger size than those now caught would more frequently be on the hook. The reason why trout grow with such amazing rapidity in this lake arises probably from the abundant feed they obtain on its mossy bottom. The Llyn is in no part exceedingly deep; its greatest depth is probably eight or ten yards, but its general average is only from six to twelve feet. No angler who knows the lake would dream of fishing in the deeps, which by the knowing ones are aptly named "the Sahara," or barren waters. Even on the most favourable days, you can hardly ever obtain a rise on this part of the pool. We have often been highly amused watching the "griffins" anchor their boat on this sterile ground, with little probability of even stirring a single fish. The quality of the trout in Tal-y-Llyn is very indifferent; they are best when cooked immediately after they are caught, and then, especially if you happen to catch some that are pinky in the flesh, they are palatable enough to hungry fishermen; but they are vastly inferior to the trout found in some of the lakes of Caernarvonshire and in the northern portion of Merioneth.[1]

Shore-fishing at Tal-y-Llyn is seldom pursued except in stormy weather, when it is almost impossible to manage a boat. You should provide yourself with a pair of Cording's wading-boots, and be able to throw your flies well in the eye of the wind, otherwise your labour will not be rewarded with much success. We never knew but one or two fishermen who frequented Tal-y-Llyn, who could boast of having obtained a good day's sport from shore. The fact is, that many anglers fancy the further they can throw their fly into a lake the better chance there is of a "rise." This is frequently a great mistake; some of the heaviest fish we have ever caught in the Welsh lakes have been actually taken almost on the "surf." You will almost always obtain the best "rise" on a lee-shore; this, of course, unless in a boat, involves the necessity of throwing against the wind. The reason is obvious : the wind drifts the fly to the shore, and instinct guides the finny

---

[1] The trout caught in Tal-y-Llyn are so exceedingly delicate that they will not bear transport to any distance, so that if you want to make presents to your friends, you must have them potted down and seasoned well with spice. In this state they are far more palatable than when cooked fresh.

tribe to the most favourable position to seize upon their prey.
Fishing from a boat is comparatively much easier to learn than
shore-fishing, and in a pool like Tal-y-Llyn, where the trout are
generally "free," even a perfect "greenhorn" may sometimes
obtain very fair sport. There is less art in the manipulation of
your flies, and if the lake is rough, the wind will carry them from
the boat with very little labour to yourself. We have said that
the trout in Tal-y-Llyn are generally "free," but, like most of
their congeners, they are sometimes fickle and capricious, and
occasionally even the most accomplished anglers make what is
called a "blank day."

Fourteen or fifteen years ago, very capital sport was frequently
obtained here. One or two first-rate anglers, who knew the "ways
of the lake" well, would take from six to nine dozen trout each in
a day, including some of large size. Although not "gluttons in
the matter of trout," we have also enjoyed some very good sport.
We find, upon referring to our journal, that in June, 1850, our daily
average amounted to from forty to fifty fish, some of which weighed
from three-quarters to one pound each. At the present time, we
have been informed, that from the increased number of boats, and
the still greater increase of anglers, the sport has fallen off. The
fact is, that the lake is so incessantly "flogged" that a great
many fish are scared, "pricked," and lost off the hooks, so that
they have not only become more wary, but are also not so plentiful.[1]

It may be useful to anglers fresh to the lake if we here impart
some information as to the best portions of it for sport. The
largest quantity of fish are undoubtedly taken at the lower end,
but the size, with of course exceptions, is much smaller than
those caught at the upper extremity. There is good fishing to be

---

[1] In 1855, during a stay of eight days at Tal-y-Llyn, we killed twenty-three
dozen, which makes an average take of thirty-four trout per diem; but it is
proper to add, that on the two last days the weather became bright, calm, and hot,
so that few fish were taken, and which reduced considerably the average of the
preceding six days, on two of which, we severally killed forty-seven and fifty-
three. During this visit the heaviest fish taken did not exceed fourteen ounces.
The chief elements of success on this lake, are clouds, plenty of rain, and a
brisk breeze. Without these concomitants, little is to be done.

obtained on both sides of the lake from Ty'n-y-Cornel until you arrive off a point on the south shore, which stretches into the pool at the narrowest part, and where the water for some distance is very deep. Nearer the head of the lake the water shoals off, and from the mouth of a rivulet which here flows into it, the source of which is in Llyn-y-Cae, larger trout abound than in any other part. The shore on the side of Cader Idris is the best. Indeed, there is good fishing near the edge on the north side to the mouth of the stream above-mentioned, especially off some tall rushes which fringe the margin. Near what is called "the island" good sport is frequently obtained. This "island" is seldom visible above water unless the lake is very low. It appears to be a large *carn*, or tumulus of stones, and is believed to cover the remains of some ancient warrior or chieftain. This is mere conjecture, but it certainly bears a resemblance to such a monument.

The principal flies in use depend on the season of the year. In the months of May and June—the best months—the March brown, red spinner, partridge and green, alder, pea-hen, cinnamon, Shaw's governor, fernshaw, and the cow-dung, are all excellent flies. There are many others occasionally used, according to the whim or fancy of the fishermen, all of whom profess to have a "wrinkle" or two; but, from long experience, we have had better sport with these flies at this season than with any others.

Llyn-y-Cae.

This solitudinous sheet of water, which lies in a deep hollow under the frowning precipices of Cader Idris, is of considerable elevation, and there are few lakes in Wales more difficult of access. It is called Llyn-y-Cae, which signifies the "Pool of the Chasm," or, more literally, the "Pool of the Enclosure." It is, beyond comparison, superior in sublimity and grandeur to any other mountain scene in Wales, with perhaps the exception of Llyn Idwal. The lake is bounded on the west side by the lofty rock—inaccessible from the pool—called Craig-y-Cae, one of the highest peaks of Cader Idris, the abode of the kite and the raven; the hoarse, ominous croaking of the latter bird, hovering around or perched upon the rocks far overhead, being sometimes the only break to the solemn silence which pervades this desolate spot. The north and south sides are also encircled by lofty precipices which, in some parts, run down sheer into the water, but you can generally approach the shores, although your footing is precarious, from the loose rough *débris* with which they are lined; with the exception, however, of the east shore, the descent to the lake is rough and difficult from all points. The easiest access is from the east, where the shore is low and open. A limpid, sparkling brook, abounding in small trout, issues from the Llyn, at the north-east corner, and, after a succession of picturesque falls, beautifully fringed and adorned with trees and coppice-wood, empties itself into Tal-y-Llyn, about three-quarters of a mile below Minffordd. Llyn-y-Cae, from its immense depth, which is said to be at least sixty fathoms (360 feet), has been supposed by some authors to have once formed the crater of an extinct volcano: there is, however, little, if any, evidence in support of this theory, as no remains or appearance of remote volcanic action at present exist. The lake is of small extent, not exceeding sixty or seventy acres; it is about three furlongs in length, and is about half that distance broad in the widest part from north to south. Two persons fishing on opposite shores can easily hold a conversation when the lake is calm. The pool swarms with trout; occasionally they "rise" freely, but are oftentimes exceedingly sullen, so much so, that some anglers— amongst others, Captain Medwin—have gone away from the lake with the impression that it contained no fish. Medwin says, "As I expected, I never got a rise, nor saw a fish move, though they tell me it abounds with trout." Fine bright hot weather we have generally found the most favourable time to visit Llyn-y-Cae, but even then you are often disappointed, and scarcely obtain a rise, or even see a fish stir. We have enjoyed upon several occasions some excellent diversion here. On referring to our journal of sport in 1847, we find that during a sojourn of a few days at Minffordd, we made two or three excursions to the lake with the following results:—"June 3d.—A lovely summer's morning, cloudless and oppressively hot. After an early breakfast, breasted the steeps of Cader Idris, *en route* to Llyn-y-Cae. A very slack

inconstant breeze at the pool all day: this is always the case at this place in hot bright weather. Fished round the precipitous rocks on the south side—some of which shelve down into deep water—as far as the 'island,' a small rock nearly surrounded by water, lying under Craig-y-Cae. From this rock the largest trout are generally caught. Notwithstanding the slack breeze, the trout for some time rose remarkably well, and at three P.M. I had nearly filled my basket, having killed fifty-three; average weight, nearly a quarter of a pound each: a few were six ounces. June 4th.—Weather as before; hot and cloudless, with a gentle breeze. Arrived at Lyn-y-Cae at nine A.M. A fair rise from about one to four o'clock, with the following results: Thirty-four trout of the same size as on the previous day. If we had had sufficient breeze in the forenoon, we should at least have equalled the previous day's take." One of the best day's sport we ever obtained at this pool was in July, 1849, on a very hot day, when there was scarcely the slightest ripple on the water. We chiefly took our fish from one spot, near the small rock or island under Craig-y-Cae. The "rise," while it lasted, was really astonishing, and, what was still more surprising, it occurred at noon, when the heat of the sun, from the confined nature of the place, was almost insupportable, as there was not at the time the slightest breath of wind. We extract the following account from our journal :—
"July 11th, 1849.—Ty'n-y-Cornel, Wednesday. Started for Llyn-y-Cae about nine o'clock A.M., *vid* the rocks above Minffordd. Dry, hot, and cloudless. A very slack breeze at the Llyn; notwithstanding, there was a most extraordinary 'rise' at the artificial fly. I caught forty-four in little more than an hour, which nearly filled my basket, and weighed about nine pounds. Returned to Tal-y-Llyn at half-past five." On this occasion we several times caught two fish at a cast, besides losing many others, the shores of the lake being steep and rocky. The trout here seldom exceed a quarter of a pound, but occasionally much larger fish are taken. During the same year (1849), about a week previously, a friend of ours staying at Ty'n-y-Cornel, caught thirty-eight in the course of a few hours, one of which weighed ten ounces. The weather at the time was rather unsettled and squally. As a general rule, little, if any, sport can be obtained

on a lake when calm, but there are exceptions, as on the occasion
we have referred to. The trout in Llyn-y-Cae are much superior
in quality to their congeners in Tal-y-Llyn; they are firmer in
flesh, and better tasted, but they are not so handsome in appearance. It is a singular fact, that trout in lakes high up in the
mountains will seldom "rise" after the sun is off the water; if
the day has been ever so good, the "rise" is over almost as soon
as the sun is hid by the mountain. This we have repeatedly
found to be the case at Llyn-y-Cae and elsewhere. It is seldom
that a good breeze gets to the lake in hot summer weather, unless
after a thunderstorm, when the wind frequently blows in violent
squalls from all parts of the compass. Medwin says, "it is so
abrité on all sides from the wind," that even when it blows hard,
scarcely a ripple affects its surface. This, however, is a great
mistake, an easterly breeze always ruffles the lake amply sufficient
for the purpose of the angler. On some parts of the lake the
fishing is both difficult and dangerous, in consequence of high
precipitous rocks, which afford a precarious footing, overhanging
the water : a slight stumble would precipitate the unfortunate
angler headlong into the pool. The best sport is frequently
obtained from these rocks, both in size and number, and it is
curious to observe the trout strike at your flies with lightning
rapidity from a great depth, which is the case on a sunny day, the
water, though green in colour, being in reality as clear as crystal.
The flies in use on this pool are similar to those at the sister lake.
We have found the alder and the fernshaw, in June and July,
sometimes very successful.

There are two ways of reaching this mountain solitude. The
nearest from Ty'n-y-Cornel is up one of the arms of Cader Idris,
that rises above Cwm Ammarch; the distance is about two miles.
Though a tolerably smooth road, the ascent is steep and toilsome,
and it will take at least one hour and a half to reach the lake,
unless you are more nimble of foot than the generality of pedestrians. There is another and a better way, we think, by following
the course of the brook at Minffordd. From the back of the
parsonage-house there is a very zigzag, precipitous path, which,
although it gives you "a breather," the "collar work" is not
nearly so great as the road up Cwm Ammarch. If you are staying

at Minffordd inn, this is by far the best and nearest way, as the distance is less than one mile and a half, which can generally be accomplished in an hour. From experience, we infinitely prefer the latter route, even if staying at Ty'n-y-Cornel, although the distance is about one mile and three-quarters farther.

The scenery at Llyn-y-Cae is very imposing; in stormy weather, when huge masses of dark clouds overhang the mountain and lake, the solemn gloom which invests this fine scene leaves an impression not easily effaced. Richard Wilson, R.A., the celebrated painter, made one of his finest and most effective pictures from Llyn-y-Cae. There is a fine engraving in line—now scarce—from the painting, by Earlom or Sharpe.

During the fearful storm which ranged around Cader Idris and its neighbourhood on the night of July 2d, 1849, and which fell with extreme severity on Llyn-y-Cae, immense quantities of large stones and *débris* were washed down from the sides of the mountains surrounding the pool, and the water, shortly before clear and pellucid, became much discoloured, and remained so for several days. This was an event of very rare occurrence, and shows what a deluge of water was poured into the lake. The walking along shore, previously difficult, became still more so, from the loose stones which strewed the narrow strand. This lake is seldom frequented, owing to the difficulty of the ascent to it. A few parties from Dolgelley, during the summer, and an occasional angler from Ty'n-y-Cornel, are its chief visitants.

Cader Idris.

" How bold its outline ! It looks like a seat fit for a giant, the monarch of mountains, or a Cybele with her rocky diadem ! "—MEDWIN.

"Dreaminess, grandeur, and sterility intermingled," is an appropriate description of this celebrated mountain, long erroneously supposed to be inferior in altitude to Snowdon only of all the Cambrian Alps. "How grand those mountains that shut in this gem of a lake[1] on all sides ! Look how it glows in the sunbeams like a sapphire ! How steep those rocks that seem to form ramparts—an inaccessible barrier to this little world ! Those specks

[1] Tal-y-Llyn.

are the wild flocks without a fold; see how they hang on the precipice, or cross in files the broken crags to pick up a scanty vegetation that here and there relieves their barrenness!" Such is a truthful and eloquent description of Cader Idris by Captain Medwin, although he falls into the vulgar error of describing the mountain as "the second highest in Wales." The comparatively recent trigonometrical survey by officers of the Board of Ordnance, and the accurate admeasurement of the altitudes from the sea-level of the loftiest mountains in the Principality, have established the fact that seven other mountains take precedence of Cader Idris, amongst which the least lofty is Aran Mowddwy, 2,955 feet, which rears its head into the clouds above the retired hamlet of Llan-y-Mowddwy, on the road from Bala to Mallwyd. The height of Cader Idris is 2,914 feet. But though inferior in altitude to its rivals in Caernarvonshire, few of the Cambrian hills display such picturesque effects, such colour, such "play of light and shade," as the "giant Idris." In lowering, stormy weather, the dark purple colouring of the stupendous precipices on the south and south-western sides present to the eye a sublime aspect, and few scenes in Britain afford a grander combination of lights and shadows—"elegance with grandeur"—than that seen from the road near Minffordd, where the beautiful lake of Tal-y-Llyn first appears to view on the left, with the little primitive hamlet of Dol Ffanog reposing near its borders in the vale below.

The ascent of this mountain, and a description of the scenic beauties from its summit, have been described by numerous authors, all of whom have more or less extolled the magnificent prospects unfolded to view, when seen in favourable weather. Warner appears to have ascended from Minffordd, taking the usual route to Llyn-y-Cae through Cwm-y-Cae; after skirting the south shore of the lake, he ascended the western arm or peak, Craig-y-Cae, and from thence to the summit, Pen-y-Gader, "the head of the chair." He descended to Dolgelley from the northern side, crossing what he calls a "flood of stones," but which has elsewhere been more accurately termed "an immense wreck of stones:" this is the route generally taken by the guides in the ascent from Dolgelley. Warner's account is so graphic that we are tempted to give a few extracts. After ascending the tertiary range by the zigzag path from Minffordd we have already described, he says, "Another half hour brought us into a second valley, called Cwm-y-Cay, a deep hollow in the heart of the mountain, shut in to the north, west, and south, by huge rocks of porphyry, and black perpendicular precipices of five and six hundred feet in height. The centre of this *coomb* is filled by a clear and extensive lake, of unfathomable depth, which, together with other surrounding circumstances, give the whole hollow the appearance of an ancient volcanic crater. This piece of water is called Llyn-Cay, and, according to the account of our guide, covers fifty acres, and is filled with trout of large size and exquisite flavour." If such was the case, the trout must have materially fallen off in size and quality within the past sixty years; but a tourist who places implicit faith in the marvellous tales invented by guides, even now-a-days, must be a disciple of "Mr. Verdant Green." The appearances of volcanic agency, alluded to in the foregoing extract, have long since been exploded by the researches of modern science. "We at length approached a dark, beetling rock, of shaggy aspect and tremendous height, which stands entirely detached from the neighbouring cliff. Its real name is Craig-Cay; but our guide, with a pardonable vanity, had christened it after himself, and assured us it was called Pughe's Pinnacle. . . . Arriving at the extremity of the pool, we began to ascend the western summit of Cader Idris, a task not only of labour, but of some peril also, it being a different route from that which travellers usually pursue: six hundred feet of steep rock, covered, indeed, with short grass, but so slippery as to render the footing very insecure. As we approached the top, the ascent became more abrupt, whilst the scene below us, of craggy rocks, perpendicular precipices, and an unfathomable lake, did not operate to lessen the alarm that a person unaccustomed to so dangerous a situation naturally feels. Our companion, the mountaineer, skipped on the meanwhile with the agility of a goat, and whilst we were dumb with terror, descanted on the beauties of Cader Idris and the excellence of its mutton. . . . At length, after excessive labour and repeated efforts, we gained the top of this noble mountain, and were at once amply recompensed for all the fatigue and alarm of the ascent. The afternoon was gloriously fine, and the atmosphere perfectly clear, so that the vast unbounded prospect lay beneath us, unobscured by cloud, vapour, or any other interruption to the astonished and delighted eye, which threw its glance over a varied scene, including a circumference of at least 500 miles.   To the north-west is seen Ireland, like a distant mist upon the ocean; and a little to the right, Snowdon, and the other mountains of Caernarvonshire.   Further on, in the same direction, the Isle of Man, the neighbourhood of Chester, Wrexham, and Salop; the sharp head of the Wrekin, and the undulating summit of the Clee hills. To the south we have the country round Clifton, Pembrokeshire, St. David's, and Swansea; and to the westward a vast prospect of the British Channel unfolds itself, which is bounded only by the horizon. . . . We now proceeded in an eastern direction, to the Pen-y-Gader, the highest peak of the mountain, passing on our left the saddle of the giant Idris (from whom the mountain receives its name), an immense *cwm*, its bottom filled with a beautiful lake called Llyn-Cair (Llyn-y-Gader, the 'Lake of the Chair'), and its sides formed by perpendicular cliffs, at least 1,000 feet in height.   Here we found a stone much resembling that volcanic substance called pumice-stone. . . . The air, notwithstanding the rays of an unclouded sun beamed upon us, was piercingly cold. . . . From the rude heap of adventitious stones which form what is called the bed of the giant, for several hundred yards the mountain wears a singular appearance.   Its surface is covered with a stream of rocky fragments of different magnitude, and lying in all directions, their shape for the most part columnar and quadrangular, and many being from three to seven feet in length.   All of them bear marks of attrition, and probably were thrown into their present rude disjointed situation by that great convulsion of nature, when 'the fountains of the great deep were broken up, and the windows of heaven were opened.'"

Warner's account upon the whole is accurate: the great features of Nature, how different from the mutability of the works of man, remaining the same after the lapse of centuries! But we must altogether protest against Warner's description of the "terrors" and "dangers" of the ascent.   The route he pursued is certainly more arduous and difficult than the path followed by the Dolgelley guides; but it is in no part dangerous, and it

has this advantage over the Dolgelley route, it is infinitely more
grand and imposing.   We have in the course of our wanderings
in Wales, now extending to nearly a quarter of a century, ascended
Cader Idris four times, on each occasion, except the first, being
highly favoured by the weather.   Our first visit was on the 20th
of June, 1840.   We ascended by the usual route, accompanied
by two friends, under the guidance of Richard Pugh, possibly a
descendant of the quaint guide that accompanied Warner.   The
day was fine, but the higher portion of the mountain was enveloped in clouds, which, however, occasionally sailed off from the
loftiest peaks, leaving them clear; the vapours which shrouded
the mountain came from the Irish Sea, the wind being due west.
We shall not attempt to give a minute description of our excursion.   We proceeded in the first part of the route along the old
road to Towin, as far as Llyn Gwernan, a small lake about two
miles on the road; here we turned to the left, and at once got
upon the tertiary ranges of the mountain, threading your way over
which is by far the most disagreeable part of the route.   As we
approached the region of the clouds, which were drifting along at
a brisk rate, impelled by a strong breeze, we passed by a Welsh
cottage, very primitive and ancient, supposed to be at least four
hundred years old, with scarcely any shelter to protect it from the
storms of winter.   Here, formerly, resided a dwarf of great strength,
named Cow Idris.   Upon entering the cottage, we were introduced
to an aged crone, reputed to be rich, and were struck with the
rude character of the furniture, seemingly very old, and the
sombre appearance of the apartment, not wanting, however, a
certain degree of comfort.   We then proceeded up a gradual ascent
until we at last reached the plateau on the west shoulder of this
hill monarch.   Warner calls this the "bed of Idris:" all we can
say is, that if the giant made this his couch, we fancy his bones
must have ached after a night's rest.

With the exception of the summit of Glyder Bach, a description
of which we shall give in a future chapter, we never passed over
such a rough, chaotic, confused "wreck of stones" as that presented at this point of the ascent, and we were really glad at last
to find ourselves in the narrow well-worn path which leads to
Pen-y-Gader.   Here we became enveloped in vapour, which

continued to boil and curl around us during the whole of the time
we remained on the summit, with the exception of a few brief
intervals.   We visited Pugh's hut, what he called his "hotel,"
a rudely built pile of large stones, but it was so damp and dark
in the interior, that we were glad to exchange our quarters for
the lee of the huge Carnedd, or mound of stones erected by the
Ordnance surveyors.   Here, although damp and rather cold from
the high wind, we were comparatively comfortable, and we proceeded to discuss, with infinite zest, the contents of a basket of
viands provided for us by our worthy hostess, Dame Walker, of
the "Golden Lion."   Whilst discussing our repast, we were
entertained with sundry anecdotes by our loquacious guide.
Amongst others he related an accident he had witnessed a few
years previously, to one of a party of Oxonians, on the abrupt
descent usually called Llwybyr Cadnaw, the "fox's path."   These
gentlemen, after arriving at the summit, had indulged rather too
freely in stimulants, and commenced "larking," and performing
sundry hairbrained tricks.   In descending the "fox's path," one of
them, more excited and daring than the others, started off at full
speed down the precipitous path, to the horror of his now sobered
companions.   He of course, from the impetus acquired by his
frantic career, lost all control of his movements, and fell headlong
on the slippery way, which consists of loose rolling shingle : he
was picked up insensible, severely cut and bruised about the
head, and with one of his arms broken : for some time his life was
in great danger.   At the foot of this path, a short distance to the
left, lies a small deep pool, called Llyn-y-Gader, the "lake of the
chair," and in its immediate vicinity, Llyn-y-Gafr, a shallow tarn
full of trout, and where sometimes there is good sport.   We
returned to Dolgelley by this route, following for some distance
the rapid brook which flows from Llyn Aren, a very small pool
under the precipices of Mynydd Moel.   We have before observed
that our view from Pen-y-Gader was obscured by clouds, but occasionally we had some marvellous peeps—magical glimpses—of
the surrounding country, which, although almost momentary, were
grand beyond description.   We were especially delighted with a
view of Bala lake, Llyn Tegid, which appeared the colour of a sapphire, the sun shining on its waters giving it this gorgeous effect.

Our second ascent occurred on the 10th of July, 1843. We left Dolgelley about 9 o'clock A.M. accompanied by a friend. The day was magnificent; large masses of clouds hung over the peaks of Cader Idris, but at a considerable elevation; the effects of light and shade and the occasional bursts of sunshine lightened up the landscape with marvellous tints. On this occasion we dispensed with the services of a guide, but we were for some time entangled amongst the copsewood which clothes the tertiary ranges, and it was not until after several hours of rather severe toil, that we finally accomplished the ascent. We were, however, amply repaid, and enjoyed the magnificent prospect spread around us on all sides with feelings of delight. After spending more than an hour on the highest summit, and taking a peep at the dark blue waters of Llyn-y-Cae, we commenced our descent over the "awful steeps" immediately hanging over the lake. We found our downward progress infinitely more difficult and fatiguing than the previous portion of our labours; but at last, after crawling and scrambling down one of the numerous deep rifts or gullies which serve as water-courses in wet weather, we at length stood on the northern shore of Llyn-y-Cae. We were *en route* for Aberystwith, distant at least thirty miles from this spot. Being on an angling excursion, we for the first time essayed our skill to move some of the "large trout," spoken of by Pugh, Warner's guide. Although disappointed in this respect, we succeeded in killing about a dozen trout of the size previously mentioned. After remaining at the lake for about an hour, we proceeded to the "Blue Lion," Minffordd, there refreshed, and proceeded to Machynlleth, where we arrived about 8 o'clock P.M. We afterwards travelled to Aberystwith, and arrived there, after a most exciting day, about half-past 12 at night, having walked a distance of not less than thirty-seven miles. Fatigued and thirsty from the length of the walk and the heat of the day, we were glad to betake ourselves to repose in one of the most comfortable inns in Wales, the "Gogerddan Arms."

On two subsequent occasions we have ascended Cader Idris from Tal-y-Llyn, proceeding up a wild dingle called Cwm Ammarch, on the north shore of the lake, and then turning to a path on the right up the steep sides of the mountain. This leads you to the precipices of Craig-y-Cae, and from thence the ascent to the summit is comparatively easy. There is from this point a fine bird's-eye view of Llyn-y-Cae, which lies in the deep hollow at your feet. This route is very arduous and fatiguing, but scarcely so difficult as the route from Minffordd.

Railway extension will in a few years render the fishing station of Tal-y-Llyn of easy access. The lake which lies under the southern side of Cader Idris, is in Merionethshire, and is seen to great advantage on the coach road from Machynlleth to Dolgelley. It is distant from these towns, either way, about nine miles; but, as the inn at Ty'n-y-Cornel is situate at the lower end of the lake, the posting distance is ten miles. There are two or three ways of reaching Tal-y-Llyn open to the sportsman; decidedly the most interesting is by rail from Shrewsbury to the Llangollen-Road Station, and from thence by coach to Llangollen, passing through its romantic and beautiful vale to Corwen, Bala, and its famous lake, Llyn Tegid, to Dolgelley; at the latter town you must take a car, the expense of which, including driver and turnpikes, is about 13s. 6d. The distance from Llangollen-Road Station to Dolgelley is forty-four miles. Another route—which on a fine summer morning is a very pleasant one—is from Shrewsbury by mail to Machynlleth. This road runs through Welshpool, Newtown, and Llanbrynmair, and is distant from Shrewsbury about sixty-two miles. The Aberystwith mail leaves the "Lion" hotel, Shrewsbury, at a quarter to four o'clock in the morning; and, though it is rather early to turn out, you are amply rewarded, if the weather is fine, by the magnificent views you obtain of the Breidden hills, at the base of which the road runs on approaching Welshpool, and by the verdant and richly timbered country, watered by the Severn and Vyrnwy, through which you pass. The mail reaches Machynlleth about twelve o'clock. Here you leave the coach, and, if you are inclined, you can proceed to Tal-y-Llyn at once; the distance and expense about the same as from Dolgelley. The disadvantage of proceeding from Shrewsbury by this route is, that you have not only more coaching by nearly twenty miles, but the inconvenience of a broken night's rest at Shrewsbury. The fare outside the mail is fourteen shillings.

CHAPTER II.

> " The wild brook babbling down the mountain-side,
> The lowing herd, the sheepfold's simple bell,
> The pipe of early shepherd dim descried
> In the lone valley ; echoing far and wide
> The hollow murmur of the ocean-tide."—BEATTIE.

MACHYNLLETH, " supposed to have been the Maglona of the
Romans," derives its Welsh appellation from being " a town or
place at the upper end of the flat or swamp." It is pleasingly
situate near the banks of the Dyfi, at its confluence with the rapid
mountain torrent, the Dulas. Surrounded by lofty mountains,
and sheltered beneath some broken rocks of picturesque outline
and varied tints, Machynlleth and its environs form a charming
summer retreat for the sportsman and the lover of Nature.

THE DYFI, in its course from Mallwyd to its confluence with the
sea, passes through one of the most pastoral valleys in Wales.
In some parts of its course the banks are adorned with wood, but
it is frequently open for some distance, the verdant meadows on
either side the stream, which is generally of crystalline purity,
being pastured with groups of cattle, some of the lords of which
are at times not a little troublesome to the angler. The Dyfi
has long been celebrated for the excellence of its salmon and
sewin fishing : as regards trout, we quite agree with the remarks
of a correspondent in a sporting newspaper, who advises his
readers to avoid " all inducement to loiter on the banks of the
Dyfi, which, as a *trout* stream, is a perfect 'sham.' " The river
for some years past has been strictly preserved from Mallwyd to
below Machynlleth, but tickets, to fish either by the day or year,

can be procured at a moderate rate during the season, which ranges from April to October.   Capital salmon and sewin fishing can occasionally be obtained, especially after "a fresh;" but in dry weather the river is so clear and low that the angler will find little or no sport.   Nevertheless, Machynlleth has always with us been a favourite locality.   If the river fails, you are in the neigh-bourhood of several excellent lakes, amongst which are Tal-y-Llyn, already described, Llyn Penrhaiadr and Llyn Bugeilyn.   The scenery in the neighbourhood of Machynlleth is exceedingly beau-tiful, and, on a fine summer's day, the peak of Cader Idris, and the Aran group of mountains stretching away to the north-east, loom out grandly beyond the estuary of the Dyfi, and form a most impressive background to the magnificent landscape which greets the eye of the traveller as he approaches Machynlleth by the road from Aberystwith.   The vale of Dyfi, from Mallwyd to Machyn-lleth, distant by road twelve miles, has also been much and deservedly admired; and though its clear and silvery stream does not afford much attraction to the angler, yet a ramble on its banks is very enjoyable.   Machynlleth possesses one great advantage, and that is a most excellent hotel, the "Wynnstay Arms."   Here the sportsman will find first-rate accommodation on most reason-able terms, and it is only doing an act of justice to the worthy landlord, Mr. Charles J. Lloyd, to add that, for comfort, civility, and attention, we know of no house in the Principality to surpass it.   Mr. Lloyd grants tickets of permission, gratis, to fish in Llyns Bugeilyn and Penrhaiadr, and also provides tickets for fishing the Dyfi.   Mr. Lloyd requires no eulogy from us; suffice it to say that his hotel during the season is crowded with visitors from all parts of the country, and in August and September there is great difficulty in securing accommodation.

LLANBRYNMAIR, a village about eleven miles from Machynlleth, is sometimes frequented by anglers.   There is a very comfortable inn there—the *beau ideal* of a fisherman's retreat—kept by Mr. Robert Lloyd, a brother of C. J. Lloyd, of Machynlleth.   This place is worth a visit, if only for the beautiful wooded valley watered by the Twymin, through which the road winds down a sharp declivity from Newtown to Machynlleth.   The Twymin is a rapid mountain stream containing both trout and sewin; when the water is in good order, fair sport may be obtained, but much of course depends on the weather : angling in this river, we believe, is *free*. The Twymin flows near the inn in its course to the Dyfi, which it joins about five miles from Machynlleth.

CEMMAES, a small roadside village, nearly midway between Machynlleth and Mallwyd, is also a favourite resort of anglers. · It contains a very comfortable inn, and is prettily situated near the banks of the Dyfi, which here certainly looks a tempting stream, as it gently meanders along the valley from its wild mountain-home. It is a somewhat singular fact, that Craig-Llyn-Dyfi, a small pool under the steeps of Aran Mowddwy, from whence the Dyfi rises in a solitary *cwm*, is destitute of fish, and is said to contain only lizards, and probably horse-leeches ! There are few mountain lakes that are without trout ; even in lakes on the summits of very high mountains trout are generally found. Where there are no fish, it possibly arises from the waters containing some mineral poison. We have heard it argued by anglers that the reason why the Dyfi is deficient of good trout arises from the poverty of its waters. It flows over a gravelly bed, and trout rarely grow to any size when such is the case. The largest trout are almost invariably found in rivers which flow through an alluvial soil ; the water becomes impregnated with rich deposits, which cause the fish to grow and fatten. It is certain that great difference as to size and quality occurs in many streams. Trout are plentiful in Devonshire, but they are generally small ; whilst in the Hampshire rivers many very large fish are found.

Llyn Bugeilyn,

the "Shepherd's Pool," is a dreary, sequestered piece of water, surrounded by turbaries, and might with propriety be called "the Lake of the Dismal Swamp." It is situated on elevated ground, amongst the bleak, barren hills to the north of Plinlimmon, about ten miles from Machynlleth, on the old mountain road to Llanidloes, "which is one of the wildest in the kingdom." This road, for a considerable portion of the way, is one continued ascent ; and as you approach the lake by a rough road which turns off to the right, you find yourself in the midst of the wilds—a portion, in fact, of the "Great Desert of Wales"—scarce a habitation or a human being to be met with for miles. On a fine summer's day, with the "blue above" partially obscured by clouds—for mountain scenery is comparatively tame under a cloudless sky—a magnificent landscape presents itself from this elevated spot to the north and east. The lofty summits of Cader Idris, the Aran range, the Arenigs, and a convulsed region of mountains, of various colouring, in every direction arrest the attention; and in the more immediate foreground, the beautiful estuary of the Dyfi, with "the dark blue sea" in the distance, sparkling in the beams of the morning sun, present a superb prospect which cannot fail to charm the senses of the admirers of nature. We know of few mountain scenes in Wales superior to that presented to the eye from the mountain road to Bugeilyn; nor are there many wilder or more desolate spots in the Principality than this locality. When the lightnings flash, and the thunder rolls in long continuous deafening peals, amongst the savage heights around, the dark waters of the lake rendered still more black and gloomy from the masses of heavy clouds and vapour which at such times hang over them, you might almost picture yourself standing by the shores of Avernus; or, like Sadac, by the "waters of oblivion." Warner, in his walk across the mountains from the Devil's Bridge to Machynlleth, thus describes the scenery. "After passing at the foot of 'huge Plinlimmon,' and climbing a steep hill, we were suddenly surprised with a magnificent mountain scene. The jagged head of Cader Idris and the solitary summit of Snowdon make conspicuous figures in the picture, which is rendered complete in its kind by the 'thousand subject hills' of all shapes and forms that rise around them."

Fifty years ago there were no trout in Bugeilyn, but "millions of horse-leeches." The pool was originally stocked with trout from the Rheidol by two gentlemen who happened to be grouse-shooting in proximity to the pool. For some years a war of extermination was carried on between the leeches and the trout; the latter, however, proved victorious, and no leeches are now to be found. The lake is preserved by Mr. Jones, of Garthmill Hall, Montgomeryshire, but leave to fish can be obtained from Mr. C. J. Lloyd. "Bugeilyn pool," says Captain Medwin, "is of an irregular form, shut in on all sides by drear hills and crags, and may be a mile and a half or two miles in circumference. The bottom is covered in many parts with weeds, and it is very shallow : the water of a pitchy blackness, from the peaty bed in which it lies, and islanded here and there by masses of rock." In June, 1832, Captain Medwin states, in his "Angler in Wales," that he one night obtained extraordinary sport from a small islet near the shore, taking a great many fish of two and three pounds weight with a white moth. The account is so marvellous that we are tempted to extract it. Having waded to "a small craggy island" he sat "on a fragment of the rock," and commenced to fish. "The night was calm, and only now and then a breeze following the curve of the lake gently ruffled its surface; the moon, like the wheel of a vast flaming chariot, rolled over the precipitous dark clouds, and between them some spare stars peeped dimly out : it could scarcely be called night. At the second cast I took a trout of three pounds; at the third, one on my stretcher and second dropper, and landed both. All the fish in the pool seemed collected round the place—the fools! The moths were irresistible in their attractions. . . . . The day broke, and found us with eighty-one fish, none small." An old fisherman, named Humphrey, accompanied him in this expedition. This account, however, we believe to be merely a fisherman's fable. A great many years ago —we were told by an aged angler from Llanidloes, whom we sometimes met at the Llyn—large trout of three or four pounds were *occasionally* taken ; but of late years, few, if any, are caught exceeding half or three-quarters of a pound. The lake round the sides is generally shallow, and the ground exceedingly boggy, so that unless you wade in for some distance you cannot obtain any sport. We found the best to be where the little rocky islet lies, celebrated by Captain Medwin's myth. The water here is tolerably deep near the shore, and the fish run larger. How Medwin *waded* to the island we are at a loss to conjecture, for it lies at some distance from the shore, and the water is apparently deep. The trout in Bugeilyn are of excellent quality, and are much esteemed. They cut quite red, but are not handsome, and have a dark inky colour, from the nature of the water they inhabit. The colour of their flesh probably arises from the nature of their food ; but it cannot now be owing to the leeches, for they have entirely disappeared. The trout are so exceedingly delicate that they will not keep good even for a day; they ought, in fact, to be eaten almost as soon as they are caught. The sport in this lake is very uncertain. If you happen to hit on the *right* day, and have the *right* fly, a good basket may be obtained. We have generally found the Alder and Fernshaw excellent flies in June, but much depends on the weather. We have had good sport in a thunder-storm, taking some fine fish; but, as a general rule, a nice warm grey day is the best, with the fog down on the tops of the hills. Of course a good breeze is indispensable, and, we may add, a pair of wading-boots. A portion of the southern shore is unapproachable, owing to a turbary: indeed, the shores generally are exceedingly wet and boggy. In consequence of the distance, Bugeilyn is seldom visited by anglers from Machynlleth, as it involves the expense of a car; you can, however, obtain rude accommodation for man and horse at a small farm-house about a furlong from the pool; but the car must be left on the moor, about half a mile off. You must provide yourself with a store of "creature comforts" at the "Wynnstay Arms," and with these necessaries you can make yourself tolerably comfortable, even in stormy weather. Some of the trout in Bugeilyn are *said* to be hog-backed; we, however, have never caught or seen any. It is most likely one of those legends common to several other lakes, and which have not any substantial foundation. Bugeilyn is a lake of limited extent; it is less than half a mile long, lying in a direction from N.W. to S.E.: in its broadest part it is little more than a furlong. About three-quarters of a mile to the north is Glasllyn, a small oval-shaped pool with a bright gravelly shore; it wears a smiling aspect in comparison with its gloomy neighbour. It contains no fish: it has been stocked several times, but the fish all die; so that its waters are supposed to contain mineral poison, probably lead. The road leading to Bugeilyn runs close to its southern extremity.

Llyn Penrhaiadr

is a wild secluded mountain lake about five miles to the south of Machynlleth. The road to it—and it richly deserves the praise—has been called "one of the gems of Wales." After proceeding for about a mile on the Aberystwith road, you turn off to the left up a romantic mountain glen, beautifully adorned with wood. The scenery reminds us of some portion of the "land of the waterfalls" in the Vale of Neath, and that is no mean praise. The road is better adapted for horseback than a car, as it is somewhat rough in places, but you can approach to within less than two miles from the lake: at this point you must leave your car at a farm-house, and proceed on foot. On your road, about three-quarters of a mile, you arrive at a waterfall over high precipitous rocks, called Pistyll-y-Llyn, the "Cataract of the lake," which is formed by the river Llyfnant, which issues from the pool above. There is a narrow winding path, which is rather formidable to look at—but it is neither difficult nor dangerous to climb—over the precipice which forms the waterfall. Most parties proceeding to the lake go this way, as it is much nearer than the path over the mountain to the left. The view of the waterfall in ascending the precipice is impressive and magnificent, especially after a fall of rain; the water comes tumbling over the tremendous shelving rock, and dashes in headlong fury into the *cwm* below. It is certainly one of the finest Falls in Wales, but is little known, which is surprising, considering its near proximity to Machynlleth. The Fall is destitute of timber, and, in consequence, has a naked unfurnished appearance. Nevertheless, the scene is exceedingly grand and imposing. In some respects Pistyll-y-Llyn resembles the waterfall at Aber, but it scarcely equals that romantic dingle from the bridge, that "wild and untouched scene," the view from which, backed by the majestic waterfall, presents to the eye one of the most charming vistas—full of the poetry and sublimity of Nature—which we ever remember to have seen.

Llyn Penrhaiadr is strictly preserved by Mr. Pryse, of Gogerddan, who keeps a boat on it; but Mr. Lloyd can give permission to gentlemen staying at the "Wynnstay Arms:" you cannot, however, obtain the use of the boat. The fishing on this pool is best in May and June, when capital sport can be obtained, the trout being large and tolerably free. We infinitely prefer Llyn Penrhaiadr to Bugeilyn; not only as regards distance, but also for sport. There are few more enjoyable trips from Machynlleth than a visit to this lake; it is wholly destitute of wood, and its aspect is wild, bleak, and desolate.

TOWYN is a "small, quiet, thoroughly Welsh town," situate on the sea-coast, about four miles from Aberdyfi, near the mouth of the river Dysynni, "one of the best salmon and sewin streams in Wales," if properly preserved. We know of few more delightful rambles than the road from Tal-y-Llyn to Towyn; as far as the celebrated "Bird Rock," Craig Aderyn, it is a succession of exquisitely beautiful and varied scenery, watered by the Dysynni, one of the sweetest streams in Wales. This is one of the most striking scenes in Merionethshire, and is best seen in the evening. The river scenery from thence to the sea, through a flat country, is tame and uninteresting, possessing no romantic features. The "Bird Rock" is so named from being the constant resort, in the breeding season, of black cormorants, hawks, and other birds of prey, whose discordant clamour adds much to the effect of this sequestered spot. There is a very excellent inn at Towyn, the Corbet Arms, where the angler or artist can obtain cheap and comfortable accommodation; we, however, in accordance with a general rule, have preferred private lodgings; although we have reason to believe that a sojourn at the Corbet Arms is much cheaper. Lodgings at Towyn, in summer, are much sought after by families, chiefly from the neighbouring Welsh counties, who come hither for the purpose of bathing, and, in consequence, are rather high. The sea-shore is uninteresting; but the sands, for miles, are firm and level, the air is pure and bracing, and the inland scenery, including Cader Idris and the Aran range of mountains, is really exquisite.

THE DYSYNNI, a river whose course may be roughly estimated not to exceed twelve or fourteen miles, is chiefly fed by several rivulets which take their rise from Cader Idris, and the mountains lying between Tal-y-Llyn and the estuary of the Dyfi. By some writers the small stream which flows out of Tal-y-Llyn is called the Maes-y-Pandy, "which joins the Dysynni a few miles below;" but we have always been informed that the true source of the Dysynni was in Tal-y-Llyn. It flows down the valley, until its course is impeded by a picturesque hill, called Gamallt, which here divides the vale, and is joined by a small brook at the retired

village of Abergwynolwyn—a sweet scene—and it then turns
abruptly to the north-west, until it receives a considerable tributary, which rises in a lonely nook not far from the west side of
Craig-y-Cae, and flows near Castell-y-Bere, an ancient Welsh
castle, situate on "a long isolated rock, much covered with
foliage," in the parish of Llanvihangel-y-Pennant. It then proceeds in a south-west course past Craig Aderyn, where it is
crossed by a rude bridge of one arch, called Pont-y-Garth, one of
the most beautiful and romantic scenes on its course. From
thence it flows to Peniarth, the seat of Mr. Wynn; receiving
several small tributaries, until it enters the flat, uninteresting
district called Avon Dysynni: here its waters are considerably
increased by its junction with the river Vathew, a few miles from
the sea, where the united rivers form a small sandy estuary, the
mouth of which is choked by shoals. The best part of the river
for angling is from Pont-y-Garth to below Pont Dysynni; but
there is tolerable fishing above to Abergwynolwyn, and to Tal-y-
Llyn, except where the banks of the stream are impeded by wood.
We, however, cannot speak favourably, of trout-fishing in the
Dysynni, although we are aware that it bears a high reputation.
We have fished it repeatedly from Tal-y-Llyn to below Craig
Aderyn, always with indifferent success. The trout generally run
very small, and it requires you, when the river is clear and low, to
keep as much out of sight as possible, otherwise you will scare
the fish. A gentleman who frequented Tal-y-Llyn some years ago,
sometimes obtained a good day's sport with the worm, when there
was a "fresh" in the river; occasionally he caught some large
trout, supposed to have run out of Tal-y-Llyn, of a pound and
upwards. We cannot give any results of this mode of angling,
which is, after all, a poaching sort of practice. Sewin, and sometimes salmon, find their way into Tal-y-Llyn; some have been
caught in the lake, with a trout fly, as large as twelve pounds.
Salmon-pink are frequently taken in the pool in April and May;
we have taken some even as late as the middle of June. Several
of the small streams which join the Dysynni afford sport after
rain; the best of which is the Vathew. Good fishing was formerly
obtained in Llyn Cregenan, a small pool, situate near Capel Arthog,
on the coast road from Towyn to Dolgelley; but it has been much

injured, of late years, by poaching with the "board" or "otter."
As an angling station, except perhaps in April and May, we cannot recommend Towyn. Poaching is carried on in the rivers to a
great extent, and immense quantities of salmon and sewin are
taken by the net. "Two tons of salmon are said to have been
caught in this river in a fortnight!" What a noble stream for
salmon this would be, if properly preserved!

PENLLYN POOL.—We can only speak from hearsay of this lake,
which is a shallow expansion near the sea-shore of a small brook
which runs along the old road to Machynlleth. The trout are
said to run large—two or three pounds—but are exceedingly
wary. There are boats on the pool. Medwin, in the "Angler in
Wales," describes the lake as full of red trout, but says "they
were the most cunning of all the finny tribes," rising freely, but
'short;" so that you might fish all day, and probably longer,
'without catching more than one or two brace. A successful lure
was, however, practised, some years ago, by Lord ——, a most
accomplished angler, who obtained splendid sport by adopting the
expedient of "tipping" his "dropper" with a *gentle;* by this
means he killed a number of good fish, some of them exceeding
two pounds. This story, however, appears to be somewhat on a
par with the account of the moonlight sport at Bugeilyn with the
white moth.

There used to be an excellent fisherman and guide living in
Towyn, named Jonas; and such of our readers as purpose a visit
there, will do well to avail themselves of his services: we believe
his terms are five shillings per day. The distance from Machynlleth
to Towyn is fourteen miles; an omnibus, we think, runs three
times a week in the summer, between Newtown and Towyn,
passing through Machynlleth and Aberdyfi. The old mountain
road, which turns off at Penal, four miles from Machynlleth, saves
about two miles, and the pedestrian will find this a very pleasant
route in fine weather.

MALLWYD.—It is scarcely possible to overrate the romantic
position of this retired village, surrounded by wild mountains,
thus forming a vestibule to the deep repose of the pastoral vale
below. In quiet, picturesque beauty, few places in Wales excel
this "green and sylvan temple;" the "bowered river" serpentines

through the valley, enriched with the "sublimest near prospects of mighty mountain slopes," some way up whose bases, nestling in sheltered nooks, farm houses of antique and primitive appearance, the patriarchal abodes of the "mountayne men," peep out here and there amidst their umbrageous retreats. To the studious and contemplative, to the disciple of the "gentle arte," Mallwyd —as the poet Gray eloquently observes in his description of Monmouth — " is the very delight of the eyes, and seat of pleasure." The scenery here is exquisitely beautiful near the close of a fine summer's day; we scarcely remember a more delightful prospect than that from the inn looking across the valley, when the misty top of Rhiw Penhairn, a lofty spur of the gigantic Aran, became suffused with the roseate tints of, the departing orb of day. Warner, in his " Second Walk through Wales," thus describes the scenery of the Vale of Dyfi, in this locality:—" The course of the Dyfi presented us with many striking beauties of landscape. The valley consists chiefly of rich pasture, inclosed by lofty mountains, some of which, particularly the Aran, vie in point of height with the most lofty in Wales; through this the river rolls, a silent majestic stream, in sweeping meanders, ornamented here and there with neat cottages, the humble but happy abodes of content and peace. . . . . You cannot picture to yourself a more quiet, peaceful, picturesque situation than that of Mallwyd—an inclosed vale, round which enormous mountains shoot into the clouds in the form of an amphitheatre; shading it from the heats of summer, and affording shelter from the blasts of winter. At a small distance from the village, an alpine torrent rushes through the valley, tumbling amid large masses of disjointed rock, beautifully circumstanced with trees and shrubs pendent over the rapid stream. . . . . The distant view of the village, with the spire of its humble church, enlivened the scene, and brought to our remembrance those pastoral pictures which live in the elegant descriptions of classical bards."

The site of the venerable church—described as "one of the prettiest scenes in the Principality"—is remarkable for a grove of yew-trees, several of enormous girth, said to measure from fifteen feet to twenty-seven feet in circumference. Yew-trees are frequently seen in old churchyards; probably, in olden times, they were considered as types of the imperishable spirit, after the body had been consigned to the tomb; but various conjectures have been made as to the origin of the custom. Thus, the bard in Ossian, speaking of two lovers, says, "Here rests their dust, Cathullin! These lonely yews sprang from the tomb, and shade them from the storm." Yew-trees may be considered as appropriate companions to the grave: their dark sombre melancholy aspect clothed with perpetual verdure, render them "a happy emblem of that eternal youth and undecaying vigour the soul will enjoy," when "this corruptible shall put on incorruption, and this mortal be clothed with immortality."

Mallwyd contains an excellent inn, much resorted to during the spring and summer by anglers and artists; it is, in fact, one of the neatest and most comfortable hostelries to be found in the Principality. The landlord, Mr. Lloyd, is, we believe, a brother of Mr. Charles J. Lloyd, of Machynlleth.

As an angling station, Mallwyd enjoys an excellent reputation; but the Dyfi is certainly not a good trout stream—as far as our experience goes—in any part of its course. Trout are more plentiful in the river above Mallwyd, and about Ddinas Mowddwy; but they are generally small, and after the months of April and May, little sport is to be obtained. The stream is frequently low and clear during the summer, and the banks are besides much impeded by trees and bushes. The Dyfi is joined by a large brook—the Cleffion, or Clyvion—above Mallwyd, which has its source in Cwm Tafalog; a deep valley lying between two ridges of mountains called Mynydd Cemmaes and Craig Coch, part of the long range of hills which stretch to the north, from Plinlimmon to the Berwyn mountains. It runs near the road leading from Mallwyd to Garthbibio and Cann Office, for several miles. It flows into the Dyfi below Pont-y-Cleffion, which crosses it on the road to Ddinas Mowddwy. It is said to contain good trout. Warner, in his description of this district, gives the following account of an excursion up the banks of this stream, the scenery of which is singularly romantic:—"The character of this brook is so truly alpine, that we could not omit tracing its course for nearly two miles, during a great part of which it rushes through a profound channel, hollowed out of a black rock by its own incessant agitation, and rendered additionally dark by deep overshadowing woods. . . . The best mode of seeing the beauties of a mountainous country, is, without dispute, to follow the meanders of its rivers." Few will be inclined to deny this opinion, but few tourists follow Warner's example.

There are several waterfalls and cascades in this neighbourhood worth a visit. At Pont Fallwyd, near Mallwyd, there is a cascade of singular beauty, which has been much and deservedly admired; in its way—heightened as it is by striking accessories—it is one of the most lovely scenes on the Dyfi.

THE COWARCH, a small brook which rises high up in the Aran group, near Craig Cowarch, joins the Dyfi between Llan-y-Mowddwy and Ddinas Mowddwy. The Cerist, a more considerable stream from the same range, runs near the Dolgelley road for several miles, and falls into the Dyfi at Ddinas Mowddwy. These streams contain trout, and good bottom fishing may be had occasionally—especially after rain. We believe they are quite free to the angler.

Aran Mowddwy, and the Source of the Dyfi.

Aran Mowddwy is the highest mountain in the county of Merioneth, being forty-one feet higher than Cader Idris. It is a stiff pull to the summit, but the view from it is very extensive, and, under proper lights, magnificent in the extreme. The best ascent is from Blaen Pennant, which is about two miles from Llan-y-Mowddwy, on the road to Bwylch-y-Groes, the "Pass of the Cross," on the road to Bala. "Here," observes an eloquent writer, "an extraordinary rock scene presents itself on the left hand, which commands a mountain prospect so sublime as to set verbal description at defiance. The mountains, retiring as it were from each other, sink their craggy heads, and form a sweeping hollow, consisting of beds of rock so curiously arranged as to give no inaccurate idea of a stupendous flight of stairs. This depression suffers the eye to range into Cwm Aran, the awful recesses of one of the mightiest mountains in Wales. Thither we went, and were filled with astonishment at the objects before us—enormous rocks heaped on each other, vast hollows scooped by the gigantic hand of Nature, their dark precipitous sides many hundred feet in depth, frowning upon the little valleys that were crouching at their feet."

On leaving Blaen Pennant, you turn to the left up a profound *cwm*, savagely grand in its aspect—in many respects rivalling Cwm Llan in Snowdon;—a road here leads you to the infant Dyfi, hurrying into the vale below from the wild solitudes whence it has its birth in the lonely mere under the frowning steeps of the mountain. By following the course of the stream you cannot mistake your course, which leads you up Llaith Nant, at the head of which to the right lie the dark waters of the Llyn. Here rest awhile, for you have had a sharp incline to surmount, and survey the dreary savage aspect of the scene around, scarcely exceeded in wildness by any in Britain. The sides of the mountain above the lake are inaccessible, being rifted and hollowed into "vast semicircular *cwms*." You must proceed to the north up a *cwm* to the left, called Erw Ddafad Ddu, which leads to the plateau upon which the highest peak is situate. Here stands the "huge carnedd" erected by the Ordnance surveyors, the materials of which are said to have been furnished by the "men of Ddinas Mowddwy, who, on hearing that Cader Idris was about six feet higher, were determined not to be outdone by their Dolgelley neighbours, and by this means raised their parochial hill to a surpassing height." Cader Idris, however, as we have before observed, is about forty feet lower than Aran Mowddwy. There is a grand view of Bala Lake—Llyn Tegid—and the magnificent group of mountains in the background, the Arenigs, the highest of which is 2,809 feet. The scenery on the ascent of Bwlch-y-Groes has been pronounced among the grandest and most remarkable in Wales, passing through "an immense ravine of great depth and length running through mountains whose declivities are nearly perpendicular." The view of Bala pool on the descent of the other side of the mountain is exquisite: indeed the road for nearly the entire distance between Mallwyd and Bala—twenty miles—is a succession of scenes of wild beauty, which rivet the gaze of the pilgrim as he slowly passes through one of the most magnificent *Bwlchs* in Cambria.

D

CHAPTER III.

HARLECH — LLYNS — SCENERY — MOEL GOEDOG — LLYN VEDW—
BRITISH CAMP—LLYNNIAU TECWYN — SCENERY—LLANBEDR—
LLYN CWM BYCHAN — GLYN ARTRO — CRAIG-Y-DDINAS — CWM
NANTCOL—DRWS ARDUDWY.

> " In this track,
> How long soe'er the wanderer roves, each step
> Shall wake fresh beauties, each short point presents
> A diff'rent picture ; new, and yet the same."

ANTIQUE romantic HARLECH! situate in a land which affords so
much to interest the imagination, and possessing no ordinary
claims to the attention of the artist and the antiquary ; "with its
grand skeleton of a famous fortress, its round towers lifted to the
sky by a noble promontory *not* jutting over the wild sea waves,
but distant a good mile of sand hills, its precipice of a street,
green and uncouth with slabs of the mountain's own rock starting
through the soil ; its houses of oldest thatch bristling down lower
than a man's head ; the doors half a man's height high, dark
within, weather-stained without, and lichened all over as damp
rocks in the thick of woods," such is a truthful picture of
Harlech in its decay, not as it was in the wars of the Roses,
when the unfortunate Margaret of Anjou found a temporary
asylum within the walls of the majestic castle after the blood-
stained field of Northampton.   Harlech possesses also claims to
the notice of the angler.   Amongst the lofty mountains in the
background, stretching from Maentwrog to Barmouth, are
numerous solitary Llyns ; and though on some of them there
is little to attract in the shape of sport, yet the wanderer will
find ample gratification in exploring these "eyes of the mountains,"
the shores of some strewed with the relics of a remote age, the
scene of many a bloody skirmish and ruffianly atrocity.   This
portion of Merionethshire is one of the most barren solitudinous

regions in North Wales. To the English tourist it is almost a
terra incognita; but such adventurous travellers as have dared to
dive into its hidden *cwms* and recesses, unaided and alone, with
the Ordnance Map and pocket-compass as guides, have enjoyed, as
we have done, the wonders of Nature, and exclaimed in the
fulness of their hearts, "These are thy glorious works, Parent of
good!" The mountain scenery in the neighbourhood of Harlech
is said to resemble, in many of its external aspects, the savage
sterility of the *Sierra Morena;* it has, however, in the midst of
this wildness, some gleams of beauty, a few lovely and romantic
valleys, set like oases in the desert, to one or two of which we
shall in due time conduct our readers. Before we proceed with a
description of the scenic features of the Harlech district, we
cannot omit to notice the quiet village of Llanbedr, distant from
Harlech about three miles on the road to Barmouth. At this
retired spot there is a comfortable inn, "The Victoria," kept by
a brother and sister named Richards; and although in the long
course of our rambles in various parts of the Principality we have
often met with comfort and civility, yet for liberality and real
kindness we never found anything to equal the host and hostess
of this humble village inn. To the angler especially, the place is
perfection; and many pleasant and profitable days have we passed
there in bygone years. We must, however, for the present,
return to Harlech, and take up our quarters at the "Blue Lion,"
a well-conducted hostelrie—where excellent board and lodging
can be obtained early in the season—overlooking the time-worn
remains of the castle, and possessing from its terrace one of the
noblest prospects in the British Isles. On a lovely summer's
morn, here you can behold "the disrobing to the sun of all
Snowdon's mountains. . . . . Here are to be seen high up
Snowdon, peculiar tints of umber red, mixed with grey and blue,
the former ferruginous probably, but whispering to fancy of
ancient volcanic ruins. The chaotic lofty view of their confused
groups—the rolling blackness of the mist, itself now become
their most exquisite beauty—is food for lofty phantasy."[1] Seaward, perchance, the eye rests on a white sail, midway between
Harlech and Criccieth, with its ruined castle, perched like its

[1] Mountain Decameron.

nobler sister on a weather-stained rock, and frowning over the blue and sparkling waters. To dilate worthily on all the varied natural beauties of Harlech, and the adjacent locality, would require a far more gifted pen than ours.

Harlech Castle and its history have been so often described, that it would be foreign to the purposes of this work to recapitulate what is now so well known to every reader of Welsh history and topography. We shall therefore proceed to examine the interior of the hill country in the neighbourhood—comparatively little known to the tourist—and to conduct the sportsman to some of the numerous llyns in the more immediate vicinity, offering occasional passing remarks on the scenery and antiquities most worthy of notice. The number of lakes, great and small, in the Harlech and Llanbedr district, amount to about twenty-four. For the sake of convenience, we will confine ourselves for the present to those most easily reached from Harlech, reserving an account of the southern portion until we arrive at Llanbedr. Merionethshire contains more lakes than any other county in Wales; it is difficult to furnish a correct list, and still more difficult to afford accurate data as to sport. Changes occur year after year, we fear for the worse, and so long as the mining population are allowed to poach *ad libitum* several of the finest pools, so long will the chances of sport annually diminish. As far as we can ascertain, we are warranted in asserting that there are at least sixty-six llyns in the county; some of them mere ponds, others destitute of fish. Out of these we have visited upwards of half; a few of them, it is perhaps not too much to say, we are more intimately acquainted with than any other Englishman living. It may be convenient *en passant* to enumerate, *seriatim*, the northern position of the group, reserving further particulars, route, etc., for the present.

Llynniau Tecwyn Uchaf and Isaf are situate in the mountains in the parish of Llan Tecwyn, on the mountain road to Maentwrog from Talsarnau. Llyn Vedw, near Moel Goedog, about four miles north-east of Harlech; Llynniau Eiddew Mawr and Vach, one mile and a half north-east of Llyn Fedw; Llyn Caerwych three-quarters of a mile north-west of Llyn Eiddew Vach; Llyn Lennerch, or Llenyrch, a small pool one mile to the east of Tecwyn

Uchaf; Llyn Dywarchen, three-quarters of a mile north-east of
Llyn Eiddew Vach. These comprise nearly all the lakes worth
notice in the vicinity of Harlech. We have not included Llyn
Cwm Bychan, because although that fine pool is sometimes visited
from thence, it more properly belongs to the Llanbedr series, and
is from that village of easy access. All the pools above mentioned
lie in the mountainous district at the back of Harlech, bounded
to the east by the wild, sterile, desolate rocks called Craig Ddrwg
and Craig Wion. To the south of these mountains, and divided
by the Bwlch Tyddiad, the Rhinog range commences, which
stretches across the country in a southerly direction to the
estuary of the Mawddach. Within the recesses of this secluded
district, there are at least thirteen llyns, at nearly all of which
we have had sport. More of these hereafter.

Llyn Eiddew Mawr,

a beautiful sheet of water about four miles and a half from
Harlech, lies a short distance to the west of Craig Ddrwg: its
length from north to south is about half a mile; its breadth in
the widest part not much exceeding a furlong. The road to
it, especially after rainy weather, is rough and fatiguing; in
no case should we advise a stranger to proceed thither without a guide, unless provided with the Ordnance Map. It is
our intention, however, to furnish such information as may
enable the angler, should he feel inclined, to wander into these
wilds by himself, and to dispense with the services of a guide.
We may premise that the routes to the lakes in this locality are
none of them nearer Harlech than four or five miles—some are
six or seven—and the ascent to them is arduous. The road to
Llyn Eiddew, the "Ivy lake," commences with the hills behind
Harlech, at the summit of which you get into the old road to
Maentwrog, which you follow nearly to Moel Goedog; and just
beyond y Fonllef hir, "the long loud cry"—supposed to have
been a battle-field in early pagan times—the road branches off in
the direction of Trawsfynydd: here the road bends to the north-
west, and by means of the map and keeping to the west, you cross
over a wild morass, with scarcely any path, until you reach the

shores of Llyn Eiddew. A brook discharges itself from the
lake, and runs in a southerly direction towards Llyn-Cwm-Bychan,
the river from which joins it above Dol Rheiddiog. If the brook
is full of water, you may soon fill your basket with small trout.
The scenery around Llyn Eiddew Mawr is "untameably wild,"
presenting an aspect similar to scenes Salvator Rosa loved to
depict ; and the view of Y Craig Ddrwg is as savage and desolate
as imagination can conceive. The antiquary will here revel in
some very interesting remains of an ancient British town, until
lately unknown, which lie on the north-west shore; and there
are also several Druidical circles. The trout in Llyn Eiddew are
small, but of excellent quality, and from the middle of May until
the middle of July, the sport is sometimes good ; as many as from
six to eight dozen may be taken in a day. The best side to fish
is the west shore, but sport may be obtained on either side. The
walking round the lake is tolerably easy. The flies most successful in summer are the Alder, March Brown, Coch-a-bonddù, Black
Gnat, and the Fernshaw. Altogether, although fatiguing, this is
a very delightful excursion. LLYN EIDDEW VACH lies about half
a mile to the north, and the trout here are much larger—some of
half a pound and upwards are taken; but as the pool is of very
limited extent, there is not much fishing ground, except near a
steep rock on the east side. From thence, about one mile to the
north-west, lies

Llyn Caerwych,

on higher ground, in a very bleak and dreary country. Here there
is little or no protection from the weather. Some years ago, we
obtained excellent sport on this pool for about two hours : there
was a very cold wind from the north, with occasional showers of
sleet; but the trout rose freely, and we caught about forty of a
quarter of a pound and upwards. Very large trout are said to
exist in this lake, but few, if any, are ever taken with the fly.
This is a vulgar legend, which attaches to almost all lakes where
small fish only abound. An ancient British camp, called Bryn
Cader Fawr, about three-quarters of a mile to the north-east, is
worth a visit. It is laid down on the map.

𝕷𝖑𝖞𝖓 𝖁𝖊𝖉𝖜.

The route to this Llyn from Harlech is the same as to Eid-dew Mawr, as far as Y Fonllef hir. Instead of proceeding to the west, you advance in the direction of Moel Goedog, "the woody hill," the western shoulder of which you cross, and from thence to the pool it is three-quarters of a mile in a north-east direction. The distance from Harlech is about three miles and a half. Some years ago Llyn Vedw was full of very large, handsome trout, and fine sport was frequently obtained. The only drawback was a margin of weeds nearly a rod's cast from the shore, which rendered it difficult to manage a large fish, if hooked outside this barrier, and in consequence you frequently broke off. We once caught several fine trout in this pool, upwards of one pound each, with a small blue gnat. On the same day, June 3d, 1848, we saw several fish that could not be less than three or four pounds each, disporting themselves on the surface, but they rose far out of reach. A fisherman from Llanbedr, named Roberts, informed us that he once caught a large basket of fish in Vedw, by means of a raft formed of a five-barred gate; this he launched, and drifting across the middle of the lake, was enabled by this contrivance to throw over and capture some very good trout. Llyn Vedw can scarcely be called a lake; it is about one furlong and a half in length, and about one furlong broad. It supplies a corn mill, and there is a sluice on it to regulate the supply of water. It appears deep towards the centre, but the water round the sides is shallow and weedy. A fine sunny day, with occasional clouds, is best for this pool. Were it for nothing else, Llyn Vedw is well worth a visit, for the very exquisite view of Snowdon, the Traeths, the highlands on the south-east, and the peninsula of Lleyn, "land of the bleak, the treeless moor," which you obtain from the summit of Moel Goedog. From hence, on a fine, clear summer's evening, especially before or after rain, the lights and colouring of distant objects are perfectly gorgeous and entrancing. It must be seen —it cannot adequately be described. Moel Goedog was anciently a fortified British post; traces of the circular double-walled camp

are very perfect.   The Roman military roads to Maentwrog and
Trawsfynydd pass near this eminence.   From its name, it was
doubtless formerly covered with wood, and it must have been a
strong fortification.   This Roman road branches off to Trawsfynydd, near Y Fonllef hir; several of the ancient mile or direction
stones still exist, and there may also be seen some Druidical
circles.

Llynniau Tecwyn Uchaf and Isaf.

These lakes may be reached by car or ponies.   You proceed
along the road to Tan-y-Bwlch, as far as the village of Talsarnau; here you turn off to the right, up a steep, rough
mountain-road, past a farmhouse called Cefyn Trevor Fawr,
passing on your right Llyn Tecwyn Isaf, which lies in the
bottom, to a farm at Llantecwyn, where you can put up your
horse and car.   From thence there is a good road to Llyn
Tecwyn Uchaf, which runs along the entire length of the pool.
This is a very beautiful lake, nearly half a mile long, and
abounds with small trout.   Llyn Llenyrch, a small lake about
one mile to the east, is also full of trout, many of them large;
but these lakes are much poached by the quarry men from
Ffestiniog and Maentwrog, and the trout are therefore shy.   We
believe there are no trout in Llyn Tecwyn Isaf, but there are
perch and eels.   We cannot recommend the fishing in these pools
as far as our own experience goes, but the excursion to them is
highly interesting and romantic.   The scenery at Llyn Tecwyn is
really exquisite; a wild dingle leading to the Harlech road also
deserves exploring.   A small horseshoe-shaped pool, called Llyn
Dywarchen—which must not be confounded with its more
celebrated namesake in Caernarvonshire—lies in the wilds about
two miles and a half south of Llyn Llenyrch.   This tarn is also
poached by quarry men; we have heard it contained good trout,
but we never tried it.   In completing our description of these
lakes, we should strongly recommend the angler to confine his
attention, if bent upon sport only, to the Eiddews and Caerwych.
Vedw is at best very uncertain, and of late years much fallen off,
probably from poaching.

Llanbedr.

Some of the most enjoyable days of our life have been passed at this retired spot. We prefer it infinitely to any other fishing station in North Wales, not on account of sport, for that is now somewhat indifferent, but for the variety of walks and excursions it affords, all of them most delightful. The vicinity of Llanbedr is also rich in Celtic antiquities. Probably few districts exist in Wales where there are so many evidences of an ancient people, and the superstitious relics of a dim age. Some of the Druidical Cromlechs and Cistvaens are amongst the finest which at present exist in the Principality; and there are also several fortified British camps, with *cyttiau*, which are well worth inspection. Most of those interesting antiquities we have visited in our solitary wanderings in quest of sport. The botanist and geologist will also find an ample field for exploration at Llanbedr; many rare plants are to be found in the hill district, and the geological formation of the country is also well worth inspection. A sketch of the geology of the county of Merioneth appeared in the *Mining Journal* in 1849. With the Ordnance Map, the "Book of North Wales,"—which is an excellent guide —and a few odd numbers of the *Archæologia Cambrensis*, no man need be at a loss to find out the antiquarian curiosities of the district.

Brothers of the "gentle craft," allow us now to introduce you to "mine host and hostess" of the Victoria. Picture to yourselves a hearty welcome, a cordial shake of the hand, a glass of *cwrw*, brewed of the best, and tapped in anticipation of your visit; many kind inquiries after your health, absent friends, &c.— such is the reception you are likely to meet with at this paragon of village inns. The only fault to find is, that you are nearly "killed with kindness"—you absolutely revel in "creature comforts." Fancy yourself sitting down to dinner at 8 o'clock P.M. after an exciting day in the wilds, and a walk of twenty or twenty-five miles, with the appetite of a cormorant, and finding a repast fit for a prince. Broiled sewin and trout, roast lamb, chickens, ducklings, young peas and potatoes, besides a variety of excellent sweets prepared by the kind hostess, who does not appear happy unless you make a vigorous onslaught on these delicacies *seriatim*. Fancy yourself reclining in an easy chair, in a dreamy state, after your gastronomic feats, with a balmy weed between your lips, or meerschaum filled with choicest Latikia, between whiles sipping from a glass of carefully compounded whiskey punch, or "cold without." Such is life at Llanbedr. Are we not justified, then, in asserting that there is not such another comfortable hostelrie in Wales ? But a truce to these reflections; it is time that we should shoulder our basket, grasp our rod, and forthwith conduct our brethren of the angle to the various Llyns in the adjacent hills; and, with one exception, a pretty tug it is to reach them. What can be more spirit-stirring —what can produce more buoyant feelings—more real enjoyment —than a walk amongst the wild mountains, or by the side of one of those merry, joyous, flashing streams which fill the moorland solitude with the melody of their rippling waters ?

The lake and river fishing at Llanbedr may be divided into at least four or five separate excursions, which for the sake of convenience we will classify as follows : First, Llyns Cwm Bychan and Pryved; second, Llyns Prefeddau, Cwm Howel, and Ybi ; third, Glowlyn and Llyn Dû; fourth, Llyns Irddyn, Bodlyn, and Dulyn; fifth, Cwm Nantcol. Besides these there are several brooks and rivers which sometimes afford sport, or are worthy of a visit for their picturesque beauties. In point of interest none of these can bear comparison to the wild secluded

Cwm Bychan,

—"the little hollow,"—and its fine lake. The road to this romantic *Cwm*, through Glyn Artro, is excelled by few in Wales. Watered by the river Artro, sometimes a mighty torrent, which flashing from its mountain source—the surplus waters of Llyns Eiddew and Bychan—runs joyously through this enchanting valley, and pursues its way to Llanbedr, after which, running through a marsh, it flows into the sea at Mochras. The road to Llyn Cwm Bychan is tolerably good ; a car can be driven, if required, to an old farm-house near the head of the lake, in imme-

diate vicinity to Bwlch Tyddiad, through which it is supposed
was an ancient Roman road, probably from Heriri Mons, or
Castell Prysor; the stone steps, or rather stairs, said to be laid
by Roman soldiers, are still tolerably perfect. The best plan,
however, is to leave the horse and car at Dol Rheiddiog, and
crossing the Artro over a rude bridge proceed over some meadows
leading to the lake on foot. Imagination can scarcely depict a
more savage, desolate scene than that surrounding the waters of
Llyn Cwm Bychan. In some of its sterner aspects—" when the
waters rage and swell, and the mountains shake" amidst "clouds
and darkness"—we question if there is a more impressive picture
of naked sterility and barrenness in the Principality. Some
attempts have been made to relieve the desolate appearance of
the place at the southern side of the lake, by planting larch and
spruce fir amongst the rocky *debris* which cover the shores; but
these attempts to beautify are sadly obstructed by the goats and
sheep, and an occasional conflagration of the heather.

Llyn Cwm Bychan is nearly half a mile long from east to west;
it is however narrow, scarcely exceeding two furlongs. It is
supposed to be of immense depth in the centre, and from the
colouring of surrounding objects, the waters assume a dark,
melancholy aspect. Generally speaking we have met with very
indifferent success at this pool—the trout are shy and sullen as
the waters they inhabit. Few of large size are ever caught: we
have taken some of half a pound; these are a beautiful yellow-
bellied trout, small head, with bright red and black spots. Some
of them, when cooked, cut red, and are delicious eating. In May
and June, the salmon fry, which at that season abound in the
lake, sometimes afford excellent sport; they are about six ounces
in weight, and of a bright gray colour. The best day's fishing
we ever had on this pool, was on a very wet day,—June 1, 1848
—when we caught forty-four, including several very fine salmon
pink. Fish on the south side, near and under Craig-y-Saeth, "the
crag of the arrow," which is one of the finest scenic features of
the lake. When the Artro is full, after heavy rains, some fair
trout fishing may be obtained; but after leaving Dol Rheiddiog,
the banks of the river are so clothed with trees and coppice wood
as to prevent throwing the fly. We should imagine, however,

that an expert "bottom" fisher, either with salmon paste or worm, would obtain good sport in some of the deep pools which occasionally occur in the river's progress through the umbrageous dingle.

Llyn Pryved,

the "lake of the worm"—why so named we could never learn—is a small, narrow, sequestered pool, of very difficult access, in a hollow on the east side of Craig Wion. You can ascend to it from the farm-house already mentioned, at the head of Cwm Bychan. We know of few harder pulls. From the experience of several visits, we found the trout in this pool exceedingly shy, and from the paucity of "rises," both to the natural and artificial fly, we should imagine not very numerous. The trout are, however, generally large, and when they do rise, you are almost sure of hooking them. We find in our journal, that on June 20, 1848, we caught six trout weighing four pounds; we did not begin to fish until half past four P.M.; this was the best sport we ever had on the lake. Llyn Pryved is the most dangerous lake to fish that we are acquainted with; the sides are bluff and precipitous, and the rocks being covered with a tall growth of heather serves to conceal many deep and dangerous crevices, and unless you are very careful, you might easily break your limbs. On the road to the pool, you pass near a small piece of water called Llyn Twr Glas, "the lake of the Blue Tower"— a singular cognomen—it lies about one third of a mile to the north-west. It contains no fish. Though we cannot report very favourably of Llyn Pryved, yet we strongly recommend an excursion to it; the healthy pleasurable excitement of the walk amongst these desolate wilds, fully compensates for lack of sport. An old fisherman at Trawsfynydd once informed us that he had caught, at different times, several large fish in the llyn of from three to four pounds each, which he said "fought horrid savage." All we can say is, that this lake has every appearance of containing monster trout.

Glyn Artro.

We must now return to DOL RHEIDDIOG, "the meadow of the salmon," and proceed down the lovely vale of Glyn Artro, rendered still more lovely by the contrasts it affords to the scene of desolation we have just emerged from. The valley for several miles is clothed with wood, and the river as it dashes along, peeps here and there out of its mantle of green, rolling merrily away over rocks and stones. The lofty spurs of Rhinog Vawr enclose the scene on the east, and sometimes you "have grand breaks: islands covered with red and purple heaths," standing out from "abysses of foliage." The air is "breathing incense" from the perfume of the whitethorn, honeysuckle, and other sweet-smelling wild flowers; "this many-scented perfume" is combined with the aromatic odour wafted from the mountains, proceeding from wild thyme and bog myrtle: the evening sun sheds a flood of golden radiance on the distant mountain-tops, whilst the air resounds with the sweet melody of birds. A more thoroughly placid scene full of pastoral delights it is scarcely possible to imagine. Long will the recollection of Glyn Artro dwell in our remembrance. At Aber Artro is a pretty cottage, delightfully situate at the "meeting of the waters," the junction of the rivers Artro and Nantcol, over which there is a stone bridge. This residence is built on a pleasant *dol* or meadow, adorned with trees and evergreens, and was erected some years ago, by the late Bell Lloyd, Esq., of Cors-y-Gedol. Some confusion exists as to the names of these rivers. The Ordnance surveyors call the brook that runs out of Llyn Howel and other sources, down Cwm Nantcol, the Artro, and the valley Afon Artro; no name appears on the map, to the river which flows from Cwm Bychan. The latter is properly the Artro, and as such we have distinguished it. The views on the road from Aber Artro to Llanbedr are very pleasing; the rocks, adorned with wood ivy and other parasitical plants, form in some instances a strong resemblance to the walls of a ruined castle.

Glowlyn,

or Gloywlyn, which signifies the "Bright Lake," is a small
and very narrow llyn about five miles and a half north-east
of Llanbedr, under the north-west steeps of Rhinog Vawr, and
lying between that mountain and Craig-y-Saeth.   The altitude of
Rhinog Vawr is 2,463 feet above the sea-level, and looms out
majestically from Llanbedr; Glowlyn therefore lies at a considerable elevation, and is not unfrequently buried in the clouds.   It
is one of the smallest pools in the district, being scarcely two
furlongs in length, whilst its breadth in no part much exceeds
100 yards.   Except at the north end, where the water is rather
deep, it is generally so shallow that a man may actually wade
across it in one part when it is low in summer.   At the southern
extremity the bed of the lake is covered with weeds and rushes,
which form an admirable preserve for the finny tribe, and a place
of shelter for wild duck and other aquatic birds.   Sandpipers
frequent this lake in the breeding season.   These beautiful little
birds are here so tame and fearless, as to pass within a few inches
of your feet at the very edge of the water whilst you are fishing
on the shore.

Notwithstanding Glowlyn is small and shallow, it is decidedly
the best lake in the neighbourhood of Llanbedr.   The trout are
generally large and free, and afford excellent diversion.   The fol-
owing extract from our journal will give the reader some idea of
the sport we have obtained there :—" *Wednesday*, June 20, 1849.
—Went to Glowlyn: good fishing-day, with a moderate breeze.
Caught eleven trout, weighing altogether nine pounds two ounces.
The largest, a magnificent fish of three pounds, gave a splendid
run for some time; he was taken with the pea-hen or Llyn
Gwynant fly.   The second-largest weighed one pound two ounces;
the third one pound, the fourth three-quarters of a pound; the
remainder eight ounces each."   Many of the trout are very
beautiful to look at when fresh caught, being of a bright golden
colour, but are of an inferior quality for the table.   The best side
to fish is from the eastern shore, especially from some rocks
which shelve off into deep water.   There is, however, sometimes

good fishing to be had nearly all round the lake. Throw as near as you can to the weeds on the south side; very large trout lie there. The best flies in June and beginning of July are the alder, pea-hen (the latter a most killing fly), the wren's tail, fernshaw; a small red spider made from a cock's huckle, with black legs and some gold twist on the body, is also an excellent fly. A March-brown, dressed pale, wings and body, is also useful in wet weather. Glowlyn, of late years, has been much injured by poaching, which has rendered the trout less "free" than formerly. That pernicious implement "the board" is often used here by the quarrymen from Ffestiniog, Trawsfynydd, and elsewhere. It is a great pity that a lake of such superior character should gradually have become spoiled from this cause. Of all the pools in the neighbourhood of Llanbedr, Glowlyn, with the exception, perhaps, of Llyn Pryved, is the most difficult of access. The route as far as Crafnant is the same as that to Llyn Cwm Bychan. Here you turn off to the right over a bridge which crosses the Artro, and after passing over some swampy meadows, and through a wood, the real toil of the ascent commences. You emerge at once into the "open," upon a narrow road paved with loose stones of all sizes, which give way under your feet, and add greatly to the fatigue of the journey. Once, however, at the summit of this pass (Crafnant), the rest of the walk is comparatively easy. You cross a high dry stone wall on your left, and proceed over a peat morass for some distance, intersected by a brook running from Glowlyn, until you arrive at the range of mountain, behind which, in a hollow, the lake reposes. Although the Ordnance Map will enable the stranger to find the road tolerably well, yet it would perhaps be better on the first visit to make use of a guide; as the path, if it can be called one, across the turbary, is, after rain especially, somewhat heavy. The aspect of the scenery here is dreary and desolate, but the effect is in some measure relieved by the lofty peak of Rhinog Vawr, which rises in grandeur before you, whilst the barren, tempest-riven summit of Craig-y-Saeth appears on the left. Glowlyn lies between these two mountains. The view of Snowdon, and the Snowdonian group of mountains generally, from the north end of Glowlyn, in clear weather, is very grand and imposing. We should also recommend a visit to the summit of Rhinog Vawr from this lake, taking "a cast" on Llyn Dû, "the Black pool," *en passant*, which lies immediately under the highest peak of Rhinog Vawr, the distance being about half-an-hour's walk from Glowlyn. We once witnessed the most extraordinary rise of fish in this lake that we ever saw. It seemed as if the whole surface of the water was absolutely alive, as though hundreds of pebbles were being thrown into the water from all quarters. The trout, however, would not look at the artificial fly; whether they were merely disporting themselves, or actually feeding on the surface on something we could not see, we cannot say. In the course of one hour's stay we only caught two trout, which were as black, big-headed, and ugly as any we ever saw. They were very strong for their size, about half a pound. A local fisherman informed us that the trout in Llyn Dû were sometimes very "free," but their coarse quality and lean appearance hardly repaid the trouble of fishing for them. On the summit of Rhinog Vawr, the Ordnance surveyors have raised a large carnedd, or heap of stones, which can be seen for some distance off. A splendid panoramic view can be obtained here on a fine clear day. Snowdon, the Traeths, Lleyn, Bardsey Isle, Cader Idris, &c., are all visible, and bird's-eye peeps of several llyns. We cannot bid farewell to Glowlyn without looking back to the many very pleasant excursions we have made to it in former years; and a regretful feeling steals over us when we reflect that, in all human probability, we shall revisit it no more.

Llynniau Prefeddau, Cwm Howel, and Ybi,

is the next group of lakes we purpose introducing to the notice of the reader. These pools lie at a greater distance from Llanbedr than those previously noticed. The route is through Cwm Nantcol, the "hollow of the sunken brook," which leads to the Drws Ardudwy, "one of the sublimest scenes in Wales," of which more anon. After following the path up the vale for several miles, you come to an ancient farm-house, the tenant of which, an extensive sheep farmer, lately dead, was said to be worth £30,000! He had several thousand sheep on these barren wilds, and notwithstanding his reputed wealth, lived almost as coarsely as the poorest peasant. It is by such means, combined with low rents, that Welsh mountain farmers acquire such wealth. After passing the farm-house, the road gradually becomes more difficult. About two miles further, you must turn off to the right, up the side of the mountain, until you reach

Llyn Prefeddau,

this requires some "heavy collar work," as the ground you pass over is rocky and precipitous. This is a very small Llyn lying under the steeps of Llether, containing some very handsome trout, but it is difficult to fish in the best part on account of weeds ; when there is a good breeze, some nice fish of six ounces or half a pound may be taken, which are of excellent quality. The trout here were formerly very "free," but of late years have become more wary, probably from poaching. The south shore of the lake is of fine gravel, and the water is beautifully clear. The route from hence to

Llyn Cwm Howel

is steep, but not of very great length. Were it not well worth a visit as one of the finest and most impressive mountain scenes in the district, Llyn Howel is utterly valueless as regards sport. The deep hollow, which contains the waters of the lake, is under the southern precipices of Rhinog Vach, a mountain of little inferior altitude to its giant sister. It is hardly possible to picture a more gloomy, savage spot than this. The shores of the lake are in parts covered with large masses of rock, piled on each other in chaotic confusion, evidently detached by the effects of time and weather from the precipices above, and it requires no little care and exertion on the part of the angler to scramble along them with due regard to the safety of his limbs. In several respects this lake resembles Llyn-y-Cae, previously described. The water is exceedingly deep, particularly under the precipices on the east side, which run perpendicularly down into the pool, and the deep basin or *cwm* in which it lies is of volcanic appearance. The trout in Llyn Howel are exceedingly numerous, but very small, many of them with ugly flat heads, and eyes that

E

leer upon you with a strange expression; they are also of the
worst quality, and so delicate, that they keep fresh only for a
very short time. You can frequently take two or three at a cast,
and generally fill your basket in a few hours. The average size
is about three ounces. Llyn Howel is about two furlongs in
length.

A very steep, narrow ridge, connecting Rhinog Vach with
Llether, separates Llyn Howel from Llyn Ybi; over this ridge or
" divide," you must wend your way to get to

Llyn Ybi.

The easiest way, however, to this lake is through the sublime
Pass of Drws Ardudwy, at the head of which, you turn to the
right over the morass. By keeping under Rhinog Vach you
arrive at the lake. At the summit of the ridge before mentioned,
there is a high dry stone boundary wall, and when it blows or
rains, we have found under the lee of it comfortable shelter. The
scenery around Llyn Ybi is dreary and comparatively uninteresting; it lies under Llether, the rugged precipices of Rhinog Vach,
bearing north-west. Ybi is the parent of the Camlan, which
stream runs through Cwm Camlan, until it joins the Mawddach,
near Tyn-y-Groes. Its course from the lake is about seven miles.
On this river the celebrated Rhaiadr Dû, the "Black Cataract,"
better known as the Dol-y-Melynllyn Fall, occurs. On the "lanes"
of water in the Camlan above the "falls," some excellent trout-
fishing may be had when there is a good breeze. The trout in
Llyn Ybi are superb fish, both in appearance and quality, but they
are exceedingly shy, and you may, as we have done, visit this
pool time after time, without being rewarded with even a "rise."
The best sport we ever had there was in a very stormy day, when
we succeeded in landing four fine trout, averaging one pound
each. This lake is much poached at night with the "otter," by
men from Dolgelley; this practice contributes to render the trout
still more sullen than they naturally are, and at present it is
almost useless to fish Ybi with the angle. Before the "otter"
or "board" was in vogue, very large trout have been taken in
this lake with the rod: a Llanbedr fisherman informed us that

one afternoon in summer, he caught two trout which weighed four pounds each, besides several of one pound and upwards. Trout *have* been taken here with the fly exceeding five pounds. The shores of Llyn Ybi are flat and open, of easy walking, although rather wet and boggy in some parts. The best dish of fish we ever saw from Ybi was at Dolgelley, in the month of June, 1855: they had been caught at night with the "board." There were about two dozen trout of from half a pound to one pound each, in high condition. It is a pity that such a valuable lake as Ybi is for fine trout, should be so utterly spoiled. The distance to this pool from Llanbedr is about eight miles, and the road is, at least for half the distance, exceedingly rough, and the climbing arduous. There is a path from Llyn Ybi over the steep shoulder of Llether, and from thence along the high ridge called Crib y Rhiw, at the foot of which lies the small pool Llyn Dulyn; we prefer, however, returning to Llanbedr by Cwm Nantcol, as Dulyn belongs to another group of lakes which lie about one mile nearer to Llanbedr than those near Cwm Nantcol.

Llynniau Irddyn, Bodlyn, Dulyn.

The road to these lakes is along the old mountain horse-road to Dolgelley, over the wild hills called Llaw Llech. These hills are a continuation of the Rhinog group, and terminate at Barmouth. The excursion from Llanbedr to these llyns is one of the most enjoyable and interesting that this romantic country affords; and in fine breezy clear weather, the combined features of mountain, sea, and lake are very fascinating. How elastic a man's spirits feel as he bounds over these wild rocky moorland solitudes! how the mind expands in the contemplation of Nature's works—ever the same, "to-day, yesterday, for ever." The ground around you covered with evidences of a byegone age—the battle-field, the graves of the dead, or the ruined cromlech, sacred to the rites of a crafty and barbarous superstition. Below, the deep blue sea, "near enough to look beautiful, but not to be heard," studded with white sails as they plough their way towards the sparkling waters without; "the breezy blue aërial freedom of a whole sea sky, newly uncurtained—its mists not yet quite scattered," partially unveiling

a boundless horizon of restless ocean; the ruined causeway*
submerged centuries ago, which the "wild waves" in their never-
dying rage and fury have for more than twelve hundred years
ceaselessly battered: its site visible by a long track of foam—such
is a faint description of the scenic beauties which surround you on
your ramble to these solitary mountain tarns.

Fine pure mountain air is a certain cure for low spirits; you
have only to hie to the "mountain's brow," and your spirits rise
like a barometer. It is really astonishing with what ease a man
in good health can traverse these mountain wastes, and accomplish
without fatigue, considerable distances in a day. We have walked
to the lakes we now propose to describe, fished in them, ascended
Crib y Rhiw, skirted the sides of Llether, descended to Ybi,
crossed over the precipitous ridge to Llyn Howel, and from
thence through Cwm Nantcol to Aber Artro and Llanbedr, without feeling more than a pleasant fatigue. Upon reference to the
map this will be found a great distance to accomplish in a day,
particularly as a portion of the region you traverse is very rugged
elevated ground.

Llyn Irddyn,

the "Priests' Lake," lies to the south of the road leading
to Dolgelley, which crosses a brook called Ysgethin, flowing
from Bodlyn. On leaving Llanbedr, the road winds round
Moelfre, the "Bald-hill,"—a visit to the summit of which
is worth making—you then turn off to the right across some
large walled in "parks," the site of an ancient battle-field, at the
back of Cors-y-Gedol, and proceed towards the very interesting
British Post called Craig-y-Ddinas. The grounds in this locality
abound in circles, ancient barrows, remains of British houses, etc.,
and afford a rich field to the archæologist. The following brief
description of Irddyn, we extract from our diary:—"Llyn Irddyn,
a long narrow llyn near the old road to Dolgelley, about one mile
and a half from Cors-y-Gedol, and about half an hour's walk
from Bodlyn. The fish are large and of good quality, but
generally shy. This lake is for the most part very shallow near

* Sarn Badrig, or "Patrick's Causeway."

the shores, the stones along which are slippery and dangerous,
so that a boat is indispensable to insure good sport.. The distance
from Llanbedr, is from four and a half to five miles." We were
informed by William Roberts, the guide and fisherman at Llanbedr
—and a very useful, intelligent fellow he is, who can make a fly,
mend a rod, besides possessing many other qualifications—that
the best plan to insure a good basket of fish at Irddyn, is to
proceed there over night, and "camp" out in a rude hut of stones
and heather which he had constructed. In the early morning,
before sunrise, proceed to fish. At this early hour the trout come
out of the deep water to feed on the shallows, and the "rise" is,
for a short time, very good. He once showed us a very fine
basket of fish he had procured by following this plan. We can
imagine, that in a fine warm summer's night, with good store of
"creature comforts," a bivouac of this sort would create a very
pleasurable excitement. The best sport we ever obtained at
Irddyn was about ten years ago, early in June. We killed
twenty-three trout, weighing in the gross eleven pounds six
ounces. Amongst these were two or three fine fish, of beautiful
colour, about three-quarters of a pound each, the average weight
being from six to eight ounces. The trout in Irddyn are
generally considered equal in quality to those from Ybi, and far
superior to any other lake in the district.

The scenery around Irddyn is very wild and dreary, although
not without a touch of the romantic. It lies immediately under
the long range of hills called Llaw Llech, in a direction north-east
to south-west. The remains of an ancient British town are clearly
discernible on the west shore, and the rocky eminence called
Craig-y-Ddinas, formed the citadel or fort. Some antiquaries
have pretended to point out "an inclosure, where the Druids
used to keep a store of fish," at the outlet of the lake; but this,
in our opinion, is a mere fanciful conjecture. The llyn, however,
probably derived its name, "Priests' Lake," from some tradition
of this sort. Craig-y-Ddinas has not met from antiquaries the
attention it deserves. A few years ago, in company with an
ardent archæologist, a man whose imagination had imbibed largely
from the visionary creations of Rowlands, Stukely, Borlase,
and others, we made a minute survey of this ancient fortified

stronghold, and in those remote times it was probably considered almost impregnable. The remains of a "covered way" to the summit of the rock may still be traced, with numerous Cyttiau. Altogether, this is a very interesting specimen of an ancient British fortress, and well deserves inspection.

From hence to

Llyn Bodlyn,

which lies in a north-east direction, about one mile and a half higher up, under the romantic precipices of Diphwys. The walk thither lies over a wet boggy turbary, where peat is cut in summer. Bodlyn is a beautiful piece of water, about half a mile from north to south, the stones of which under Diphwys are of fine gravel, and afford pleasant walking. Further on, large rocks and boulders fringe the shore, and the water is deep close to the edge. This lake, on its south side, is forty-two yards deep; it contains char, which are sometimes caught in the winter with worm. The following description is from some notes taken on the spot: "Llyn Bodlyn, a rather large pool, well stocked with trout, perch, char, and eels, situate on the route to Dulyn. The trout in general rise freely, and are a very pretty fish, but small. Small-sized perch are numerous in certain parts of the lake. The water is beautifully clear." We have paid many visits to this pool, and have generally been successful, taking on some occasions from four to five dozen; but these trout are very capricious, and sometimes tantalize the angler by making numerous "false rises," the little rascals evidently rising in play. Bodlyn has always with us been a favourite lake, although we cannot recommend it for any *real* sport.

Llyn Dulyn

is a small pool, about one mile and a half further up in the mountains, lying under Crib y Rhiw; which literally means the summit, or head of the ascent. The situation is as wild and sequestered as it is possible to conceive. The trout in this pool are very handsome, and of good size, but rather shy; sometimes, however, you can manage to kill some if you happen to hit upon the right day. The fish are very firm and of good quality, quite equal to those taken in Irddyn. We once caught a large trout here late in the evening, weighing one pound and a half, with a fly called the "Coachman," which much resembles a night-moth in appearance. Dulyn has been much injured of late years by poaching with the net, and possibly with the "board." The best weather for success on this lake, is a nice sunny warm day; nothing can be done here when the weather is cold and gloomy. Dulyn and Bodlyn are, we believe, the property of the Crown. In the centre of the lake, a pretty rocky islet adds much to its beauty; indeed, we know of few more beautiful mountain llyns than Dulyn. The distance to it from Llanbedr is about eight miles, *viâ* Bodlyn; there is another route on the east side of Moelfre into Cwm Nantcol, which shortens the distance, but the road is very rough and boggy. If you return by the Dolgelley road, looking seaward, a fine view is to be obtained of Sarn Badrig, "St. Patrick's, or the sea-breaking causeway," distinguished by a long line of foam, caused by the sea breaking over the ancient embankment, which is supposed to have been the sea wall constructed to prevent the sea from inundating the lowland country: a catastrophe which actually took place about the year of our Lord 500. The flat country called Cantref-y-Gwaelod was entirely overwhelmed, and sixteen towns destroyed. The Welsh Triads contain an historical account of it; it is therefore certain that a great portion of Cardigan bay was once dry land, a sort of Welsh Flanders. Sarn Badrig extends for nearly twenty miles into the bay, and is about twenty-four feet broad. Large ships have at different times been totally wrecked upon it, accompanied with loss of life. An enthusiastic young friend of ours a few years ago went from Port Mochras in a small boat and landed on the Sarn, although the sea was rather rough at the time. He managed to effect a landing by swimming from the boat, and brought off several shells and stones from the slippery summit of the wall; it was, however, a somewhat hazardous exploit. Sarn Badrig is only partially dry for a short time at low ebb.

Drws Ardudwy.

We must not omit to notice a very delightful excursion to
Cwm Nantcol and the Drws Ardudwy. You can proceed
thither either by Gwynvrin and Aber Artro, where you cross
a bridge, or through woods near a slate-quarry on the banks
of the river. A fine waterfall is to be seen on the latter route,
embosomed in woods. After getting into the open country—
which is intersected by stone walls, and numerous deep drains to
draw off the water from the turbary, where a great deal of peat
is cut in summer—the vale is flat, and the river forms many
very deep "lanes" of water, which contain some large trout;
these, we need scarcely remark, are extremely shy. We have
caught seven or eight dozen of small fish in Cwm Nantcol after a
"fresh." The walking along the banks is then, however, very
wet and swampy; and several of the cuts or drains running into
the river are wide and deep. The hill scenery, though naked, is
wild and romantic; and as you proceed towards the sources of
the river, several rapids and waterfalls add much to the general
effect of the landscape. The Pass of Drws Ardudwy divides the
mountains Rhinog Vawr and Vach, and leads into the wilds
between Dolgelley and Trawsfynydd. Steps, either artificial or
cut out of the native rocks, are seen here similar to those in Bwlch
Tyddiad, already described, and are assigned by tradition as the
work of the Romans. This was supposed to be, in ancient times,
a military road leading from Dolgelley to Harlech. This secluded
Pass is little known, and still less frequented by the stranger; it
is not too much to affirm, however, that in wild beauty and sublimity it is one of the gems of Wales. Sewin cannot ascend into
Cwm Nantcol on account of the waterfall above Glyn Artro; but
great numbers both of sewin and salmon find their way up the
Artro, and we have seen several spawning beds in that river, near
Llyn Cwm Bychan. The best time to fish for sewin at Llanbedr
is in August, but the banks of the river are so much inclosed
with trees, except near the sea, that few parts afford the fisherman room for a "cast." Some years ago, fine trout-fishing could
sometimes be obtained in the marshes towards Mochras. About
half a mile from Llanbedr is the old course of the river, leading

to the left across the marsh. In this water, which is still and deep, were some large red trout; and, although shy, we managed occasionally to catch some. We have taken trout out of this water one pound and a half, many of three-quarters of a pound and one pound weight. The difficulty is to land them; and, as many tall bulrushes line the banks, nothing can be done without a landing-net. We have found a fly made with a red hackle for wing, and a dark blue body ribbed with gold twist, a very killing fly in the marsh. The Fernshaw and Governor are also excellent. Be sure and use only one fly, on account of the weeds and rushes. The trout in this water are red as salmon, and of excellent quality, better than any lake trout in the locality.

A very interesting excursion to Llyn Irddyn may be made by way of Egrin Abbey. You proceed from Llanbedr for about four miles on the road to Barmouth, and turn off to the left at Pen-y-Bryn. A lane leads you to Hendre Cirian farm-house, and then proceed up a wild dingle, destitute of wood, watered by Egrin brook, to a well-defined British post, called Pen-y-Ddinas: this camp can be seen from the Barmouth road. About half a mile beyond, on some high ground to the right, are some extremely interesting Druidical monuments, called Carneddau Hengwm, or "the stone heaps of the old defile," supposed by some to be sepulchral monuments to warriors or chieftains who fell in battle. In 1847, during a stay of some weeks at Llanbedr, we visited Carneddau Hengwm, and made several sketches of it. In our note-book we find the following particulars: " Carneddau Hengwm or Waun Cwm, near Cors-y-Gedol, is a remarkable Druidical remain, consisting of cromlechs, cistvaen, and an immense collection of stones piled together. One carnedd is sixty yards long, and in it there is a singular chamber, quite perfect, with stone benches and a chimney! Altogether, it is one of the most interesting relics of Druidism in the Principality. The horizontal stone that rested on the cromlech at the south-east end of the carnedd has been displaced, probably by the shepherds; otherwise it is tolerably perfect." Llyn Irddyn is about one mile and a half to the north-east of this spot, and is easily approached from hence ; at the back of Cors-y-Gedol is another very interesting Cromlech, in the cattle inclosures, which may be visited on

your return to Llanbedr. We have thus indicated a few of the
principal antiquities in the vicinity of Harlech and Llanbedr;
but, as we have before stated, the whole country around is
strewed with circles, ancient British dwellings, cromlechs, and
carneddau, which will afford ample gratification and amusement
to the explorer.

From the account we have given of fishing at Llanbedr, our
readers will perceive that to get sport you must work hard.
None of the lakes are nearer than five miles; some of them are
seven or eight, and the roads rough, rocky, and steep. It
is necessary, therefore, to start very early in the morning, not
later than seven o'clock, and as much earlier as possible. It
generally takes from two hours and a half to three hours and a
half to reach your fishing-ground; and every angler knows the
importance of being at the water-side *early*. To insure early
rising, you must get to bed in good time, avoiding late sittings at
night—enjoyable as sportsmen's "*noctes*" usually are, in narrating
the incidents of "flood and field," which each day's ramble produces.
Many a good day's sport is spoiled from a non-observance of this
salutary practice.

There is one great advantage possessed by the angler in Wales,
and that is free permission to sport in the lakes and rivers.
There are, of course, exceptions; but even where waters are preserved, there is, in general, very little difficulty in obtaining permission. The lakes and streams around Harlech and Llanbedr
are all *free;* some of them are Crown property, such as Dulyn,
Bodlyn, and all the Llyns near the summits of the mountains.
Llyn Irddyn belongs, or at least part of it, to the Cors-y-Gedol
estate, the property of the Hon. Edward Lloyd Mostyn. The
ancient manor-house of Cors-y-Gedol was built by Inigo Jones,
in 1594, and is well worth a visit. It lies about one mile from
the Barmouth road, nearly three miles and a half from Llanbedr.
The avenue to the house from the turnpike road is composed of
stately limes, and forms a beautiful approach. The gateway, also
ascribed to Inigo Jones, bears date 1630, on the shield over the
crown of the arch. A gallery of family portraits, a painting by
Wilson, and some curious antique furniture, are shown to the
visitor. In Pennant's time, baronial hospitality was dispensed
here with a liberal hand to all comers. He was treated and

lodged in the style of an "ancient baron" by the then possessor, William Vaughan, Esq.

In concluding our notice of this very interesting locality, it may be useful to the reader to point out the best routes to get to it. From London and Birmingham, you must proceed to Shrewsbury, thence to Llangollen-road station: here you leave the rail, and get upon a "well-appointed" four-horse coach to Dolgelley: distance forty-four miles. There is a coach to Caernarvon daily from Dolgelley, during the summer, and this passes through Llanbedr and Harlech. From Liverpool and Chester, you can proceed to Llangollen-road station, through the vale of Gresford, Rhuabon, &c.; or, if you prefer the round, you can go to Bangor and Caernarvon, and from thence through Beddgelert and Tan-y-Bwlch. The distance from Caernarvon to Harlech is thirty-eight miles. Before we conclude, there are one or two other points which deserve attention. The climate on the sea-coast of Merioneth is mild and exceedingly healthy, but a great deal of rain falls during the year, from its proximity to the sea. The prevailing wind is the south-west, which generally brings rain with it. We have known the weather at Llanbedr as fine in the morning as could be desired, without the least appearance of falling weather; a shift of the wind at noon has rapidly altered the state of affairs, and a downfall of the watery element has followed, which, for severity, an Englishman has scarcely an idea of, unless, as we have been, well used to it. It is, therefore, absolutely necessary to provide for these sudden changes, for there is little or no shelter to be found on the shores of the mountain lakes. We should recommend a good Macintosh-cape, a pair of waterproof leggings to reach to the hips, and a "sou'-wester" cap to tie under the chin; with these accoutrements you can manage to keep tolerably dry, unless, as is sometimes the case, a strong wind accompanies the pluvial deluge. Unless you wish to become a good customer to the village cordwainer, you must also supply yourself with two or three pairs of strong double upper-leather shooting-boots, with "hob" nails on the soles, and a pair of Cording's wading-boots: with these indispensable auxiliaries you will be able to get on exceedingly well, in defiance of rain, wind, and weather.

CHAPTER IV.

INTRODUCTORY REMARKS—DESTRUCTION OF FISH—POACHING—
LAKES AND RIVERS IN CAERNARVONSHIRE—FISHING STATIONS
—BEDDGELERT—SCENERY — LLYN GWYNANT — LLYN-Y-DDINAS
—LLYN-Y-GADER.

> " Amidst the vast horizon's stretch,
>   In restless gaze, the eye of wonder darts
>   O'er the expanse ; mountains on mountains piled,
>   And winding bays, and promontories huge;
>   Lakes, and meandering rivers, from their source
>   Traced to the distant ocean ; scattered isles,
>   Dark rising from the watery waste, and seas
>   Dividing kingdoms !"

IT is our intention in the present chapter to afford the most
accurate information—derived from our own practice and observation—of the angling to be met with in some parts of Caernarvonshire ; combining an occasional passing description of the
scenes of wild grandeur and beauty, some of them rarely visited,
into which we have been beguiled in pursuit of sport ; and also to
give such advice as to accommodation at inns or lodging-houses,
and expenses at such on a moderate scale, as we may deem useful
for the several localities we shall point out.   It is to the lover of
natural beauty, to one who can " sit down to creation's table as
to a perpetual feast ;" where he can gaze upon " the abrupt cliff,
the sharp ridge, glens without verdure, and all the severer forms
of mountain scenery," that we would now address ourselves.
Here you can reverently stroll amongst the numerous relics of a
rude and dim age, or of early Christian piety, which lie scattered
over the land ; wander with your rod or staff into the wild
hollows or recesses of the " everlasting hills," and look up from
Nature in awe and admiration to " Nature's God."   This is the
land for imagination to revel in, nor is it to be wondered at, that

several of the most illustrious of the Welsh Bards drew their lofty aspirations from the habitual contemplation of scenery so sublime, so vast in its details; and where in some quiet retreat they "found more lessons in the woods and stones, than in towns." Sir Walter Scott somewhere finely observes, that "the seat of the Celtic muse is in the mist of the secret and solitary hill, and her voice in the murmur of the mountain stream. He who woos her, must love the barren rock more than the fertile valley, and the solitude of the desert better than the festivity of the hall."

"The partial opening of the iron road," observes the accurate and intelligent author of the "Book of North Wales," "has excited afresh an interest in that romantic country, which had been gradually flagging since the peace." The opening of the Chester and Holyhead railway has induced many hundreds of tourists to wend their way into North Wales. In consequence of this influx of visitors, vast strides in social improvement are visible within the last ten or twelve years. Hotel and inn accommodation is now quite equal to the wants of the most fastidious travellers, and the posting throughout the country generally is excellent. In Warner's time, when he wrote his "Walks in Wales," at the latter end of the last century, there was a dash of romance in his excursions, and a zest and originality in his graphic descriptions of the "troubles of travel," which cannot be realized in this utilitarian age. There are, however, still to be met with, swarms of pedestrian tourists in the autumnal months; who, knapsack on back, sturdily take the road, avoid the great hotels, preferring the quiet old-fashioned inns, and who scorn to take advantage of coach or rail. Fifty years ago, the inns generally were of the rudest sort; there were few coaches; in some counties hardly a post-chaise could be procured; the only means of travelling was on horseback or on foot. The roads also were in general execrable—what Pennant describes as "most dreadful horse-paths"—in short, the romance of a tour in Wales now-a-days, except to such as can "rough" it among the nooks and byeways of the country, is nearly gone.

Within the last twenty or thirty years, commercial enterprise has greatly interfered with the sport of the rod. In some of the

best fishing localities of byegone days, trout, sewin, and salmon
have entirely disappeared from the rivers, and in some of the
finest lakes of Snowdonia, trout and char have almost ceased to
exist.   Several causes have combined to produce this wholesale
destruction of fish.   The most fertile source of evil, however,
has arisen from the quantity of poisonous metallic water from
the levels of the numerous lead and copper mines, and the drainage
from the extensive slate quarries.   In proof of the destructive
effects of mineral water, we may instance the beautiful lakes of
Llanberis and Nant-y-Llef, fishing in which is now not worth
pursuing.   Forty or fifty years ago these lakes were celebrated
for the quantity and excellence of their trout and char.   At
Aberystwith, such is the havoc made in the various rivers of the
neighbourhood—we may more especially mention the Rheidol
and Ystwith—that the Aberystwith Fishing Club has for some
time ceased to exist, and the poor fishermen of the town complain
that no fish can be caught for several miles out at sea, in consequence of the salt water being impregnated with the deleterious
matter from the numerous lead mines.   There is, however, another
cause which has proved almost as great a scourge to the angler
as the evil effects produced from the mines : this is poaching.
The " otter " or " board " is extensively employed on the lakes,
and the rivers suffer from the spear or net.   There is scarcely a
llyn, where the fish are of any value, that is not infested by men
—chiefly miners—pursuing their illegal calling.   This nefarious
destruction of fish is also greatly encouraged by the ready sale
the poacher obtains at the numerous hotels and lodging-houses.
Indeed, we may mention one instance, where the landlord of one
of the principal Snowdonian hotels nets the lakes in his neighbourhood once or twice a week; such is the demand for trout
and sewin by the shoals of tourists which overrun the country.
If this state of affairs is allowed to continue through the careless-
ness or apathy of the great landed proprietors, in a few years
hence the sport of angling in Wales will belong to the past.   We
put it to the hotel-keepers themselves, whether they are not
" killing the goose that lays the golden egg," by holding out such
inducement to poaching, as the purchase of salmon and trout
obtained from the rivers and lakes, where they profess to provide

sport for the gentlemen who frequent their houses during the
summer months for no other purpose than the amusement of
trout and salmon fishing?

There are numerous lakes and rivers in Caernarvonshire. Some
of the llyns are of considerable size, and nearly all of them, half
a century ago, abounded in trout and eels. In some of the
largest, very little, if any, sport—as we have previously observed
—can now be obtained. The number of lakes in the county
amounts to about fifty; the rivers—several of which are excellent
—are also numerous; but there is only one of much importance,
the Conwy, which takes its rise in Llyn Conwy. The Ogwen,
Glaslyn, Llugwy, Gwyrfai, Machno, Lleder, Seiont, and Llyfni,
are amongst the other principal streams in the county. In some
of these, fair trout-fishing may be had early in the year. There
are several fishing stations; the best of which are Beddgelert,
"Snowdon Ranger" 'hotel, on the banks of Llyn Cwellyn,
Llanrwst, Bettws-y-Coed, on the river Llugwy—a good station—
Trefriw, a small village on the Conwy, Capel Curig, and Pen-y-
Gwryd. Penmachno, on the river Machno, contains, we believe,
a small inn, where tolerable acommodation may be obtained. It
has the advantage of being within four miles of Llyn Conwy, and
also possesses one or two experienced fishermen. Llyn Conwy is
a fine pool, where sometimes there is excellent sport. Bettws-
y-Coed possesses a very comfortable inn, and is a favourite resort
of artists. The late David Cox, one of the most eminent water-
colour painters which England has produced, passed much of his
time here during the summer.

Beddgelert.

The romantic village of Beddgelert is a favourite haunt of
anglers and artists during the summer months. It is on the
high road from Caernarvon to Tan-y-Bwlch and Dolgelley;
distant from the former thirteen miles. There is a railroad now
from Bangor to Caernarvon, so that you may travel from London
to Beddgelert in a day. During the height of "the season," the
lodging-houses in the village are generally quite full; and the
"Goat" Hotel, decidedly one of the best in the Principality,

both for comfort and beauty of situation, has frequently all the beds engaged.

The situation of Beddgelert is charming in the extreme. Placed at the confluence of the rapid rivers Colwyn and Glaslyn—the waters of which chiefly derive their source from Snowdon—it is sheltered from the north by some precipitous crags, which form a continuation of the southern arm of the mighty "hill king," the lofty peak Yr Aran. To the south some verdant meadows, watered by the sister streams rushing in their impetuous course through the celebrated Pass of Beddgelert—which for colour, especially in autumn, is without a rival in Wales—form a scene of quiet delicious repose, and breathe an air of tranquillity, which soothes and elevates the mind. The *Bwlch* at Pont Aberglaslyn is certainly the finest scene of its kind, the most perfect realization of a mountain Pass to be found in Wales. In grandeur, in beauty of detail, nothing can surpass or equal it; not merely on a similar, but even on a larger scale. Then the scenery beyond! Language is inadequate to do it justice; well might it be said to "exceed the power of description."

Beddgelert, as a delightful summer retreat, is deservedly appreciated by tourists; to our taste, it is decidedly the gem of the Principality. Moel Hebog, "the hill of the Hawk," towering to the height of 2,580 feet over the west side of the village, is best seen from the lower end of Llyn-y-Ddinas. The view from the summit in favourable weather is superb, and very extensive, but the ascent is difficult.

The best months for lake-fishing are May, June, and part of July. Some sport may occasionally be obtained later in the year, by anglers who are "up to the mark," and know the lakes well; but after many years' experience we have found lake-fishing in Wales of little account after the period we have specified. After all, even at the most favourable time, success is only to be obtained by a knowledge of the water you fish in, and by the use of the proper flies. We well remember, whilst fishing in Llyn Ogwen some years ago, in company with a most accomplished angler, we observed an old gentleman in wading boots, diligently fishing from shore, without apparently raising a single fish, whilst in a boat we were obtaining excellent sport. It was not from

want of ability in the manipulation of his rod that his want of
success lay, but—as we afterwards learned—from the use of
Scotch flies! Many *professed* anglers come into Wales profoundly ignorant in that most important branch of the art, viz.
the right flies. They fancy they have only to buy a rod and
basket, and a lot of flies of all sizes and colours, from a London
tackle-maker, and success must follow—supposing that trout will
rise to anything they throw upon the water. They, however, find
themselves egregiously mistaken. We have met with numbers of
such "muffs." Many, again, cannot even throw a fly, and instead
of alluring the wily trout, scare them away. Again, lake and river-
fishing are quite distinct branches of the art, and require a very
different manipulation of the rod. Fortunately for the sportsman,
Beddgelert possesses two most excellent fishermen and guides, of
the name of Jones, father and son, who not only make very neat
flies, but are able to conduct you to the best fishing in the neighbourhood.

Before we proceed to give some account of angling at Beddgelert, let us pause for a moment to say a few words as to the
accommodation afforded at the "Goat Hotel," and the various
lodging-houses in the village, with a hint or two as to the daily
and weekly expenses. Nor must we omit to say a good word
for the "Prince Llewellyn" inn, near the bridge; which, although
old-fashioned, is comfortable, and where you meet with attention
and civility. It is just the inn for an angler or artist, and less
expensive. The charges at the "Goat Hotel" are, however,
moderate, considering its excellent accommodation and attention
to the *cuisine*. A magnificent coffee-room has recently been
erected, very handsomely furnished, in fact, the finest apartment
of the sort in the Principality. You can live well, including all
expenses, for fourteen or fifteen shillings per day. We, however,
strongly recommend private lodgings as far preferable to an inn.
There is more comfort and privacy, and it is infinitely cheaper.
Comfortable apartments may be obtained, consisting of parlour
and bed-room, at from twenty to twenty-five shillings per week;
with board, at about twelve shillings extra.

There are three lakes within a moderate distance of Beddgelert,
of easy approach; two of them, Llyn-y-Ddinas and Llyn Gwynant,

are on the road to Capel Curig and Llanberis; Llyn-y-Gader lies
about a furlong from the road leading from Beddgelert to Caernarvon. During the summer of 1857, there was a boat belonging
to the "Goat Hotel," on Llyn Gwynant, and another small boat
on Llyn Gader; and now, we believe, a boat has been placed on
Llyn-y-Ddinas. *Without* a boat, it is quite useless to attempt
fishing these pools. The charge for a guide and boatman is five
shillings per day; you cannot obtain the use of the boat without
one, unless you are staying at the hotel; and, as the majority of
anglers who resort to Llyn Gwynant, a distance of about four
miles, are too lazy to walk, it involves the cost of a car and
driver, about six or seven shillings extra. This is paying rather
high for the chance of a day's sport. Indeed, angling at Beddgelert is expensive; neither is the sport commensurate with the
expense. There is another way of getting a day's fishing on
Gwynant at a much cheaper rate. Walk there early in the
morning—the scenery on the road is exceedingly beautiful and
romantic—and engage a boat belonging to a farmer, who lives
near the end of the lake, which you can obtain at two shillings
and sixpence per day. If two or three gentlemen club together,
and can manage a boat, this will reduce the expense to a very
reasonable amount.

Llyn Gwynant

is a lake of surpassing beauty—scarcely equalled by any other
scene in Snowdonia. It fills up the bottom of a lovely valley, called
in Welsh, Gwynant, which signifies "the Vale of Waters." At the
lower extremity, its shores are fringed with thriving woods, and
adorned with two pretty villa residences belonging to Messrs.
Vaudrey and Wyatt. The lake is nearly a mile long, and towards
the middle is about one-third of a mile broad. Its principal feeder
is the Avon Lâs, which takes its rise in Llyn Ffynnon Lâs, a small
pool in a hollow high up Snowdon; and after passing through the
lonely Llyn Llydaw, a fine lake about one mile and a half long, it
dashes through Cwm Dyli, and falling over a series of lofty cataracts, called Rhaiadr Cwm Dyli, descends into Nant Gwynant. You
cannot see, but imagination will picture, the large sullen Llyn,

sheltered by the lofty storm-riven precipices of Y-Wyddfa on
your left—a lake dear to the lover of nature in her dreariest
aspect—whence, as it were, " by the slightest fracture in the rim
of its rocky basin, it sends forth this little stream (Avon Lâs) to
gladden the ' Vale of Waters ' beneath with the freshest of
verdure," before its waters—turbulent and brawling through the
Pass of Beddgelert—smoothly expand in the Traeth Mawr, on
their onward march to the sea. Except in one part, where the
lake washes the precipitous base of Y-Lliwed—the third peak in
height after the main summit of Snowdon—the water is shallow,
with a grassy weedy bottom, resembling in this respect the lake
of Tal-y-Llyn. In the early portion of the season, the trout in
this pool " rise " freely, and are exceedingly strong and gamesome ;
the larger fish of half or three-quarters of a pound affording excellent sport. There are two varieties of trout in the lake ; the
bright yellow variety, which are chiefly taken in the shallows at
the lower end, are very beautiful when first taken out of the
water, and, when cooked, cut quite red. The other species is of
darker colour, with white belly, and is of very inferior quality to
the yellow sort. The *habitat* of these is chiefly at the upper
portion of the pool. Some twelve or fourteen years ago, the
sport on Llyn Gwynant was exceedingly good. We remember in
the month of June, 1846, catching a large basket of trout, many
of them from half to three-quarters of a pound, on a bright hot
day, with a very slack inconstant breeze. Since then the sport
has much declined, in consequence of the immense number of
trout of all sizes being taken out with the net. The fact is, the
right of fishing belongs to several proprietors ; and, until some
general understanding is come to as to the preservation of the
fish, this fine lake will soon cease to afford any great attraction
to the angler. The landlord of the hotel at Capel Curig, who
rents under the Hon. Colonel Douglas Pennant, M.P., has the
right of fishing at the north-east upper end of the lake, and he
makes good use of the privilege by netting the pool at least once
a week during the summer months. In the year 1857, during a
series of visits to Llyn Gwynant, we frequently saw the net at
work ; and we were informed by our boatman that from twelve
to twenty dozen of trout were frequently taken in a day, of all

sizes.   In consequence of this wholesale slaughter, it is not to be
expected that angling can be so good as formerly.   Some years
ago, Llyn Gwynant suffered from netting in a still greater degree
to what it does at present: at that time there were no less than
three nets at work ; one from the " Goat Hotel," Beddgelert ; the
one already mentioned from Capel Curig; and a large seine-net,
constructed on purpose by a gentleman who then resided at Plas
Gwynant, a pretty villa in the immediate vicinity.   We have been
credibly informed—however monstrous the statement may appear
—that from this net alone, during a single season, 15,000 dozen
of trout were taken out of the lake !

The general size of the trout we caught in Llyn Gwynant in
1857, was about three to the pound; a few of the largest weighed
eight, nine, and ten ounces.   In former years the average was
much larger.   There are still a few very fine trout occasionally
captured.   John Jones, senior, fisherman at Beddgelert, caught
a trout with the fly which weighed four pounds, about four years
ago.   The best season of the year to fish the lake is from the
middle of May to the end of June ; when, on a favourable day, in
May, you may sometimes take from three to four dozen.   The
best part of the lake is the south or lower end, where the water
is shallow ; in the middle, where it is very deep, few fish " rise,"
but when they do they are generally *large*.   Some good fishing is
also occasionally obtained in the shallows at the north-west end,
or head of the Llyn, where the Avon Lâs flows into it ; we, however, met with very indifferent success in the summer of 1857,
partly owing to the best season being over before we commenced,
and partly to the intense heat and atmospheric influence, which
rendered it one of the worst fishing seasons, at least in Wales,
ever known.   The largest number of trout we caught occurred on
our first visit, the 20th of June ; we killed twenty-five, one or
two of which weighed half a pound.   After that the weather
became exceedingly hot and bright, so that our best day's sport
never exceeded eighteen or twenty, and frequently not half that
number.   The best time for fishing is almost always in the
forenoon, from eight or nine to eleven o'clock, and again from
two until four.   The evening " rise " is very uncertain, as it
generally is in most Welsh lakes.   The favourite fly is undoubtedly

the "pea-hen," sometimes called the Llyn Gwynant fly, in May, June, and July; the alder, red-spinner, Shaw's governor, and fernshaw, are also excellent flies. There are several boats on the pool, three of which belong to proprietors in the vicinity; and Henry Owen, the enterprising landlord of the comfortable inn at Pen-y-Gwryd, has recently put a very good boat on the lake, for the convenience of gentlemen frequenting his inn. Salmon, of from six to eight pounds, are occasionally taken with the angle, chiefly at the upper end of the lake, and afford excellent diversion from the boat; indeed, the pool would swarm with salmon, were it not for the poaching in the river at Beddgelert.

Nant Gwynant.

The view of Nant Gwynant, with the limpid waters of the Avon Lâs expanded into a lovely lake, about three miles from Pen-y-Gwryd, on the road to Beddgelert, is one of the most enchanting scenes in Snowdonia. There the grandest view of Snowdon is to be obtained: under a *proper light*, it is one of the sublimest scenes in Britain, and far surpasses the view from the Nantllef lakes, Llyn Cwellyn, or from any other point. On a fine summer's evening, the sun shedding a flood of radiance over the flashing waters of the lake below, or, later still, lighting up the lofty peaks of Snowdon, the general colouring of the surrounding mountains glowing with a rich ruddy hue, it will bear honourable comparison with any alpine scene in the British islands. Startling, however, is the contrast in stormy weather. The lightning's lurid flash—the thunder booming like successive discharges of heavy artillery amongst the mountains around—the dark mysterious hollows of Snowdon, ever and anon lit up with magical, awe-inspiring glimpses, rendered still more terrible by the Spirit of the Storm—the elemental strife and uproar, assisted by rain and hail descending with a force and fury rarely seen in lowland countries;—these manifestations of the power of Him who "created all things," kindle in the heart feelings of profound reverence for that Almighty Being, in whose hands we are, who alone can curb the stormy winds, and say, "Peace, be still!"

Llyn-y-Ddinas,

the "Lake of the Fortress."—Angling in this lake is very inferior to Llyn Gwynant. There was no boat on it in 1857, and, therefore, we had no opportunity of examining it much; but we were informed that the best sport was to be obtained in the spring, when, from a boat, twelve to twenty pounds of trout might occasionally be taken; but, as a general rule, the fish are neither so large nor so " free " as in the sister lake. We several times attempted to fish this pool from shore without any success: it is strange that the trout should be so shy, as the water is from the same source; the breed is similar: the only way to account for it is that possibly the bottom affords more food to the fish. At the latter end of July, and during August and September, some fine salmon fishing may, at times, be obtained upon this pool after a flood. The best place for the angler is at the upper end, where the Avon Lâs enters the lake. Several fine salmon, from eight to ten pounds, were caught in the pool during the summer of 1857. This llyn is generally rather shallow, and is nearly one mile in length, with an average breadth of from a quarter to one-third of a mile. The turnpike-road to Capel Curig and Llanberis runs along the west shore, and in winter, when the lake is high, must occasionally overflow the road. Llyn-y-Ddinas affords some fine picturesque effects for the artist, and, for general scenic beauty, is superior to any lake in the district, with the exception of Llyn Gwynant. Between the lakes on the left of the road leading to Capel Curig, is one of the finest Gorges in Snowdonia, CWM LLAN, the "hollow of the Church." In fine clear weather, the eye rests upon the highest peak of Snowdon, Moel-y-Wyddfa, "the bold head of the conspicuous summit." In the foreground, the murmuring crystal waters of the Avon Lâs, the varied tints of the frondage, the lower rock precipices, beautifully adorned with ivy and other parasitical plants, render the colouring, " the harmony of Nature," truly exquisite. We have "sat on rock, and mused o'er flood and fell," for hours on a calm summer's day, without being weary of gazing on the varied beauties of this magnificent *cwm*.

There are, indeed, few spots in the Principality where the beauties and sublimities of Nature are more admirably blended than on the road from Pen-y-Gwryd to Beddgelert, a distance of eight miles.

Llyn-y-Gader,

the "Pool of the Chair," is a small mere, surrounded by a dreary bare morass, about three miles and a quarter from Beddgelert on the Caernarvon road.   You follow the road, which is a continuous ascent for more than two miles, passing on your way Llam-y-Trwscol, "Trwscol's leap,"—to which a legend appends—until you arrive at a remarkable rock, on the left of the road, called "Pitt's Head," so named from its fancied resemblance to the profile of that celebrated statesman.   About three-quarters of a mile beyond lie the waters of Llyn-y-Gader.   On arriving opposite to the pool, you cross some swampy meadow land until you reach a rocky hummock which runs into the water; under the east side of which, in a small shallow creek, you will find the boat that belongs to the "Goat Hotel."

The trout in this lake are generally *very free*, and on a favourable day in May, from seven to eight dozen may be taken by a practised hand.   The trout are small, the average size being a quarter of a pound; the quality is very indifferent.   There *are*, however, large trout in the lake; one of three pounds was caught in the summer of 1856, by a young man from Beddgelert. During a series of visits we paid to this water, we occasionally took some trout of half a pound and upwards; and what was very remarkable, we, on one occasion, caught a few samlets, which were beautifully bright.   How they got into the lake is a mystery, as salmon are never caught above the waterfall at Nant Mill, and therefore cannot find their way into the brook that runs from Llyn-y-Gader to Llyn Cwellyn.   On referring to our notes, we find that the best sport we had on Llyn-y-Gader in 1857, occurred on the 11th and 13th July.   On the first occasion we killed forty-five, on the subsequent day fifty; the weight of fish for both days somewhat exceeded eighteen pounds.   The weather afterwards became very bright and hot, and so far as we know, the sport for the remainder of the season was at an end.   The flies we used

were similar to those at Llyn Gwynant.   The pea-hen was generally the favourite fly, but we also found the cinnamon and Shaw's
governor, dressed on rather smaller hooks, on some days in great
request.   The best time to fish is from nine o'clock A. M. until
four P. M., but the trout will sometimes rise freely until after
sunset.   There is only one small boat on the pool, which belongs
to the "Goat Hotel."   Some years ago, this lake was "all the
rage" with visitors at the "Goat;" in 1857, its popularity appeared to have declined, as very few fished this water besides
ourselves.   Llyn-y-Gader, although it looks deep in places, owing
to the dark peaty bed on which it lies, is not so in reality.   In
several parts it is so exceedingly shallow, that in dry weather,
when the water is low, it will hardly float a boat at some distance
from the shore.   The greatest depth is about eight yards, and
this occurs near some large stones, called "The Islands," which
peer above the water for a few feet when the lake is low, near
the shore on the west side, and form a convenient resting-place
for the black cormorants, which are frequently to be seen here.
Llyn-y-Gader is abundantly stocked with fish; and notwithstanding the large quantity that is annually taken with the rod, and
the injury it receives from the "board" and net, there appears
to be no perceptible diminution of the finny tribe.   From our
own observation, we believe that no lake of similar size in the
district is so full of trout.   You cannot fish from shore, partly
from the swampy nature of the ground, and also from the weeds,
bulrushes, and shoal water.   A boat is therefore *indispensable,*
and this involves an expense of five shillings per day at least; if
you *ride,* the charge is more than doubled.   The expense incurred
in fishing this pool, has probably been one cause why it is now
comparatively deserted.   The most favourable fishing-ground, for
large trout especially, is near the "islands," and along the west
and north shores, near some bulrushes which fringe the margin.
For general sport, across the middle of the pool; and occasionally
some fish may be taken in the shallow weedy water on the south
side.   The shores of the llyn, with the exception of a picturesque
rock at the south-east corner, are perfectly destitute of the
slightest protection from the weather; it is therefore advisable
to provide yourself with waterproof garments, in the event of

being obliged to brave the elements, as very heavy showers frequently occur in this bleak mountainous district, accompanied at times with violent gusts of wind.

The surrounding landscape is very imposing: Snowdon and his attendant Alps, loom up grandly to the east, whilst to the west and north-west, the eye wanders towards the summit of Mynydd Mawr (2,300 feet) with its finely curved outline, beneath which Drws-y-Coed, "the door of the wood," forms the entrance of the romantic Pass to the Llynniau Nantllef. On the south, Moel Hebog, and the hills around Beddgelert, form a magnificent background to the picture; and more immediately in the foreground, the vast mountain buttresses of Snowdon, "the outworks of the interior region of lakes and hills," soaring high above the naked valley at their feet, are seen to great advantage. At sunset, on a bright calm summer's eve, the surrounding panorama is truly exquisite.

CHAPTER V.

A PEEP INTO SNOWDONIA—CWM CLOGWYN—A VISIT TO LLYNNIAU
FFYNNON GWAS, COCH, FFYNNON LÂS, Y-NADROED—SCENERY—
EXCURSION TO LLYN LLAGI, LLYN-YR-ADAR, LLYN EDNO—BLACK-
BACKED GULLS—LLYNNIAU CWN—MONSTER TROUT—EXCURSION
TO LLYN EDNO IN 1849—EDNO TROUT—ACCIDENTS IN LLYN
LLAGI—DANGER OF CORACLES—YSTRADLLYN.

> "Such beauty, varying in the light
> Of living nature, cannot be portrayed
> By words, nor by the pencil's silent skill;
> But is the property of Him alone
> Who hath beheld it, noted it with care,
> And in his mind recorded it with love."

Llynniau Ffynnon Gwas, Coch, Ffynnon Lâs, Y-Nadroed.

On the west side of Snowdon there is a profound *cwm* or hollow, called Cwm Clogwyn, or the "hollow of the precipice;" this lonely spot lies immediately under the awful steeps of Moel-y-Wyddfa. In this "great hill solitude" there are four small llyns, which lie contiguous to each other, called Ffynnon Gwas, Llyn Coch, Ffynnon Lâs, and Y-Nadroed, severally signifying the "Servants'," the "Red," the "Blue," and the "Adder's" pools. These are very rarely visited by the angler, or even by the most adventurous tourist. The best way to approach these lakes, is to leave the turnpike road, near the "Pitt's Head," which the guides usually do in conducting visitors to the summit of Snowdon, and following the path for about one mile, make round the shoulder of Clawdd Coch, the "Red Ridge," and proceed over some rough broken ground, intersected by dry stone walls, and occasionally turbaries, some of them difficult to cross, until you reach Llyn Ffynnon Gwas, the most northerly of the group, and the only pool worth trying for the sake of sport. We visited

these lakes once, and as we were amply repaid for the fatigue we
endured in reaching them, we will give an account of our excur-
.sion, which occupied more than twelve hours.

It was on a fine morning in July, 1857, that we started from
Beddgelert early, accompanied by our guide and fisherman, to
visit these wild sequestered lakes. We went more for the sake
of exploration and adventure than with the expectation of sport.
The guide was nearly as ignorant as ourselves as to the exact
locality of the lakes; but, being provided with the Ordnance Map
—without which no man need travel among the byeways of
Wales—we had not much difficulty in piloting ourselves to Llyn
Ffynnon Gwas; the pool furthest from Beddgelert, and lying lower
down the mountain, and rather apart from the others. We had
both of us frequently seen these llyns from the summit of Clawdd
Coch, on the ascent to Snowdon, but until we arrived at the
locality, we were not aware of the extreme ruggedness of the
wild country we had to traverse, or the distance these lakes were
from the road.

On reaching our fishing-ground, after about four hours' toil,
we found the waters of Llyn Ffynnon Gwas violently agitated
with a furious north-west wind, which prevented any attempt to
angle until we got under the lee; it was besides exceedingly
cold, and we were glad to envelope ourselves in a waterproof cape
to keep warm. After refreshing "the inward man," we commenced fishing, but for some time we were in doubt whether
there were any fish in the llyn, as we could neither see a fish stir
nor obtain a "rise." The water appeared profoundly deep close
to the shore, and was of a dark, leaden hue; partly arising from
the boggy nature of the land from whence the lake derives its
supply, and also from the heavy masses of clouds which were
rapidly drifting over us. This llyn is said to derive its name,
"Ffynnon Gwas," which literally signifies the "Servants' well, or
spring," from a melancholy circumstance which occurred here
many years ago. A poor man, a shepherd or servant to a neighbouring farmer, was washing sheep in the lake, and by some
means or other got out of his depth and was drowned. The
lake ever after was called the "Servants' pool." After fishing
for half an hour, the sun came out, and as we had by that time

gained some shelter from the wind, we were at last favoured
with a "rise," and, after a short struggle, landed a trout of half a
pound. Thus encouraged, we continued fishing as well as the
wind would permit, until we returned to our starting point, and
by that time we had caught about thirteen of the most ugly trout
—chiefly very small—we had ever taken in any part of Wales.
They were also exceedingly lean, showing that the feed in the
lake was scarce. This circumstance is not uncommon in some of
the llyns which lie high up in the mountains. The fish generally
rose "short," and although we occasionally stirred some apparently large fish, yet it was evident they were not "in the humour:"
the more surprising, considering their lank hungry appearance.

The scenery here is exceedingly wild and impressive. On a
calm day—when profound stillness reigns, unbroken even by the
slightest sound—this "dark, melancholy" llyn, gleaming in the
midst of a trackless waste, backed by the "stony ruins" of the
vast mountain above it; the stillness broken perchance, after an
interval, by the ominous croak of the solitary raven, or the low
and hollow whisperings of the mysterious wind; the dark-brown
of the surrounding peat morass—the leading feature in these
shelterless and lofty wilds—these accessories, if anything additional was wanting, must add to the sublimity of this fine scene.

Llyn Ffynnon Gwas lies in a hollow, above which the route to
Snowdon from Llyn Cwellyn winds its way, with a deviation to
the left under the nearly perpendicular precipices of Clogwyn
Dù-Yr-Arddu, and then turning into the path through Bwlch
Cwm Brwynog, which conducts you down to the magnificent
Pass of Llanberis. It was in this immediate vicinity that the
Rev. Mr. Starr was killed, in 1846. The unfortunate gentleman,
in spite of the warnings of the guide, imprudently ventured upon
the mountains alone, got enveloped in the mist, lost his path,
became bewildered, and fell headlong over some precipices near
Clogwyn Dù-Yr-Arddu. His mangled remains, torn to pieces by
wild cats, were not discovered until the spring of 1847.

Having thus presented to the reader the results of our visit to
Llyn Ffynnon Gwas, let us now conduct him to Llyn Coch. At
three o'clock P. M., we accordingly proceeded on our way thither.
This very small tarn is scarcely more than half a mile off, but the

ground is so steep and broken that it cost us at least half an hour's toil to reach it. On our way we occasionally followed the course of the turbulent stream which issues from it, and on which are several pleasing waterfalls. After a heavy downfall of rain, the view of these falls must be very grand.

> " Here balmy air, and springs as ether clear
> Delight the eye, reanimate the heart."

The surplus water from the four pools falls into the stream which runs from Llyn-y-Gader to Llyn Cwellyn. Llyn Coch, the " Red pool," is the most shallow llyn we ever met with, and in dimension does not exceed a moderate sized pond. It appeared to us nearly, if not quite, destitute of fish; although we had been informed in several quarters that good sport and fine fish were occasionally obtained. We, however, afterwards learned, that shortly before our visit a net had been dragged through it, and doubtless nearly all the fish taken out. The pool does not exceed two or three feet in depth even in the centre, and, as the bottom is composed of mud, and tolerably free of stones or weeds, it is just the place for a net. After a few fruitless casts, we wended our way to Ffynnon Lâs, the " Blue pool," which lies immediately under the awful steeps of Snowdon. This tarn is even smaller than the former, but the water shelves down to apparently a great depth, and is of a pure azure green colour; hence, we presume, its name. Good trout are said to be occasionally taken here, and it probably supplies Llyn Coch. We could not, however, stir a fish; we suppose, as Captain Medwin says, " from the difficulty of extracting or luring them from their crystal retreats." Having with some difficulty crossed the rivulet which flows from Llyn Coch, we ascended a sharp acclivity until we arrived at Llyn-y-Nadroed, the "Adder's pool;" why so called, we could not learn. This is a small, dark, sullen piece of water, bounded on the south by steep rocks, with deep water close to their base, and the shore generally is very rough. There was such a nice ripple on the water that we were tempted to try a few casts; but we might have spared ourselves the trouble, for not a living creature exists in the llyn. This is caused probably from the existence of some mineral poison, probably copper, which abounds

in Snowdon.   Here we sat on a rock to refresh ourselves, after a
somewhat severe toil of several hours, and contemplated with
delight the sublime scene of rugged grandeur around, and it was
fully an hour ere we could tear ourselves away from this "profound, vast, and lonely mountain hollow."   The sun, however,
began to wax low on the horizon, and warned us to depart, as
the country we had to traverse on our homeward route was
exceedingly broken.   We therefore reluctantly bade farewell to
this region of "solemn desolation," so little known, but so well
worth the investigation of the admirer of nature.   Thus we successfully accomplished our exploration of Cwm Clogwyn.

Excursion to Llyn Llagi, Llyn-yr-Adar, Llyn Edno, etc.

The several routes to these lakes—neither of which are of considerable size—are some of the most interesting, as well as the
most arduous to be met with in the vicinity of Beddgelert.   These
llyns are very rarely visited by anglers ; but to such as can brave
the fatigue, they amply repay the labour of the ascent to them,
although the sport is most uncertain; but the grand scenic effects
from the summits of the mountains around, it is hardly possible
to overrate.   We include our account of these llyns in the
Beddgelert district, because, although they are situate in the
adjoining county of Merioneth, yet they lie at a more convenient
distance from Beddgelert than any fishing station in that county,
the village being on the very verge of Caernarvonshire.

There are at least three ways of reaching Llyn Edno, decidedly
the best pool of the series.   The easiest is from Pen-y-Gwryd ;
the most difficult, from Beddgelert.   There is another route,
almost equally formidable, from the shores of Llyn Gwynant.
We have, on different occasions, explored all of these routes.

We will first describe an excursion we made to these lakes
from Beddgelert, during the summer of 1857.   On Wednesday,
June 24, we started from our quarters at twenty minutes to five
o'clock, A. M.   The morning was cloudless ; and the day proved
excessively hot and sultry, with little or no breeze.   After leaving
Beddgelert, we followed the turnpike-road to Llyn-y-Ddinas;

there we crossed the Avon Lâs on stepping-stones, and followed
a path which skirted the south-west shore, until we approached
the north-east extremity of the lake.   Here we struck off to the
right, into a wild rugged country, crossing several ravines, and
through a belt of fir timber: at the bottom of the valley below
us we descried a farmhouse; and, being already excessively
thirsty, we made towards it, in the hope of obtaining some
refreshment; nor were we disappointed : the good woman of the
house readily produced some "glas dwr," literally, "blue water,"
Anglicè, skim-milk, which we found very refreshing.   We then
proceeded due east, towards a rather elevated mountain range of
picturesque outline, called Craig Llyn Llagi, which divides Llyn
Llagi from Llyn-yr-Adar.   At the foot of this range we discovered
the lake.   Llyn Llagi lies in a semi-circular *cwm*, and somewhat
resembles Llyn Bodlyn, near Llanbedr.   It is a wild sequestered
scene, but not nearly so savage and desolate in appearance as
Edno.   From the extreme beauty of the early morning, with a
thin almost transparent haze hanging over the pool, it indeed
wore a smiling dreamy aspect.   As the lake was as calm and
unruffled as the surface of a mirror, not a shadow on its waters,
save from the lofty rocks on its eastern shore, we saw that it was
useless to attempt to angle; so we slowly proceeded onwards to
visit Llyn-yr-Adar.   This portion of the route was the most
arduous and difficult of the whole excursion : it is not only very
steep and rugged, but the overpowering heat we had to endure,
added to the fatigue of crossing over Craig Llyn Llagi.   The trout
in Llagi are large and "free;" but it is dangerous to fish on the
east side, in consequence of there being deep water up to some
nearly perpendicular rocks.   We observed a few trout rising as
we passed the lake.   After gaining the summit of the barren
verdureless precipices which divide the llyns, we found the path
to Llyn-yr-Adar comparatively easy.   This pool is at a much
greater altitude than Llagi; it contains a picturesque rocky
islet, the haunt of a number of sea-gulls of the "black-backed"
species.   Here they lay their eggs, and bring up their young in
perfect security, being quite safe from the spoiler, unless he is
inclined to swim, as there is deep water between the islet and
the shore.   The appearance of this islet reminded us of the

account given by Mr. Charles St. John, in his very interesting "Tour in Sutherland;" similar rocks in the Highland lakes being the abode of the osprey.   On our approach to the lake, the gulls, which were all sitting on the islet, about 100 yards off, rose into the air, and testified their anger at our intrusion, by setting up an unceasing, wild, discordant screaming, making altogether a hideous clamour.   Here the lover of Nature may rest awhile, and contemplate the magnificent mountain scene which lies around him.   To the south, the barren, scathed, rocky peak of Cnight, by some supposed, from its steep conical form, to have been in remote ages subject to volcanic action ; the huge, daring outlines of Moelwyn, and the dark *cwms* around them, arrest the attention, and on the east and north the eye rests on a series of bare rugged mountains, where, amidst their deep recesses, several lakes lie " in grim repose."

We found Llyn-yr-Adar quite as calm as its sister lake.   It was now half-past ten o'clock, and there appeared to be little probability of the slightest breeze : fishing was out of the question. The sky at this time became suddenly overcast—dark thunder-clouds loomed up in the eastern heavens, which seemed to forebode a tempest : still no breeze—nought disturbed the death-like stillness except the melancholy wail of the gulls, which sounded ominously on the ear.   The air, even at this high elevation, was sultry and oppressive to a degree, and produced a feeling of lassitude and drowsiness which it was difficult to shake off.   After reposing for about an hour, we reluctantly gave the word to march, and bade adieu to Llyn-yr-Adar.   We now proceeded towards Llyn Edno, which lies about one mile and a quarter to the north-east, in the bosom of the same range of wild, savage, sterile mountains.   You pass, on your route, by two small tarns, called Llynniau Cwn, in the smallest of which it is said that there are some very large trout.   We were told that two gentlemen, fishing there in 1856, caught two trout, one of which weighed seven pounds, and the other two pounds.   There is also a marvellous tale of a monster trout, which is still believed to be in the pool, said to be at least eighteen pounds weight, and which has several times broken off the hooks.   The largest of these pools is destitute of fish.   On our arrival at Llyn

Edno, we were delighted to find that a slight breeze had sprung up, which we hoped would continue to freshen. We also observed that several large fish were on the move, several of which lazily rolled over the flies which were floating on the water. We therefore speedily unlimbered our rod, and put on a tempting cast of flies, viz. a woodcock wing, with yellow body, a fernshaw, and a March brown. Some heavy drops of rain now began to fall, so that we began to anticipate some sport. We were, however, doomed to disappointment. We remained nearly three hours waiting for a good breeze, without which it was quite evident nothing could be done. There were now and then a few "cats' paws," but the wary trout, although occasionally they "nibbled" at your flies by way of tantalizing you, were evidently not in earnest, and we were ultimately obliged to leave the lake— as others had done before—without "a fin" to recompense us for all our toil and labour. We returned home to Beddgelert by another route, following the course of Edno brook, which falls into the Avon Lâs near Plas Gwynant. This route, if possible, proved more toilsome and difficult than the ascent we had made in the morning, and we arrived at Beddgelert about six o'clock P.M., fatigued and somewhat exhausted, after spending the hottest day in the mountains we had ever encountered.

We now proceed to transcribe from our journal a brief account of an excursion we made to Llyn Edno in 1849, from Pen-y-Gwryd, attended with more fortunate results. In June, 1849, during a sojourn of a few days at Pen-y-Gwryd inn, we made our first acquaintance with this desolate spot. The distance from this place to Llyn Edno is about five miles, and the path, if it can be called one, though occasionally rough, boggy, and of steep ascent, is comparatively much easier than any other route. It was early on a joyous summer's day that we left our humble inn, in company with our guide and landlord, Henry Owen, bent on capturing, if possible, some of the wily trout, about whose shy habits we had had frequent talk with some of the native fishermen. The day appeared most favourable for our purpose; light fleecy clouds, with occasional bursts of sunshine, and a gentle breeze from south-east, which curled the waters of the llyn, left nothing that could be desired. *En route* we were much charmed

G

with the view of Nant Gwynant, which lay bathed in sunshine far down the mountain-side on our right. The tiny waves of the beautiful Llyn Gwynant sparkled in the sun's rays; and Snowdon, lifting his tall peaks into the clouds, which occasionally drifted across them, presented those sublime effects of light and shade, that inexpressible freshness, dignity, and grace, which we have never seen so fully realized as amongst the wild highland solitudes of Wales. As we proceeded we gradually got into a more alpine district, and after crossing a high ridge, on the summit of which we remained for a few minutes to rest, we descended into Cwm Edno, which leads to the lake. On our arrival at the pool, we speedily rigged our rod, and commenced fishing, not without some misgivings as to success. The wind and weather, however, as we had surmised, proved very favourable, and, in the course of a few hours, we were so fortunate as to capture six handsome trout, exceeding one pound each. These fish, for their size, were the strongest we had ever encountered; and as the shores of the llyn were very rough and stony, it was no easy task to land them safely. The trout were in the finest condition, firm, and of a beautiful colour. Our guide assured us that we ought to consider ourselves exceedingly fortunate, as it was only on rare occasions that trout could be taken here. Llyn Edno is scarcely more than three furlongs long from north to south, and is about two furlongs in width; it is of unknown depth, and there is hardly any shoal water even close to the shore. It is in some places difficult of access, owing to smooth rocks slanting off into deep water. This is the most celebrated lake in the district for its large and finely flavoured trout; as a matter of course these trout are exceedingly shy, and you may go several times in succession without being even favoured with the sight of one. The best side to fish is the east shore; the water on the western side is very deep, and trout —as we have before observed—seldom rise well in deep water. We killed our fish with the March brown and fernshaw. The flesh of most of the trout caught in Llyn Edno cuts red, and for quality and flavour can even successfully vie with those taken at Llyn Ogwen. Trout have been caught in Edno as large as six or eight pounds, but the general size is from three quarters to one pound and a half and two pounds. The best sport we heard of in 1857, was that obtained by two first-rate anglers from the neighbourhood of Maentwrog, who caught twenty-three trout, the weight of which averaged about one pound each. The trout in Llyn-yr-Adar are said to run large, but, like those in Edno, extremely shy. These lakes are occasionally poached with the "board" by quarrymen from Ffestiniog and Tan-y-Bwlch, but we presume with indifferent success, at least by day. The "board" is generally most destructive at night, as the tackle employed is coarse, and therefore apt to scare large fish in the daytime. It is within the memory of man when no trout existed in Llyn-yr-Adar; it is said to have been stocked from Llyn Llagi. A few years ago a fatal accident occurred at Llagi. A man was fishing under some rocks, off which he slipped, and getting out of his depth was drowned. An accident, which might have been attended with a similar catastrophe, occurred to a Mr. S. and his servant, whilst fishing Llagi, in 1856. They were in a coracle, which is a ticklish boat to manage, and were fishing over the deepest water in the lake, near to the rocks. He had hooked a fish of about one pound, and was in the act of getting him into the landing-net, when his foot slipped, and losing his balance, he fell over the coracle, which immediately capsized, carrying the servant with it. Mr. S. called out to the servant to take care of himself, as he—Mr. S.—had quite enough to do to keep himself afloat. This hint "Jack" instantly acted upon, and being more nimble than his master, struck out and reached the shore first. The coracle, fishing-rod, and we believe even the fish, were ultimately recovered. There are no boats on any of these mountain-pools, but coracles, or India-rubber boats, are occasionally employed. Unless you can swim well, they are exceedingly dangerous, as they require skilful management.

Before we conclude our notice of the lakes in the Beddgelert district, we must not omit to mention

Ystradllyn,

pronounced Strathllyn, a small pool on the west side of the range of hills leading to the sea coast near Tremadoc, which form a continuation of the ridge leading south from Moel Hebog. There is a slate quarry near the east end of Ystradllyn, and probably it is poached by quarrymen; nevertheless, good sport is occasionally obtained, and the trout, although not large, are good and "free." We derived this information from one of the local fishermen, who sometimes went to the lake. The pool, however, we were also informed, is netted weekly. There is a boat which may be had for a trifling remuneration. The distance to Cwm Ystradllyn from Beddgelert is about four miles and a half, and the views of the surrounding scenery on the route, including the Pass of Beddgelert, are exquisitely beautiful. There are one or two other small tarns amongst these hills; but we cannot give any information about them.

CHAPTER VI.

RIVER FISHING AT BEDDGELERT—AVON LÂS—PONT ABERGLASLYN
—CRAIG-Y-LLAN—RIVER-POACHING—COLWYN—ANECDOTES—
MOEL HEBOG—EXCURSION TO SUMMIT—CNIGHT—MOELWYN—
TREMADOC—SCENERY—PORTHMADOC—PENMORFA—DOLBEN-
MAEN.

> " I love the walks where Nature's track is seen,
> And riot mid rent rocks and forests wild,
> Huge precipices, cataracts, and groves
> Of venerable oak, impervious half
> To Sol's bright beams, o'erhanging waterfalls,
> And half admitting chequer'd rays to dance
> Adown the silver Naiad's murmuring stream."

The Abon Lûs,

commonly called the Glasllyn, is the most beautiful stream in
Snowdonia—in our opinion it is the most picturesque river in
all Wales. Cradled in the clouds, nursed by the frost and
snows of winter, the dews and rains of summer, it issues
from its parent, Ffynnon Lâs, "The Blue Spring," a small deep
pool of crystalline purity lying in a profound *cwm*, under
the northern precipices of Snowdon, and passing through the
"wild and lone Llyn Llydaw," it flows over a series of cataracts
called Rhaiadr Cwm Dyli, into the lovely "Vale of waters;"
thence to Beddgelert: a situation, as Mr. Pennant justly observes,
"one of the fittest in the world to inspire religious meditation,
amid lofty mountains, woods, and murmuring streams." A
ramble along the banks of the Avon Lâs below Beddgelert is
very delightful, and offers, in fine weather, "a most delicious
evening scene;" indeed the whole course of the river from its
mountain home until its waters arrive at Pont Aberglaslyn, is a
succession of contrasts. In one part you behold, bountifully

spread out, the luxuriant beauties of nature; in another, her wild
and barren sublimities; and should the "pale moonlight" at a
later hour lend additional grace to the picture, portraying in
softer outlines the darkening shadows of the rocks on one side of
the Pass, while on the other they are brightly illumined by the
moon's rays, the wanderer may silently contemplate the decreas-
ing shadows of the lofty mountains, as the moon becomes more
elevated, or listen to the ceaseless roar of waters plunging and
foaming in their mad career over the huge rocks and stones—
"fletynge and raging," in the language of quaint old Leland—
which vainly attempt to stay their course through the magnificent
Pass of Beddgelert.   Before arriving at Llyn-y-Ddinas, the river
receives an additional supply from the superabundant waters of
Llyn Edno; at Beddgelert, it is joined by its wild romping sister
the Colwyn, a mountain torrent, which chiefly derives its source
from Snowdon and Moel Hebog, and flows, as already observed,
through the Pass of Beddgelert to PONT ABERGLASLYN, "the gate
into Merionethshire."   This spot is deservedly considered one of
the most wonderful scenes in Wales; but to see the view to perfection, you must proceed about one hundred yards on the Tremadoc
road.   Here the venerable bridge clothed with ivy, and the lofty
rocks on either side the entrance to the Pass,

> " Raised tier on tier,
> High pil'd from earth to heaven,"

form a fine scene; the view is incomparably grand, and makes
a lasting impression on the mind and memory.   "We were
inexpressibly struck," remarks an observant writer, "with the
Bwlch at Pont Aberglaslyn, certainly the finest scene of its kind,
the most perfect realization of a mountain pass to be found
in Wales."   The river, after passing under the bridge, forms a
deep pool, a favourite haunt of salmon, and from thence proceeds tranquilly on its course to the sea, through a flat marshy
traeth—meaning a sand—until it reaches Porthmadoc, where it
passes into the sea through sluice gates, which shut when the
tide flows.   This *traeth* was formerly covered at high tide, but
reclaimed at vast expense by the late Mr. Maddocks.   The
embankment, a mile long, which accomplished this great im-

provement, was finished in 1807, at a cost of £100,000.
There are several deep, dark green pools in the Avon Lâs above
the bridge. Here the salmon and sewin lurk on their passage
from the sea to the lakes, and higher portions of the river.
The "salmon leap," described by Hansard in his work on
angling, published about twenty-five years ago, has been destroyed
for some time, probably through elemental agency. It used to
form a stock subject in the guide books and tours. This "leap"
was just above Pont Aberglaslyn. The precipitous sides of the
chasm through which the river flows, are composed of schistose
rocks of a black, grey, and ochry tinge, betraying evidence of
copper ore. These are in some parts clothed with heather, which
when in blossom in the autumn, presents a rich purple tint, and
adds much to that colour for which the Pass is so celebrated.
These rocks—Craig-y-Llan—rise to an altitude of 700 feet, and
in some places scarcely leave a secure footing to the angler, as
the wild waters rush tumultuously at their feet. Several levels
have been driven into the rocks on both sides the river in search
of copper, but we understand that ore has not been found in sufficient quantity to repay the expense of working the mines.
With one or two exceptions, these levels are now abandoned. So
far as angling is concerned it is fortunate ; for, had copper been
found in any quantity, the mineral water from the levels would
speedily have destroyed all the fish in the river.

Some years ago, the Avon Lâs was a most excellent stream for
salmon, sewin, and trout fishing, in fact, one of the very best
rivers in North Wales ; but of late years poaching has been
carried on to such a great extent as materially to interfere with
the legitimate sportsman. Notwithstanding the efforts of the
poachers, who at Beddgelert, day and night, pursue their illegal
calling with net and spear, a great number of sewin and salmon
ascend the river from Porthmadoc ; but numbers are netted before
they reach Pont Aberglaslyn, and comparatively very few indeed
fall to the share of the angler. Below the bridge, the river is
strictly preserved by a wealthy solicitor of the name of Williams,
residing in the vicinity ; and gentlemen angling, even for trout
only, are liable to be warned off by the keepers, unless they
possess a card of permission. Strictly speaking, this portion of

the river can hardly be said to be *preserved*, as Mr. Williams's keepers are daily employed sweeping the river with a net during the summer and autumn.   A few years ago, a fishing club was established at Tremadoc, mainly, we believe, through the efforts of a Mr. Spooner, a gentleman then residing in the neighbourhood, and day or season tickets could be obtained at a moderate rate. We were informed in 1857, that the *traeth* at that time was preserved entirely for angling, so that first-rate trout and salmon fishing could be obtained.   Trout, of large size, still abound in the river below the bridge, of from one to three or four pounds. These fish are occasionally taken with the fly above the bridge in the autumn, on their passage up the river to spawn.   From the circumstances we have detailed, angling in the Avon Lâs in 1857 was a profitless pursuit, and very few salmon or sewin were taken by visitors.   Those fish that were caught by the rod were chiefly taken by one or two professional fishermen residing in Beddgelert, who knew the river well, and were at work early or late, as it suited their convenience.   We knew of several gentlemen who had come a considerable distance, expressly for the purpose of salmon-fishing, who went away disgusted with the disgraceful practices openly followed by the natives of the village.   The Avon Lâs above Pont Aberglaslyn belongs, we believe, to the Crown, and is therefore a *free* river; but surely some steps might be taken by proprietors of land in the neighbourhood to put a stop to these unlawful pursuits, and thus prevent one of the very best rivers in Wales from becoming comparatively worthless.

We have considered it a duty to place before the salmon-fisher the vexatious annoyances he will be exposed to, should he fix upon Beddgelert as the scene of his piscatorial pursuits ; unless, therefore, affairs are much altered for the better since our sojourn at Beddgelert in 1857, we emphatically warn anglers against a visit to that village for its salmon or river fishing.   The season for sewin commences in June, and salmon begin to ascend the river in July and August.   The average size of sewin is from half a pound to two or three pounds ; salmon weigh from six to twelve or fourteen pounds; but few very large fish are caught until late in the autumn.

The Colwyn.

We cannot report favourably of the fishing in the Colwyn. This river in the spring and summer is frequently very low and clear, so much so, that in many places you can easily cross it almost dryshod. Comparatively few sewin or salmon ascend this stream, as two or three miles above Beddgelert their further progress is stopped by a waterfall. The trout in the Colwyn are generally very small; but they are pretty little fish, and in the spring, or during a flood, will bite freely at a worm. Near the waterfall, an old woman, who lives hard by in a cottage, occasionally earns a few shillings by catching sewin in their attempts to leap over it. She places a basket at the foot of the fall, and the fish actually fall back into it. This puts us in mind of a somewhat similar practice, which we have somewhere read of being pursued in Scotland, the precise *locale* we do not now remember. A laird, who lived near a salmon stream on which there was a fall, used to catch sea-trout by placing a caldron of boiling water beneath it, into which the fish fell in their attempts to ascend, and they were actually cooked ready on the spot for the entertainment of his friends whom he had invited to witness this singular sport. The Colwyn is a joyous mountain torrent flowing through Nant Colwyn, and, to the stranger who is fond of a stroll into the wilds, we strongly recommend a ramble to its sources. Near Beddgelert, the banks of the river are clothed with native oaks and other trees, and it rushes for about two or three miles over a rocky bed, which during a high flood assumes a similar aspect to its turbulent sister, the Avon Lâs. An immense body of water after heavy rains comes down this river from the mountains, and at Beddgelert it sometimes presents in a few hours a most formidable appearance.

Excursion to the Summit of Moel Hebog.

In favourable weather, mountain-climbing forms a most delightful pursuit, and by some enthusiastic spirits it is followed up with a degree of ardour which scorns alike danger or fatigue. Amongst the Snowdonian Alps one of the most striking and attractive is

Moel Hebog, and as there are very few recorded accounts of an ascent to its summit, we purpose giving a brief account of a visit we made to it in 1857.   There are several routes, all of which are more or less difficult; but the path generally followed is through a lane to the right of the Goat Hotel, which gradually leads to the tertiary ranges of the mountain, and is easily followed without the assistance of a guide.   There is another way from the summit of the hills overlooking Ystradllyn.   The ascent from this point, however, is exceedingly arduous and difficult, as the sides of the mountain on the south-east are very steep, and in some parts scarped and covered with rocks and loose rolling *débris*, which perpetually give way under your feet; but the summit of Hebog once attained, we can promise a rich treat to such as *dare* its performance.   We are surprised that Moel Hebog is so seldom visited by tourists.   To our mind, the view from it, if not so extensive as Snowdon, is equally as pleasing, and in some respects superior, because you are now upon a level with several of the surrounding mountains, and obtain such a magnificent prospect of Snowdon himself.

> " The mountains huge appear
> Emergent, and their broad backs upheave
> Into the clouds ; their tops ascend the sky."

It is singular that, with the exception of Lord Lyttelton, who ascended Moel Hebog some time in the last century, there is no recorded instance—as far as our reading goes, which is tolerably extensive—in the various "tours in Wales," of any topographer of note having attempted it.   The fact is, that only one leading idea pervades the heads of the numerous tourists who annually arrive at Beddgelert, and that is, the ascent to the "King of Mountains."   There is, however, a great deal to see and admire in this delightful locality, besides the view from Snowdon, and an excursion to the summit of Moel Hebog is by no means the least attractive.   It is a much more difficult task to perform than it looks from the old bridge at Beddgelert, and, although not nearly so lofty, requires a great deal more exertion—really harder "collar work"—than the usual route from Beddgelert to the summit of Snowdon.

We accomplished our ascent of Moel Hebog on a fine warm morning in August, 1857, commencing from the north-east side, until we had rounded the vast deep *cwm*—the grandest feature of the mountain—looking north-east; we then advanced towards the ridge before mentioned, and boldly breasted the almost perpendicular steeps at the south-east side. We had no guide, and therefore cannot say whether this is the usual route; but, at all events, it proved fatiguing enough, and even dangerous, as in some places a single false step might have produced a broken limb. The day—although the sky was sometimes partially obscured by dark masses of clouds, producing those fascinating effects of light and shade, those "stirring mountain effects"—was excessively hot and sultry, and even on the highest point of the mountain it was quite 'calm. Moel Hebog, according to the latest trigonometrical survey, is 2,580 feet above the sea level: this altitude is 1,091 feet lower than Moel-y-Wyddfa, the highest peak of Snowdon. There are two *carnedds* or mounds of stones on the summit of Moel Hebog; one of them, apparently very ancient, near the edge of the precipice which overhangs the deep *cwm* or hollow already described, and the other erected a few years ago by the Ordnance surveyors. This *carn* lies to the west of the other, and is built over a dry stone wall boundary. It is not laid down on the Ordnance map, and has perhaps been erected since its execution. The summit of the mountain between the two *Carnedds* is table-land, and affords a very pleasant promenade. There is also from the Ordnance *carnedd* a very smooth, easy incline, mostly short velvet-like turf, from hence towards Cwm Ystradllyn and Dolbenmaen. The view from the summit looking south to the sea over the peninsula of Lleyn,

"Land of the bleak, the treeless moor,"

the bay of Cardigan, as far south as St. David's Head, the hill country of Merioneth, including the "ruined towers" of Harlech and Criccieth, is magnificent in the extreme :—to the north and north-west, the eye embraces some of the loftiest points in Snowdonia,

"Sterile mountains seared and riven," ,

with peeps here and there of some of the most beautiful lakes
and valleys. "It is long before the eye," eloquently observes the
author of the Beauties, Harmonies, and Sublimities of Nature,
"unaccustomed to measure such elevations, can accommodate itself
to scenes so admirable—the whole appearing as if there had been
a war of the elements : . . . . rocks and mountains are blended
with others as dark, as rugged, and as elevated as themselves :
the whole resembling the swellings of an agitated ocean."

> " The increasing prospect tires our wandering eyes,
> Hills peep o'er hills, and Alps on Alps arise."

Moel Hebog is generally the quarter to which the guides look
before they start for Snowdon; it is in fact their weather-glass.
If the peak of Hebog is covered with clouds, and assumes a dark
and threatening aspect, they consider that it is hopeless to attempt
the ascent of Snowdon; if on the contrary it is clear, they
prognosticate that the ascent will be accompanied by favourable
weather.   We remember that in June, 1840, when we ascended
Snowdon for the first time, under the pilotage of Richard Edwards,
" the father of guides," as he was called, the old and experienced
guide would not permit us to leave our quarters at the Goat
Hotel, until Hebog had "doffed his night-cap." We may add,
that we afterwards found from experience that the guides were
generally right.

Cnight.

Before we finally bid adieu to Beddgelert, we cannot refrain
from calling the attention of the reader to one or two other
charming excursions within reach, and which, if he is fresh to the
country, he will be especially delighted with.

The tourist, on the road from Tremadoc to Pont Aberglaslyn,
will observe on his right two mountains of singularly bold and
picturesque outline, these are called Cnight and Moelwyn; the
former is 2,372 feet, and the latter 2,566 feet above the sea-level.
It is not too much to assert that there is no mountain in Wales—
not even Snowdon—that presents to the eye such elegance of
outline as the conical summit of Cnight.   One of the best views

of this mountain is from the point just named; but there are several other exquisite peeps to be obtained on the road between Pont Aberglaslyn and Tan-y-Bwlch.   One of them, especially that near the bridge on the Merionethshire side, is certainly one of the finest mountain vistas in Wales.   In the course of several solitary rambles along the streams and amongst the woods which clothe the bases of these mountains, we were seized with the desire of ascending to the summit of Cnight; this exploit we knew, from the appearance of the mountain, would be attended with some difficult and arduous climbing; but nothing daunted, and having recently performed the feat of ascending Moel Hebog unaided and alone, we determined to carry out our purpose on the first fitting opportunity.   The weather in September, 1857, was singularly fine in North Wales; magnificent lights, magical transitions from light to shade, brilliant sunsets, were the usual daily concomitants for several weeks.   Such weather is rarely seen in Wales at this advanced period of the year; mists and heavy rains being the usual characteristics.

Few Englishmen have ever stood upon the summit of Cnight: we never met with but one individual who had performed the feat, and this was a clergyman, a perfect enthusiast in mountain scenery—a most intellectual companion—and whom in a future chapter we will introduce more prominently before our readers.

Friday, the 4th of September, being a singularly fine day, and exactly suited to our purpose, we left Beddgelert early in the afternoon, on an excursion to the summit of Cnight.   We proceeded by way of Pont Aberglaslyn, and, crossing the bridge, followed the road to Tan-y-Bwlch for about half a mile, when we struck off into the old mountain road to the left through some woods, passing Nantmor, "the vale of the sea," and after crossing several ravines and a mountain rivulet (which contains some fine trout), we at length gained the open country.   The scenery here is "untameably wild," and the magnificent outline of the lofty mountain—the object of our excursion—loomed up grandly before us to our left.   After crossing some stone walls—which, built without mortar, are often dangerous to get over, from being generally in a ruinous, tottering condition, the usual boundaries in the Welsh highlands—we began, after leaving the old road, to

gradually ascend the secondary ranges of Cnight. The view to
the south was very extensive, embracing the estuaries of Traeth
Mawr and Bach, Cardigan Bay, the noble ruins of Harlech and
Criccieth castles, the hill country of Merioneth, stretching from
Ffestiniog to Barmouth, backed up by Rhinog Vawr, Cader Idris,
and the Arans. To the west, the eye rested on Moel Hebog, and
the picturesque range of hills trending down to the sea at Tremadoc; a portion of the wild peninsula of Lleyn, including the bold
headland, off which lie St. Tudwal's Isles, which stretches into
the sea beyond Pwllheli, and the "isle of saints," Bardsey, looming in the far west. "A landscape, like a picture," remarks an
intelligent writer, "requires a good light; it looks flat under
broad sunshine, although all its elements are essentially picturesque, and those who view it under a morning or midday sun,
or cold gray sky, and depart near a fine sunset, can hardly believe
that the same scene could exhibit contrasts so great, if they did
not see it with their own eyes. Then, the natural beauty, the
grandeur of the parts of which the landscape is composed, is
understood." The truth of these remarks will hardly be disputed;
and we fully appreciated them;

"The gay beams of gladsome day,"

however, in no way interfering with the beauty of the landscape,
as the striking contrasts of light and shade, produced by a
canopy of broken clouds, some of them occasionally resting on
the summits of the more lofty mountains, left their due breadth
of shadow and produced a combination of "effects" we had
rarely seen equalled. After a gradual ascent of about an hour,
we approached the *plateau*, from which rises the cone of Cnight;
and here the real labour of the ascent commenced. On our
approach to the foot of the cone, we saw at once that our antici-
pations of the difficulty of ascending, or rather *clambering* to the
summit, were not magnified. Path there was none; the steep
incline was covered with small loose *débris*, and on the south
side, looking down into Cwm Croesor, the mountain was a sheer
precipice, absolutely inaccessible. It was some little time before
we could summon up courage to commence our task; and it was
not until after several repulses, from the difficulty of keeping our

footing, that we succeeded in accomplishing the ascent. Our approach to the mountain was from the south-west; we then turned to the north-west side, and after excessive toil, and some danger, we at last stood upon the summit of the cone. Here the Ordnance surveyors have erected a *carnedd ;* and, being exposed to the wind, which began to blow freshly, we were glad to repose under its lee. We had no conception that the view would have been so extensive or so magnificent, and it was some time before we could take in all the details of the splendid panorama around us. To the north and east, Snowdonia lay unveiled; the mighty monarch Snowdon, carnedds Llewelyn, Dafydd, Moel Siabod, and the Glyders, rose up in all their majestic grandeur; whilst to the east, the waters of Llyn Conwy glistened in the sunshine amidst the sea of mountain tops which arose in that quarter. The view to the south, seaward, we have already noticed : but what struck us more than anything else was the deep *cwm* that lay immediately below—Cwm Croesor. Picture to yourself a bird's-eye view of an enormous ship—a " Great Eastern "—on the stocks before her decks are laid, or the depths of some mountain lake left dry through some fearful convulsion of the elements ; this gives you only a faint idea of this sublime scene. Cwm Croesor is the profound hollow which separates Cnight from Moelwyn ; from the height on which we stood, that huge mountain of course lost some of its grandeur, because we were within some 200 feet of being on a level with it ; still we were inexpressibly charmed as we dived into some of the dark, shadowy, mysterious *cwms* which surround his base, amongst which we observed the waters of the romantic Llyn Cwm Orthin, sparkling in the rays of the evening sun. These bird's-eye peeps of lakes in the wildly-picturesque landscape, which characterise the mountain scenery of Wales, add greatly to the general effects observable from a lofty position. No less than eighteen or twenty llyns are visible from the summit of Cnight, amongst which our old acquaintances, Edno, Llagi, and Llyn-yr-Adar, were conspicuous. Cwm Croesor is watered by a little streamlet which threads its way at the bottom, gladdening the vale beneath in its onward course before its waters join the Avon Lâs at Cerig-y-Rhwydwr, on the Traeth Mawr.

After spending more than an hour in the silent contemplation

of these stupendous works of nature—these glories and sublimities of the

> " Mountain and the flood,"

we reluctantly began to retrace our steps, which we found almost
more arduous and fatiguing than the ascent.

> " These are thy glorious works, Parent of good,
> Almighty! Thine this universal frame,
> Thus wondrous fair; Thyself how wondrous then!
> Unspeakable, who sitt'st above these heavens
> To us invisible, or dimly seen
> In these thy lowest works; yet these declare
> Thy goodness beyond thought, and power divine."
>
> PARADISE LOST.

Traces of volcanic action are said to have been discovered on
Cnight. Vitrified stones, showing the effects of fire, are also said
to have been picked up; but we are free to confess that we
could discover nothing leading to the conjecture, and must therefore leave it to wiser heads to determine. We descended into
the road by nearly the same route as the ascent, and were glad
to reach our quarters after six hours' pleasurable excitement,
feeling only a slight fatigue.

Moelwyn.

The ascent to Moelwyn is easily performed over the western
arm, up which a pony may be ridden. The route part of the way
is the same as to Cnight. At the entrance into Cwm Croesor, you
pass by Ffynnon Helen, on the old road to Tan-y-Bwlch; and
after proceeding on the road for about three-quarters of a mile,
you turn off to the left, and get upon the south-west arm of the
mountain, which gradually leads to the summit. The view is
very extensive, and almost equally as impressive as from Cnight.
Cwm Croesor, however, is scarcely seen to such advantage, the
sides of Moelwyn being less precipitous. There is a fine view of
the vale of Ffestiniog from the summit of Moelwyn, which also
includes the Arenigs and the mountainous region around Bala.
The distance from the highest point of Moelwyn to Beddgelert

cannot be less by road than seven miles. This mountain is surrounded by numerous llyns, but they are all more or less poached
by the workmen employed at the slate quarries, and now afford,
we believe, indifferent sport.

Tremadoc.

This pretty quiet village is delightfully situate beneath the
precipitous rocks which terminate the Moel Hebog range to the
south. The distance from Beddgelert is seven miles, and forms
a very pleasant pedestrian excursion. We can hardly extol too
highly the exquisite scenery which greets the eye at almost every
step from Tremadoc to Beddgelert; "lofty rocks, well-wooded
slopes, cascades, green recesses, retired valleys," which make you
long to explore them, diversify the scene. The perpendicular
cliffs, some of them adorned with ivy, are steep and inaccessible
from their foot, bearing some resemblance to the walls of an
ancient fortress, while here and there, lying on the roadside, you
behold huge boulders torn off from the crags above, the combined effects of time and weather; and narrow escapes from
fearful accidents are recorded, when these large masses of rock
have fallen with a tremendous crash from the adjacent precipices.
These disruptions occur chiefly in the winter, after heavy rains
or long-continued frosts. The road runs occasionally by the side
of the Avon Lâs for several miles, and about two miles from
Pont Aberglaslyn, a fine mountain view—an evening scene especially of great beauty and grandeur in fine clear weather—unfolds
itself to the eye. The highest peak of Snowdon gradually appears
in the extreme background—the entrance to the Pass of Beddgelert, with its richly-wooded rocks covered with purple blooming
heather, and with mosses and lichens of delicate green—the
summits of Cnight and Moelwyn, and the convulsed scenery at
their feet, glow under the effulgence of the setting sun,—the
whole presenting a picture of mingled sublimity and softness
which absolutely fascinates the beholder; and we much question
whether there is any other landscape in Wales which is comparable
to this, when seen under favourable lights.

Porthmadoc.

This improving seaport is distant from Tremadoc about one
mile on the road to Tan-y-Bwlch. It is situate at the outlet of
the Avon Lâs into the sea, and has rapidly become a place of
considerable trade. When we were there, in the year 1857, a
great many new houses were in progress of erection, several of
which were intended for shops; and the town and port wore the
appearance of busy industry. This is the principal outlet of the
district, and a large export trade in slates is carried on from the
quarries of Ffestiniog, Moelwyn, and neighbourhood. There is a
good and safe tidal harbour for shipping, most of which lies afloat
even when the tide is out. A great many vessels were in the
harbour loading with slates; and one day we counted at least
twenty vessels outside the " bar " on their outward voyage. The
sluices which shut the tide out from the *traeth* are above the
town, and extend across the river. A road is bridged over them,
and at half-ebb the water rushes with great velocity through
these sluices from the fine lake of water formed by the river
being thus dammed up at high water, or more properly during
the flow of the tide, when the sluice-gates close. Salmon and
sewin find egress to the river, above the sluices, at the slack of
the tide after high water, or during the ebb. The lake appeared
to us generally shallow, and extends along the inner side of the
great embankment. Whilst standing on the summit of this, we
have, when the sun shone on the water, counted numerous fine
salmon and sewin, sailing about like so many chubb, fresh from
the sea. Fine sport is here to be obtained from a boat, as the
fish will rise greedily to the fly; but you must first obtain leave
from the proprietor of the fishery, Mr. Williams. The walk
across the embankment extends for about one mile, and forms a
delightful promenade in fine weather. Charming land and sea
prospects may here be obtained. The tramway from the slate
quarries runs along its summit, which is 100 feet high from the
foundation. The coach-road is formed on a lower portion of the
embankment on the landward side.

ᵽ It may be useful to anglers and others to know that there is a
ferry from the harbour across the estuary to Harlech; but there

is a wide expanse of sands on the other side of the river when the water retires, and care should be taken to ascertain the time of flood-tide. In fine weather, the passage across the ferry is agreeable enough; but when the wind blows fresh from the south-west it raises a heavy sea; at such times we should much prefer to take the road by Tan-y-Bwlch, although it is a considerable distance round. There is another passage across the river, higher up, but we have not tried it.

Penmorfa,

the "head of the marsh," is a small village, situate on an eminence about one mile from Tremadoc, on the old road to Caernarvon: a visit to this place, where there is a comfortable village inn, forms a pleasant evening's stroll from Tremadoc. Farther on, distant four miles, is the wretched village of Dolbenmaen, "where was a round tower like that at Dolbadarn, now demolished." The country here is extremely wild and dreary, on the confines of the Peninsula of Lleyn, and the natives appear equally as wild and primitive as the country they inhabit. Before reaching Dolbenmaen you cross a considerable brook, the Dwyfor, which rises in the mountains called Mynydd Tal-y-Mignedd, a few miles to the south-east of Llynniau Nantllef. Its waters are here joined by a small rivulet, combining the waters flowing from Ystradllyn and Llyn Dù. In the spring, we were informed that there was excellent trout fishing here; we, however, did not try it, as at the time of our visit it was very late in the season; we only made an exploratory excursion. The chief drawback to the angler is the want of accommodation at Dolbenmaen. We had expected to have found a respectable village and a comfortable inn, being deceived by the conspicuous letters in which the name of the place appears on the map; it, however, consists of only a few mean cottages, a small church, and one of the most filthy, miserable pothouses we had ever the misfortune to enter. Imagine our disappointment, hot and thirsty as we were—for we had walked from Beddgelert, *viâ* Tremadoc, a distance of twelve miles, in a very warm day—to find some difficulty in procuring any refreshment whatever. On entering the ruinous-looking tenement, we were going to turn to the right, when we found the damp, dirty hole, called, we suppose, the "parlour," filled to the brim with the family at dinner, with scarce room to move round the table, which occupied no inconsiderable share of the apartment; what the dinner consisted of we did not stay to examine, but there was nothing of a very savoury character, judging from the effluvia which proceeded from it. We then directed our steps into the kitchen, where our nostrils were assailed with a vile compound of nauseous tobacco-smoke and stale porter. Several men, half savages in appearance, were here carousing, and to judge from the jargon—to us incomprehensible—which was going on, were already (*temp.* one o'clock) given to Bacchus. As Welshmen generally on such occasions are very much inclined to be quarrelsome; and knowing from experience that a man "in his cups" is a very disagreeable acquaintance, we hastily summoned to our aid the best Welsh we could command, and asked a dirty handmaid for "*Gwydraid-o-cwrw da,*"—a glass of good ale—instead, we were indulged with some sour, stale porter, having drunk which, we hastily made our exit, and bade adieu to Dolbenmaen. From this description of Dolbenmaen accommodation, we should strongly recommend the angler to take up his quarters at Penmorfa or Tremadoc; at the latter place there is a most excellent inn, the Madoc Arms, where he will meet with every comfort and attention.

We have thus indicated a few more places that present attractions to the angler and the lover of nature in the district surrounding Beddgelert, but there are others almost equally worthy of a visit—wild hill solitudes, dark dreamy hollows, smiling vales, flashing waterfalls, or shadowy mountain tops—whither the angler, perchance tired of sport, may repair, and jot down in his memory vivid recollections of

> "Scenes so charming,"

where the mind of the wanderer becomes so deeply impressed with a sense of his own littleness, and where he is ready to exclaim, in the beautiful and impressive language of the Psalmist—

> "O Lord, how manifold are thy works: in wisdom hast thou made them all, the earth is full of thy riches."

CHAPTER VII.

LLYN CWELLYN — SCENERY — NANT MILL—CASTELL CIDWM—
MYNYDD MAWR—CHAR—TROUT—ANGLING—GWRFAI—SNOW-
DON RANGER—ASCENT TO SNOWDON—BROOK FISHING—LLYN
DYWARCHEN—DRWS-Y-COED—NANTLLEF—SCENERY OF NANT-
LLEF LAKES—EXCURSIONS THROUGH PASS—LAKE FISHING.

> " High on the south, huge Ben-venue
> Down to the lake in masses threw
> Crags, knolls, and mounds, confusedly hurled,
> The fragments of an earlier world ;
> A wildering forest feathered o'er
> His ruined sides and summit hoar,
> While on the north through middle air,
> Ben-an heaved high his forehead bare."
>   LADY OF THE LAKE.

Llyn Cwellyn.

THERE are few scenes in Snowdonia where finer contrasts, more
picturesque effects, are to be observed, than in the vale of Llyn
Cwellyn. The scenery in this romantic valley has been compared
to that which occurs between Grenoble and Susan ; and, though
on a smaller scale, " magnitude is not essential to beauty, nor can
sublimity be measured by yards and feet." Llyn Cwellyn, in its
various aspects, is a beautiful sheet of water : under some phases,
it is scarcely to be surpassed by any other lake in Wales. The only
drawback is what Gilpin calls the "lack of furniture," that is, the
treeless, naked appearance of the banks ; indeed, few trees of any
kind are to be seen in the vale, and these wear a stunted, weather-
beaten, melancholy appearance. This nakedness, however, is in a
great measure relieved by the sublime near aspects of the mighty
mountains around, whose bases, covered with verdure, relieve the
eye as it rests upon the savage desolation of the higher ranges ;

which bounded on the west by the frowning precipices of Mynydd Mawr, rise in majestic grandeur at the lower extremity of the lake; on the east and north appear the smooth, verdant slopes, and graceful outline of Moel Aeliau, which here divides the valley from its more celebrated neighbour, Llanberis. After leaving Nant Mill, which you pass on your road from Caernarvon—and which we shall presently notice by a few passing observations—a grand view of Llyn Cwellyn is obtained; very lovely, then, is this fine lake on a calm summer's evening—the tall shadows of the lofty mountains reflected across its mirror-like surface, its placidity perchance broken by the tiny eddies caused by its finny inhabitants, disporting themselves, or feeding on the myriads of insects which hover over its pellucid waters. Llyn Cwellyn, although it lies at the foot of Snowdon, and is nursed and cradled in his lap, is what may be called a lowland lake, or rather a lake of the vale, notwithstanding its comparatively high elevation; and in many of its external aspects it certainly bears a resemblance to its gentler sister, Tal-y-Llyn. The distant views of the lake, from either extremity, are very beautiful; but we prefer, upon the whole, the view we have already mentioned, that which suddenly bursts upon you after leaving Nant Mill. Llyn Cwellyn is of easy approach; it lies along the high road from Caernarvon to Beddgelert for nearly the whole of its length. It is distant from the former town about seven miles and a half, and it is nearly five miles from Beddgelert to the head of the pool. The tourist will see little to interest him for the first five or six miles from Caernarvon; the country is tame and dreary, and although the eye is occasionally relieved by grand distant mountain vistas, yet "the strength of the hills," "the severer forms of mountain scenery," are not fully revealed untill you approach

Nant Mill,

celebrated of yore as a "favourite scene for artists," but which, in our opinion, has been vastly overrated. The fact is, there is no mill at all there now; the ruinous old building indeed is still standing, but the dam which supplied the wheel with water is dry, the weir is broken down, and the mill has been dismantled

for some years.   Except under certain lights, of rare occurrence,
and during a heavy flood over the falls, the scenery of Nant Mill
is comparatively tame, and vastly inferior to the really fine views
on the lake.   Our first impressions of Nant Mill, however, many
years ago, were decidedly favourable.   We had, in company with
a valued friend and relative, now no more, made an excursion from
Caernarvon, *via* Pen-y-Groes and Llanllyfni, on foot to visit the
Llynniau Nantllef.   The season of the year was autumn, October,
the weather was showery and broken, and the "lights," in alpine
districts, usually fine in such weather, were on this occasion more
magnificent than we ever remember.   After passing the Nantllef
Lakes—of which more anon—and before we reached the Caernarvon road at Rhydd Dû turnpike, the rain descended in a deluge,
the higher portions of the mountains became wreathed in mist,
and, as we descended the road at Nant Mill, we were much impressed with the sublimity and grandeur that pervaded the scene;
and the waterfalls appeared to us, as we passed them near the
close of an autumnal day, to be really magnificent.   If we had
viewed this scene by broad daylight, our impressions might have
been very different.   Subsequent visits have not sustained our
"first impressions," and Nant Mill has long ceased to present to
our eye any peculiar scenic attractions.

After leaving Nant Mill, you pass on your left Plas-yn-y-Nant,
where formerly stood a shooting or fishing lodge belonging to Sir
R. W. Bulkeley, Bart.; it is now in ruins.   The ancient chapel
adjacent, also we believe ruinous, is still partly standing.   The
sites of the house and chapel are embosomed among trees, and
therefore not easily discernible from the road.   The approach is
through a dilapidated gateway, and the whole scene wears the
aspect of decay and desolation.   Cwm Bychan, a morass, watered
by the Gwrfai, lies on the right, and leads to the lake.   Hence
the road approaches to the shores of Llyn Cwellyn, where

> "No murmur waked the solemn still,
>   Save tinkling of a fountain rill;
>   But when the wind chafed with the lake,
>   A sullen sound would upward break,
>   With dashing hollow voice, that spoke
>   The incessant war of wave and rock."

Half a mile farther, near the banks of the lake, formerly stood
an ancient roadside public-house, known as the "Snowdon
Guide," and marked on the Ordnance map. The "chances and
changes" of time, however, make havoc with the works of man,
and the late occupier of this rude tenement being gathered to his
fathers, gave way to his son, Evan Roberts, who has recently
erected, nearly on the site of the ancient hostelry, a neat well-
built hotel, which he has called the "Snowdon Ranger," and for
economy, combined with comfort and cleanliness, may fairly vie
with any establishment of its size in the Principality. Situate at
the foot of Snowdon, the highest peak of which looks less lofty
from hence than from the east side—arising, probably, from the
greater altitude of the situation—the hotel commands a fine view
of Llyn Cwellyn, and the magnificent mountains, Mynydd Mawr
and Moel Aeliau.

Castell Cidwm,

the "Wolf's Castle," on the north-west extremity of the lake, is
a prominent object from the "Snowdon Ranger;" that is the
picturesque, rugged, and almost inaccessible precipice on which it
stood, for no vestige now remains of the "early British fortress,"
said to have existed on its summit. We are more inclined to
believe, however, from personal inspection, that it was literally
what its name imports, a haunt of wolves, which ferocious animals
abounded in Snowdonia in olden times, and probably ascended
this rock either for safety or in pursuit of goats or deer; for
Snowdon in those days was a forest, and the declivities of the
mountains were covered with wood, and full of wild game.

> "These scenes are desert now and bare,
> Where flourished once a forest fair,
> When these waste glens with copse were lined,
> And peopled with the hart and hind."

The vast rounded summit of MYNYDD MAWR, which name
signifies the "Great Mountain," sometimes assumes, after rain,
the appearance of being slightly powdered with snow or hoar frost.
This probably arises from the summit being covered with minute
particles of granite or silica, which may produce this singular

appearance. The rays of the evening sun, gilding the highest precipices, frequently present a roseate hue of surpassing beauty; and when the Queen of Night lends her charms and casts her soft glances in unclouded majesty and grace over the rippling waters of the lake, the dark precipices of Mynydd Mawr glistening under · the influence of the silvery light,

> "The wanderer's eye could barely view
> The summer heaven's delicious blue;
> So wondrous wild, the whole might seem
> The scenery of a fairy dream."

Llyn Cwellyn derives its appellation from an ancient family of that name, now extinct. An old farmhouse near the head of the pool, called "Cwellyn," was, we believe, formerly the manor-house, but there is now little about it which indicates its original state. Indeed, from appearance, we are rather inclined to believe that the present mean-looking habitation has either been erected over its site, or that it formed a portion only of the ancient manor-house.

The lake is nearly a mile and a half long, lying in a direction from north-west to south-east. Its circumference may be roughly estimated at about three miles and a half; but it is in no part more than half a mile wide. Around the shores, the walking is generally good, either turf or a gravelly beach : in some parts the shore is swampy, or strewed with large stones or fragments of rock. From its situation in a vale of moderate elevation, although lying at the foot of lofty mountains, it is difficult to believe in its immense depth. We have been assured, however, that at the lower end, immediately under the precipices of Mynydd Mawr, upon a part of which is the rock called Castell Cidwm, the depth exceeds 130 yards ! At the head of the pool, where it receives a brook containing the superabundant waters of Llyns Dywarchen and y-Gader, the water is rather shallow for some distance from the shore, with a grassy bottom and some weeds. Here the best sport is usually obtained, and the trout which frequent this part are generally larger and in better condition. With the exception of a few stunted bushes, and some solitary hawthorns few and far between, the banks of Cwellyn are destitute of wood. If the shores were planted in certain parts it would add much to the beauty of the scenery; but we are afraid, unless the land was well drained and improved, there would be some difficulty in forming plantations. In the middle the lake is very deep, and generally round the sides the water shelves off rapidly to a great depth. In such parts very few fish will rise, although we have occasionally taken trout whilst rowing a boat down the centre of the pool by leaving the rod in the stern: the "way" on the boat keeps the line at full stretch, but care must be taken to let the winch run *free*, or else you will break off even a small fish. As a general rule, fish as much as possible in shoal water. The best portions of the llyn for angling are at the upper and lower ends, and along the north-east shore for about two-thirds of its length. After passing a walled enclosure for washing sheep, very few fish are taken until you enter the bay at the termination of the pool.

CHAR are still caught in Llyn Cwellyn, chiefly in the winter season, but not in such quantities as formerly. They will rise occasionally to the artificial fly in summer, when they are best in season; but they are rarely taken except by the net. Evan Roberts, of the "Snowdon Ranger," informed us that he caught one during the summer of 1857, near the hotel, in rather deep water. The *habitat* of the char or *torgoch*,—"Red Belly"—as they are termed by the Welsh, is in the deepest part of the lake, near Castell Cidwm, but an old fisherman informed us that in winter he had caught them in a net in different parts of the pool, quite in shoal water. The fact is, they come out of the deeps in winter into the shallow water to spawn, and they are then virtually out of season. This beautiful and delicate fish is only found in lakes that contain very deep water, and as they lie during summer in their deepest retreats, that may possibly be a reason why they do not rise to the fly. The char is a very handsome fish, with a small head, more symmetrical than a trout, and the red and black spots more brilliant. The belly is red, wherein it differs from its congener the trout, and may be immediately detected by this criterion. They do not run to a large size, at least in Llyn Cwellyn, the general run being from three ounces to a quarter of a pound. The flesh is firm, quite red, and of a delicious flavour.

TROUT.—In April and May, when the lake is full of water

after heavy rains, very good sport may sometimes be obtained from the shore, more especially in the bay immediately opposite the hotel; but for a good day's sport the use of a boat is absolutely indispensable. Trout of large size have occasionally been taken both by the hook and net. Some years ago, an old poacher informed us that he caught a trout weighing seven pounds with the " board;" one also of ten pounds was caught in a net in the bay at the lower extremity of the lake a few years since; and in the summer of 1857, a farm labourer, in the employ of Mr. Evan Roberts, the landlord of the hotel, caught a very well fed trout of two pounds with the artificial fly, on the shore under Mynydd Mawr. These are, however, exceptional captures; but we have no doubt that, in a few years, many fine trout will be taken by the rod, if the present judicious management and preservation of the lake is continued. The angling on Llyn Cwellyn has much improved the last three years, that is, since it came under the care of Mr. Evan Roberts. In a few years more, we have no hesitation in asserting, that angling on this lake will be found superior to any other llyn in Caernarvonshire, and excellent sport may be obtained now in May or June, or even earlier, should the season be favourable. Some years ago, Llyn Cwellyn was much injured by the "board" and net. There was scarcely a day that the lake was not poached by quarrymen from Llanberis and other neighbouring quarries and mines. Now, however, the llyn is strictly preserved, and no sort of fishing is allowed except angling, which is *free* to all. In consequence of the injury the lake sustained from these malpractices, the trout at present do not generally run to a large size. The average weight does not exceed four or five ounces, but some of the trout will vie in beauty and quality with those even of the best reputed lakes in the county, Llyn Ogwen excepted. The trout are exceedingly strong and lively, sometimes jumping a yard or more out of the water when struck, and afford good sport from a boat. When we visited the lake in 1857, there was only one good boat on the pool, but the landlord informed us that he intended to put several new boats on the lake during the following season, as much disappointment was occasioned from the want of a sufficient supply. There is no direct charge for a boat if you are staying for a few days at the hotel;

if you come only for the day's fishing, the charge is then two shillings and sixpence, exclusive of the boatman, who is generally satisfied with one shilling. The hire of a boatman is not imperative, but optional; when two or more gentlemen engage a boat, they can generally manage themselves. The wind best adapted for fishing Llyn Cwellyn from a boat is south or south-east; a steady westerly breeze is also good, as it enables you to sweep the shallow water at the head of the lake. Llyn Cwellyn is subject to very heavy squalls, more so, as far as our observation extends, than any other lake in the district. When the wind blows fresh from the south-west, it brings on a very heavy swell, which renders rowing against it from a lee shore laborious work, and it is almost impossible to prevent a rapid drift, as the water generally is so deep, twenty to thirty yards from the shore, that you cannot get a "pull" from the anchor. The anchor, so called, is merely a heavy stone tied to a boat-rope or "painter," which, when thrown overboard in shoal water, drags along the bottom, and thus steadies the "way" on the boat. We have seen "squalls" come down on the lake from the sides of Mynydd Mawr with terrific fury, carrying with them sheets of spray in columns from one shore to the other. At such times boating is dangerous to "greenhorns," and care should be taken to keep well under the windward shore, and avoid letting the boat drift into the white water. We have seldom found fish rise well in very stormy weather on this lake. When you see the waves with "their jackets off," or what is sometimes called the "white horses," it is more labour than profit to angle from a boat.

We must now say a few words as to the sport we obtained on Llyn Cwellyn in 1857, and the flies we generally used. We must premise that we did not angle on the lake until some time after the best fishing was over; it cannot be expected, therefore, that our success was very great: nevertheless, in the course of several visits, and notwithstanding frequent interruption from wet and stormy weather, we find, on reference to our journal of sport, that we killed fifteen dozen and ten fair-sized fish—some of half a pound and upwards—besides many small trout that we consigned again to their native element. In the early part of the season, in 1857, we were assured that first-rate sport was obtained. On one occasion, two gentlemen from Caernarvon severally caught, from two boats, eighty-eight and ninety-one trout on the same day, some of good size. Our greatest take never exceeded two dozen *per diem.* A moderate breeze, with a cloudy day and light rain, is the best time for sport. From the experience we had—limited we admit—we found the morning "rise" much the best, but sometimes the fish would rise tolerably free in the evening until dusk. A good macintosh, leggings, and a "sou'-wester" cap will keep you perfectly dry in the boat. The flies we found most successful—of course we speak of the latter end of the season, August and September—were the red spinner and dark mackerel, a most killing fly, dressed either with orange or purple body ribbed with gold twist. The pea-hen, or Llyn Gwynant fly, was also occasionally serviceable; but the mackerel was the *favourite* fly.

Some good bottom-fishing with the worm may sometimes be obtained in the Gwrfai—the stream that issues from the lake— towards the end of September, especially after a "fresh;" the trout are then leaving the lake to spawn in the river. It is, however, a pity to catch them at this time, although those we saw caught still appeared in pretty good season. It is a singular fact, and one for which we can vouch, that trout in the lake will not look at a worm, at least in the daytime, but as soon as they leave their still retreats and enter into running water, they will bite greedily at ground-bait. We have seen large trout taken with a worm within a few yards of the lake, just where the Gwrfai leaves it. It is difficult to account for this peculiarity in the habits of trout; possibly they prefer in the lake the food they obtain amongst the weeds and moss at the bottom, the lack of which in the stream compels them to seek for worms or other live bait. We may here also mention, that but for the waterfall at Nant Mill, plenty of salmon would ascend the Gwrfai into the lake, and would probably also find their way into Llyn-y-Gader. Mr. Evan Roberts informed us that he had some intention of cutting down a portion of the waterfall above mentioned, in order to afford a passage for the salmon, which could be accomplished at a small expense. If this project was carried into effect, capital salmon-fishing in the lake would add to its attractions, and the pool in the spring would swarm with salmon peel. In concluding our account of Llyn Cwellyn, which is much fuller, probably, than was ever given before, we have confined ourselves to facts and matters of detail; and, however slight and imperfect our sketch, we have carefully avoided the regions of romance, and at least truthfully set before the reader the lake as it was at the time of our visit, and the means at present pursued to improve its attractions to the sportsman. If these are fully carried out, we have no hesitation in saying that Llyn Cwellyn will in a few years become the most favourite angling station in North Wales.

THE "SNOWDON RANGER" HOTEL. — We can affirm, with perfect truth, that we know of very few places in the Principality better adapted to supply the wants of the angler or artist than the "Snowdon Ranger" Hotel. To comfort, you find added the greatest attention and civility from the worthy host and hostess; indeed, the charges are hardly commensurate with the good fare provided for you. You may live well for six or seven shillings per day, but you can, if you like, "sail still closer to the wind" than that. Of course this does not include wine, beer, or spirits. If you make any stay, we believe you may, if you prefer it, board and lodge on very reasonable terms; and if you happen to be lucky enough, you can engage a small sitting-room for your own use. Mr. Evan Roberts, the obliging landlord, is well known on the road between Caernarvon and Dolgelley; until lately he drove one of the coaches on this road many years, and was highly respected. During the summer, in 1857, he provided, for the entertainment of his guests, Pugh, the celebrated harper of Corwen, whose dulcet strains upon the three-stringed or Welsh harp—now so seldom heard in the Principality—especially Welsh airs, were much and deservedly admired.

ASCENT TO SNOWDON.—The path or pony-track from the "Snowdon Ranger" to the summit of Snowdon is tolerably easy, and many tourists now ascend by this route. In 1857, they generally came from Caernarvon under the guidance of a Mr. Hamer, who advertised to ascend Snowdon once a week, "weather permitting," by a new route found out by himself, called "Hamer's route," but which we have reason to believe is

much the same as the one followed by the guide from the
"Snowdon Ranger." At all events, it professes to be "Snowdon
made easy." The charges attendant upon an ascent to the
summit of Snowdon from the hotel are, we believe, five shillings
for a pony, and seven shillings for a guide: many tourists, however, both ladies and gentlemen, prefer to walk. We reserve our
account of Snowdon until a future chapter.

BROOK FISHING.—We have previously described the group of
lakes which lie in Cwm Clogwyn, on the south-west side of
Snowdon, Llyn Ffynnon Gwas, Llyn Coch, &c. These pools are
within a moderate distance from the "Snowdon Ranger," and
the route to them is probably easier than the one we traversed
from Beddgelert. To such as are fond of "bottom-fishing," the
brooks that run from these lakes will afford diversion. Though
the trout are small, they are very numerous, and after rain a
good basketful may be obtained. After a strong "fresh," some
tolerable fly or worm-fishing can also be had in the brook that
flows from Llyn-y-Gader to Llyn Cwellyn.

Llyn Dywarchen.

At the small straggling hamlet called Rhydd Dû, which lies
on the Beddgelert road, about one mile distant from Llyn Cwellyn,
you turn up a narrow turnpike road to the right, which leads to
Drws-y-Coed, the "door of the wood," the entrance to the
sublime Pass of the Llynniau Nantllef. Before reaching
Drws-y-Coed, a little to your right, lies Llyn Dywarchen, the
celebrated "Pool of the Sod," mentioned by *Giraldus Cambrensis*,
in his Itinerary, anno 1188, as containing a "floating island"—
insula erratica. Most, if not all the guide-books, allude to this
wonder, and assert that it is still in existence. Some go so far
as to say that sheep get upon it to graze, and are frequently
drifted from one side of the lake to the other! This statement
is, however, erroneous. There is *now* no floating island, nor has
there been one for many years. Llyn Dywarchen is small, of
irregular shape, and apparently very deep. We only fished it
once, on a very hot bright day in June, with a gentle breeze, but

did not obtain even a single " rise." The day of course was unfavourable for sport; but besides, the trout, which are said to
run to a large size, and of good quality, are exceedingly shy and
wary, and therefore seldom on the hook. A stormy rough day is
the best time to fish this pool. It lies in the midst of a turbary,
and its murky waters partake of the colour of the peaty soil
which surrounds it. Llyn Dywarchen is indeed scarcely worth a
visit for the chance of sport; but the angler is more than amply
rewarded with a survey of one of the most romantic scenes in
Cambria.

Drws-y-Coed—Nantllef Lakes and Pass.

The entrancing prospect, which suddenly bursts upon you at a
sharp turn in the road, from the head of the Pass of Drws-y-Coed,
is really superb, and exceeded in grandeur and sublimity by few
scenes in Britain. To the right you behold the dark bristling
precipices of Mynydd Mawr, called Craig-y-Bera; the Llyfni, a
small streamlet which rises on the south side of the mountain,
meanders gently down the Pass at your feet on its course to the
Llynniau Nantllef, after running through which, it falls into the
sea at Clynnog Vawr, a distance of eight miles.

> " Like streamlet of the mountain north,
> Now in a torrent racing forth,
> Now winding slow its silver train,
> And almost slumbering on the plain
> Like breezes of the autumn day,
> Whose voice inconstant dies away :
> Yet pleased, our eye pursues the trace
> Of Light and Shade's inconstant race;
> Pleased, views the rivulet afar,
> Weaving its maze irregular;
> And pleased, we listen as the breeze
> Heaves its wild sigh through autumn trees."

Looking towards the farther extremity of this striking scene, the
Vale of the Llyfni, you behold the beautiful lakes of

Nantllef,

so eloquently described by the gifted author of the "Mountain Decameron," their waters radiant in the sunshine, and the tall shadows of the dark precipices around reflected on their placid surface.

Warner, in his "Second Walk through Wales," in 1798, thus briefly records his impressions of the scenery at these lakes. After describing the adjacent slate quarries, which even in his time appear to have been extensively worked and "extremely valuable," he says, "From this elevation we descended to the two lakes, stretching one behind the other in an eastern direction. The scenery of these, particularly of the large one, is exquisitely beautiful. Here the eye ranges over a fine sheet of water a mile and a half in length, and above half as much in breadth, surrounded on all sides with mountains, whose dark slaty heads tower above it to a sublime height, in shape most singular and fantastic, and in appearance most wild and rude. As they fall, however, towards the lake they drop this savage aspect, and before they unite with it, become verdant slopes, covered with vegetation, ornamented with little cottages, and fringed with various trees."

· The view of these lakes, it will therefore be perceived, up the vale from Llanllyfni is scarcely less striking than from the head of the Pass. We are here tempted to add the following hasty, but graphic and original, sketch from the pen of a lamented friend, an enthusiastic admirer of landscape scenery; and although this description of Nantllef was written nearly eighteen years ago, and the works of man

> "Like April morning clouds, that pass
> With varying shadow o'er the grass,"

yet the scene in its essential features—"the mountain and the flood"—is still the same; the "glorious works of the Lord" are unchangeable until the end of time. "Each step," observes the writer, "brings you nearer to enchanting scenery. Mynydd Mawr forms the boundary of the valley to the right, and Graig Coch to the left. The dark *cwms* and details of the hills present

I

a constant variety of charming views. The scenery along the lower Nantllef lake is marred by the operations of the slate quarries. In some parts, huge banks of slate rubbish have been driven out on the edge of the lake, and the whole district for at least a mile is a scene of busy industry. There are, we believe, two quarries, Pen-y-Bryn and Tal-y-Sarn, upon the former of which an immense sum has been expended. The upper lake is not deformed by any mean accessories, and its eastern side is finely fringed with wood, which runs up the hill side beautifully, and is a great additional ornament to the landscape. You now enter a *Bwlch* of great magnificence, Snowdon looming in the background with indescribable majesty. The steep of Mynydd Mawr—Craig-y-Bera, to the left, is by far the finest example of its class that we have seen in Snowdonia, especially under advantageous lights. The Pass increases in wildness and grandeur as you proceed. Alpine scenes of intense seclusion, mountain homes, constantly arrest attention, or awaken thought. A copper-mine, which consists of a level driven into the mountain, is passed on the right : it is only imperfectly worked. Some of the few farmhouses are of high antiquity ; and we were especially struck with one which rests on the hill side near Llyn Dywarchen. Shortly before emerging into the Caernarvon road, we opened Llyn-y-Gader to the right. Rhydd Dû pike is seven miles from Pen-y-Groes, and nine miles from Caernarvon. Here it came on to rain furiously, and we had a wet and dreary late walk home through the rain, and were glad when we once more hailed the ' Sportsman,' and got into comfortable shelter about half-past seven in the evening."

A railway has been constructed within the last few years, between the Nantllef lakes and Caernarvon, and in addition to "business traffic," numerous tourists and pleasure-seekers are attracted to those once secluded and romantic lakes.

Richard Wilson, R.A. the British Claude, painted his celebrated view of Snowdon from the Pass of Drws-y-Coed. This eminent artist was a native of Mold, in Flintshire, and his remains lie interred in the churchyard there. He died in 1782, ætat. 69.

Excursion through the Nantllef Pass.

In the year 1843, during an angling tour in North Wales, accompanied by a friend, we revisited the lakes of Nantllef. We left Beddgelert early in the morning for the purpose of enjoying a day's fishing at Llyn Cwellyn; but as the day advanced, huge masses of clouds overspread the face of the sky, and the wind blew with so much violence, that we were obliged to forego our intention of angling. We therefore determined to proceed to Caernarvon by the Nantllef pools. Having accomplished the circuit of Llyn Cwellyn, we retraced our steps to Rhydd Dû. From hence, through the Pass to Caernarvon, the distance is twelve miles, and as the afternoon wore on, we felt the necessity of pushing forwards, as there was every appearance of a wet, stormy evening. As we approached Drws-y-Coed, we were much impressed by the profound gloomy aspect of Mynydd Mawr, the dark purple colouring of which, rendered still more stern and impressive under the dark canopy of storm-threatening clouds which overhung it, caused the mountain to assume a portentous appearance. As we proceeded onwards, large drops of rain occasionally fell, and the wind came moaning up the valley in fitful gusts. The lakes in the distance gleamed under the solemn light, and their waters quivered under the influence of the blast. Then it was that we saw this valley under its finest phase, and felt doubly impressed with its sublime aspect. We never before felt so much under the influence of mountain scenery; indeed, we may say, *awed*. Fortunately the weather favoured us in our journey through the vale; hardly, however, had we got to Pen-y-Groes, when the rain began to descend in torrents, and long before we got to Caernarvon, we were literally drenched to the skin. Never, from that day to the present, have we forgotten our impressions of the scenery of Nantllef and Drws-y-Coed; which, when seen under a lowering light, is scarcely equalled—it cannot be excelled—by any other valley in Wales. We prefer, upon the whole, the descent into the vale; the distant view of the lakes is much more interesting and beautiful than the nearer approach you make to them from Llanllyfni.

" The western waves of ebbing day
  Rolled o'er the glen their level way ;

   *   *   *   *   *

But not a setting beam could glow
Within the dark ravines below,
Where twined the path in shadow hid,
Round many a rocky pyramid.
Shooting abruptly from the dell
Its thunder-splintered pinnacle ;
Round many an insulated mass,
The native bulwarks of the PASS,
Huge as the towers which builders vain
Presumptuous piled on Shinar's plain.
For from their shivered brows displayed,
Far o'er the unfathomable glade,
All twinkling with the dewdrop sheen,
The briar-rose fell in streamers green,
And creeping shrubs of thousand dyes,
Waved in the west wind's summer sighs."

LAKE FISHING.—A few hints on lake fishing, and the
"means and appliances" to be employed, may here, perhaps
prove acceptable. We offer them as the results of many years'
experience. The best rod for a boat is a short one, not too pliant,
about twelve or twelve and a half feet long; the cost of which,
including a couple of spare top joints, which should always be
handy in case of accident, would be about thirty shillings. George
Bowness, of 33, Bell Yard, Temple Bar, has supplied us for many
years, and we have found his rods endure hard work well, being
made of the best materials, and throw a line beautifully. Mr.
Bowness, we believe, has lately retired from business, but his
successor may probably supply equally as good articles. Messrs.
Jones and Co., 111, Jermyn Street, we have also heard highly
spoken of. It is better to pay a little more for a good even-
balanced rod, made according to your own directions, than purchase a jim-crack implement cheap, which frequently turns out
perfectly worthless. In fishing from a boat—especially when there
is a lazy inconstant breeze—a long line and fine tackle are
required, and then it is when the science of the angler is brought
most into play, as the difficulty is so to throw that your fly
"lights like gossamer" on the water. The way to accomplish

this desirable result, is to let your line fly to its full stretch behind you before making a fresh cast, and this is accomplished by staying your arm for an instant, so as to allow time for the line to straighten itself.

If you follow this method, you will not only throw a neat, clean, straight line, but you will seldom or never "crack" off your flies, which bungling anglers frequently do, especially in windy weather. Unless also the line is straight previous to the "cast," it frequently "fouls" or makes a serpentine on the water; so that should a fish "rise," you would most probably miss him from not being able to strike quick enough. Young fishermen are very apt to be deficient in manipulation, and are frequently disappointed or disgusted with their want of success, which arises from non-attention, or want of knowledge of the most useful part of an angler's education, patience and perfect manipulation. Shore-fishing on a lake is often "slow" and monotonous enough, especially where the trout are shy or sulky, and requires both practice, skill, and perseverance to ensure sport. You require a longer rod than in boat-fishing, because you are not only often obliged to throw against the wind, but also, where the water is very shallow for some distance into the lake—as at Bugeilyn, for example—you require a long rod to enable you to reach the fish. We generally use a rod from thirteen feet and a half to fourteen feet for shore-fishing; but it does not always follow that the trout lie from the shore. We have often caught large trout close to the edge. A good rod of this description will cost from two pounds two shillings to two pounds five shillings; a line of spun silk and hair, about thirty-five to forty yards long, is quite sufficient for trout-fishing in Wales, in addition to which we always use a three-ply plaited gut line, about two yards long, to which we affix our "cast" of flies. A great difference of opinion exists among anglers as to the requisite number of flies to affix to the "foot link." For shore-fishing, we consider two or three flies ample; for a boat, not to exceed four; as we have found from experience that the fewer the number of flies the heavier are the fish taken. Some anglers, boat-fishing, who are very skilful manipulators, sometimes use as many as eight or nine flies; but it requires very dexterous management to prevent "fouling," and

the use of a landing net adds to the difficulty. We should advise
the beginner not to put on more than two flies to his line until
after some practice. Where the water is weedy, especially under
water, large fish are apt to bore to the bottom after being hooked.
In such ground, you should not use more than two flies, as, if you
"foul" at the bottom, you are not only almost certain to break
off, but in a boat you run the risk of snapping the top joint of
your rod, from the line getting under the boat. We have always
been in the habit of using a multiplying winch, but some anglers
prefer a check one. A multiplier is, however, exceedingly handy
in boat-fishing; but from the shore it matters not which sort you
use. The cost of a good multiplier for a moderate-sized trout-
rod is from fifteen to eighteen shillings. *Never purchase* London
flies for Welsh lake-fishing, unless they are faithful copies from a
Welsh pattern, or from a *Welsh* natural fly. We have sometimes
sent the natural fly to London to copy, and have generally had a
good imitation by return of post. You can be at no loss for flies,
however, in Wales. At Shrewsbury, Dolgelley, Bala, Beddgelert,
Caernarvon, and other places, excellent flies may be obtained;
better in most respects, *except gut*, than any London flies. We
do not mean to say that the flies are so neatly tied, but in *colour*
they are generally far superior. Wading-boots are essential to
the comfort of the shore-fisherman: those made by Cording, in
the Strand, are durable and watertight, and the best we have
met with. To be perfectly comfortable, you require two fishing-
jackets; one made of thick waterproof cloth for cold, wet weather,
and another of some cool, light material. Of course there should
be waistcoats to match. The weather in Wales is extremely
variable; one day it is exceedingly hot, the next one after very
cold and wet. Waterproof double-upper-leather shooting-boots,
to button or lace in front, are the best for walking over the rough
roads and up steep mountain sides. The soles should be well
nailed for obvious reasons. These few "wrinkles" we offer for
the benefit of the neophyte. There are other essentials which he
will soon learn by experience.

CHAPTER VIII.

AN EXCURSION TO CLYNNOG VAWR, YR EIFL, AND NANT GWRTHEYRN—ST. BEUNO'S CHURCH—CROMLECH.

> "Methinks some musing wanderer I see,
>   Weaving his wayward fancies. Round him rock
> And cliff, whose grey trees mutter to the wind,
> And streams down rushing with a torrent ire :
> The sky seems craggy, with her cloud-piles hung,
> Deep mass'd as though embodied thunder lay
> And darken'd in a dream of havoc there."

THERE are few countries—to an Englishman at least—that offer greater scenic or historical attractions than Wales. The land of the *Cwmry* is indeed a region of romance ; her history abounds in stirring episodes, from the remote times of Vortigern down to the untimely end of her greatest monarch, the heroic Llewelyn, and to the successful rebellion of a prince almost equally great, Owen Glyndwr. To such as possess a taste for magnificent and soul-inspiring scenery—the interest of which is enhanced by the wild legends and memories of the past—or a love of antiquities, "those silent, yet expressive and instructive, records of our forefathers," we cannot too strongly recommend the peculiar charms of this romantic country ; whilst some of the ruined fanes or lordly castles still existing, both in North and South Wales, may vie in grandeur and interest with those in "merrie England." In Celtic remains the antiquary will find an abundant field for exploration, and many interesting pilgrimages may be made to the *Beddau*, or graves of celebrated warriors, bards, or other distinguished characters. Some of these ancient memorials exist in the wildest and most untrodden districts ; it is our intention, therefore, in the present chapter to introduce the reader to one or two of those "nooks of the world" which are seldom intruded on by the footsteps of the stranger.

Some years ago, during a brief sojourn at Caernarvon, we were tempted by the exceeding fineness of the weather to make an excursion to the summit of Yr Eifl, or "the Rivals," as they are commonly called, and from thence to that "profound, vast, and lonely mountain hollow" lying at their western bases, celebrated as the supposed site of the grave of Vortigern. The season was autumn—September—and when the weather is fine and settled, we prefer that period of the year to any other for a tour in Wales.

Accompanied by two friends of congenial tastes, we left Caernarvon at an early hour, as the objects of our excursion were some miles distant, and from Llanael-haiarn—a little village situate near the west coast of the Peninsula of Lleyn, on the road between Clynnog and Nevin—we knew we should have some rough walking ere we reached the terminus of our ramble in that wild, romantic region. The day was cheering, the air cool and invigorating, and in every respect favourable. Snowdonia was seen under striking effects of light and shade; and the Rivals loomed out darkly in majestic grandeur through the long vista formed in the road, for nearly two miles, by the trees of Lord Newborough's park at Glynllifon. The objects and antiquities on this route are so well described in the Rev. P. B. William's "Caernarvonshire," that we will confine ourselves to a mere hasty glance, *en passant*, at some of the principal antiquarian curiosities of this secluded district. Nearly opposite Glynllifon, about half-way between Caernarvon and Clynnog, you will observe on the right, at the distance of a mile and a half, near the coast, a strong earthwork or fortified post, called Ddinas Dinlle. This fort is thirty acres in extent, and was a Roman station, supposed to have been constructed by Agricola; but the Rivals riveted nearly all our attention as we gradually drew nearer to them. There rose the range ahead of us, of singular majesty and grace of outline, far outstripping in this respect their English *rivals*, the Malvern and Breidden hills. From this distant point of view they appear to run into the sea, and bar all progress to the north. Nearer at hand, to the left, rose Gyrn Goch (1,823 feet), a fine mountain with two summits, often confounded with the Rivals, but perfectly distinct, and which run in a different direction, although the two groups harmonize finely, running nearly parallel to the coast.

Before we reached Clynnog we crossed the Llyfni, the mountain torrent which flows through the Llynniau Nantllef. It seems an inviting stream to the angler, but we are afraid its waters are too much impregnated with the mine-water, which flows from its native source, to abound with the finny tribe; nevertheless, we longed for a ramble along its banks.

Soon after we pulled up at the " Newborough Arms," the very comfortable and inviting little inn at

Clynnog,

distant ten miles from Caernarvon, and ten miles from Pwllheli. Here we devoted an hour for the purpose of visiting the ancient church and *cromlech.* With the former we were, on the whole, disappointed, notwithstanding Mr. Pennant's assertion that it was the finest church in Wales. We will not attempt to go into the history of St. Beuno's church. The edifice is cruciform of the latest English style, but presents several incongruities in its architecture, for which we can only account by supposing that it has been altered at several periods. Adjoining the church is St. Beuno's chapel, at the time of our visit used as a parish school. It was in a state of neglect and decay. The tomb, or reputed tomb, of the saint was standing here at the latter end of last century; it was "plain and altar-shaped:" but Bardsey and Nevin also lay claim to his remains. St. Beuno's chest is the most remarkable relic of antiquity in the church. It is oak, and decaying under the influence of dry-rot, but is strongly secured by iron clamps and three locks. We were also shown a curious old instrument called the *gefail cwn,* or dog-tongs. It was formerly the custom to employ these tongs to expel canine intruders during divine service. The points of the tongs are serrated, and we should fancy them capable of inflicting severe punishment. There are fourteen stalls in the church, and amongst the monuments is one to Geo. Rd. Twistleton, 1667, in which the inscription is cut in relief. The screen is of good design, but deformed by a modern railing. The church is surrounded by a large grove of aged trees, which are literally weather-beaten, and almost denuded of foliage to seaward: they produced, on the whole, a quaint and striking effect. About 200 yards from the church, on the left side of the turnpike road, is St. Beuno's well, which is in a most filthy degraded state, and not worth the trouble of a visit. In olden time, this well was famous for healing the sick, and "particularly for curing the rickets in children." Its peculiar virtues have, however, long since ceased. Leland, in his "Itinerary," thus notices Clynnog:—"The church that is now there, with cross aisles, is about as big as St. David's; but it is of a new work. The old church, where St. Beunow lieth, is hard by the new. This is a great parish, and the church is the fairest in all Caernarvonshire, or better than Bangor." St. Beuno was a Welsh saint of peculiar sanctity, who flourished in the early part of the seventh century, founded a college or *ban-cor* at Clynnog, and afterwards retired to Holywell, in Flintshire. He was uncle to the celebrated St. Winefred, whose miraculous well was one of the "seven wonders of Wales."

Having concluded a hasty inspection of the church, we proceeded to the cromlech, called the *Bachwen Cromlech*, which means "holy creek." It stands in a meadow towards the seashore, not far from the *eglwys*, or church, and is in a very perfect state. It consists of four uprights, which support a large horizontal stone of triangular shape, gradually tapering off nearly to a point, and resembles, as far as we can recollect, "Kitt's Cotty House," near Maidstone. We could see nothing of a stone pillar, said to be standing near the *cromlech* by Williams and other topographers. What a curious contrast is presented to the eye and mind of the inquirer whilst surveying these monuments of the past! Here you behold, almost side by side, the Temple of the living God, erected through the zeal of early Christian piety, and the rude altar-stone set up by the votaries of a blind, degraded, and barbarous superstition. The question is still undecided whether the *cromlechs*, as they are termed—several of which still lie scattered, in a more or less perfect state, in different parts of the Principality—are the grave-stones of eminent chiefs or heroes, or connected with the mysterious religious rites of the Druids. For more than 2,000 years have these relics of ancient days endured the vicissitudes of climate, the fury of the elements, and, to some extent, the hands of the spoiler; to all appearance, they may still survive for many more centuries. The neighbourhood of Clynnog abounds in antiquities; amongst others, the *Penarth Cromlech*, about one mile from the village, near the Llanllyfni road, and a hill-fort at Craig-Cynan.

On leaving Clynnog, the road to Nevin runs for some miles between the Gyrn Goch mountains and the sea. The Rivals rise straight ahead, and become more impressive than ever as you approach nearer to them. As you advance, the road, about three miles from Clynnog, winds suddenly from the coast through a fine *bwlch*, between Gyrn Goch and the Rivals. It is called the Pass of Llanael-haiarn. In the Pass is a primitive roadside inn, the "Waterloo," where we found excellent bread and cheese—*bara-a-caws*—oat-cakes, schiedam, and rum and milk. Here we left our car, and having done ample justice to these *delicacies*, we prepared for our mountain adventures. The pedestrian, especially if he is limited to time, had better leave the main road near the foot of the *bwlch*, proceed along a lane to the right, and ascend the western Rival over Vortigern's Grave; which can, we believe, be most easily approached in this direction. We, however, proceeded *up* the Pass, through the village of Llanael-haiarn : the church lies close to the road on the left. The distance to this place from Caernarvon is seventeen miles, and is about four miles to Nevin. We now proceeded to ascend the mountain, and crossed the intervening waste. The prospect to the east and south-east was magnificent in the extreme. Immediately below us, however, the surface of the Peninsula of Lleyn was mean and flat : this district has evidently been overflowed by the sea at a distant period. A llyn, which stands near a gentleman's house, and some timber, are the only objects which arrest the eye in its glance towards the Pwllheli coast, except Criccieth Castle, which frowns on its bold sea-rock, opposite Harlech, on which sun-gleams occasionally fell. The view of the Harlech district of mountains was, however, indistinct; beyond, Cader Idris could be made out, and a long and misty line of coast terminated the view to seaward. The days are too short in September to attempt a minute survey of Yr Eifl, together with an exploration of Nant Gwrtheyrn, so that we were only able to find time for the ascent of the central peak of the Rivals, which is sur-

rounded by a stupendous mass of *débris,* and forms as wild a
scene as can well be imagined. The Ordnance surveyors have
erected a lofty wooden post in a heap of stones on the summit.
The post is covered with inscriptions and the initials of numerous
visitors. This custom is a habit belonging exclusively to the
English. How frequently we see even the most handsome monuments disfigured by this vulgar and barbarous practice.

The view from this elevated spot—1,886 feet above the sea—
embraced objects of great interest, extent, and variety.

> " To sit on rocks, to muse o'er flood and fell,
>   To slowly trace the forest's shady scene,
>   Where things that own not man's dominion dwell,
>   And mortal foot hath ne'er or rarely been ;
>   To climb the trackless mountain all unseen,
>   With the wild flock that never needs a fold ;
>   Alone o'er steeps and foaming falls to lean ;
>   This is not solitude ; 'tis but to hold
>   Converse with Nature's charms, and view her stores unroll'd."
>
> BYRON.

We have already described the view to the southward and
eastward. To the north and north-east, Snowdon rose without a
cloud : an observation which may be extended to all Snowdonia·
The Menai Strait was made out through its whole extent, from
its entrance in Caernarvon Bay upwards. Anglesea, with Holyhead and Parys Mountain stretched to the north-west. The west
and south-west views embraced the wide sweep of Caernarvon
Bay, the elevated and mountainous western coast of the Peninsula
of Lleyn—hill succeeding hill—till Bardsey Isle loomed to seaward,
beyond the far headland of Aberdaron—the *Canganum Promonto-
rium* of Ptolemy. The picturesque shores of St. Tudwal's Bay,
with its islands off Pwllheli, were well made out. All these
objects were seen under an exquisite light. We, however,
observed an extensive range of *cumulo-strati* which hung to seaward, and as the wind (south-west) set in from that quarter, we
were not without apprehension that the fine weather which had
so far favoured us might not be changed into rain and tempest.
How far our apprehensions were realized will be seen in the
sequel. At this moment, however, the declining sun threw a flood
of radiance on the ocean that greatly heightened the effect of the

land views.   The narrow promontory and harbour of Porth
Dinllaen with its bay, including the coast line, was a graceful
illustration of this.   Below us, to the south of the Western peak
of the Rivals, yawned

Vortigern's Grave,

the vast and profound hollow so eloquently and floridly described
by the author of the "Mountain Decameron."   To this interesting "nook" we now wended our way, as every moment
became precious.   To be caught in this valley in the dark,
was an event we were extremely anxious to guard against; we
were therefore unable to ascend the eastern peak of the
mountain, the Tre'r-Ceiri—the "Town of Fortresses"—which
we greatly regretted, but the fast-waning day warned us to
depart.   Before doing so, however, we will briefly devote our
attention to this "most perfect and magnificent, as well as
most artfully constructed British post" to be found in Britain.
The ascent to the summit appears very steep, and covered
with loose *débris*.   At the highest point, the strongest part of
the fortification, there is "a double range of walls and entrances,
one of the latter being still covered over.   Within the circuit
are the habitations (small oval houses), and several circles
of stones, amounting to fifty or sixty in number.   On the very
summit is a *cairn*, whence the body has been abstracted, and below
it the remains of a small *cromlech*."   The only accessible side is
defended by three walls, which appeared to be very lofty: the
area is irregularly shaped.   Mr. Pennant, in his Tour of North
Wales, made a most minute survey of this ancient British fortified town, and also of Nant Gwrtheyrn.   Of the latter he says,
"embosomed in a lofty mountain, on two sides bounded by stony
steeps, on which no vegetables appear, but the blasted heath and
the stunted gorse; the third exhibits a most tremendous front of
black precipice, with the loftiest peak of Yr Eifl soaring above.
The only opening is the sea, a northern aspect! where that chilling
wind exerts all its fury, and half freezes during the winter the
few inhabitants."   We can add nothing to the force and truth of
this description.

Nant Gwrtheyrn.

Nant Gwy Bedd Gwrtheyrn, or "the Brook of the Valley of Vortigern's Grave," is one of the most solemn sequestered spots in Britain. It lies under the south-west base of the central peak of Yr Eifl, and is almost as difficult of approach as it is of egress. It was therefore with a peculiar thrill of excitement that we prepared to descend from the lofty eminence on which we stood, into the lonely solitude at our feet. We soon found a sheep path, which led us along the south side of the mountain, and we gradually reached the bottom, lost in admiration of the wildness of this awe-inspiring retreat, in which, says tradition, the perfidious British king (A.D. 465) had chosen to hide himself from the merited vengeance of his subjects. As we looked seaward—for the ocean laved the extreme boundary of the valley—we could hear "the solemn, low, thundering music of the sea's breaking unseen on the far down beach," and soon we saw the agitated waters heave in white-crested surges against the everlasting barriers Nature has provided, and which seemed to say, "Thus far shalt thou come, and no farther!"

At length we stood on the earthen mound supposed to have been raised over the remains of Vortigern nearly fourteen centuries ago! As if to corroborate this supposition, Dr. Downes informs us, in his "Mountain Decameron," that "a stone coffin, enclosing a gigantic skeleton, was discovered within that assigned site about a century back, and recommitted to its burial-place; giving 'a plausibility at least to tradition, supported as that is by the name of the spot, 'Vortigern's Hollow.'" There are, however, now no vestiges of the grave, as far as we could observe, at present existing on the barrow. We longed to be *alone*; we felt that

> "There is a rapture on the lonely shore,
> There is society, where none intrudes,
> By the deep Sea, and music in its roar."

As we lingered over the sepulchre of fallen greatness, and listened to the uproar of the wild billows dashing against the front of Craig-y-Llam, a terrific precipice impending over the sea, signs of elemental strife of a still more terrible description almost suddenly presented themselves.   Thunder-storms in this region are as sudden as frequent, attracted perhaps by the forked summits of these magnetic mountains.*

The day was drawing to a close, but a deep gloom came on so suddenly that it made us aware a fearful tempest was on the point of bursting over our heads.   The wind, which had previously been blowing freshly from the sea, became calm—that treacherous calmness which usually precedes the storm.   The music of the wild waves, the melancholy wail of the sea fowl as they skimmed along the surface of the agitated waters, sounded portentously upon our ears.   The storm-clouds were rapidly coming up over the summit of the lofty steeps above us, *against* the wind; the deep valley in which we stood having prevented us from noticing them in time to avoid their fury.   Anxious to escape the effects of the tempest we made what haste we could over some stone walls and broken ground from Vortigern's Grave; but ere we could reach the friendly shelter of a neighbouring cottage, the storm began to rage with a violence rarely equalled, except in mountainous countries.

> "The mists that round yon peak concentring spread,
> Changes portend that mountain-dwellers dread.
> Clouds, dense and lowering, throng the western sky,
> A pause proclaims aërial conflicts nigh;
> Save when—the equal prelude that dismays—
> On summits bleak, the winds their voices raise,
> Heard 'mid the stillness, like the sullen roar
> From ocean's distant wave assaulted shore—
> Now storms conflicting burst upon the ear;
> The wild goat hurries to his covert near—
> Whilst quivering flags before the tempest bend,
> Rains, with brief warning, torrent-like descend,
> And the loud gust, ascending peal on peal,
> Comes with a might that probes the heart of steel."

---

* The Rivals are said to abound in magnetic iron-stone, and it is generally believed by sailors that when ships approach them, the *compass* becomes much affected.   We have ourselves observed a curious phenomenon whilst in the neighbourhood of these mountains.   In the finest weather, when not a cloud or vapour was discernible in any direction, small ragged spots or *lumps* of vapour would suddenly form, and rapidly drift along the sides of the mountain, and then almost as quickly disappear.

Vivid forked lightning, succeeded momentarily by prolonged deafening peals of thunder, quickly following each other, and solemnly reverberating amongst the hollows around, were accompanied by a deluge of rain that drenched us to the skin; so that no alternative remained but to wend our way out of the valley as soon as possible. The storm fortunately lasted but for a short time, leaving us just enough light, after toiling to the summit from whence we started, to discern in the distance the *locale* of the "Waterloo" tavern. We now endeavoured to descend between the central Peak and the Tre'r Ceiri; but, after clambering down a steep for about 500 feet, we found, to our dismay, all further progress arrested by a lofty loose stone wall, below which was a precipice, which forbad all further efforts in this direction. We therefore were compelled, tired and almost exhausted, to climb up again; and, after rounding Tre'r Ceiri, we providentially struck a "broad trail," which led us first over some stone walls; but we discovered a nearer route than the path, over turf fences, which at length brought us into the *Bwlch*, and to the comfortable shelter of the "Waterloo" inn.

In going home in the evening, we overtook a fine pack of otter hounds, which had killed two foxes on Gyrn Goch, after capital sport. Several of the huntsmen had long poles, constructed for mountain hunting. We arrived at Caernarvon, after a most exciting day, about half-past nine.

The Yr Eifl range, although not lofty, assume a bold appearance, from their proximity to the sea; dividing, as it were, the generally flat dreary Peninsula of Lleyn from the flat marshy coast between Clynnog and Caernarvon. Their graceful outline and picturesque appearance render them amongst the most attractive features of Caernarvonshire : but they are rarely visited by tourists, being out of the beaten path, and the Peninsula of Lleyn is almost a *terra incognita*. A ramble into that wild primitive country, however, is very enjoyable; its antiquarian treasures are of the highest interest; and a pilgrimage to Bardsey Isle, an event never to be forgotten.

CHAPTER IX.

SNOWDONIA—PEN-Y-GWRYD—INN AT PEN-Y-GWRYD—LAKES—
ASCENT OF GLYDERS—SUMMIT OF GLYDER BACH—SINGULAR
APPEARANCE — TRIFAEN — DIFFICULTY OF ASCENT—LLYDER
VAWR—Y-WAUN OER—LLYN CWM FFYNNON.

> " Some ruder and more savage scene,
> Like that which frowns round dark Lochskene :
> There eagles scream from isle to shore,
> Down all the rocks the torrents roar ;
> O'er the black waves incessant driven,
> Dark mists infect the summer heaven ;
> Through the rude barriers of the lake,
> Away its hurrying waters break,
> Faster and whiter dash and curl,
> Till down yon dark abyss they hurl ;
> Rises the fog-smoke white as snow,
> Thunders the viewless stream below."—MARMION.

Pen-y-Gwryd.

"BARREN, solitary, dignified Nature," in her ruder aspects, is
aptly portrayed in the desolate Nanty Gwryd. The gigantic
mountains around,

> " Stern and full of dread,"

lift above it their bare and rugged heads, and fold it, as it were,
in their embrace ; and the wanderer, as he slowly travels on his
way towards the Pass of Llanberis—a scene of still wilder grandeur and sublimity—may call to mind the cold and selfish world
he had left for a brief space, to enjoy that quiet and tranquillity,
that freedom from the carking cares and anxieties of human
existence, amidst the solitudes of the mountainous wilderness we
now propose to explore. In the midst of this solitudinous region

K

formerly stood a wretched roadside ale-house, known as "Pen-y-Gwryd Inn." Occasionally a weary, benighted tourist, after the toilsome ascent of the Pass of Llanberis, would direct his steps to it, glad to receive such shelter and entertainment as the slender resources of the place afforded. In process of time, however, and in accordance with the march of improvement, which is gradually spreading over the nooks and byeways of Wales, the humble roadside pothouse becomes transformed into a very comfortable inn; where not only the wayfarer meets with civility and attention, but even in the culinary department he will have no reason to complain. The enterprise of the landlord, Henry Owen, has in a great measure accomplished this desirable result; and, in a few years more, we confidently predict that "Pen-y-Gwryd Inn" will occupy a still more important position amongst the hotels of Snowdonia. The inn is happily situate at the junction of three roads, severally leading to Beddgelert, Llanberis, and Capel Curig. It is literally an oasis in the wilderness, a palm-tree in the desert, a solitary spot of verdure, snatched by the industry of man from the wreck of Nature; and notwithstanding its elevation—for it is oftentimes in the clouds—and its exposure to the frosts and snows of winter, you will observe several kinds of garden flowers and vegetables flourishing luxuriantly; and hereafter, we have little doubt that human industry will still further improve the out-door character of the place. Behold us, then, reader, comfortably installed in a neat parlour at "Pen-y-Gwryd Inn," which, though small, is sufficient for our wants, discussing, with a zest and appetite unknown to any save a mountain wanderer, the savoury viands prepared by the hands of Mrs. Prichard, our host's mother-in-law—an old dame who, in days of yore, was a domestic in the service of Thomas Pennant, Esq. of Downing; whose fame, at the close of the last century, as an antiquary and topographer, is so well known and appreciated.

Whilst we are occupied in discussing our repast (a leg of mountain mutton), which an eight miles' walk from Beddgelert has caused us to do ample justice to, let us draw the attention of the reader to a few of the more prominent attractions which a sojourn of a few days at this healthful and really delightful locality ought to make him acquainted with. In a previous chapter we pointed out Pen-y-Gwryd as an angling station, and though it does not possess resources equal to one or two other localities we have previously described, yet the fisherman, if he can "rough" it among the mountains, will sometimes be able to obtain fair sport. But even this sequestered and thinly-peopled district is not free from that pest to the angler, the "Board," and more or less, all, or nearly all the neighbouring llyns are poached. Peny-Gwryd has, however, several other claims to favourable mention besides the pursuit of angling. To "the fond lover of Nature's charms," to the botanist and the artist, we scarcely know a more attractive spot, being in the midst of the greater portion of the most celebrated scenery of Snowdonia, and within easy distance of all of it. The inn is situate at the foot of those lofty sterile mountains, Glyder Vawr and Bach, the ascent to the summits of which forms a delightful excursion. Then there is the ascent to Snowdon, by Llyn Llydaw and Glas Llyn, the "Azure Lake," under the awful precipices of Moel-y-Wyddfa, "one of the finest scenes in Britain"—a scene of stupendous grandeur and fearful sublimity, in some respects unequalled in Wales. The gloomy and savage scenery around the solemn and sullen Llyn Idwal may also be explored, and the Pass and Lakes of Llanberis. The botanist will revel in the acquisition of rare ferns and other plants in the vicinity of Rhaiadr Cwm Dyli and the "Vale of Waters," at the head of Llyn Gwynant; and the artist will obtain some charming points for the exercise of his pencil in the same neighbourhood. These are a few of the most attractive features, which we now only slightly glance at; but it will be our pleasure hereafter to accompany the reader, and examine more minutely the varied beauties and wonders of the several localities we have enumerated.

The lakes in the neighbourhood of Pen-y-Gwryd worthy the notice of the angler, are few in number; these are Llyn Gwynant and Llyn Edno, previously described, Llyn Llydaw, Llyn Cwm Ffynnon, and Llynniau Duwaunedd, on the east side of Moel Siabod. The little river Gwryd, which takes its rise in Llyn Cwm Ffynnon, is also worthy of mention. Of these lakes, the only one now possessing boats is Llyn Gwynant, one of which belongs to Henry Owen, who, in 1857, placed a boat on the lake for the accommodation of anglers frequenting his inn. The distance to the lake through Nant Gwynant is about two miles and a half. The old road, which runs lower down the valley than the new one, is perhaps shorter, but we prefer the turnpike road. As either road is a continuous descent to the lake, you will find the walk home, unless you prefer a car, rather sharp "collar work."

Our first sojourn at Pen-y-Gwryd was in 1849, before the inn was partly rebuilt and enlarged. At that time the accommodation consisted of a small, rudely-furnished room, and two or three bedrooms of the same primitive character. In those days comparatively few anglers or tourists frequented it, beyond merely a passing call for a glass of *cwrw*, or some *bara-a-caws*. We made an excursion hither from Bangor, taking the wild mountain road from thence to Dolbadarn, situate near the narrow neck of land which separates the upper and lower Lakes of Llanberis. After passing a few hours at the "Dolbadarn Castle" inn, we determined to visit

Llyn Cwm Dwythwch,

a small pool lying in a peat morass under the precipices of Moel Aeliau, where, from local report, we expected to meet with some good fishing. We were, however, doomed to be disappointed, for, after lingering two hours at the llyn, we came away with only one small trout in our basket. In the evening, we proceeded up the Pass of Llanberis to Pen-y-Gwryd, distant six miles. As the day was hot and sultry, we did not leave Llanberis until seven o'clock, and as we slowly travelled up the Pass, lost in admiration of the sublime mountain scenery on either side, it was dusk when we arrived at our humble quarters. A hearty welcome from our host, Henry Owen, a good supper, consisting of homely eggs and bacon, and some excellent *cwrw*, soon made us forget our fatigue; and an early acquaintance with bed found us perfectly refreshed in the morning, and ready for an ascent to the summit of Glyder Bach, a description of which, in Pennant's tour, had awakened a strong curiosity to visit it.

Excursion to the summit of Glyder Bach.

GLYDER VAWR and GLYDER BACH are two of the loftiest and most rugged mountains in Snowdonia; the former, according to the latest survey, being 3,300 feet, and the latter 3,000 feet, above the level of the sea. The frosts and rains of ages, combined with other elemental agency, have operated upon the external face of these elevated mountains. Rocks have been shivered to pieces, huge masses or protuberances, called "horns," stand out occasionally from the sides of the mountains, and fragments of rock of all sizes strew the sides and bottom, which renders progress at times painful and difficult. This is one of the sternest regions of desolation in Britain—a wilder or more impressive scene imagination cannot conceive. Pennant thus describes the summit of Glyder Bach, and though this eloquent description was penned as far back as nearly eighty years ago, we found it as accurate as it is forcible :—" The plain which forms the top is strangely covered with loose stones, like the beach of the sea, in many places crossing one another in all directions, and entirely naked. Numbers of groups of stones are almost erect, sharp-pointed, and in sheaves ; all are weather-beaten, time-eaten, and honeycombed, and of a venerable grey colour. The elements seem to have warred against this mountain—rains have washed, lightnings torn, the very earth deserted, it, and the winds make it the constant object of their fury. The shepherds make it the residence of storms, and style a part of it Carnedd-y-Gwynt, or the 'Eminence of Tempests.' "

The morning proved exceedingly favourable for our projected ascent. Huge masses of clouds, some of which slightly rested on the summit of the mountain, with occasional bursts of sunshine, and a gentle breeze, the bracing and invigorating effects of which greatly assisted us in our progress, left nothing that could be desired. At nine o'clock A.M. the order was given to march, and, accompanied by our *compagnons de voyage,* two friends, and our guide, Henry Owen, we started on this most interesting mountain excursion. Previously to leaving home, we had made a

rough pen and ink sketch of the engraving in Pennant's tour of
the tall "columnar stones" on the summit of Glyder Bach, to test
the accuracy of the description given in the text: this, we need
hardly say, was fully realized; not a stone seemed moved out of
its place since Pennant's visit, nearly eighty years before. After
leaving Pen-y-Gwryd, our route lay over a peat morass, through
which flows the Gwryd on its course to the Llynniau Mymbyr,
commonly called the Capel Curig Lakes. After crossing the
river, we soon commenced the ascent of the mountain, which,
though rough, was less toilsome upon the whole than we expected.
After proceeding slowly for at least two hours, we neared the
summit, and resting for a brief interval under one of the "horns,"
refreshed ourselves with some deliciously cold pure spring water;
which, slightly flavoured with *cognac*, proved very refreshing.
The water we partook of flowed, or rather welled, out from the
mountain side, creating one of those green oases so pleasing to
the eye amidst the verdureless waste—with eternal barrenness and
desolation around it. Here we paused to survey the grand array
of huge mountains, which rise up and encompass this elevated
region in almost every direction. Amongst the chief attractions
of this magnificent scene were Snowdon and his attendant Alps;
the lovely Nant Gwynant, and its lake; Moel Siabod, "its sides
and base covered with verdure, its upper part a great pile of
broken rocks;" and the lakes and mountains in the neighbourhood
of Capel Curig. We now gradually neared the area on the
summit, which we found covered with groups of columnar stones,
some of vast size, from ten to thirty feet long, lying in all directions. The scene before us, in fact, resembled the ruins of some
vast *Druidical temple*—a mountain *Stonehenge*—which had been
overthrown ages ago by some awful convulsion of nature. Indeed,
so strong was our impression that we were in the midst of
venerable Druidical remains, that it was some time ere we could
convince ourselves that what we saw was in reality a chaotic mass
of stones thrown into inconceivable confusion—the work of time
and the violence of the elements. Pennant's description is so
truthful, that we cannot do better than give it. "I climbed up,"
says he, "one of these stones, twenty-five feet long and six broad,
and stamping it with my foot, felt a strong tremulous motion from

end to end. Another, eleven feet and six in circumference, was
poised so nicely in the thinnest part on the point of a rock, that,
to the appearance, the touch of a child would overset it. One
side of the mountain is formed into a gap, with sharp rocks
pointing upwards to a great height." The stone Pennant alluded
to lies in a horizontal position, supported by nine or ten upright
stones, forming a sort of natural altar. On this stone we also
climbed, and stood with reverential feelings on the very point of
the stone that this eminent topographer and antiquary trod full
eighty winters before. This natural *carnedd* of columnar stones
would appear to be of basaltic formation, as other portions of the
steep sides of Glyder Vawr, overhanging the Pass of Llanberis,
"exhibit ranges of basaltic rocks, much convulsed, and one
columnar cluster stands apart from the rest, quite upright."
Several rocky fragments which have fallen down into the Pass are
described as being sixty feet in length, exhibiting "marvellous
variations in colouring and outline."

> "It is a barren scene, and wild,
> Where naked cliffs are rudely piled."

Having spent nearly an hour in the examination of this wonderful work of nature, we proceeded to the northern side of
Glyder Bach, from whence we had a sort of bird's-eye view of
the summit of

Trifaen,

the singular conical mountain which rises from the vale far below.
This mountain in fact is a spur, or gigantic "horn" of the Glyder.
The ascent to the summit of Trifaen is both arduous and difficult,
and requires considerable nerve, as the mountain on all sides is
exceedingly precipitous. Two columnal stones on its peaked
summit, similar in formation to those on the Glyder, are frequently
mistaken by travellers on the Holyhead road—which runs at the
foot of the mountain—for human figures. Some years ago, a
gentleman who had ascended Trifaen, performed the hazardous,
foolhardy exploit of jumping from one of these stones to the
other. If his foot had slipped, or he had lost his balance, he

would have been dashed to pieces on the rocks below. Trifaen derives its name from these remarkable stones; formerly there were three of them, hence the name. We now obtained a magnificent view of the romantic Nant Ffrancon, the "Beaver's hollow," the celebrated Llyn Ogwen, famed for its trout, and the lofty summits of Carnedds Llewelyn and Dafydd. At our feet, in a tremendous hollow, lay Llyn Bochlwyd, and on our left we beheld the vast precipice called Castell-y-Geifr, the "Castle of the Goats," which connects the Glyders with Llyder Vawr. This lofty eminence, upwards of 3,000 feet in height, hangs over the dark waters of Llyn Idwal, situate in the most savage solitary *cwm* in Wales.

Mr. Roscoe, in his "Wanderings in North Wales," describes, in glowing terms, the marvellous contrasts, the sublime effects, of this wild, solitary region. "Situated in the very gorge of the craggy and beetling heights, the aspect of this lake had a thoroughly wild and sombre appearance, and produced a corresponding feeling in the mind. It was a combination of the picturesque and terrible, not unsuited, in its sternest mood, to the genius of Salvator. Had the foot of Wilson penetrated these grand recesses of Caernarvon hills, the noble taste of that enthusiast of nature must have seized some of its striking features. . . . The antique bridge, the wooded abyss, the picturesque coloured rocks, and the Trifaen, with its giant semblance of the human features; and through the terrific chasm below, the Ogwen pouring in three foaming cataracts, down heights of above 100 feet, into the green spreading meadows below."

We now proceeded to the verge of Castell Geifr, and reposing here for a short time, we surveyed with pleased emotions the sublime scenery around, and at length reluctantly turned on our homeward route, passing over Y-Waun Oer, the "cold, chilly waste," as it is fitly termed by the native shepherds. Y-Waun Oer is the connecting between that of the Glyder, called Glyder Bach, and the loftier portion of this vast double-headed mountain, Glyder Vawr. We at length reached the summit, passing near Clogwyn-Du-Ymhen-y-Glyder, "as dreadful a precipice as any in Snowdonia." The surface of the highest part of Glyder Vawr, we found comparatively smooth, but it wore a tempest-beaten, sterile aspect. From

hence we had a fine view of the Pass of Llanberis, and the country
to the west, including Caernarvon and its majestic castle.   We
descended in high spirits down a precipitous *cwm* or hollow in the
mountain—again partaking in the descent from a well of crystalline purity—towards Llyn Cwm Ffynnon, a small pool near the
foot of the mountain, about half a mile from Pen-y-Gwryd inn.
From this dark, savage, stormy-looking sheet of water, the river
Gwryd takes its rise.   We finally regained our quarters about
half-past five o'clock P.'M., amply repaid for our exertions, and
fortunate in our choice of a day on which, from its beauty, and the
extreme purity and clearness of the atmosphere, mountain scenery
appeared to such advantage.

> " Fill'd with the face of heaven, which, from afar,
>   Comes down upon the waters ; all its hues,
>   From the rich sunset to the rising star,
>   Their magical variety diffuse :
>   And now they change ; a paler shadow strews
>   Its mantle o'er the mountains."—BYRON.

CHAPTER X.

LLYN LLYDAW—ANGLING EXCURSION—INCIDENT—SCENERY—A
MOUNTAIN CLIMBER—LLYN CWM FFYNNON—RIVER GWRYD.

"This sober shade
Lets fall a serious gloom upon the mind.
Such are the haunts the mountain wanderer loves."

Llyn Llydaw.

THIS fine lake,

"Embosomed in the silent hills,"

reposes in a dark and gloomy recess under the north-east precipices of Snowdon. The pool is about one mile long—*not* one
mile and a half, as some guide-books have it—and is of profound depth. It is narrow, and contained a few years since a
small islet near the south-east shore, which from time immemorial
was the summer haunt of black-backed gulls. We have previously
described these birds in our excursion to Llyn-yr-Adar. Since
our visit to this lake, in 1849, we found on revisiting it, in 1857,
a considerable alteration. There is a copper-mine on the north-
west side of the pool, on the path to Llyn Ffynnon Glas and the
summit of Snowdon, and the miners, to facilitate their approach
to the mine, have lowered the depth of Llyn Llydaw from four to
five yards, to enable them to make an embankment across the lake
near the north-east extremity, at its narrowest part. Across this
embankment is the road to the mine, and it is now also the path
of the guides to the summit of Snowdon. The lake is thus
divided into two parts, and might, with some propriety, be called
Llynniau Llydaw Vawr and Vach. In consequence of the lake
being drained to the extent of at least from twelve to fifteen feet
of water, the islet has become a portion of the mainland, and its

former inhabitants, the gulls, finding their retreat insecure, have
deserted the place altogether. It is not unlikely that these were
the birds we found at Llyn-Yr-Adar. In 1849, there was also a
large flat-bottomed miner's boat, used to transport the ore and
the workmen across the lake; this has disappeared, there being
now no further use for it, since the lake has been divided by the
embankment.

Excursion to Llyn Llydaw.

Our first acquaintance with Llyn Llydaw occurred in 1849, an
account of which, and the sport we obtained, we now proceed to
furnish. We started from Pen-y-Gwryd on a fine cloudy morning,
with a mild southerly breeze; after getting upon the mountain
road, a few light showers occasionally fell, and

" All the air was breathing balm."

The distance from Pen-y-Gwryd inn to Llyn Llydaw is about three
miles, and the road, for the latter part of the route, is rough in
some places from being covered with loose stones. You first
proceed for about one mile and a half up a continuous ascent,
along the Pass of Llanberis as far as Gorphwysfa, which signifies
"the resting-place." Here you can "rest," if you feel inclined,
at a roadside public-house, where coaches and cars generally pull
up after toiling over the highest and steepest part of the Pass,
known as the Bwlch-y-Gwyddyl. The road to Llyn Llydaw here
turns off to the left, and the distance to the nearest part of the
lake is about one mile and a half. The steepest portion of the
ascent is, in fact, accomplished on your arrival at Gorphwysfa; so
that upon the whole, the road to the llyn is much easier than you
would imagine, considering its elevation. Near the lake, you see
below on your left, a row of mean-looking deserted miners' cottages, overlooking a small pool called Llyn Teyrn. This pool contains trout, and sometimes sport may be had; but we did not try
it, there not being at the time any breeze. Soon after you come
in sight of Llyn Llydaw, its dark-green sullen waters finely con-

trasting with the terrific precipices surrounding it, blackened and
scathed by the storms of ages.

> " The mountain shadows on her breast
> Were neither broken nor at rest;
> In bright uncertainty they lie,
> Like future joys to fancy's eye."

On our arrival we were soon made aware of the presence of
numerous gulls, by the discordant screams they set up, their
clamour increasing when they saw us land upon the islet, which
we did by means of the large flat-bottomed punt before mentioned.
Mr. Pennant, in his account of Snowdon, alludes to the presence
of gulls of the black-backed species on this islet. Here we put
our rods together, and prepared for a cruise upon the lake. A
gentle breeze curled its waters, and we commenced fishing on the
south-east side near the islet. The trout, however, were sullen,
notwithstanding the favourable weather, and after several hours'
hard flogging, and trials of several sorts of flies in the vain attempt
to lure the finny tribe from their crystal retreats, we only succeeded in capturing two brace of small trout. We afterwards
learned that we had fished the wrong end of the lake; the trout
are much larger and of better quality at the north-east extremity,
what now in fact constitutes that portion of the lake separated by
the embankment, and which, for distinction, we have named *Llyn
Llydaw Vach*.

For Alpine grandeur and sublimity—for picturesque effects of
the highest character—Llyn Idwal, Llyn Llydaw, and Llyn-y-Cae,
are unquestionably the three finest scenes in Wales. Of these,
the most sublime and terrible in aspect is Llyn Idwal; but
scarcely less inviting to the student of nature in her severer
moods are the sister lakes, Llyn Llydaw and Llyn-y-Cae. Reposing under the steeps of the two most celebrated mountains in
Wales, these lakes, to a certain degree, possess an advantage over
the gloomy Llyn Idwal: this advantage, however, is fully coun-
terbalanced by the savage cleft, Twll-Dû, and the still wilder
character of the rocks and precipices which surround it. From
our boat in the middle of Llyn Llydaw, for awhile we forgot our
more immediate object, being lost in admiration of the magnificent mountain—the "Monarch of the Hills"—towering imme-

diately above. The sun, which had shortly before broken out from amidst a canopy of clouds, dispersed the white vapours which had previously obscured his summit, and there he stood, with all his majestic beauty of outline, before our enraptured gaze. We must, however, leave it to the imagination to picture the magical effects produced by the combination of lights and shadows, the *chiaro scuro* of this sublime mountain wilderness. To be deeply impressed with the scenery of Llyn Llydaw, it must be seen from the water.

Revenons à nos moutons.—A short time after we gave over angling, we approached the west shore for the purpose of landing; our object being to obtain a view of Llyn Ffynnon Las, which is higher up, and lies in another deep basin more immediately under the precipices of Y-Wyddfa. As we neared the shore, steering for the mouth of the brook which flows from Llyn Ffynnon Las, an incident occurred, which, though sufficiently ludicrous at the time, might have been attended with unpleasant consequences. When about twenty or thirty yards from the shore, we observed a young colt about three months' old without its dam, which we supposed it had for the time lost, come galloping down to the edge of the lake, neighing at us with all its might, and before we could prevent it, the poor creature jumped into the water and made for the boat. Our first intention was to sheer off, hoping that the colt would discover its mistake—for it evidently had mistaken us, that is, the boat, for its mother —and return to the shore. But to our astonishment and annoyance, the colt persevered; and as we had by this time rowed out at least forty yards from land, the creature still pursuing us, we were obliged to return and meet it, as its strength was fast giving way, and in a minute or two more it would have sunk. As it was, we were just in time, and having run alongside the animal, Owen, our guide, got hold of it by the head, and we, with the help of our companion, by the tail, and after some exertion, we at length safely hoisted him aboard. The next step to take was to land him; but as soon as he was fairly on *terra firma*, he was again seized with the same strange desire to board us; and if we had left the shore, there is little doubt he would have again followed us as far as he could swim. At last it was suggested that Henry

Owen should be despatched to look for the dam, and fortunately he found her in a few minutes afterwards. The mare had got out of sight over some high rocky ground, and the colt had strayed from her towards the lake. After a hearty laugh at this strange adventure, and sundry jokes had passed, we recrossed to the other side of the pool, picked up our younger companion, whom we had left upon the islet amusing himself with the gulls, and finally returned home to our quarters about four o'clock; one of our companions jocosely remarking, that if we could not catch trout in Llyn Llydaw, we had caught something "very like a whale."

The general aspect of Llyn Llydaw resembles that of several other alpine lakes we have visited—Llyn-y-Cae, for instance— being in almost every part exceedingly deep close to the shore. The Llyn, in common with almost all the lakes in this district, is poached by the "board." During our last visit to Pen-y-Gwryd, in September, 1857, a very fine dish of trout—apparently of good quality, the weight of some of them being from half a pound to three-quarters of a pound, and similar in colour and appearance to those caught in Llyn Gwynant—were brought for sale to the inn by two quarrymen, who stated that they had taken them with the "board" in Llydaw, at the north-east end. They told us that the fish were generally small and inferior in the larger portion of the lake. We did not try this llyn in 1857; there was no boat: the walking round the shores is rough, and besides, being late in the season, the prospect of sport was very dubious. We have very little doubt, however, that earlier in the year, from all we could learn, as good sport may be obtained in Llyn Llydaw as in Llyn Gwynant. The best season for the angler is, from the middle of May to the middle of July.

Llyn Llydaw lies at a considerable elevation, probably not less than 2,500 feet above the sea, and is perhaps the largest *alpine* lake in Wales. The dark and stormy character of the scenery around it, the singularity of its bleak, gloomy situation, its waters often lashed into fury by the impetuous howling blasts which rush down from the lofty beetling crags which overhang it, ridge above ridge running upwards, dark and terrible in aspect, until they meet where the towering Y-Wyddfa rises in majestic grandeur, proclaim the workmanship of Him

"Who layeth the beams of his chambers in the waters, and maketh the clouds his chariot, and rideth upon the wings of the wind."

During our stay at Pen-y-Gwryd a few years ago, we made the acquaintance of a gentleman, a clergyman of the Church of England, who was possessed with a most extraordinary mania for climbing mountains. He would make, for instance, Pen-y-Gwryd, Capel Curig, Llanberis, and several other stations in Snowdonia, his head-quarters for a week or ten days, until, in fact, he had "exhausted the scenery." Picture to yourself a tall man, about fifty-two years of age, of a wiry, spare habit, rather slightly built, dressed in a pair of dingy slop trousers, a linen spencer of the same complexion, without hat or covering of any sort for the head, no neck-tie, his shirt-collar unbuttoned, with an enormous *Alpenstock* or climbing pole, seven or eight feet in length, in his hand, and you may perhaps be able to form some idea of the strange grotesque figure we have endeavoured to describe. His object was, to use his own expression, "to follow the sky line" of every mountain he visited. For example, he would ascend Snowdon from Llanberis, but instead of following the beaten track, he would take the edge of the mountain along the verge of the highest precipices, following what he called the "sky line" until he reached the summit; he would then descend the other side of the mountain towards Beddgelert, in a similar manner. He most frequently performed his excursions alone, although occasionally, when not so familiar with the locality, he availed himself of the services of a guide. He would follow up these rambles *de die in diem*, regardless of the weather, and was generally on his legs from about nine A.M. until eight P.M. The most extraordinary thing was, how he could keep up such violent daily exercise without any refreshment whatever during the period he was among the mountains. To prevent thirst, he carried a small pebble in his mouth; and Henry Owen, the guide, assured us that he never saw him partake of anything to eat or drink, not even a cup of cold water, whilst on an excursion. We have several times met him on his return to the inn, drenched with perspiration, and whilst his dinner was being prepared, he would continue at gentle exercise (staff in hand), to "cool down"—like a race-horse after a "breather"—preparatory to partaking of his repast—in fine weather generally *al fresco*—exhibiting not the least apparent fatigue. He was a man of very temperate habits: two or three glasses of sherry were the extent of his libations; he avoided smoking, and he would be up early in the morning performing his ablutions for several hours. He appeared to have no other object in climbing to the wild mountain tops than merely (as he said) to behold the wonderful works of the Almighty. Such was the remarkable individual with whom we became acquainted at Pen-y-Gwryd. We found him a most refined, intellectual companion, well read and informed on all subjects of general interest, thoroughly versed in Welsh topography, and in his demeanour most affable and courteous. He informed us that he spent several weeks annually in North Wales, following up the same pursuit—mountain climbing, either revisiting old scenes, or finding out, if possible, some fresh mountain path still more difficult and arduous to surmount than what he had previously attempted. In following the "sky line," no rocks, however rough, no precipices—unless perfectly inaccessible—ever daunted him. This singular mania or hobby horse, he appears to have followed up for years, and continued with unabated ardour. The last time we saw him was on a wet, stormy morning, preparing to "hie away to the mountain's brow," on his route from Pen-y-Gwryd to Capel Curig; the said route being the "sky line" over the summit and entire length of the lofty Moel Siabod.

Llyn-cwm-Ffynnon.

We have stated in a former chapter, that Pen-y-Gwryd would afford fair sport to the angler at the proper season. We have previously described Llyn Llydaw and Llyn Gwynant; and it now only remains for us briefly to notice Llyn-Cwm-Ffynnon, and the little river Gwryd. We have already described the character of the scenery around the lake, which is bleak and dreary enough. It is situate at the foot of the Glyder, in the midst of a peat morass, and when the lake is low in summer it is quite impossible to fish its northern boundary, on account of the turbary. Indeed, except at the south-east corner, where there are some precipitous rocks, which in one part almost abut upon the water, the walking along shore is mostly over the peat bog, which in wet weather becomes impassable. On the north-west shore for a short distance there is a low ledge of rocks washed by the llyn, off which, on one or two occasions, we have killed a few fair-sized trout. The lake in this part is rather weedy and shallow. Llyn Cwm Ffynnon is small—scarcely two furlongs in length from north to south, and not much above half that distance in breadth. The trout, though generally small, have been described as "good and often free." We, however, are obliged to confess that we have found them neither the one nor the other. The usual size of the fish is about a quarter of a pound; some, we believe, have been taken larger. We have fished this water several times during the best season (June), but we never succeeded in capturing more than two or three brace on any occasion. The trout are exceedingly sullen, and the angler's skill and patience are alike exhausted in the attempt to lure them to the surface. It is very possible that poaching may have caused the trout to become shy; at all events, we never visited the lake without finding one or two men in possession of some of the best water, zealously pursuing their unlawful occupation with the "board." We never had many "rises" on this pool, nor have ever observed the fish rising freely to the natural fly. From this circumstance we deduce that either the trout are comparatively scarce or extremely shy. Llyn Cwm Ffynnon is situate at a very convenient distance from Pen-y-Gwryd Inn, not more than three-quarters of a mile, and the ascent to it, over some rather wet boggy ground, is not particularly steep. We cannot, however, as far as our experience goes, hold out any hope of much sport. There is a very fine view of Snowdon to be seen on a clear day from the south-east side of the pool; this alone renders Llyn Cwm Ffynnon at least worth a visit.

The Gwryd.

The bleak and dreary waste, Nant-y-Gwryd, watered by the infant Gwryd—a stream flowing, as most rivers do in Cambria, from a solitary mountain lake until its waters expand into the Llynniau Mymbyr—presents little to attract the eye of the traveller as he passes on his way to Capel Curig. Sheep or mountain cattle are amongst the few living objects to be seen on the moorland solitude, roaming wherever inclination leads them on these wild uplands; occasionally a lone farmhouse, or deserted *Hafodtai*, few and far between, present themselves, but

> "The world, and all that love that world,
> Are far away."

The country is sparely inhabited; and, were it not for the shoals of tourists who roll along the road in their cars and carriages during the summer months, enlivening in some degree the monotonous stillness that prevails at other periods, you might not meet with a single human being for miles. The Gwryd swarms with trout close to the inn; and as it becomes larger in its course through Nant-y-Gwryd to the Llynniau Mymbyr, being fed by several smaller brooks, on the "lanes" of deep water which occasionally occur in its course, large trout are sometimes taken with the fly or worm, particularly during a flood. These fish are supposed to have run into the river out of the lakes. We have frequently had tolerable sport with the fly about two miles below the inn; the trout, though rather small, are pretty, well fed fish. The angler fond of "bottom" fishing may soon fill his basket, by merely keeping out of sight of the quick-eyed trout, and begin his pursuit at less than five minutes' walk from the inn. Lower down the vale, especially near Pont-y-Gwryd, he may also regale himself with a magnificent prospect of Snowdon and the adjacent lofty mountains. We take it for granted that every true lover of the angle is also an admirer of fine scenery.

CHAPTER XI.

SNOWDON—USUAL ASCENTS—SERMON ON THE MOUNTAIN—GUIDES
—SUPPOSED DANGERS OF ASCENT—GRANDEUR OF SCENERY—
EXCURSION TO SUMMIT—VIEW FROM Y-WYDDFA.

> " I climb'd the dark brow of the mighty Helvellyn,
>   Lakes and mountains beneath me gleam'd misty and wide;
> All was still, save, by fits, when the eagle was yelling,
>   And starting around me the echoes replied."—SCOTT.

Snowdon.

THE " hill king" of Cambria, Snowdon, is termed by the native
Welsh Craig-Eira, which means the "snowy mountain;" hence
the Saxon appellation, Snowdon.   Some writers, however, have
asserted that Snowdon and the adjacent range of mountains are
called Creigiau-yr-Eryri, the "eagle's cliffs;" but Pennant, whose
authority ought to be indisputable, says the former is the correct
appellation.   Whatever might be the case in olden time, eagles
are never seen soaring over the peaks of Snowdon nowadays;
therefore "snowy mountain" is at all events the more significant
title.   The highest peak of Snowdon is 3,571 feet in elevation
above the sea-level, according to Ordnance admeasurement, and
is therefore 779 feet below the level of perpetual snow; so that
it is not true—as has been erroneously asserted—that snow may
be found in some of its clefts throughout the year.*   Never
theless, even in the middle of summer, the temperature is sometimes low.   The thermometer has been observed at 34° just after
sunrise, and even in August as low as 48° early in the afternoon

---

* "Snowdon, as its name implies, is covered with perpetual snow."—
MEDWIN'S *Angler in Wales.*

"In 1850, snow fell here in June;" a phenomenon, we should suppose, of rather rare occurrence.

MOEL-Y-WYDDFFA, "the bald head of the conspicuous summit," is the highest mountain elevation in South Britain; and several eminent topographers, amongst others Pennant and Bingley, have favoured the world with glowing and eloquent descriptions of their ascents to it. It may therefore appear presumptuous on the part of a humble disciple of Isaac Walton to attempt the description of an excursion to the summit of this celebrated mountain; but we are encouraged to do so, partly because we have had some experience, having ascended Snowdon on several occasions from different points, and also because we are anxious to record our impressions of the scenic effects we have observed from the summit and on the route less frequently described than the others, the ascent from Pen-y-Gwryd:

In perusing the accounts given by the older topographers, of the difficulties to be encountered in the ascent of Snowdon, one cannot help being amused with the air of exaggeration, the inflated terms employed in their descriptions, leading you almost to believe the ascent to be as difficult and dangerous as if you were ascending one of the Alps in Switzerland. Even the usually accurate Pennant is scarcely free from the charge of exaggeration in recording the "perils" of the ascent. Far be it from us, however, to question the merits of Pennant's narrative; for, taking it altogether, it far exceeds in descriptive power any account we have ever perused. It must be remembered, also, that during the last century and even down to the earlier portion of the present one, the ascent of Snowdon was seldom undertaken by the English tourist. The "Saxon in Wales" was rarely to be seen in those days; Welsh tours were not much in vogue; and few indeed of those individuals who did find their way into North Wales, ventured upon the ascent of Snowdon. We must not, therefore, be much surprised at the timidity exhibited, or the "nervous horror" which pervaded the minds of such of those early pioneers who have recorded their experiences of the ascent of Snowdon, or his almost as celebrated neighbour, the "giant Cader Idris."

There are four usual ascents of Snowdon—that is, the routes

followed by guides—viz. from Llanberis, Beddgelert, Pen-y-Gwryd, and the " Snowdon Ranger," on the shores of Llyn Cwellyn. The Capel Curig route is *via* Pen-y-Gwryd; it is, however, four miles longer. Of these, Llanberis enjoys by far the greatest share of popularity, for two reasons; the first is, that from thence it is indisputably the easiest ascent; and secondly, the expense is comparatively trifling. These two powerful persuasives will always preserve to Llanberis the largest amount of patronage. The Llanberis route, however, has this drawback; it is, in our opinion, inferior in sublimity either to Beddgelert or Pen-y-Gwryd. The majority of topographical writers, among whom we may mention Bingley, have, however, ascended Snowdon from Llanberis, and some of them have selected this route in preference. Bingley also ascended from Llyn Cwellyn, Dolbadarn, and Beddgelert. In consequence of " low fares " and " easy gradients," a very large majority of tourists and pleasure-seekers ascend from Llanberis, 200 or 300 a day during the height of the season being no unusual amount; and as many have, on one or two occasions, been on the summit of the mountain at the same time. We were told by one of the Beddgelert guides that, a few years ago, a church dignitary preached extempore a very eloquent sermon from Moel-y-Wyddfa, to a numerous congregation, selecting for his text, " Behold the Lamb of God! " What an interesting occasion! What an opportunity for the preacher to dwell upon the "mighty works " of Him in whose hands

"Are all the corners of the earth :
And the strength of the hills is his also."

From this it will appear that the romance of the ascent to Snowdon belongs to the past. The summit of the mountain is absolutely *mobbed* in the summer and autumn; and such as prefer a quiet journey must seek it in the evening, hold communion with the Queen of Night, view the stars, " the poetry of heaven," flickering above the misty mountain peaks, and watch for the effects of early sunrise—"the solemn splendour of colouring, the chaotic prospect around "—in stillness and solitude.

Within the last few years, two or three of the Llanberis guides have erected some rude huts, called the " Snowdon Hotel," on the highest peak, adjoining the Ordnance *carnedd*, or heap of stones, in the centre of which is a tall signal-post, where tea and coffee, ale, porter, spirits, and other refreshments, can be obtained. Of course you cannot expect these commodities at the usual prices, the labour of conveying them to so great an altitude being taken into consideration. Where such a number of hungry and thirsty visitors are congregated, the demand is great, the prices commensurate; and we have no doubt that the guides have found it a good speculation, and reap a rich harvest during the season. You can also "procure a bed," if you are desirous of remaining on the mountain all night; but, as there is only one bed, in a very small, rude apartment, as far as we know, the great majority of the visitors who arrive over or during the night are obliged to "rough" it in the best way they can. The charge, if we recollect rightly, is six shillings and sixpence, for bed and breakfast. The appearance of the huts is unsightly; and the solitudinous stillness of the "lonely mountain top"—the great charm to us in mountain excursions—is now, in a great measure, destroyed. The innovations of man, however, cannot alter in this alpine region the external charms of nature. The prospect from Moel-y-Wyddfa presents the same magnificent combinations —the same majestic views of mountains, valleys, lakes, and streams, bounded by the sea, or the faint outlines of the wild Wicklow mountains in the far distant western horizon—until the eye of the observer almost strains itself in the vain attempt to look beyond them.

In some of the guide-books we find emphatic warnings of the "dangers" of the ascent—"even in the finest weather it is dangerous to do so without a guide." We may here remark that these assertions are entirely erroneous. Snowdon is sometimes for days together entirely free from clouds or vapour; it was so in 1857; and we have on several occasions ascended to the summit alone from different routes, without the least danger or inconvenience. The fact is, the various paths to the summit are now so well worn, the "trail" so distinctly marked, that on a fine day it is almost impossible, especially if you have any previous knowledge of the locality and the various landmarks, to mistake your path. In a day of "darkness and of gloominess," when fogs, rolling from the sea, infold the mountain in their chilly embrace, or at *night*, a guide is then, of course, indispensable; but comparatively few persons in stormy weather, think of encountering the ascent.

Before we proceed to give a description of one of our excursions to the summit of Snowdon, *without* a guide, it may be useful to offer a few hints as to the expenses attendant on a guide and ponies from the different stations we have named. The charge for ponies is, we believe, the same at all the inns; viz. five shillings to the summit, if practicable; but, if you proceed over the mountain—say, for instance, from Beddgelert to Llanberis—the charge is then doubled. The guides' fees vary. From Beddgelert, the guides charge seven shillings to the summit; if afterwards they proceed with a party to Llanberis or Pen-y-Gwryd, the fee is ten shillings; sometimes, when there is a large party, a higher sum is voluntarily paid. A night ascent to Snowdon from Beddgelert is ten shillings, which is moderate enough. The expense of a guide from Pen-y-Gwryd—a much more fatiguing ascent, and nearly the same distance—is only five shillings. Llanberis is far in advance on the score of cheapness. When a large party join together, as is almost always the case, the guides' fee for a single individual is a mere trifle. The charge from the "Snowdon Ranger" is about the same as Beddgelert. From Capel Curig, which is a great deal the longest journey, the guides' charge, we believe, is ten shillings. The guides are also usually provided with some refreshment, either on the route, or at the summit. Ponies may be ridden from Llanberis or Llyn Cwellyn, to the highest summit of the mountain—these routes being by far the easiest. From Pen-y-Gwryd, it is desirable to dismount on reaching Llyn Ffynnon Lâs, as the path from thence becomes rough, steep, and very narrow. From Beddgelert, the visitor may ride nearly, if not quite, to the top; but many nervous persons proceed on foot after arriving at the narrow ridge called Clawdd-Coch, a part of the route formerly so much dreaded by tourists. On this subject, Mr. Bingley remarks, "There is no danger whatever in passing Clawdd-Coch in the daytime, but I confess that I should by no means like to venture along this tract in the night, as many do who have never seen it. If the moon shone very bright, we might, it is true, escape unhurt; but a dark cloud coming suddenly over would certainly expose us to much danger. Many instances have occurred of persons who, having passed over it in the night, were so terrified at seeing it by the daylight the next morning, that they have not dared to return the same way, but have gone a very circuitous route by Bettws [Bettws-Garmon, we presume he means]. I was informed that one gentleman had been so much alarmed, that he crawled over it back again on his hands and knees." In reply to this statement, notwithstanding it is backed by the opinion of such a distinguished authority as Bingley, we confidently affirm that, in ordinary summer weather, there is not the slightest danger by night, whether by moonlight or not, with an experienced guide; and, as Beddgelert possesses three most excellent ones, all rejoicing in the name of Jones, the most timid person need not feel in the least alarmed whilst crossing over the narrow ridge of Clawdd-Coch. We ourselves have repeatedly seen both ladies and gentlemen leave Beddgelert even so late as nine o'clock, P. M., and when the night afterwards was both dark and cloudy, under the safe conduct of one of these guides. It usually occupies from three and a half to four hours, to reach the summit of Snowdon from Beddgelert at night. In the daytime, the distance, about six miles, is frequently performed in from two and a half to three hours. It would thus appear, from the accounts given by Bingley, Warner, and others, that the "terrors" of the ascent have been much magnified; that, in reality, there is nothing formidable in the ascent of Snowdon in fine weather; nothing to terrify the most nervous person. Surely the nerves of tourists in former days were made of much more fragile materials than the modern ones.

The view of Snowdon from the Beddgelert road is unquestionably the finest *near* view that can be obtained of the "Monarch of the Hills." This view occurs about one mile from Pen-y-Gwryd inn. Not only is the magnificent outline of the mountain more clearly and exquisitely defined, but you obtain a more perfect prospect of the neighbouring eminences, the group of mountains forming Snowdon, Crib-y-Dystul, the "Dripping Peak," Crib Coch, the "Red Summit," and y-Lliwed, the peak third in height after y-Wyddfa, and forming the highest point of the range of precipices along the whole northern face.   Crib-y-Dystul is the highest point in elevation next to Moel-y-Wyddfa.   The eye in passing to these lofty peaks, is refreshed with a charming view of Nant Gwynant and its beautiful lake in the distance, and in the immediate foreground, the fine falls of the Avon Lâs—Rhaiadr-Cwm-Dyli—which come tumbling and foaming over the lofty precipices above, in their descent to the "Vale of Waters."

The distance from Pen-y-Gwryd inn to the summit of Snowdon is about six miles, and there can be no question—notwithstanding the assertion of one or two of the guide books, that the ascent from Beddgelert is "the most difficult"—that in this respect, during the latter part of the route, the path is much more steep and rugged from Pen-y-Gwryd than from any other point.

Mr. Warner, in his "Walk through Wales," in the autumn of 1797, made an ascent from a different point to any we have read in the various published tours, and judging from the description he gives, it appears to have been exceedingly toilsome and difficult.   As far as we can understand his narrative, he, in the first place, followed the turnpike road from Beddgelert, passing on his way Ddinas Emrys, "a huge perpendicular rocky mountain, finely shaded with wood," and the "beautiful pool of Llyn-y-Ddinas," nearly to the road leading to Llan farm, which is situate at the entrance to Cwm Llan.   Here he struck into a path to the left, near a meeting-house and cottages ; by this track he toiled to the summit of Snowdon.   It lies between the peak of Yr Aran and the "deep hollow" of Cwm Llan to the right.   He thus describes the ascent :—"The summit of Snowdon, towering above us to the north, had hitherto been involved in a fleecy cloud, which hung around it in the manner of a curtain, undulating with the wind.   This now appeared to be drawn up higher than it had yet been, and to rest like a crown on the very point of the mountain ; the misty mantle being likely to melt away altogether before the sun, which was now approaching towards his meridian.   Our guide observed, that should we determine to visit the top of Snowdon, we should find the ascent much more steep and disagreeable than the regular road [from Beddgelert] ; that notwithstanding, it was a practicable way, and had been trodden by *some* travellers before us. . . . . The first stage of our journey was up a rugged steep by the side of a mountain torrent, which, falling from ledge to ledge, stunned us with its unceasing noise. The principal branch of Yr Aran [y-Lliwed], little inferior to his mighty neighbour, heaved his unwieldy bulk into the clouds on the right hand; under which a frightful hollow, called Cwm-Llan, spread its hideous profundity, stretching a mile and a half in length, and nearly as much in breadth, a precipice of Snowdon forming one of its black perpendicular sides. We contemplated this scene with marks of astonishment and dread. . . . . After two hours of very severe labour we gained the summit of Snowdon, a sharp narrow crag of rock, not more than two yards over. Our toil, however, seemed at first to be ill repaid; a crown of clouds still covered the top, and we remained involved in a mist that produced the most intense cold. . . . . In this truly hyperborean climate we waited half an hour, at the instigation of our guide, who assured us the cloud would shortly leave the head of the mountain; the mist gradually sailed away, and left us to contemplate for a few minutes, a wide unbounded prospect, diversified with mountains and valleys, cities, lakes and oceans. . . . We were not long indulged with this free, uninterrupted gaze; the cloud again came rolling on, and the covering soon became thicker and darker than hitherto, and our guide warned us to descend with all expedition, lest we should be involved in a storm amid these exposed unsheltered regions. We accordingly proceeded through the gloom, following the steps of our conductor, who walked immediately before us, as we literally could not see the distance of a dozen feet. The situation was new to us; it produced, however, an effect that was very sublime. Occasional gusts of wind, which now roared around us, swept away for a moment the pitchy cloud that involved particular spots of the mountain, and discovered immediately below us, huge rocks, abrupt precipices, and profound hollows, exciting emotions of astonishment and awe in the mind, which the eye, darting down an immense descent of vacuity and horror, conveyed to it under the dreadful image of inevitable destruction."

Very erroneous impressions of the altitude of Snowdon, as compared with some of the mountains in the Scottish highlands, are to be met with in some of the earlier works on Welsh topo-

graphy. Thus Warner, amongst others, calls Snowdon the
"highest mountain in the three kingdoms;" and Cader Idris was
almost universally believed to be second only in height to Snowdon
amongst the Cambrian Alps. There are, however, nine or ten
mountains in Scotland that are all loftier than Snowdon; four of
them are considerably higher. Ben Mhuicdhu, in Aberdeenshire,
is 4,418 feet; Ben Nevis, Invernesshire, is 4,358 feet; and Cairn
Gorm, in the same county, is 4,050 feet. Ben Lawers, in Perth-
shire, is nearly as lofty, being 3,944 feet. Ben Mhuicdhu, on its
highest point, is sixty-eight feet above the limit of perpetual
snow, and Ben Nevis is also a few feet above that altitude.

An Excursion to the Summit of Snowdon.

Our ascent of Snowdon from Pen-y-Gwryd was unpremeditated.
It was on a very fine morning, about the middle of August, 1857,
that we started from Beddgelert with some intention of angling
in Llyn Cwm Ffynnon, near Pen-y-Gwryd. We were, however,
on a "roving commission," and circumstances might occur which
would possibly alter our intention. We were much struck during
our walk—certainly one of the most delightful in Wales—with
the magnificent "lights" which prevailed over the landscape, the
gorgeous colouring, the *crispness*, if we may use the expression,
of the outlines of rocks and mountains, woods, lakes, and glens,
which we passed in succession. Never before had we felt so
much impressed with the *majesty* of Snowdon. "A scene like
this," eloquently remarks the author of the "Beauties, Harmonies,
and Sublimities of Nature," "commands our feelings to echo, as
it were, in unison to its grandeur and sublimity; and the trans-
ports of imagination seem to contend for the mastery, and nerves
are touched that never thrilled before." As we silently proceeded
on our journey, we saw that this was one of those marvellously
brilliant days which occur only at rare intervals in mountain districts, and which, from the humidity of the atmosphere, generally
portend a change in the weather. By the time we had arrived at
Pen-y-Gwryd our mind was made up, our piscatorial intention
was abandoned, we resolved to *dare* an ascent of Snowdon. As
we had never before ascended from this side of the mountain, a

few queries to our host, Henry Owen, were requisite. We were acquainted with the route as far as Llyn Llydaw, but not farther; however, a few directions from Owen, and a careful survey of the Ordnance Map, convinced us that no apparent difficulty presented itself; and after a frugal meal, and a glass or two of excellent *cwrw* to fortify us against the fatigue of the ascent, we prepared for our excursion. Whilst, however, we were thus refreshing ourselves, one of those sudden changes in the weather occurred, so frequent in mountainous countries, which almost caused us to alter our intention. A change in the wind had taken place; it had veered to north-west, and brought on a thick fog, which boiled down the sides of the mountain and rapidly enveloped Snowdon in a mantle of mist. In reference to these sudden changes of weather, Pennant says, "It is very seldom that the traveller gets a propitious day to ascend Snowdon; for often, when it appears clear, it becomes suddenly and unexpectedly enveloped in mist by its attraction of clouds, which just before seemed remote and at great heights. At times I have observed them lower to half their heights, and notwithstanding they have been dispersed to the right and to the left, yet they have met from both sides, and united to involve the summit in one great obscurity." What was to be done? To ascend Snowdon in such weather was simply impossible—in fact it was useless. Whilst we were hesitating as to whether to proceed or not, Robin Hughes, the celebrated Capel Curig guide, hove in sight, convoying three ponies, upon which sat a lady, a gentleman, and a very pleasing intelligent-looking boy. We immediately accosted Hughes, and asked him if it was his intention to attempt the ascent in such weather. He replied that the lady and gentleman were determined to proceed if possible, and added that he thought the fog was below the summit of the mountain; that he had no doubt the y-Wyddfa was perfectly clear and cloudless, and probably the fog would disperse almost as suddenly as it had appeared. Encouraged by this opinion, and relying upon the great experience this veteran guide —whom we had known for many years—possessed of the weather in this elevated region; notwithstanding the remonstrances of our host, who emphatically warned us of the danger we might encounter, we determined to proceed unaided and alone, in the first

instance to Gorphwysfa; there to await and avail ourselves of
any favourable change in the weather that might occur, and then
immediately proceed on our mountain adventure.　There was a
spice of romance in the idea of accomplishing the ascent which
chimed in with our feelings, and irresistibly urged us to carry out,
if practicable, our previous intention.　With this determination
we arrived at Gorphwysfa; but the weather, so far from improving,
became, if possible, more unfavourable than ever.　The fog increased in volume, and descended lower and lower, until we
became enveloped in it on the road ascending through the Pass of
Llanberis.　We found on our arrival, Robin Hughes and his party,
who decided, after some hesitation, and evidently labouring under
feelings of great disappointment, to proceed to Llanberis; a
favourable ascent to the summit on this occasion being now
deemed hopeless.　We were thus left "alone in our glory," and
were for some time in doubt and hesitation as to what steps to
pursue under these discouraging circumstances.

The day wore on, it was now three o'clock, and it was time to
make up our minds either to advance or retreat.　At all events,
we argued, we could find our way as far as Llyn Llydaw, and by
that time perhaps, some favourable change might take place, so as
to enable us to proceed.　We therefore, after some hesitation,
decided to start.　We carried our rod with us for a staff, our
fishing-basket served us for a canteen, and thus accoutred, we
arrived at the shore of Llyn Llydaw.　We had observed on our
route several "lifts" in the fog, and that it by degrees folded
itself up, and gradually rose from the lower portion of the mountain.　Every now and then, swift as thought, a magnificent burst
of light suddenly illumed a distant peak, which absolutely glowed
like burnished copper of a deep ruddy hue, and threw over the
waters of the lake a fearful supernatural glare, and then,

"Like the rainbow's lovely form,"

vanished "mid clouds and thick darkness," which again "spread
upon the mountains."　The contrasts between these brilliant
magical glimpses of light, and the black murky threatening gloom
which hovered over the deep *cwms* or hollows of Snowdon, were
so startling, that we felt almost spell-bound, and a deep thrilling

awe crept over us, such as we had never felt before. "The very air of the place seemed solemn and lonely;" and although we confessthat we felt some what daunted, we were wrought up to such a pitch of excitement, that if the scene presented to us had been even still more threatening and terrible, we should have endeavoured to pursue our way.

> " Such are the haunts the mountain wanderer loves."

Matters, however, now began to improve, and by the time we had reached Llyn Cwm-Ffynnon-Glas, the fog continued to rise higher and higher, until we could, to our extreme delight and relief, at last see dimly the peerless summit of Moel-y-Wyddfa like a beacon light of Hope to the tempest-tossed mariner, the sun evidently gilding its peak in unclouded majesty and splendour. We were thus at last rewarded for what, at one time, we had deemed a hopeless attempt, and obtained thus far the prospect of a grand and marvellous scene amidst the "damp of clouds" and the wailings of the chilly mysterious wind, which at brief intervals, came *soughing* down the gullies and ravines, in the struggle to obtain the mastery over the vapours which shrouded them.

In our anxiety to advance, and in the state of nervous excitement we laboured under, we forgot the roughness of the road, which for the most part consisted of a bed of rolling stones, fatiguing to pass over, and which produced an unpleasant sensation of pain to the feet, and a constant strain upon the ancles. We had now performed the greatest portion of the journey; what remained, however, was by far the most difficult part of the ascent, namely, from the foot of the rocky steeps of Crib-y-Dystul and Crib Coch. Here we reposed a short time at the copper mine, and refreshed ourselves with some of the coldest and purest water we ever tasted. By the time we had rested ourselves, the sun broke out in full splendour, illuminating with his rays the summits of the mountains, and rapidly dispersing the vapours which still lingered upon the highest acclivities. Y-Wyddfa now loomed up before us clear and unclouded, and we commenced the ascent up the side of Crib-y-Dystul with renewed strength and ardour, in the confident hope of successfully accomplishing our feat. We had never before ascended so high on this side of

Snowdon, and stood for the first time on the shore of Llyn-
Ffynnon-Glas. This solitary pool looked even still more savage
and gloomy than Llyn Llydaw, which lies immediately below it.
The path, after leaving the copper mine, leads nearly due north;
it is very narrow, and covered with loose *débris* from the precipices above. It afterwards winds in a serpentine direction
towards the west, on a very sharp incline, until you near the
summit. About half way up, we discovered the figures of
several persons near the Ordnance *carnedd*, and we concluded
that we should meet a host of people at the "hotel." As we continued slowly to ascend, pausing occasionally to look around, the
sublimity of the scene above and below increased every moment.
It was fearful to look back on the precipitous path up which we
had toiled, and which to the eye looked almost inaccessible; the
cold green glassy waters of the lake below reflecting on its crystal
depths the crags which overhang the yawning gulf in which its
waters repose.

> " How fearful
> And dizzy 'tis to cast one's eyes so low !
> The crows and choughs that wing the midway air,
> Scarce show so gross as beetles."

It was half-past six o'clock ere we stood on the summit of
Moel-y-Wyddfa; it was evening, not a soul was there: we
were alone. The mountain, during the day, had been visited by a
number of people, but all had now departed. We had accomplished the ascent in about two hours and thirty minutes from
Gorphwysfa:

> " Soft fell the night, the sky was calm."

The view we obtained from this elevated spot was a singular one.
Above us the sky was beautifully clear; all below, to about half-
way down the mountain, looking towards the vale of Cwellyn,
Anglesea, and the whole of the country to the west and south-
west, was enveloped in a dense mass of white vapour, resembling
the ocean billows after a storm. The effect was

> " Beautiful exceedingly,"

surpassingly grand, and marvellous beyond conception. You
could almost imagine that what you beheld were the raging

waters of the foam-covered ocean rolling beneath your feet.   The ridge of Snowdon appeared to have formed a barrier to the mist on the east side; for, looking towards Capel Curig, Moel Siabod, the mountainous country beyond, and in every direction, not a cloud or vapour was to be seen.   Llyn Conwy and several other llyns could plainly be discerned; some of these we recognised as old acquaintances.   We had also a fine view of the Merionethshire mountains; it was, however, too late in the day to distinguish very distant objects.   The curtain of vapour which shrouded the western side of Snowdon did not extend far, not even to the roots of the mountain, as we afterwards ascertained; still there seemed no present prospect of its clearing off, although an occasional gust of wind, which caused the clouds to boil and heave as if suddenly about to be torn asunder, gave us faint hopes that it would do so.   But we were doomed to be disappointed.   After feasting our eyes for some time on the magnificent prospect before us, for "language is indigent and impotent when it would presume to sketch scenes on which the Great Eternal has placed his matchless finger," and warned at length by the rapidly waning light, we slowly descended from our position; and after partaking of a slight refreshment at the huts, we resumed our journey, it being our intention to return to Beddgelert.   We soon after passed the Clawdd Coch,·

> " Nec temere, nec timide; "

the abyss on either side being concealed by the thick vapour furiously boiling and circulating below us, and without any danger, as the path was perfectly visible.   We did not finally quit the clouds until we had advanced to the lower acclivities of the mountain.   Here the evening was calm and peaceful; the sky was almost cloudless, and

> " The moon half hid in silvery flakes,
> Afar her dubious radiance shed,
> And summer mists in dewy balm,
> Steep'd heathy bank and mossy stone."

CHAPTER XII.

LLANBERIS — HOTELS — LLYN PERIS — LLYN PADARN — PASS—
SCENERY—VILLAGE—CHURCH—WELL OF ST. PERIS—CAENANT
MAWR—LLYN DWYTHWCH—LLYN-DÙ-YR-ARDDUDWY—BOTANY
OF LLANBERIS—HETTY'S ISLAND—SLATE QUARRIES.

> " Lives there the man so lost to Nature's charms
> That would not shun—when scenes like these invite—
> The crowded city ?
> The lonely Llyn—the sparkling rivulet—
> The hoarse cascade—the frowning steep
> Of yonder mountain lost in clouds—
> Hath charms for me far, far beyond
> The busy haunts of men, where, as
> A solitary pilgrim, through fair Cambria,
> I trace my devious way."

FORTY or fifty years ago, the romantic Pass of Llanberis was little frequented by tourists; it was, in fact, one of the most secluded spots in the Principality. In Pennant's time, the roads in North Wales were in a wretched state, and Llanberis formed no exception, so that a pilgrimage through it could not be made, except on horseback or on foot. At a later period, Bingley calls it "a bad horse path;" and most writers, at the beginning of the present century, complain of the execrable roads they had to traverse. Since then, a great alteration has taken place; the wild seclusion of Llanberis is broken, and the "romantic melancholy" which formerly pervaded the scene has for ever departed.

In 1818, an excellent posting-road was made through the Pass to Caernarvon; and it has since become a place of fashionable resort to some thousands of visitors every summer. Llanberis derives some of its notoriety from the visit of Queen Victoria and her royal mother, the Duchess of Kent, in 1832. The Queen, then the Princess Victoria, was exceedingly struck with the scenery of the Pass, and is reported to have said, that it commanded her admiration more than anything else she had seen in Wales.   Praise from such a high quarter naturally excited the curiosity of the public, and since then the popularity of Llanberis has been annually on the increase.   There are now two excellent hotels, both in the vicinity of the " time-worn " tower of Dolbadarn, viz. the " Royal Victoria," a handsome edifice erected by the late Mr. Assheton Smith, some time after the visit of the royal party, and the " Dolbadarn Castle," built, in 1818, at the time the road was constructed.   The " Dolbadarn Castle," although not so showy as its rival, is spacious and exceedingly comfortable ; and pedestrian tourists, " knapsack " men, and especially anglers and artists, will do well to try it.   There is now also a respectable inn at the village, called the " Vaenol Arms."   In 1840, and until 1845, the village inn was a wretched pothouse.

Llyn Peris and Llyn Padarn.

The lakes of Llanberis have long been celebrated as two of the finest and most beautiful sheets of water in Wales.   The upper lake, called Llyn Peris, is nearly one mile in length and about half a mile broad.   Its known depth is greater than any other lake in the Principality, being in some places 140 yards deep. The lower lake, Llyn Padarn, is the largest pool in the county, being about a mile and a half long, but it is rather narrow, and very inferior in grandeur and picturesque effect to the sister lake.   The upper lake is surrounded by hills of very grand form, which on two of its sides project precipitously into the lake itself, but at its extremities leave an opening for the entrance and escape of the waters.   With the exception of Llyn Tegid, better known as Bala Lake, Llyn Padarn is said to be " second in size of all in Wales."   This assertion is very erroneous, as Llyn Savaddon, or Llangorse Pool—the *Clamosum* of Giraldus Cambrensis—is three miles long, and in some parts more than one mile broad.   This lake is in Brecknockshire, and is inferior only to Bala Pool, which is nearly four miles long.   The upper and lower lakes of Llanberis are separated by a narrow neck of land, through which the Seiont flows into Llyn Padarn.   These Llyns, as we have previously mentioned, in former times abounded with trout and char but since the formation of copper mines and slate quarries in their immediate vicinity, both these species of fish have become exceedingly scarce. It is said, that after the opening of the copper mines, the mineral water from the level had the effect of driving the char out of the lakes into the river Seiont which flows through the pools ; and numbers of char were afterwards caught in nets in the Menai Strait, at the mouth of the river.

Our first impressions of Llanberis were extremely favourable. It was towards the close of a lovely summer's day, in 1840, when we entered the Pass. We were on horseback ; and as we slowly descended towards the village, which has been justly styled " the *beau ideal* of a mountainous retirement and its attendant simplicity," the rays of the departing luminary lit up the summits of the towering rocks and precipices on either side of the tremendous hollow through which we passed; " the olive-coloured gloom," russet heights, lone cataracts, and " cloud capt " mountains which greeted our gaze on every side, and the sparkling waters of the beautiful Llyn Peris, with the ancient tower of Dolbadarn in the distance, glimpses of which occasionally came in view, gave a softened character to a scene so full of majestic grandeur and sublimity.

> " O Nature, how in every charm supreme !
> Whose votaries feast on raptures ever new."

The scenery of Llanberis, however, like all other mountain hollows, is susceptible of startling contrasts. In stormy, tempestuous weather, when the thunder rolls and the lightning's blue glare flashes over the basaltic rocks and almost perpendicular crags which hem in the Pass for several miles, momentarily revealing the fantastic outlines of the rugged rocks and sombre *cwms* which ever and anon present themselves, and are again lost in the deep gloom which succeeds the flash—these are phases which sometimes almost suddenly occur, and leave a lasting impression on the memory of the beholder.

Llanberis.

The village of Llanberis is situate in a narrow grassy dell at
the upper end of Llyn Peris. In romantic beauty, we know of
few places which excel it—one of those "nooks of the world"
which convey to the imagination a charming picture of patriarchal
simplicity and retirement. Camden, in speaking of the scenery
of Snowdonia, says :—"Nature has here reared huge groups of
mountains, as if she intended to bind fast the bowels of the earth.
. . . Here are so many crags and rocks, so many wooded valleys,
so many lakes, that these mountains may be truly called the
British Alps, for they are, like the Alps, bespread with broken
crags on every side, all surrounding one (Snowdon), which, towering in the centre, far above the rest, lifts its head so loftily, as if
it meant not only to threaten, but to thrust it into the sky." It
is supposed that in ancient times the lower parts of the mountains
in the Vale of Llanberis were covered with wood, and abounded
with deer, which were not finally extirpated until the early part
of the seventeenth century. This opinion receives confirmation
from one of the laws of the great Welsh Lycurgus, Howel Dda,
"Howel the Good," which directs, that "whoever cleared away
timber from any land, even without the consent of the owner, he
should for five years have a right to the land so cleared; and
after that time it should again revert to the owner." At the
present time, Llanberis, like nearly all the other portions of the
Welsh highlands, can boast of but very few trees.

The primitive church of Llanberis, which some years ago was
restored by Mr. Kennedy, of Bangor, is "a highly curious building,
partly of the fifteenth century," and the timber-work is described
as being unique. The church (*eglwys*) is situate in a deeply
sequestered glen, called, in Leland's time, Nant-y-Monach, the
" Monk's Valley," about half a mile above Llyn Peris, and, to the
lover of ecclesiology, is well worth a visit. It is dedicated to
St. Peris, a British saint contemporary with Padarn, an anchorite,
who, about the sixth century, is said to have dwelt at a cell or
chapel in a meadow near Dolbadarn Castle, from which the castle
derived its name. *Dol*, in Welsh, signifies a meadow; hence the

name Dolbadarn, the "Meadow of Padarn." There is a holy well near the church, called Ffynnon Peris, the "Well of St. Peris," formerly famed—as most holy wells were in olden time—for the miraculous cure of diseases. A few tame fish, we were told, still exist in the well. The way to it is over a stile from the turnpike-road.

Caenant Mawr.

A short distance to the south of Castell Dolbadarn, is a fine waterfall, called Caenant or Caunant-Mawr, the "cataract of the great chasm," or, more properly, the "valley of the great chasm." The accumulated waters that flow from Moel Aeliau, Cwm Brwynog, and the streams that descend from the north-west side of Snowdon, unite at the head of a deep glen, and rushing through a cleft in the rocks above, form a fine Fall of at least sixty feet in height. After heavy rains, this cataract is, doubtless, well worth a visit, and the water then descends with thundering fury into a deep pool, or basin, at the bottom. We were not fortunate enough to view this rather celebrated fall to advantage, the water at the time of our visit being rather scant; even Rhaiadr-y-Wenol, and other falls we have seen in dry weather, are comparatively tame. Caenant Mawr, however, under any circumstances deserves mention, and is one of the "lions" of the locality.

> " Smooth to the shelving brink a copious flood
>   Rolls fair and placid, where, collected all,
>   In one impetuous torrent down the steep
>   It thundering shoots, and shakes the country round.
>   At first an azure sheet, it rushes broad ;
>   Then whitening by degrees as prone it falls,
>   And from the loud resounding rocks below
>   Dash'd in a cloud of foam, it sends aloft
>   A hoary mist, and forms a ceaseless shower."

Llanberis can now be scarcely called a fishing-station. We never angled in the lakes, and therefore cannot afford any information from personal experience; but from all we could learn, little or no sport either from boat or shore could now be obtained. There is a small pool under the tremendous precipices of Moel Aeliau, in a dreary morass—one of the sublime solitudes of

Snowdon—called Llyn Dwythwch, which bears a good reputation, and is reported to contain red trout; but our experience of it proved anything but satisfactory; we were, however, strongly recommended to try it by an old fisherman. It is true, we hardly gave the pool a fair chance, as we only angled there for a few hours one afternoon in June, 1849, during a short stay at the "Dolbadarn Castle" hotel, whilst on an excursion from Bangor to Pen-y-Gwryd. It is highly probable that this lake is poached by the miners and quarrymen of the neighbourhood. Another small, but deep pool, called Llyn-dû-yr-Arddudwy, lying at the foot of the nearly perpendicular rocks called Clogwyn-dû-yr-Arddudwy, near Bwlch-Cwm-Brwynog, can also be visited from Llanberis. This lake lies about a quarter of a mile to the left of the guides' route to the summit of Snowdon. The water from the Llyn flows through Cwm Brwynog, and is one of the principal feeders of the united streams which form Caenant Mawr, the water from which flows into Llyn Peris, beneath the walls of Castell Dolbadarn. Of the fishing in this pool we literally know nothing; it is very possible that it contains no fish of any kind.

Llanberis has long been a favourite resort of the lovers of botany. Bingley, who was an excellent botanist, gives a list of a number of rare alpine plants which he discovered amongst the wilds and precipices of Snowdon and Llanberis. Since his time, however, many of the plants he mentions are entirely extinct, or become exceedingly scarce. One of the guides at the Victoria Hotel, who is a very civil, intelligent man, is in great request during the summer by the numerous botanists who frequent the locality, as he knows "the *habitat* of every plant in the surrounding mountains." The last time we saw him was at Pen-y-Gwryd, and he then gave us some valuable information on several particulars of which we were previously ignorant. He told us that some of the rarer species of plants were, in consequence of the incessant researches of botanists, yearly becoming more scarce, and that in winter, when the snow was on the ground, and deep in some parts of the mountains, he had several times risked his life amongst the precipices and hollows of Snowdon, in pursuit of some rare plant which he had been commissioned to procure for some botanical enthusiast.

About two miles from Llanberis church, on the side of the road through the Pass, is a huge mass of stone called "The *Cromlech*," possibly from a fancied resemblance to a Druidical altar of sacrifice. At some remote period it formed a portion of the precipices above it, and must have been rent asunder by some convulsion of nature. It is several thousand tons in weight, and is said to be much larger than the celebrated Bowdar stone in Borrowdale, Cumberland. Under the angle of this stone an old woman formerly made a habitation, and in summer resided there to feed her cows on the scanty herbage around it. The name of the place is *Ynys Hettws*, "Hetty's Island."

The slate quarries on the sides of the Llyder, along the shores of Llyn Peris, opposite to Dolbadarn, are very extensive, and large quantities of slates are shipped annually from Port Dinorwic, on the Menai Strait. They belonged to the late T. Assheton Smith, Esq., the celebrated fox-hunter, who died at Vaenol, near Bangor, on the banks of the Menai, on the 9th of September, 1858. The Llyn Peris copper-mine, which in great measure destroyed the trout and char many years ago, has been discontinued for some years, having ceased to be productive. For nearly a century after the mine was opened large quantities of copper ore were extracted, but the vein of ore has now become nearly exhausted.

Llanberis, like a great many other mountain parishes in Wales, is of considerable extent, and is divided into two districts, Nant-Uchaf and Nant-Isaf; which comprise some of the loftiest mountains in Snowdonia, and portions of the most romantic scenery in Wales; and in that part of the parish called Nant-Isaf, or Nant-Padarn, stands the ancient watch-tower of CASTELL DOLBADARN, a description of which we reserve for the next chapter.

CHAPTER XIII.

CASTELL DOLBADARN — GILPIN ON SCENERY — SCENERY OF DOL-
BADARN — WARNER'S DESCRIPTION OF DOLBADARN — EFFECTS
OF SETTING SUN.

" As I stood by yon roofless tower,
    Where the wa'flower scents the dewy air;
Where the howlet mourns in her ivy bower,
    And tells the midnight moon her care,

" The winds were laid, the air was still,
    The stars they shot along the sky;
The fox was howling on the hill,
    And the distant echoing glens reply."—BURNS.

Castell Dolbadarn.

THIS " aunciente ruine," supposed to have been originally erected
in the sixth century, by Maelgwyn Gwynedd, to guard one of the
principal Passes into the Cambrian stronghold, Snowdon, from the
incursions of the Saxons, has long been ruinous; for even in
Leland's time, temp. Henry VIII., the tower only remained. It
was, however, perfect during the rebellion of Owen Glyndwr, at
the beginning of the fifteenth century, and underwent several
sieges, being taken and retaken on various occasions by the con-
tending forces. At that time also it was probably a place of
some strength, being defended from a near approach " by a narrow
causeway over a marische," and from its situation, being placed
on a rock which commands the narrow isthmus which divides the
Upper and Lower lakes, was considered in those times a strong
and important fortress. After the death of Llewelyn Ap Gryffydd,
the last and greatest of the Welsh princes, in 1282, it was
garrisoned for a short time by the unfortunate Llewelyn's brother,

Davydd; but it was taken from the Welsh after a short resistance, by the Earl of Pembroke, in the following year, 1283.   Since the time of Owen Glyndwr, history has been silent, so far as we know, and being no longer of use as a defence to the Pass of Llanberis, the castle has, probably, "silently decaied."

The Rev. William Gilpin—whose "Observations on Picturesque Beauty" in several parts of England and Wales are so deservedly appreciated and admired by all lovers of landscape scenery—made a tour through a portion of North Wales in 1773, and amongst other places visited Dolbadarn and Llanberis.   Gilpin was the first topographer who reduced to certain fixed rules the various "combination of parts," the harmonies, the "picturesque passages" of a landscape; rendering the whole subservient to a science; in fact, endeavouring to prove that landscape gardening, in some instances, is superior to nature.   By these rules Gilpin thus criticises Snowdon:—"With regard to Snowdon, I fear, not much can be said, as it nowhere appears connected enough as *one whole* to form a *grand* object; so neither has it any of those accompaniments which form a *beautiful* one.   It is a bleak dreary waste, without any pleasing combination of parts, or any rich furniture, either of wood or well constructed rock."

We are certain that Gilpin's condemnation of the scenery of parts of Snowdon will meet with but few sympathisers in these days.   Gilpin admits that he never ascended Snowdon, and to condemn the "Monarch of the hills" from a hasty and imperfect view of him in the Pass of Llanberis is hardly fair.   Indeed, the higher rocks and eminences of Snowdon, including the magnificent outline of his peaked summit, cannot be observed from where Gilpin made his observations.   If he had viewed Snowdon from the entrance to Cwm Llan, or from the Beddgelert road, near Pen-y-Gwryd, we think his criticism would have undergone at least some modification.   Succeeding writers have, however, rendered to Snowdon that homage which Gilpin has alone denied; and it is really difficult to conceive how a man like Gilpin, with a mind so eminently gifted, and so well qualified both with pen and pencil to criticise and illustrate picturesque beauty, should—unless blinded by prejudice or a determination to judge scenery only by certain fixed rules which he had arbitrarily laid down—have con-

demned a mountain allowed by all who have seen it to be the
most magnificent and romantic in the British isles.

Gilpin, in his account of the scenery of Dolbadarn, is more
favourably disposed. He says, "Our trouble in traversing this
rugged country was not totally unrewarded. Though Snowdon
itself afforded us little amusement, we met with two or three
beautiful scenes about Dolbadarn Castle, which lies at its foot.
The castle appeared before us at the distance of two miles,
standing on the confines of a lake. The mountains around it—
which are called appendages of Snowdon—fall into pleasing lines,
forming a deep valley, and folding over each other in easy inter-
sections. Indeed, a body of water among mountains, if it have
no other use, has at least that of showing, by the little bays it
forms, how one mountain falls over another, which strengthens
the picturesque idea of a graduating distance. As we descended
towards the castle, we were drawn aside by a pleasant retreat, called
Combrunog,"—Cwm Brwynog, Gilpin's Welsh orthography was
very defective,—"where a little river flows through two circular
valleys, each about a mile in circumference, and each surrounded
with mountains. Both areas being nearly plains, and on different
levels, the river, having passed through one, falls in a cascade
(Caenant Mawr) into the other. As we left Combrunog, and
descended still nearer Dolbaddern, the scenery about it became
more interesting. In one place we descended nearly a hundred
stone steps, or rather stones laid irregularly in the form of steps,
and if our horses had not been those of the country, we should
not easily have persuaded them to attempt a passage so ill adapted
to quadrupeds. Through these and other little difficulties, at
length, however, we arrived at the bottom, where we found two
lakes, separated by a neck of land, near which arose a knoll much
higher than the banks of the lakes, but inconsiderable when compared with the surrounding mountains. On this knoll stands the
castle, which has never been a capital fortress, and now exhibits
little more than one solitary tower; but it is a very picturesque
fragment, and is more in union with the scene than if it had been
a larger building. A lonely tower is itself an emblem of solitude.
Having ascended the castle-hill, we had a good view of both the
lakes. The lower one is about two miles long, and half a quarter

of a mile broad. Its lines are beautiful, and it goes off in good perspective; but it has a contracted appearance, being sunk too much, like a gully, under lofty mountains, to which it is in no degree equivalent. In every lake view the water and skreens should be proportioned, or there can be no very pleasing effect. In the lakes of Constance and Geneva, and still more in the great lakes of America, the skreens are as little proportioned to the water, as in such a lake as this the water is to its skreens. In neither case the scenery is complete. The upper lake at Dolbaddern is still more a gully than the lower, having scarce any banks but mountains. Both lakes have a desolate naked appearance, being wholly destitute of furniture. In Cumberland and Westmoreland such lakes would attract no attention; here a dearth of objects gives them consequence. The upper lake, however, afforded an opportunity of observing the singular use of reflection in uniting land and water."

From Gilpin's account, Dolbadarn in his time was a desert. "It was now a late evening hour, and though we had seen little we had laboured much, and began to want refreshment both for ourselves and horses. Among the mountains of Cumberland one might generally have found it; but here all was desolation. We did not meet with a single village, and but few separate houses, and these were locked up. . . . The limpid rills of Snowdon were our only repast."

What a contrast does Dolbadarn now present, after a lapse of eighty-seven years! Excellent hotels, a good road, a coach daily through the Pass from Caernarvon to Llangollen-road station, elegant villa residences, lodging-houses, and comfortable conveyances.

Warner, after accomplishing the ascent of Snowdon, descended afterwards to the Pass of Llanberis, his description of which is so graphic and amusing that we are tempted to give it, by way of contrast with the foregoing sombre extracts from Gilpin's tour:—

"After two hour's walking, or rather stumbling over masses of rocks for two hours, we reached a cottage situated amidst some coarse meadows, the sparing produce of which the labourers were at this late period (August 21st) getting in. Uncertain what direction to pursue to Dolbadarn Castle, we inquired of a woman who stood at the cottage-gate, but received no other answer than an intimation that she did not speak English. After all the expressive gesticulations that we could think of, and pronouncing the name of the place with every possible variation of accent, we made her comprehend our meaning, and she ordered her daughter, a girl about twelve years old, to direct us to Castell Dolbathren. Our little guide, tripping on before us like a lapwing, and without the incumbrance of shoe or stocking, led us over rocks and bogs for about two miles, when we found ourselves on the margin of the Lake Llanberis, and near the old fortress of Dolbadarn. This piece of water is divided by a small field, through which, however, there is a communication by means of a narrow stream into two lakes, the northern one being the larger, and stretching nearly three miles in length : the latter called, after the castle, Lake Dolbadarn, and measuring little more than one. Upon the summit of a hill rising at the southern extremity of Lake Llanberis, stand the ruins of Dolbadarn Castle, forming a good accompaniment to the rude and desolate scenery that surrounds it. The only remains of the original fortress consist of the foundations of the exterior buildings, and the greater part of the citadel or keep. This is a circular building, thirty feet in diameter, containing four apartments—the dungeon at the bottom, and three others in succession over it, the ascent to which is by spiral staircases. By whom it was erected does not appear, though it certainly belonged to the ancient Welsh princes, and is consequently of high antiquity. Owen Goch, the unsuccessful rebel, and opponent of his brother Llewelyn, languished twenty years within its walls. It is constructed of the schistus of the country, and though of small extent, is well situated, and was originally very strong. On the declivity of the mountain, immediately facing the castle, are considerable quarries of a fine purple slate." Warner thus describes the state of the road :—" We now turned into a regular road, which led to Caernarvon, and was the first we had seen in the course of the day. Like all the other mountain roads, however, it consisted entirely of large loose stones and pointed solid rock, not a little incommodious to pedestrians who had already followed the undulations of this hilly country for twenty miles. Another hour brought us to the river Ryddell (Sciont), which flows from the northern extremity of Llanberis lake, and pursues a winding course to Caernarvon. We crossed it by means of a stone bridge, rude in appearance, and unworkmanlike in construction."

We cannot forbear quoting the following eloquent description, by the same author, of the magnificent effects produced by the setting sun on the landscape near the close of a lovely evening in autumn :—

"The day now drew towards a close, and the unclouded sun, sinking gradually to the ocean, produced a magic scene, which nature only exhibits in countries where she prints her boldest characters. A fine fleecy cloud was drawn around the mountains we had left, and curtained in its embrace nearly half their height. On this the declining orb of day threw its rich departing radiance, and displayed an illumination that neither pencil nor pen can imitate or describe : the misty covering of the mountains every moment varied its tint; it now assumed the appearance of a fleece of azure, the next minute it brightened into a rich golden colour; shortly afterwards it took a deeper yellow. As the sun approached the wane, its tinge changed successively to a brilliant red and solemn purple, and at length, when he sunk from the horizon, it became gradually colourless and dark. The effect was further heightened by the variation which the cloud exhibited in its form. For a short time it would confine itself to the higher regions of the mountains, then, sinking considerably, would nearly encircle their base; and again, rising and condensing itself, it hung upon their summits like a crown of glory. The picture on the opposite side was equally beautiful and grand. The solemn turrets of Caernarvon Castle, contrasted with the gay scenery of ships and villas in its neighbourhood, formed the foreground; to the left appeared the dark precipices of the Rivals (three mountains of great bulk and immense height), which were now in the shade ; and beyond them the ocean, glittering with the rays of the departing sun, stretching as far as the vision extended. Nothing could exceed the glory of his setting; as he approached the waves, his radiance became more tolerable, and his form more distinct, exhibiting the appearance of an immense ball of fire. When he reached the ocean, he seemed to rest upon it—as upon a throne—for a moment, and then buried his splendid rotundity in its waters, reminding us of that beautiful apostrophe to the orb of light, and sublime description in the father of Erse poetry: 'Hast thou left thy blue course in heaven, golden-haired son of the sky? The west has opened its gates; the bed of thy repose is there. The cranes come to behold thy beauty. They lift their trembling heads. They see thee lovely in thy sleep; they shrink away with fear. Rest in thy shadowy cave, O sun! Let thy return be with joy.'"

Warner, in his first "Walk in Wales," falls into some blunders, which must have arisen either from careless inquiries or gross ignorance. In one of the extracts we have just given, he confounds the names of the lakes of Llanberis; and the river Seiont, which flows out of the lower lake, he calls the "river Ryddell"! He surely did not mean the Rheidol, which rises in Plinlimmon, and flows into the sea at Aberystwith. Warner's ideas of *distance* are also rather amusing. It will be observed that he makes Llyn Peris—the *lesser* lake—to stretch for "nearly three miles in length;" whilst Llyn Padarn, which is considerably the larger lake of the two, measures only "little more than one." So much for the accuracy of some of the tourists of former days.

CHAPTER XIV.

CAPEL CURIG—CARNEDD LLEWELYN—CARNEDD DAFYDD—
FFYNNON LLOER—STORM IN THE WILDS.

> " High
> The rock's bleak summit frowns above our head,
> Looking immediate down, we almost fear
> Lest some enormous fragment should descend
> With hideous sweep into the vale, and crush
> The intruding visitant.   No sound is here
> Save of the stream that shrills, and now and then
> A cry as of faint wailing, when the kite
> Comes sailing o'er the crags, or straggling lamb
> Bleats for its mother."

Capel Curig.

"WHAT a Sabbath of rest from all troublous, anxious, or overwrought feelings" does the solitary romantic Capel Curig present to the mind of the wayfarer! Such were our impressions upon our first introduction to this really delightful locality some twenty summers ago.   First impressions sometimes lead to disappointment upon further acquaintance, but at Capel Curig it is otherwise; and it is perhaps not too much to say, that few places in the Principality combine a greater variety of picturesque and sublime scenery.   The village—if such it can be called—consists chiefly of the hotel, which has been increased in length from time to time since the days of its founder, the late Lord Penrhyn, until it seems almost to form one side of a short street; and a few cottages on the great Holyhead road, where comfortable lodgings, we believe, can now be obtained by such as prefer them to the hotel.   The incumbent of the humble village church, at the period of our first visit, was also the landlord of the inn, and it

is singular enough, that some years ago the landlords of three of
the principal inns in North Wales belonged to the three profes-
sions of Law, Physic, and Divinity. Such, however, we have
been informed, was the fact.

This "curious" inn has been so frequently described, and is
now so well known, that much comment on our part would be
superfluous, but it is only doing an act of justice to the present
landlord, Mr. Hughes, to state, that for general comfort, attention and civility, the hotel may vie with any of its great rivals in
Snowdonia. The inn is generally crowded with visitors during
the summer and autumn months; and at that period great difficulty is frequently experienced in obtaining accommodation.
Since the introduction of the rail into North Wales, the influx of
tourists has been annually on the increase, and should it go on
increasing, before many years are passed, numerous fresh hotels
will probably have sprung up.

That paragon of waiters, "Old Jackson," so well known to the
habitués of the hotel for many years, has been gathered to his
fathers for some time, and few, if any, of the ancient denizens of
the place now remain, except Robin Hughes, the guide and
fisherman, whom we encountered three years ago, apparently as
hale and vigorous as ever. This guide is mentioned by Roscoe,
in his "wanderings" in this locality some twenty-five years ago.
Hughes was one of the guides employed in the search after a
Mr. Philip Homer, a young gentleman who perished on Moel
Siabod, a few years anterior to Roscoe's visit to Capel Curig.
Mr. Homer's remains lie interred in the churchyard at Capel
Curig. We remember, whilst on an excursion to Llyn Idwal, in
the autumn of 1841, Robin Hughes gave us a very graphic and
interesting account of this sad event. Mr. Homer appears to
have been exceedingly rash and venturesome, and, regardless of
advice and warning, wandered on Moel Siabod, got lost in the
mist, and at last perished from exhaustion.

We must, however, for a brief space, return to our worthy
friend Jackson, a "fellow of infinite humour," and in his way a
perfect original. In some respects he reminded us of old Caleb
Balderstone, the faithful seneschal of the Master of Ravenswood,
in the very interesting tale of "The Bride of Lammermoor."

Jackson was an Englishman, who had lived the greater part of
his life in Wales, married a Welsh woman, and in short had
become almost a Welshman himself.   He had passed through the
bustling times when the great Holyhead road, after its completion
by Telford, was the fashionable route to Ireland.   No railroads in
those days to interfere with the great highway through a portion
of the grandest scenery in Cambria.   The road was thronged
daily during all times of the year with coaches and carriages of
all sorts, and the inns at Capel Curig and Cernioge were then the
"chief halting-places on the route from London to Dublin."
Tempus edax rerum.   The inn at Cernioge, which we well remember in its declining state twenty years ago, situate in the midst of
a bleak, barren, naked wilderness, has been closed some years,
and now, we believe, converted into a farmhouse.   Capel Curig,
however, from the entrancing scenery which surrounds it, commands at this moment, if possible, still greater popularity than in
the good old times when the Holyhead road was in all its glory.
The description of visitors has now of course materially changed.
Formerly the frequenters of Capel Curig were chiefly on "business
intent"; now they are almost entirely pleasure-seekers, and consist
of tourists from Bangor or Caernarvon, making the "round"
through the Pass of Llanberis.   One coach, we believe, still
remains upon the road; it runs daily between the Llangollen-road
Station and Caernarvon, through Pen-y-Gwryd and Llanberis.
Travelling through the country is chiefly performed by means of
cars, both single and double; the latter on four wheels are quite a
recent invention, and are not only much pleasanter, but safer and
more commodious vehicles than the old-fashioned two-wheeled
ones.   They are drawn by a pair of horses, and will hold a family
party.

We have already observed that Capel Curig presents many
attractions, not only to the lover of natural beauty, but also to
the botanist and geologist.   Our intention, however, is to introduce more particularly to the reader such places in the vicinity
as are less known and frequented than the "lions" which are
pointed out by the guides and guide-books, and to explore
amongst the wild hills those hidden "nooks" and recesses seldom
if ever visited, and little known save to the rude dwellers in these

mountain wastes. In previous chapters we have also endeavoured
to furnish a truthful picture of the different angling stations as
they at present exist; not misleading the sportsman, as some of
the miscalled guide-books do, which assert that "in any direction
the angler cannot fail to find sport," but pointing out the changes
which have taken place during the last twenty or thirty years.

Before we proceed upon our exploration of the country, we will
endeavour to describe the angling as it now is in the neighbourhood of Capel Curig, contrasting its present state with what it
was thirty years ago. As an angling station, Capel Curig has
gradually declined: the causes of this we have previously explained,
and may be comprised under three heads — excessive netting,
poaching, and the vast increase of mining population. Thirty
years ago, first-rate sport was obtained on the

Llynnian Mymbyr,

which form such an attractive feature "in the magnificent panoramic picture" presented to the eye, from the rude wooden bridge
that spans the infant stream flowing from the lower lake on
its course to join the Llugwy, and which is in fact a continuation
of the river Gwryd, after its expansion in the Capel Curig lakes.
In those days these lakes abounded in fine trout. Hofland, the
eminent landscape painter, states in his "Angler's Manual" that
he killed in August, 1831—late in the season too—upwards of
four dozen trout, averaging from half a pound to upwards of one
pound each. Other anglers of those days have even exceeded
this take. Such, however, is not the case now; in fact, for the
last eighteen or twenty years, the Capel Curig lakes have ceased
to afford any attraction whatever to the angler. The disciple of
Isaac Walton, however skilful, must be content with few rises,
and very small fish. Whence does this extraordinary falling off
arise? It cannot proceed from mining operations, since there are
no mines in the vicinity, neither can the "otter" or "board"
have so completely spoiled the sport. The only reason we can
assign is, that the lakes have been greatly injured by the net. In
a former chapter we mentioned the destructive effects occasioned
during one season from the use of a seine net in Llyn Gwynant;

and the Llynniau Mymbyr for a long series of years have afforded
one of the principal supplies of trout to the tables of the visitors
at Capel Curig.   In June, 1843, during a week's sojourn in this
locality, we gave these lakes a thorough examination, both from
boat and shore ; and although the weather was exceedingly
favourable for our purpose, after repeated trials we killed only a
very few small trout.   We have met with the same result on
several subsequent occasions, and this, coupled with similar
reports from other anglers, confirms our opinion that these lakes
are now "utterly spoiled."

Amongst the other llyns in this neighbourhood, are Llynniau
Duwaunedd, two small pools, about four miles distant, lying under
the eastern side of Moel Siabod; Llyn Ogwen, on the great
Holyhead road, at the head of Nant Ffrancon ; Llyn Idwal, Llyn
Bochlwyd, Llyn Cwm Cowlyd, Llyn Ffynnon Lloer, Llyn Ffynnon
Llugwy, Llyn Crafnant, Llyn Eigiau, and Llyn Geirionedd, a few
miles from the village of Trefriw, a fishing station on the Conwy ;
and celebrated for being the residence of Cambria's greatest Bard,
Taliesin, whose dwelling was on the east shore of the lake.   Some
twenty-five years ago, the sequestered

Llynniau Duwaunedd

afforded magnificent sport.   The present Lord A—— and the Rev.
A. S., on one occasion, caught a large quantity of trout, many of
them exceeding one pound, in these pools, which are separated by
a narrow strip of shingle that is sometimes covered with water.
The quality of the trout is only exceeded by those of Llyn Ogwen.
These lakes, however, like the neighbouring pools, Llynniau
Mymbyr, have gradually fallen off, in consequence, it is believed,
of the introduction of the "otter."   The lakes we have enumerated
are nearly all within a moderate distance of Capel Curig, although
the route to most of them is rough and difficult ; but to the
sportsman, the pleasurable feelings of excitement, engendered by
the love of adventure amongst the wild mountain solitudes of
this desolate region, and the healthy flow of spirits that arises
from inhaling the refreshing breezes which are wafted over the
extensive wastes around you, curling the dark waters of some

savage-looking lake, or sweeping in hollow murmurs through the
cwm which leads to it, compensate for the sensations of fatigue
which you experience after an arduous day in the wilds, or by the
rugged shores of the several llyns you may have explored.

Ascent to the Summits of Carnedd Llewelyn and Carnedd Davydd.

"Dame Nature drew these mountains in such sort,
  As though one should yeeld the other grace;
 Or as each hill itself were such a fort,
  They scorned to stoope to give the cannon place.
 If all were plaine and smooth like garden ground,
  Where should hye woods and goodly groves be found?
  The eyes delight that lookes on every coast,
 With pleasures great and fayre prospect were lost."
                THOMAS CHURCHYARD'S *Worthiness of Wales.*

It was in the days of " old Jackson "—his declining days—but
still the " old horse " seemed up to his work, that with his accustomed cheerful inquiry of " What sport, gentlemen? " he proceeded to place upon the table a magnificent dish of large Ogwen
trout, which for colour and flavour are certainly unrivalled in
Wales.   But hold! we anticipate—before we do justice to the
delicacies provided for us by our worthy *maître d'hotel,* let us first
proceed to give an account of our excursion to the summits of the
lofty mountains, Carnedds Llewelyn and Davydd.

The season was summer—the " leafy month of June "—the
weather magnificent.   We had for some time previously contemplated an excursion to these celebrated mountains; and tired
with lashing to no purpose the Capel Curig pools, we determined
to put our intention into effect; which afterwards proved one of
the wildest and most exciting adventures we had ever " dared"
to perform in the desolate region around.

Accompanied by a friend, but *without* a guide, save the
Ordnance map, we started early on a fine bright morning to
achieve, if possible, a visit to the summits of both those mighty
hill monarchs.   The day proved very favourable for our purpose;
as the morning advanced, huge masses of clouds formed over the

mountains, though sufficiently elevated as to be clear of their
tops, whilst their dark shadows added a grandeur and breadth of
effect to the landscape which every one conversant with mountain
scenery must have frequently observed. We had resolved to
dispense with the services of a guide; for guides at Capel Curig,
as elsewhere, are expensive, and we were determined to try
whether it was possible to find out our way without one. These
men are frequently indeed of little or no use, and are only a clog
upon the conversation and movements of a party. Our advice is
—whenever safe and practicable—*dispense* with the services of
a guide.

After proceeding for about three miles on the Holyhead road,
within a short distance of Llyn Ogwen, we found ourselves
abreast of Carnedd Llewelyn. Our companion, who had a splendid
eye " across country," immediately detected what seemed a practicable route, which we resolved to follow. We pursued for some
distance the course of a rippling brook—the infant Llugwy—
which issues from Llyn Ffynnon Llugwy, a dark, gloomy piece of
water which reposes in a vast abyss beneath Ysgdlion Duon,
Anglicè, "the Black Ladders." As we advanced on our route
towards the tertiary ranges of this vast double-headed mountain,
the heat of the day, and at times the slackness of the breeze, produced a temporary faintness and lassitude, which, however, was
speedily dissipated by some of the deliciously cool water we met
with by the way, tempered with a slight "dash" of *cognac*. The
"collar work" commences at Craig Llugwy, where you leave the
streamlet of that name; and, as you advance nearly due north,
the scene gradually becomes grander and more magnificent, until
at last you reach Bwlch Cyfryw Drym, the narrow ridge which
connects Carnedd Llewelyn with its gigantic sister, Carnedd
Davydd. Here the scene becomes "untameably wild." We
question whether the deep abysses on either side this ridge are
not more awful to the eye than the prospect from the Clawdd
Coch of Snowdon. Of course, much depends upon weather;
with dark, lowering clouds impending over the scene, the effect
must be fearfully sublime. Here we reposed, and proceeded to
refresh ourselves preparatory to our walk over the ridge towards
the summit of Carnedd Llewelyn. This ridge is stated in the

guide-books to be three-quarters of a mile long. We think, however, the distance is somewhat exaggerated. We now surveyed
with great delight the grand prospect which unfolded itself from
every quarter. The valley of Nant Ffrancon, with the lofty
summits of the Glyders and Llyder Vawr, and the gloomy Llyn
Idwal reposing at its base, the sparkling waters of Llyn Ogwen,
the Trifaen, and the mountains to our left, furnished a scene
which for grandeur, beauty of detail, and colour, could scarcely
be surpassed even on a larger scale. At our feet, in a " yawning
abyss " far below, lay the sullen, secluded Llyn Ffynnon Llugwy,
the parent of the joyous stream which gladdens the eye of the
wanderer as he proceeds to Bettws y Coed. How refreshing to
contemplate these limpid basins of water, teeming with life amidst
the unpeopled desert which everywhere surrounds them.

> " Here I could muse
> The livelong day, and wandering down the dell,
> Along the grassy margin trace the stream
> Meandering ; now confined from crag to crag,
> Where bursts the headlong flood, or widely spread
> Mid the broad channel, where the undimpled wave
> Bathing the wild flowers bending o'er the brink
> Glides silent by."

Here there is society " where none intrude "—the shrill whistle
of the mountain sheep, the melancholy croak of the solitary raven,
or the far-off bark of the shepherd's dog, being the only break to
the portentous stillness which reigns ; and you are still more
deeply impressed " with the magnitude, the desolation, the intense,
heart-thrilling solitude," of the lofty mountains you are among.
Such were our sensations, as we once more addressed ourselves
to the task of accomplishing the crowning object of our excursion
—the summit of Carnedd Llewelyn.

The chief labour of the ascent is accomplished on gaining the
crest of Bwlch Cyfryw Drym ; the path hence to the highest
point of the mountain is comparatively easy, and we were soon
beside the Ordnance *carn*. We were disappointed to find only
very slight traces of Llewelyn's fortified camp, from whence he
descried Bangor in flames, the work of his revengeful father-in-
law, the tyrant John. "A few *cytiau* and part of a wall," are all

that are left. A huge *carnedd* of stones, erected by the Ordnance surveyors to mark the highest portion of the mountain, occupies the site of the camp; and it is probable that during their stay there the entrenchment around the stronghold was in some measure effaced. The view from hence is scarcely exceeded by any other mountain prospect in the Principality, and seen under striking effects of light and shade, adds much to the dreaminess, grandeur, and impressive aspect of the more distant heights. The eye wanders over the vast wilds that encompass you on all sides, including the lonely descent to the Waterfall at Aber—endeared to our memory by an incident of bygone days—and from the commanding heights we occupied, was in the highest degree romantic and sublime.

It was at one time uncertain whether Snowdon was really the highest mountain in South Britain; it was affirmed by some authorities that Carnedd Llewelyn was several yards higher; but the recent accurate trigonometrical admeasurement of the rival monarchs by the officers of the Board of Ordnance puts this *quæstio vexata* beyond a doubt. The altitude of Carnedd Llewelyn is 3,469 feet; whilst Snowdon is 3,571 feet, or something over 100 feet higher. Carnedd Davydd is scarcely inferior to its neighbour, being 3,427 feet.

We observed several small llyns from the summit of Carnedd Llewelyn; amongst them, nestling under the rugged steeps of Craig Mawr and Craig Dulyn, the solitary pools Melynllyn and Dulyn. There are llyns thus named in other parts of the Principality; one we have already described—Dulyn—in the Harlech district, in a former chapter.

We now prepared to return over the narrow ridge which divides these mountains. As we slowly proceeded, we were both silent from similar feelings, being lost in wonder and admiration at the fitful gleams which flitted over the landscape. To the south-west, a vast canopy of dark thunderclouds, "nursing their wrath," seemed almost to rest on Moel-y-Wyddfa, the highest peak of Snowdon, and the profound gloom which obscured the recesses of the *cwms* or precipitous hollows on the sides of that mighty mountain, or rather group of mountains, was relieved by the comparatively smiling aspect of the rugged, weather-beaten

Glyders. A storm was evidently brewing, although some hours might elapse before it gathered to its full strength. We were anxious to visit the summit of Carnedd Davydd before our return; and as the ascent to it was not difficult from the elevated position we were in, we hastened our movements. The distance between the summits of these mountains is about two miles, and in the course of less than an hour we found ourselves on the peak of Carnedd Davydd. The view from hence is perhaps even finer than from the lofty point we had so recently quitted. You have here a magnificent bird's-eye peep of Nant Ffrancon, with Bangor and the Menai Straits in the distance; and the Isle of Anglesea is spread out before you like a map. In a deep *cwm* at your feet repose the waters of Llyn Ffynnon Lloer, which signifies in English the "Fountain of the Moon"—quite a poetical appellation. This pool is of very limited extent, but abounds in small trout, which rise eagerly to the fly. After again resting for a short time at the side of the *carnedd*, we commenced our descent, which we found extremely rough and difficult, as the sides of the mountain are very precipitous. Indeed, it was almost a continuous scramble until we reached the brink of the llyn. Here we halted for a brief space, for the purpose of angling, as we observed that the fish were on the move. We had taken our rods with us, for the purpose of trying this pool and Llyn Ogwen on our return. It was really quite astonishing to witness the multitude of rises we obtained; but the trout were not in earnest, and evidently rose in mere frolic. After remaining nearly an hour, we basketed only about a dozen, the largest of which did not exceed a quarter of a pound. They were very pretty yellow trout, and were probably of good quality. Ffynnon Lloer, however, is not worth the angler's notice; besides, it is difficult and fatiguing to reach it. From hence we proceeded on our course to the shore of Llyn Ogwen, and without any exception we found the descent the most difficult and perplexing of any mountain scramble we had ever encountered. The mountain sides are strewed with large masses of stone, torn and riven from the effects of the violent storms which so frequently occur in these regions. There are also several high and tottering dry stone walls to cross, which are really dangerous unless you are very careful. After a most fatiguing descent, which occupied more than an hour, we found ourselves at sunset on the banks of Llyn Ogwen. The evening was tranquil, and the glorious effulgence of the departing sun gilding the loftiest summits of the surrounding mountains had a gorgeous and imposing effect. This was, however, the treacherous calm that preceded the storm. A nice ripple agitated the waters of the lake, and we were once more tempted to try a cast before we turned our steps to Capel Curig. Ogwen, however, like Tal-y-Llyn, is not a shore-fishing lake; nothing is to be done except from a boat. We essayed in vain to lure the finny tribe from their retreats, and in the course of half an hour we abandoned the pursuit as hopeless. It was now quite time to hurry away from the exquisite scenery around; night was coming on, and the tempest which had so long threatened was now, it was evident, rapidly approaching the vale. Distant thunder was booming like the report of artillery amongst the hills of Snowdon, and fitful flashes of pale lightning might be observed flickering over the mountain tops. How rapid are the changes which occur in mountainous countries! The wind, hitherto calm, now warned us of the approach of the tempest; it suddenly rose, and as it swept rapidly up the valley, we could observe for some distance a column of what appeared smoke, but it was in reality clouds of dust driven on by the fury of the gale, and mingled with a deluge of rain, which caught us before we could gain the road. Shelter there was none; we had no course to pursue but brave the fury of the storm. We had lingered too long at Ogwen, and had now at least four miles to travel through one of the most violent tempests we had ever encountered. It soon became almost pitchy dark, although midsummer; the rain was a perfect deluge, and the lightning incessant; whilst the thunder rolled over our heads with prolonged and deafening peals. It was indeed an awful night, and our situation was anything but pleasant. The tempest continued with unabated violence for several hours after we had gained the comfortable shelter of the hotel. We were glad indeed —wet, hungry, and well nigh exhausted—to hear old Jackson's voice, as he welcomed us in. An excellent dinner, and a bottle of his best port, soon reconciled us to the discomforts of the storm, and rendered us unmindful of the elemental uproar without.

CHAPTER XV.

LLYN IDWAL — LEGENDS — TWLL DU — EXCURSION TO ·LLYN · IDWAL — ANECDOTE — LLYN OGWEN — ANGLING — TRAVELLING IN WALES.

> " By that lake, whose gloomy shore
> Skylark never warbles o'er,
> Where the cliff hangs high and steep,
> Young St. Kevin stole to sleep.
> *   *   *   *
> Glendalough ! thy gloomy wave
> Soon was gentle Kathleen's grave."—MOORE.

Llyn Idwal

has been styled by an eminent writer the Avernus of Wales; and certainly in savage grandeur and sublimity it far exceeds any other scene that we are acquainted with in the Principality. It lies in a gloomy hollow under the steeps of Llyder Vawr, and its dark and sullen waters, in lowering stormy weather presenting a deep leaden hue, give a still more terrible aspect to this desolate spot. Although it is in the immediate vicinity of Nant Ffrancon and the Holyhead road, it is comparatively little frequented by strangers; a stray angler or two, a few ardent botanists in search of the very rare plants which grow amongst the precipices and deep-worn chasms, or the artist who ventures into the wilds to delineate the "severer forms" of Nature's handiworks, are almost the only visitors. The fact is, the majority of tourists in Wales are acquainted only with the landscape which presents itself from the road. Reclining at their ease in their car or carriage, they hurriedly pass through the finest scenery, contented with the hasty glance which the rapidity of travelling affords, and carry away with them merely a confused recollection of scenery—which, to be indelibly impressed on the memory, must be minutely examined. Many of the finest mountain scenes, for instance, lie away from the beaten track, and require nerve and vigorous activity to reach. Then, again, *time* is required to effect a general knowledge of the picturesque beauties of a country; and how few, even amongst pedestrian tourists, can afford to spare it. In the course of our wanderings in the Principality, we have hardly ever met amongst coffee-room acquaintance a single individual who was not pressed for *time;* and when we have mentioned some of the most celebrated scenes as well worthy of a visit, and comparatively easy of access, we have been met with the reply, "Yes, we should much like to go, but we are limited as to time."

Llyn Idwal formed the subject of one of the finest works of the late G. F. Robson, a water-colour painter of great genius and ability. The drawing was engraved, if we recollect rightly, for Jones' "Views in Wales." We have since seen other drawings and engravings of Llyn Idwal, but none of them could bear a comparison to Robson's picture, who seems to have been imbued with the spirit of a Wilson, so accurately has he depicted the "bleak and stormy character of the scenery" of this remarkable spot.

The lake derives its name from Idwal, a son of Owen Gwynedd, one of the most famous of the Welsh princes. His father had entrusted him to the care of a ruffian named Dunawt, who is said to have been a descendant of one of the fifteen tribes of North Wales. This treacherous guardian, according to the legend, murdered the unfortunate youth, by hurling him headlong into the Twll Dù, or "Devil's Kitchen," a horrible black gully or fissure, through which the surplus water of the little tarn called Llyn-y-Cwn finds an exit into the waters of Llyn Idwal. The motive for this dreadful deed is not stated; but it has at all events given an infamous reputation to the locality, and even now it is looked upon with dread by the superstitious mountaineers of the country. Many are the fables which this legend has given birth to ; amongst others, it is said that the spirit of the young prince is still heard wailing from the Twll Dù in stormy weather, which noise may be attributed to the wind, which at such times rushes down the gap with furious impetuosity. It is also said to be the haunt of demons, and that no bird is ever seen to fly over its waters.* A modern tourist has averred that no fish are now to be found in the lake, and there are a host of other tales equally as absurd and improbable narrated by the lovers of the marvellous.

Twll Dù.

The most singular feature about Llyn Idwal is the Twll Dù, which signifies the "Black Cleft;" it is, however, sometimes called the "Devil's Kitchen." We believe that we are amongst the few that have ever ventured to explore this gloomy fissure to its full extent, that is, until you arrive at a perpendicular precipice, which, black and slimy from the water that trickles over it, forbids further approach. It is only during dry weather that you can attempt the exploit; after heavy rain there is sometimes a considerable body of water rushing through the gap, which prevents ingress even at the outset. It was in June, 1843, during an angling excursion to the lake, that we accomplished this somewhat hazardous feat. We were tempted to do so by a spirit of adventure, and as there was scarcely any water flowing through the cleft at the time, it seemed apparently so easy, that we determined to explore it. It was, however, much more difficult than we had calculated, for the rocks over which we clambered were so slimy, that it was with considerable risk we surmounted the obstacles we had to encounter, and narrowly escaped on one or two occasions of falling down the rocks we clung to, to the hazard of our limbs. We had some hopes when we had got well into the cleft of making our way fairly through it, but we soon found this to be impossible. The rocks in the fissure are covered with a black slimy moss, which, constantly moist with the spray of the falling waters, renders this narrow gully dark and horrible

* In Dr. Campbell's "Strictures on the Ecclesiastical and Literary History of Ireland," we find the following passage descriptive of a lake in Ireland which greatly resembles in general features the remarkable scenery surrounding Llyn Idwal. "There is a lake in Donegal, one of the most dismal and dreary spots in the north, almost inaccessible, through deep glens and rugged mountains, frightful with impending rocks, and the hollow murmurs of the western winds in dark caverns, peopled only with such fantastic beings as the mind, however gay, is from the strange association wont to appropriate to such gloomy scenes."

enough.   We were therefore glad to make our exit as soon as
possible from this gloomy place, as there was still sufficient water
falling from above to cause a considerable spray, which would
speedily have wet us to the skin.

Twll Dù is stated to be about 150 yards long, about 100
deep and six feet wide, "perpendicularly open to the face of
the mountain."   This is hardly correct, as it is not perpendicular, until you enter some way into the cleft.   The ascent to
Twll Dù is by a very rough slippery path, resembling the dry
bed of a mountain torrent full of large boulders, from the south-
west side of the lake.   This path leads over the precipices called
Castell-y-Geifr, the connecting link between the Glyder and Llyder
Vawr.   Once on the top, you can either turn to the left towards
the summit of Glyder Bach, or proceed over the "chilly mountain
waste" to the vale of Llanberis.   There are few harder pulls in
Wales than this, and especially after rain the path is so slippery,
that, unless very careful, you stand a chance of "measuring your
length" on the ground.

Miss Costello, in her highly coloured sketch of Llyn Idwal, has
adopted some of the absurd legends of the country, and avers
that "in memory of the tragedy acted here, the fish, of which
there was formerly a profusion, were all deprived, according to
received tradition, of one eye, the left being closed; as there are
now no fish in the lake, it is impossible to verify the truth of this
legend."   There is, however, no foundation for these assertions.
The fable of the monocular fish belongs to a neighbouring lake,
Llyn-y-Cwn, which, as we have already mentioned, pours its
waters into Twll Dù.   If we rightly recollect, this "singular
variety of trout" was first alluded to by that generally accurate
topographer and historian, Giraldus Cambrensis, in his "Itinerary,"
and afterwards adopted by Daines Barrington and others.   Unfortunately, no fish at present exist in Llyn-y-Cwn to attest to the
truth of the assertion.   There are other pools in Wales which are
also said to contain monocular perch and trout, but we never yet
met with an angler who was fortunate to catch any.   The story
is altogether improbable, and has its origin in some of the traditionary records of the murder of Prince Idwal.   The assertion
that no fish exist in Llyn Idwal is equally erroneous.   Here at

least "the truth of the legend" is completely contradicted: Llyn Idwal abounds with small trout, furnished with *eyes* similar to their congeners, and if you happen to hit upon a favourable day, you may soon fill your basket. The quality of the fish, however, is vastly inferior to those caught in Llyn Ogwen; indeed, as regards *quality*, the Llyn Ogwen fish are far superior to any variety of trout found in Wales, and resemble those caught in some of the best Scottish lakes. The most delicious trout, by the way, we ever remember to have tasted, were caught in a small llyn, or *loch*, as it is termed in Scotland, lying about four miles from Gatehouse of Fleet, in the Stewartry of Kirkcudbright. In size they were from one-quarter to three-quarters of a pound weight, and were so fat, that they actually fried themselves. The flesh was quite red, and the flavour exquisite. In our youthful days we spent some time on a sporting excursion through Gallo-way, and several times visited this lake, which was called after a *gaelic* word, Whynnion. On one occasion, on a mild misty day in June, we caught from a boat four dozen magnificent fish, which weighed about twenty-five pounds. The Loch Leven trout have also a high reputation, and are frequently during the season to be met with in the London market. Trout, however, are so delicate a fish, that they will not bear carriage, and are never so good as when cooked immediately after being caught.

LLYN IDWAL is supposed in some places to be immensely deep; and if *colour* is any index, the supposition would appear to be correct. Some years ago, during a short sojourn at Bala, a Mr. W——, a gentleman well known as a keen sportsman in that neighbourhood, informed us that when a boy he had had a very narrow escape from drowning in Llyn Idwal. He was fishing at the lake, in company with his father, who had temporarily scaled one of the adjacent rocks in search of a rare plant. During his father's absence, Mr. W—— had posted himself on the summit of a rock impending over deep water; and whilst angling there, a sudden gust of wind carried off his hat, and in endeavouring to save it, he lost his footing and was precipitated headlong into the lake. Although unable to swim, on coming to the surface, he providentially came in contact with a portion of sunken rock: upon this he got, and loudly called for help. Fortunately his father heard his cries, came to his assistance, and speedily rescued him from his dangerous position.

There was formerly a small boat upon this pool; if we rightly remember, at the period of our last visit, the remains of the sunken wreck were still visible near the shore. We are not sufficiently well acquainted with Idwal to be able to point out any particular parts most favourable for the angler. We have generally fished the east shore, and on one or two occasions have had fair sport.

Excursion to Llyn Idwal.

Our first visit to Llyn Idwal occurred early in the autumn of 1841. We were sojourning for a few days at Capel Curig, the weather at the time being wet and stormy. Early one morning, we were aroused from our bed by the guide, Robin Hughes, who imparted the pleasing intelligence that the rain had ceased, and the morning was fine and cloudless. We hastily obeyed his summons; and never shall we forget the magnificent spectacle that greeted us from the garden terrace. The clouds had certainly cleared away overhead, but the mountain tops were shrouded in mist. The summit of Snowdon appeared covered with a bright luminous vapour, resembling the aurora borealis, which seemed like a crown of glory on his hoary brow, and brought to our remembrance the sublime words of the Psalmist :—

"Bow thy heavens, O Lord, and come down : touch the mountains, and they shall smoke."

"Nature," remarks an eloquent writer, "in her own majestic features remains the same; the everlasting hills, the unchangeable changes of the seasons are the same for us as for the departed nations whose homes and tombs are beneath the clods around us." This sublime appearance lasted but a very short time, and

"Like the snow-flake on the river,
A moment seen, then lost for ever."

We have never subsequently observed the same effects at sunrise in this region, but we have several times witnessed some remarkably gorgeous colouring' during foggy weather, on the summits of the neighbouring hills, as the sun was retiring on the western horizon. But to return to our narrative. Having despatched breakfast, we summoned our guide to council, and decided to visit Llyn Idwal, and afterwards, if practicable, to ascend the mountains by Twll Dù, and from thence proceed to Llanberis, and up the Pass back to Capel Curig. As the morning advanced, the sun in some measure dispersed the mist, and occasionally we caught passing glimpses of the majestic heights of Carnedds Llewelyn and Davydd, and some other mountains of lesser magnitude. As Roscoe forcibly observes, "Glorious in their silent, shadowy grandeur, were those half-seen mountains, rearing their storm-riven heads like giant spectres, and looking sternly and scornfully on little things below." Llyn Ogwen lay before us as placid as the surface of a mirror, the air was crisp and bracing—all nature appeared at rest, and we thought we had never seen the scenery of that romantic valley to such great advantage. Owing to the deluge of rain that had fallen for several previous days, the path was not only very wet but slippery: and during our walk from the high road to Llyn Idwal we experienced a severe fall, which had very nearly brought our enterprise to a conclusion. We were engaged at the time in contemplating the magnificent Falls of Benglog, which were considerably heightened in effect from the recent heavy rains. In turning suddenly round we trod upon the slippery rock, and fell upon our back with considerable force; for a time we were much stunned and shaken, but a "nip" from our flask soon restored us, and we proceeded on our way with greater caution.

In passing Llyn Ogwen, our guide related a singular fact with regard to the hearing of fish, a question still in dispute amongst naturalists. It has sometimes been supposed that the alarm of fish proceeds from the vibration of the water, and not from a sense of hearing. Be this as it may, the following account we were assured by the guide was strictly true. Some years ago, whilst some men were engaged in netting Llyn Ogwen, a violent thunder-storm came on; and after several ineffectual endeavours to catch fish, they suddenly at the upper end of the Llyn had an immense haul; it seemed as if all the fish in the pool had huddled together in that particular part. This phenomenon can only be accounted for by the supposition that the vibration of the water, caused by the heavy thunder, had alarmed the fish and driven them from their usual haunts.

" Has the reader ever found himself alone on some unfrequented path, amidst the 'everlasting hills' and bold gigantic forms of primeval nature, shaped and fashioned, it may be, in some sense, by the slow wear of almost unnumbered ages ? " Has he ever found himself warmed into enthusiasm, and, forgetful of the diffi-culties which beset his path, lost in contemplating the stern grandeur, the desolation of some of the solitudes, amongst the wild blue hills of Cambria ? If not, let him forthwith make a pilgrimage to Llyn Idwal. Such were our thoughts as we paused to survey from Castell-y-Geifr the ruins of nature which lay scattered around us. From this point Nant Ffrancon, the "Beavers' Hollow," is seen to great advantage; and such was the intense stillness, that we could hear the roar of the cataract of Benglog with startling distinctness. We were, however, unfortunately prevented from minutely examining the scenery of Llyn Idwal, owing to one of those sudden changes of the weather which so frequently occur in alpine countries. The smiling aspect of the morning passed rapidly away, and was succeeded by glooms on the mountain tops, and dark clouds began to hover over the lake. This gave the scenery that savage aspect which is its finest phase. . . . Long before we reached the vale, the rain began to descend in torrents, and soon the whole of the mountains and valley were enveloped in impenetrable mist. On arriving at Llanberis, we were glad to seek the nearest shelter, and speedily found ourselves before a roaring peat fire discussing the merits of a jug of excellent *cwrw*, and such rude entertainment as the "public" afforded. Here we were detained several hours; our guide in the meanwhile amusing us with a detail of sundry adven-tures he had met with in the mountains. Our host was a York-shire miner; he had migrated hither forty years before, married a Welsh girl, and in short had become so completely forgetful of "fatherland" as to speak his own native language very imper-fectly. He had, in fact, been completely transformed into a Welshman in everything except his appearance, which retained unmistakeable evidence of his Saxon or Danish origin. Our homeward journey to Capel Curig was performed in the dark, and with plenty of wind and rain to add to our discomfort; we afterwards regretted that we did not remain at our humble quarters and "rough" it through the night.

Llyn Ogwen.

This fine pool lies in a valley called Nant Ogwen, at the head of Nant Ffrancon, and is bounded on the north by Braich Der, the "Black Arm," a portion of the lofty precipices of Carnedd Davydd. The Great Holyhead road runs along its southern shore for the whole of its length. Llyn Ogwen is about three-quarters of a mile long from east to west; its breadth at the widest part is probably about three furlongs. The scenery around it is exceedingly grand and impressive, but in point of picturesque beauty it is not to be compared to Llyn Gwynant or the lakes of Llanberis; neither will it bear comparison in sublimity' to its sullen neighbour Llyn Idwal. This lake, like several others in Caernarvonshire, is chiefly fished from a boat. There are at least four boats on the pool, two of which belong to the hotel at Capel Curig, and the others to the miners or quarrymen in the vicinity. From the superior quality of the trout, this lake enjoys a high reputation amongst anglers, and is now the principal attraction to sportsmen frequenting Capel Curig. Angling here, as at Beddgelert, is expensive, as the lake is about four miles from the hotel, and most of the anglers who visit it prefer to ride. The charge for a car and driver is about six shillings; this, in addition to a boatman, would involve an expense of eight or nine shillings per day. If, however, you walk, and manage your own boat, you can have it, we believe, gratis, provided no cars are going there, which of course command a preference.

The Ogwen trout are amongst the most beautiful in Wales, and they are certainly far superior in quality to any others we have met. They are generally of a bright rich yellow colour, and the flesh when cooked is quite red. There are, however, as in most lakes, at least two varieties. In former days, before the increase of a mining population, the sport on this lake must have been first rate, as the trout run from half a pound to a pound, or even larger; now, during the summer months, there are seldom less than four boats at work from morning until night on favourable days, and the trout have in consequence become wary. Although they still rise freely, you are tantalized with a great many "false rises," and seldom, unless a very expert hand, get good sport. We have, some years ago, met with very fair sport here, taking some fine fish; but, generally speaking, first-rate sport at Ogwen belongs to the past.

The most successful angler we ever met with at Llyn Ogwen was the late Mr. A——d. This gentleman seldom came without filling his basket; but he knew the lake well, and the most killing flies, all of which he made himself. He used a short, supple Irish rod, and had generally eight flies on his "foot link." With one exception, he was the most accomplished fisherman we ever met with. His manipulation was perfect, a most important *desideratum* in boat fishing.

Llyn Ogwen belongs to the Hon. Col. Douglas Pennant, M.P. of Penrhyn Castle, near Bangor, who most liberally permits all *fair* anglers free permission. This lake is, we believe, carefully preserved during the spawning season from the depredations of poachers, as at that period the large fish full of spawn get into the brooks, and would fall an easy prey to the peasantry and others in the locality.

Llyn Ogwen at the lower extremity is shallow, and the bottom is strewed with large stones, which, when the lake is low, frequently peep above water. We have found good fishing ground at the head of the pool, but we prefer a "drift" through the centre of the llyn, especially if the wind is blowing from the west. There is also some good water along the south shore. The flies here are in general similar to those used in other lakes in the country. In June the "Llyn Ogwen fly," "peahen," "alder," and "fernshaw," are generally "sure cards." Much, however, depends on wind and weather. Generally speaking, on a dull misty day, with a good breeze, the best sport is obtained; indeed, it is useless to fish Ogwen without a rattling breeze.

Nant Ffrancon.

This celebrated valley, the "Beavers' Hollow"—so called from being in former times the resort of beavers—is situate amongst the grandest and most stupendous scenery in North Wales. Telford's great work, the London and Holyhead road, passes through its whole extent, crossing the brawling Ogwen above the "Falls of Benglog." The scene presented to the eye is one of stern desolation; steep and craggy piles of naked rock rise abruptly from the base of Carnedd Davydd, and which, from the effect of the elements, are sometimes detached from the impending cliffs above, and fall in immense masses, with thundering impetuosity, into the valley beneath. Narrow escapes have been recorded on different occasions to travellers passing through the vale. On one occasion, some years ago, the road was completely blocked up for a time by one of these rocky *avalanches;* and a gentleman in a carriage, on his way to Bangor, had just passed before the disruption took place; a few minutes later, and he would have been completely overwhelmed. At the bottom of the valley the eye rests upon a narrow strip of verdure, through which the infant Ogwen winds its course. It is, however, the oasis of the desert, the adjacent rocks being "scathed, verdureless, and shivered." The scene, in consequence, is exceedingly wild and dreary—a combination, in short, of the "picturesque and terrible" in some of its most sublime features. The finest view of Nant Ffrancon is, perhaps, on the approach from Bangor; this more especially in dark, lowering weather, when the colouring of the landscape is wonderfully fine and imposing. Under any phase, however, this wonderful spot affords magnificent, soulstirring effects.

TRAVELLING IN WALES.—There are three methods of travelling in Wales; either on horseback, on wheels, or on foot. The first method, if you are well mounted, enables you to get over a great deal of ground without fatigue, and to rapidly traverse such parts of the country as are dreary and uninteresting. When you arrive at a town or village where a great deal is to be seen *off* the road, take the opportunity to rest your steed, and explore the scenery on foot. By following this plan, you not only keep your horse up to his work, but being *fresh* yourself, you are benefited by the change of exercise, and much better enabled to stand the fatigue of mountain climbing than such as are jaded by the toil of long marches on the turnpike-road. This applies also to the second method, but you are more *independent* on horseback. As regards expense, a horseback-tour is decidedly more economical: your horse *frees* your bed, and the cost of his keep ought not to be more than four shillings and sixpence *per diem*, ostler included. Travelling by one-horse car costs one shilling per mile, which, with tolls and drivers, amounts to a great deal in the course of an extended tour. This, of course, where two or three join together, reduces the expense; but even then it is much more expensive than horseback. Pedestrianism is by far the most independent mode of travelling; but as regards economy, taking *time* into consideration, we much question whether it is not in the long run nearly, if not quite, as expensive as horseback. For instance, you cannot, in hot summer weather, get over more than eighteen or twenty miles a day on foot, and even this distance kept up *de die in diem*, for any length of time, produces fever and lassitude. On horseback, when necessary, you can ride forty miles without experiencing more than a pleasant fatigue when you arrive at the end of your day's progress. The pedestrian traveller, unless very robust and in good training, is more fit for his bed than his supper at the end of a long, hot, dusty day's march, and is, moreover, frequently footsore and lame, the painful effects of which we have ourselves often experienced. To preserve your feet from galls, wear lamb's-wool socks, previously anointing the feet, particularly the heels, with mutton fat. This plan we have found from experience completely prevents galling. From what we have thus stated, we think we have proved the superior advantages to be derived from horseback travelling; this, when combined with occasional pedestrian rambles, is not only far more enjoyable, but enables you, even after a month or six weeks' excursion, to come home benefited in health from the effects of the pure mountain air you have inhaled, or the delightful invigorating sea-breezes you have enjoyed; and your steed, by careful management, will also look all the better for his work.

In the course of many excursions into the Principality, we have travelled by all the modes of transit we have just described, and, from experience, we infinitely prefer horseback, not only on the score of economy, but for health and enjoyment.

In the summer of 1840 we made a tour through North Wales on horseback, beginning at Monmouth. We rode to Conway, the *Ultima Thule* of North Wales, and from thence back through Llangollen and the English border to our starting-point. We were out twenty-three days; and during that period accomplished a distance of 409½ miles on horseback, 37 miles by car, and about 107 miles on foot; making an average rate of twenty-four miles per day. This, however, does not include Sunday, on which day we always rested. At some places, also, we remained a day or two, and to make up "lee-way" we frequently rode upwards of forty-five miles a day, when detained by bad weather or by sundry excursions on foot:

CHAPTER XVI.

THE TEIFI—ITS SOURCE—FISHING STATIONS—SALMON AND TROUT
FISHING—TREGARON—BEAVERS—LLYN BERWYN—EXCURSION
TO THE LAKE—ANGLING—SINGULAR CAPTURE OF A TROUT—
TEIFI FISHING—LLANDDEWI BREVI.

> " Sith I must stem thy stream, clear Teifi, yet before
> The muse vouchsafe to seize the Cardiganian shore
> She of thy source will sing in all the Cambrian coast :
> Which of thy castors* once, but now canst only boast
> Thy salmons, of all floods most plentiful in thee.
> Then Teifi cometh down from her capacious llyn
> 'Twixt Mirk and Brenny led, two handmaids that do stay
> Their mistress, as in state she goes upon her way."
>
> DRAYTON.

The Teifi.

OF all the streams that gladden the vales of Cambria, the
" beauteous Teifi," as old Drayton poetically terms it, is one of
the most picturesque and romantic. Its parent is Llyn Teifi, a
dark, sullen pool, in one of the wildest mountain retreats in
Wales, and, with the exception of Llyn Egnant, the largest of the
group called the " Teifi lakes." These are five in number, and
lie in close contiguity on the summit of a bleak, barren, dreary
range of hills, called by Giraldus, Ellenith, which signifies " the
heights of marshy places." These hills stretch away to the
north-east of the once famous abbey of Ystrad Flur, or Strata
Florida. Ystrad Flur, " the Blooming Vale," so called, we suppose,
to distinguish its comparative fertility from the desolate wilderness
above it. *Ystrad* in Welsh means a vale or flat formed by a
river. Through this " deep, wild solitude," the Teifi winds its
devious way, the ground " horrible with the sight of bare stones,"

* The beaver.

—as Leland expresses it in his own peculiar phraseology—until it arrives at Pontrhydvendigaid, the "Bridge of the Blessed or Holy Ford," evidently a monkish appellation. This retired village contains a tolerably comfortable inn, the Red Lion; and here the Teifi fishing may be said to commence.

The river from hence to Tregaron flows in a gentle stream through an extensive peat morass, called Gors Goch Lan Teifi, and presents to the eye a dreary appearance, similar to that so frequently observed in the wilds of Ireland.

Although the Teifi is in its youth, in some parts of its course through this morass it is very deep, and contains large trout, some of them from four pounds to five pounds weight, which afford fine sport when on the hook; they are, however, exceedingly wary, and a strong breeze is indispensable to ensure sport. Below Pont Trecefel, one mile from Tregaron, the river becomes fordable, and from thence flows in a rapid stream—deep pools occasionally intervening, the haunt of salmon—for many miles through a beautifully diversified valley in its course to Lampeter, one of the most important fishing-stations on its banks. The Teifi, generally speaking, is *free* to the angler through the whole of its extent; above Pont Trecefel, we believe Colonel Powell, of Nanteos, claims the manorial "right of water;" but, we apprehend, the angler would find little difficulty in obtaining leave.

On a fine balmy day in spring, when the trees are assuming their mantle of green, and

> " The voice of the turtle is heard in the land,"

we know of few more enjoyable rambles than a quiet stroll along the banks of this lovely stream. The scene is redolent of simplicity and pastoral delights; the deep repose and tranquillity of hill and dale, the music of the murmuring waters, are full of softness and harmony. The gentle "songs of spring" are heard

> " Amid the hills that shrine
> A scene so tranquil."

The Teifi is an *early* river; the best time for trout fishing is in March and April, especially when the river is clearing after a flood. As a general rule, all the Welsh rivers are *best* in early spring; when the season is mild and genial, and the rivers free from "snow broth," the angler will generally obtain sport. After the month of April, when the leaves are out, river fishing is of little account in Wales, and the angler must betake himself to the lakes. The banks of the river below Tregaron are generally open and clear of wood, but about one mile below Pont Trecefel on the right bank are several creeks of water, which apparently once formed the bed of the river, and are difficult to cross; you are therefore sometimes obliged to make a *détour*. To avoid this annoyance, we recommend the sportsman to keep on the Tregaron side, on which he will find easy access to the banks of the stream. There are many excellent "runs," or what are sometimes termed "swims" of water between Tregaron and Pont Llanio, near the ancient Roman station, Loventium; indeed, all the way to Llanfair Clydogan, there is some capital water. At Llanfair, near the lead-mines, a Roman road, called Sarn Helen, crosses the river.

The length of the Teifi from its mountain source to its influx with the sea at Cardigan, where it forms an estuary, may be roughly estimated at about sixty miles. It passes in its course several towns and villages, which are all good angling stations; amongst the principal of which are Pontrhydvendigaid, Tregaron, Lampeter, Llandyssil, and Newcastle Emlyn. The three last-mentioned places are noted for their excellent salmon fishing. For trout fishing, we infinitely prefer Tregaron, as here you have also the advantage of being in the neighbourhood of several lakes. The Teifi abounds in salmon and trout; the former are considered equal if not superior in quality to any in Wales, and during the season the "take" is considerable. The *coracle*, the ancient British boat, is used by the native fishermen employed in netting, as it still is in the Dyfi, the Wye, and other rivers. A considerable number of fish are also captured by the rod. Trout of considerable size are occasionally taken by the fly, and in some parts of the river, both above and below Tregaron, first-rate sport is obtained. A friend of ours, a few years ago, whilst angling near Lampeter, caught a number of very fine trout during the flights of the cob-fly, after the river was clearing from "a fresh." The Teifi is subject to heavy floods, and during their continuance is much discoloured, assuming for a few hours a deep red appearance; like most rapid streams, however, it soon clears, and then the angler cannot fail to kill some fine fish. It is singular that the flights of the Cob-fly are but of short duration; when they disappear from the water, the fish are so completely glutted that very little sport is obtained during the rest of the day.

Tregaron.

This secluded village is situate on the verge of the untamed and trackless mountain district of Cardiganshire; a region little known, and still less frequented by the stranger, and as primitive and solitudinous as imagination can conceive.

Tregaron is of ancient origin, a place in fact of considerable antiquity, and derives its name from St. Caron, "a Welsh prince who was canonized in the third century." There are several very old monumental stones in the churchyard, supposed to be coeval with the sixth century. At the time of our first visit, the inn at Tregaron was a wretched alehouse; of late years, however, a most respectable inn, called the "Victoria," has been erected, where the angler will meet with every comfort. The landlord, Mr. Rees, who is very civil and obliging, is a farmer and extensive flock-master, possessing a large mountain farm and several thousand sheep. We have rarely met with more comfortable quarters, or more reasonable charges, than at the "Victoria."

There is nothing very inviting about the village itself, but it is pleasantly situate on the little river Berwyn, which flows through the village from a very romantic dingle called Cwm Berwyn, at the head of which it has its source. A large tributary to the Berwyn, which flows through Nant-y-Groes, has its origin in Llyn Crugnant, and joins the Berwyn about one mile above Tregaron. The confluence of the Berwyn with the Teifi is at Pont Trecefel, a mile below the village. Altogether, Tregaron is the most pleasant fishing station we are acquainted with in South Wales; there are, besides, several most interesting remains, Roman and British, in the immediate vicinity, to engage the attention of the antiquary, and the sportsman may pass a few weeks in the enjoyment of angling amidst scenery composed of wide-spreading mountains, vast and grand in their aspect; and though not distinguished by natural beauty, yet these wild hills possess a charm in their *loneliness* which constitutes a powerful attraction to the solitary wanderer. In order to form some conception of this desolate region, Malkin, in his description of Cardiganshire, remarks, that a journey of sixty miles, in the direction of these mountain tops, might be taken almost without gate, road, or human habitation being encountered !

One of our chief enjoyments in a country such as we have endeavoured to describe, is to explore the recesses of some lonely *cwm*, watered by a "babbling brook," its source, perchance, in a sequestered mountain llyn, by the shores of which we delight to wander in quest of sport, "read sermons in stones, and good in everything."

Drayton, in his "Poly-Olbion," alludes to the existence of the beaver in Wales, that curious animal being formerly abundant on the banks of the Teifi, a portion of which, flowing through a flat marshy swamp, would appear to be exactly adapted to the habits of those creatures. Other parts of Wales were also frequented by the beaver, amongst which Nant Ffrancon; and other lakes and streams have borne the beaver's name for centuries. In the laws of Howel Dda, unquestionable evidence is afforded of the existence of this animal in the Principality, for the value of a beaver's skin is there distinctly specified. When this interesting animal became finally extirpated does not appear to be known.

Llyn Berwyn.

"Embosomed in the silent hills,
  Where quiet sleeps, and care is calm,
  And all the air is breathing balm."
                                        THOMAS MILLER.

This solitary pool lies in the mountains at the head of Cwm Berwyn, about five miles from Tregaron. You follow a tolerably good parish road by the side of the river Berwyn, until you reach the head of the vale. Here you turn off over the uplands to the right, beyond which, in a hollow at the distance of a mile from the road, the lake reposes. A more wild, dreary scene than that which surrounds the llyn, it would be difficult to conceive; this naked kind of scenery, however, is a characteristic of all the Cardiganshire lakes. There the wild waters gleam in the midst of a shelterless waste, and should rough weather occur during your visit, you must rely upon the virtues of your *macintosh*, for there is not even a crevice where you can obtain refuge from a storm.

Llyn Berwyn is not a very large piece of water; and not nearly so extensive as one or two lakes of the Teifi group. It is somewhat oval in shape, and is probably about three furlongs in length from north to south, by two in breadth. The small brook that flows from it at its southern extremity forms one of the sources of the river Dothie, which joins the Towy in the "land of the gorges." The river Berwyn has no connexion whatever with this lake, and flows in quite a contrary direction. We were informed by a local fisherman, that the middle of the lake was exceedingly deep—about fifty yards—and that it contained some very large trout. On one occasion, he said, whilst fishing there in a boat, he rose a trout at least four pounds weight, and at different times he had taken some exceedingly nice fish.

Our first excursion to Llyn Berwyn occurred early in May, 1855, during a short stay at Tregaron. The weather at the time was rather cold and showery, and in consequence of the easterly winds and frosty nights of the preceding month, the country, even at this advanced period of the year, seemed almost as verdureless and leafless as winter. Notwithstanding the unfavourable weather, we were determined to try our hand at the lake, where, from local report, we were informed that the sport was sometimes first-rate. We therefore, in company with a friend, started from Tregaron about nine o'clock, on a dull, rainy-looking morning. We had no guide except the map, but we found our way thither without the least difficulty. Shortly after our arrival, a drizzling rain set in, which with the fog down on the hills, and a nice ripple on the water, afforded promise of success. We, however, fished for some time without even a rise, but this we partly accounted for from our entire ignorance of the *proper flies*.

Fortune at last favoured us in rather a singular manner. We had patiently "flogged" the water for upwards of an hour, when, on coming round to the east shore, our attention was directed to what seemed a large trout, rising or rather moving on the top of the water, about two yards from the edge, close to a large stone which rose about a foot above the surface. After watching the movements of the fish for a few moments, we became convinced that the trout was entangled, and that his movements on the surface were occasioned by his efforts to escape. Notwithstanding the pelting of a smart shower, we hastened to doff our nether garments, and waded to the scene of action. Here we found our conjecture correct, and speedily laid hold of a " gut bottom," to which was attached four excellent flies and a large trout of nearly one pound weight, which we soon secured and brought to land. From the condition of the flies, it seemed probable that they had not been under water more than a day or two, and had evidently belonged to a gentleman, from their superior quality. Be this as it may, we immediately attached them to our own line, and shortly after killed our first fish. We caught, in all, on this occasion, nine trout, the smallest of which weighed six ounces ; several were more than half a pound. We have no doubt that if we had commenced earlier in the day, with the *right* flies, we should have taken a full basket of fish. Our companion did not obtain a rise, showing that his flies were *wrong*.

We were so much pleased with the lake and the quality of the trout—which when in full season are really very handsome fish— that we repeated our visit on the following day. The weather was very favourable—warm, with occasional gleams of sunshine, and rather showery. On this occasion we came *early*, and provided with some excellent flies made by a local angler, named Williams. In the course of a few hours we killed thirty-five trout, which weighed fifteen pounds ; the average size about the same as on the previous day. We found the best "rise" early in the forenoon ; during the latter part of the day not a fish stirred. We are convinced that in every lake it is useless to expect a *good* day's sport unless you commence early ; *lazy* fishermen, who reach their water at noon or later, may as well stay at home.

The proper flies for the Teifi and the lakes of course depends on the season of the year. We found in May the red spinner with some gold twist on the body, and a fly made with a wood-cock's feather for the wings, with a yellow body, very killing flies on the lake; and for Teifi fishing, the sand fly was excellent; but we strongly recommend the angler to apply to one of the local fishermen, who will afford him every information.

TEIFI-FISHING.—We now return to the Teifi. The weather, during the month of April, 1855, was very unfavourable; cold easterly winds prevailed throughout the month, and as little or no rain fell during that period, the rivers in Wales became exceedingly low and clear, and of course there was very little sport. We found this to be the case on our arrival at Tregaron, early in May. In consequence, little was to be done on the river, which was hardly ever known to be so short of water at that season; and the cold nights caused the fish to rise so badly, that we could only manage to kill a few brace of small trout even after a long day's ramble. A few days before our departure, however, a favourable change in the weather occurred—a southerly wind brought some warm refreshing rain, which caused a slight "fresh" on the river, and the trout began to stir more freely. The best season for stream-fishing had, however, passed away. We only tried the "lanes" on one occasion, and although there was plenty of breeze, it was very cold, and we did not succeed in moving a heavy fish. Captain Medwin's description of the Teifi is so graphic, that before we proceed farther, we are here tempted to make a brief extract from his "Angler in Wales," which will afford the reader a more accurate account of the deep-water fishing in the marshes between Pontrhydvendigaid and Tregaron, and the nature of the difficulties to be encountered, than we are able to give from personal inspection.

"The Teifi here flows in a stream, blue, rapid, and containing trout of a considerable size; later in the season, salmon. Owing to the long continuation of the spring drought, it had been little affected so near its source by the heavy rains, and was much dwindled from its accustomed volume of water; but even within a mile of the village (Pontrhydvendigaid) Charters had taken some good fish. The falls are numerous. The runnels dashed over the broken, rocky beds, and the banks are so free from wood, that a fly may be thrown anywhere without interrup-

tion. Behold us then following the river down. Had we
known the *locale*, we should have avoided giving the Teifi our
company after the first league, and have struck off into the
road, for we then came to marsh after marsh, through which
crept the sleepy stream, in a still, deep, weedy channel. A
more intricate course I never threaded than through the valley
for six or seven miles. The river had evidently some months
before overstepped its barriers, and covered the whole plain,
through which had been cut drains of great depth, which it
required the full play of the 'tendon Achilles' to leap. Occasionally too we got into a labyrinth of turbaries, when the tremu-
lousness of the ground betrayed the quagmire yawning below,
and threatening to engulf us at every step. We heartily
repented not attending to the guide's advice, during a three hours'
march, in which we had no opportunity of making a cast with any
chance of success. We, however, at length emerged from the
desolate track, and on arriving at a bridge that crossed a by-road,
our friend assumed a new face. Charters' sport now began.
The morning had been overcast, and the rain began to fall in
heavy showers; but we were too good water-spaniels to heed
their pelting. He soon called me to his assistance. 'Whish,
whish!'—I perceived the fish was one of the patriarchs. The
rapid where he had been successfully tempted by the bright
blood-red berries* was broken by rocks that gave the water the
resemblance of jet or obsidian. Down he went. 'Whish, whish!'
responded the multiplier again. Who could have dared to curb
or check him? 'There he is, out of his element—once, twice—
now wheel up!' In a few moments he was lying amid the weeds
and grass, a worthy study for Murillo. Our trout was a glorious
fish, and must have weighed, though I did not measure him, three
pounds and a half—yes, a glorious fish, I repeat, for this or any
other water, and the largest we had taken of his species in
Wales."

From the above description, which we have reason to believe
is free from exaggeration, few anglers, we think, will be tempted
to encounter the "quagmires" and deep ditches which abound

---

* Salmon roe.

in the marshes through which the Teifi flows for several miles.
Medwin states that all the fish taken on the occasion referred to,
were killed by trolling with salmon-paste, a very destructive lure;
and a skilful manipulator will sometimes capture some very heavy
fish. It is, however, after all, a poaching method of sport, and
far from a *cleanly* one. The fact is, that at the season of the
year when Captain Medwin fished the Teifi (June or July) fly-
fishing was over, except for sewin and salmon. Very few trout of
any size are ever taken in Welsh rivers after April and May. In
some streams—the Usk for instance—*skerling*, a species of
samlet, will sometimes rise well in July or August, but you
seldom capture any large trout with the fly. The grayling
season commences about the middle of August, and is *best* in
October; but few Welsh rivers contain any, except the Lugg
and the Wye.

We met with very indifferent sport in the Teifi in 1855,
although, in consequence of rain, accompanied with warm growing
weather, the river was in fair order. This, however, occurred
towards the conclusion of our stay at Tregaron. Our best day's
sport was during some thunder showers, when we killed about
two dozen trout in good season; none exceeded half a pound.
The larger fish "rose short," possibly from being glutted with
ground-bait. To obtain success on the Teifi, you must go early
in March, when the cob-fly is out: at that time, especially if you
happen to *know* your water, great sport is almost certain, if
weather and water are suitable. This river is generally considered
one of the very best trout streams in Wales, both for size and
quality; a large well-fed fish in this water is very handsome, and
for flavour is far superior to any river fish we ever tasted in
Wales.

Llanddewi Brefi.

This "out of the world" spot is little known, and still less
frequented by the stranger, although celebrated in the Ecclesiastical Annals of the Cwmry. Our first visit to it occurred in July,
1843, during a pedestrian excursion from the Devil's Bridge
(Pont-y-Monach) to Llandovery. It lies in a pleasant sheltered

situation, about three miles and a half south by west from Tregaron. Its population is small, probably not exceeding two or three hundred inhabitants. A wild dingle, which runs from hence into the hills, is worth exploring; and the country around, if not strik-ingly beautiful, is at all events pleasing.

In the year of our Lord 519, St. David, the tutelary saint of Wales, is said to have preached here to a convocation of the clergy, summoned at the call of Dubricius, Archbishop of Caerleon, to devise some means of crushing the Pelagian heresy, at that time making converts in Wales. A very ancient stone pillar in the churchyard, time-worn and dilapidated, locally called "St. David's Staff," is pointed out to the tourist as the spot where the saint delivered his discourse. Whether this pillar was afterwards raised in commemoration of the event, or existed at the period the synod was held, does not appear to be known.

Excursion from the Debil's Bridge to Llandobery.

During the remarkably fine summer of 1843, on our return from an angling tour in North Wales, we were tempted to make an exploring expedition across the almost trackless wild hill country which stretches from Llanddewi Brevi to the sources of the Towy. Our route lay, in the first instance, from the Devil's Bridge, and as we saw much to admire in the course of our walk to Llanddewi Brevi, a brief description of the most interesting objects we met by the way must claim our attention in the next chapter.

CHAPTER XVII.

> "Here balmy air, and springs as ether clear,
> Fresh downs, and limpid rills, and daisied meads,
> Delight the eye, reanimate the heart,
> And on the florid cheek emboss the rose
> 'Mid sweetest dimples and unfeigned smiles."

WHO has not heard of the far-famed Pont-y-Monach, its magnificent waterfalls, its curious double bridge, spanning a yawning chasm of profound depth, and the absurd legend attached to its origin? Its scenic attractions, however, have long been a "stock" subject in guide books and "tours," so that we can afford to spare the reader a recapitulation of what is already so well known and so deservedly admired. Hafod, too, in the immediate vicinity, another of the "lions," is also too threadbare a subject for us to meddle with. Animated descriptions of it are to be found in several topographical works, and to these we refer the reader. Nor must we forget Pont Bren, the "Parson's Bridge," one of the most secluded and picturesque scenes on a river, whose course is marked by features of grandeur and romantic loveliness, scarcely to be exceeded by any other stream in Cambria.* Our object is rather to describe scenes more out of the beaten track, and less accessible to the generality of sightseers; and which, though some of them may be well known to the *few*, are a *terra incognita* to the many. We shall therefore commence our excursion from Pont Ystwith, which lies just beyond the Hafod woods, and

---

* The Rheidol..

crosses the river Ystwith—once famed for the excellence and abundance of its trout.

It was on a fine warm misty morning in July, that we left the Devil's Bridge. The beauties of Hafod were veiled by a heavy curtain of vapour which hung over hill and vale, and the attractive and richly varied scenery surrounding this sylvan paradise, was buried in profound obscurity. Hafod, formerly a barren wilderness, has been converted into one of the most delightful retreats in Wales by judicious landscape gardening on a grand scale, executed with consummate taste; materially assisted, however, by the natural accessories of the valley in which it is situate. After emerging from these leafy bowers, the contrast afforded by the naked aspect of the country before us was striking enough. The road we now struck into led to Pontrhydvendigaid, and the aspect of the scenery was barren and desolate. A few miles before we reached that village, the sun began to dispel the heavy vapours which had obscured the landscape in the early morning, and a sudden burst of his gladsome beams, as we reached the summit of a hill, revealed to us the ancient hamlet reposing in the "blooming vale" below. Pontrhydvendigaid is a poor primitive-looking place; even its inn—since the period of our visit said to be improved—had a very *uninviting* appearance; nevertheless, we were glad to avail ourselves of its shelter, and to partake of such homely fare as the larder afforded, before proceeding on our pilgrimage to the ruins of the once celebrated

Abbey of Strata Florida.

> " The wall flower shed its perfume, as it clung
> And waved in wild luxuriance o'er the stone
> Chafed by the storms of years; . . . .
> Around me all was calm and still; the wind,
> Even that ' charter'd brawler,' seemed to feel
> A strange unwonted awe, and strove to steal
> With gentler voice amid the hills that shrined
> A scene so tranquil."

Wales is not remarkable for its existing monastic remains, nor, strictly speaking, were conventual establishments at any period

of its history exceedingly numerous. Among the most important
were Ystrad Flur, Conwy, Tinterne, and Valle Crucis. We
include Tinterne, because, until the reign of Henry VIII. that
once magnificent Abbey belonged to Wales. After its dissolution,
Monmouthshire, in which it lies, became an English county. Of
these institutions, Ystrad Flur and Conwy were considered the
most important. These monasteries divided between them the
honour of carrying on the Historical Records of the *Cwmry*,
and here these records were preserved until after the inglorious
death of the last and greatest of the native Welsh princes,
in 1282.

With the exception of the abbeys of Valle Crucis and Cwmmer,
the ruins of such others as still exist are mere fragments. Time,
the fury of the elements, and the ruthless hand of man, have
done their work; and no edifice dedicated to the worship of the
Most High has been more utterly spoliated than the once stately
abbey of Strata Florida.

It is not our intention to enter into a minute account of the
past history and fortunes of this famous monastery, but briefly
detail a few of the leading events during the time it flourished,
and more particularly the existing state of its ruins.

"The rich monastery of Stratflur"—called by the Welsh
Monachlog Vawr, the "Great Abbey"—was, when in the zenith
of its splendour and renown, the largest and most powerful conventual community in Wales. It experienced sundry vicissitudes,
the common fate of all the Welsh ecclesiastical establishments,
which, situate as it were in the midst of such a wild turbulent
race as the ancient *Cwmry*, were ever liable to pillage and insult.
This abbey was for several centuries the chief depository of the
ancient historical records of Wales, the genealogies of its princes
and nobles, and the works of its bards; its library was extensive
and valuable, and its revenues immense. It is most generally
believed that this community of monks belonged to the Cistercian
order; although there is a difference of opinion amongst some of
the best authorities on this subject. Sir Richard Colt Hoare
inclines to the opinion that the monks were of the "severe and
recluse order of the Cistercians;" this is also confirmed by Leland,
who flourished at the period of the Dissolution. Camden, how-

ever, says that it was an establishment of Cluniacs, founded by
Rhys ap Tewdwr in the reign of the Conqueror. We incline to the
former opinion, as the secluded situation of Ystrad Flur is more
in accordance with the austere discipline of the Cistercian "religious." It seems strange indeed, that any uncertainty at all
should exist on this point; the historical documents belonging to
the monastery ought to have set the question at rest long ago.
The original site is supposed by some to have been removed after
its destruction by fire, in 1295, *temp.* Edward I.; according to
tradition, this arbitrary monarch, upon the occasion of some
trifling dispute with the abbot, was the author of the calamity,
during the unhappy period which followed the wars and death of
Llewelyn, in 1282. At the distance of about two miles off to the
south-west, near the left side of the road leading to Tregaron,
the foundations of a church may be seen, which is supposed to
have belonged to the more ancient abbey. These remains are
called Hen Monachlog, which signifies, the "Old Abbey." From
the name, there appears at first sight to be some truth in the conjecture; but recent modern researches have incontestably proved
that the existing ruins are on the original foundation.

The ancient cemetery is supposed to have formerly been of
considerable extent, covering at least 120 acres; but the modern
enclosure scarcely exceeds two. In this extensive necropolis, the
ashes of the illustrious dead, princes, bards, and other eminent
persons, repose; and leaden coffins are still occasionally discovered
in the vicinity. The grave of Davydd ap Gwilym, one of the most
eminent of the Welsh Bards, tradition asserts, is under one of the
aged yew trees in the existing churchyard; the only living memorials left to lament, as it were, over the vain and transitory nature
of all human works.* An epitaph on the Bard, in Welsh, probably by some monkish writer, has been rendered with much
spirit into English by the learned author of the "Ecclesiastical
Antiquities of the Cwmry," the Rev. John Williams, late of
Llan-y-Mowddy, near Mallwyd.

---

* Malkin considers the poetry of David ap Gwilym, "the purest standard
of the Welsh language, and from his poems the modern literary dialect has
chiefly been formed."

> " Worthy David, mighty Bard,
>   Art thou laid here under the green wood ?—
>   Beneath a flourishing tree, even a beautiful yew,
>   Where he was buried, the song lies concealed.

> " Beneath a bushy green yew, the fair nightingale of Teifi,
>   David, is interred :—
>   The vigorous strain is in the dust.
>   We have now no genius by day or by night."

From the tenor of these Ossianic lines, it may be inferred that the bones of the "fair nightingale of Teifi" actually repose under one of these ancient yews; which, according to Leland, were in his time thirty-nine in number.

After the period of its restoration, the "Abbey of the blooming plain" flourished in extraordinary splendour for 200 years. It was famed for its hospitality, its learning, the beauty and magnificence of its church, its wealth and extensive possessions. More than three centuries have since then rolled away, and where is this magnificent edifice? Its "storied windows," with their delicate and elaborate traceries, its fretted roof, its paintings, its carvings "in ebon and ivory," its richly-clustered stone pillars, its stately arches, all have crumbled into dust; even the very tombs of its founders, princes, warriors, and minstrels, whose ashes lie scattered around, have vanished away

> "Like the baseless fabric of a vision,"

and become merely shadows of the Past.

At the Reformation, the once numerous community of monks had dwindled away to six or seven: these were soon afterwards driven from their sanctuary by the imperious mandate of the "Saxon" king; and the church and conventual buildings were afterwards gradually despoiled, and fell into utter ruin and decay. Even in Leland's time, "the fratry and infirmatori be now mere ruines."

> " Oh Time ! the beautifier of the dead,
>   Adorner of the ruin."
>   BYRON.

We must conclude this brief and imperfect sketch of Strata Florida, as it was in its palmy days, with a few remarks descriptive of its existing remains. The abbey, however, has been so "utterly devoured," that little appears above ground to attract the attention of the antiquary. Since the period of our visit, in 1843, some excavations have been made on a portion of the site of the conventual church, which have satisfactorily established nearly its exact dimensions; and the ruins were afterwards thoroughly explored by the members of the Cambrian Archæological Society, in 1847, at whose expense this interesting discovery was made.

The scenery surrounding the "blooming plain," with its encircling "belt of mountains," is in strict keeping with the forlorn and melancholy aspect of the ruins. A few weather-beaten trees, affording shelter to an ancient farm-house—the yews, which cast an air of sadness over the churchyard—a neglected garden, rank with weeds and desolation—are the chief accompaniments which greet the eye of the visitor. The ruins consist of a Norman gateway of considerable beauty, adjoining the east side of the cemetery. A double crozier-head is placed over the centre of the arch, and several recessed flutings add much to its general effect. In a wall adjoining the gateway there is a solitary pointed window, partially covered with a graceful drapery of ivy. The wallflower also adorns the ruined window with its beautiful fragrant flowers. These fragments constitute all, or nearly all, that remains of the " *Opimum de Stratflur Monasterium*," the "rich monastery of Stratflur." *Omnia vincit Tempus.*

A small, and somewhat mean-looking church, which a modern writer has termed "a neat building"—doubtless erected with some of the materials of its mighty predecessor—stands in the modern burial-ground, and in immediate contiguity to the ruins. The murmuring waters of the Teifi flow at less than a quarter of a mile to the north of the church. About half-way from hence to Pontrhydvendigaid, the river is joined by a considerable tributary, which rises at the head of a wild secluded dingle to the southeast, called Nant Glassffrwd, not far from Llyn Crugnant.

A feeling of regret steals over us whenever we behold the dilapidated abodes of learning and piety, the perishing memorials of a departed age. The broken arch, the crumbling pillar, the tottering tower, are types of the transitory and fleeting nature of all human works, and forcibly remind us of the words of the

Preacher, who says, "all the works that are done under the sun" are but vanity and "vexation of spirit." With such or similar thoughts, we bade farewell to the ruined Abbey of Strata Florida.

> " How many hearts have here grown cold,
>   That sleep these mouldering stones among!
>   How many beads have here been told!
>   How many matins here been sung !
>
> " But here no more soft music floats,
>   No holy anthems chanted now;
>   All hush'd except the ring-dove's notes,
>   Low murm'ring from yon beechen bough."

We now slowly retraced our steps to the "Blessed Ford," the road to which, after about half a mile, runs parallel to the meandering Teifi, which here flows in a rapid stream through the "blooming plain," from a wild ravine in the desolate hills above. The banks of the river were well clothed with wood in olden time, and were not destroyed until the reign of Edward I. Leland, in his "Itinerary," expressly alludes to it in his description of Ystrad Flur, in the sixteenth century. He says: "Many hills thereabout hath been well wodded, but now in them is almost no woode. Men for the nonys destroied the great woddis that they should not harborow thieves." The real object of the English monarch, in causing the woods and thickets to be destroyed, was to prevent them from sheltering the armed men of the country, who were at that time in resistance to his authority. Early in the afternoon we left Pontrhydvendigaid, and resumed our excursion towards Tregaron, which lies about six miles off, south by west. The road passes through a wild dreary country, extremely uninteresting for several miles. The Teifi flows, at the distance of one mile from the road, through a flat marshy plain, one of the most barren, desolate looking tracts we had ever seen in Wales. We passed Maes Llyn on our right, a small pool preserved by Lord Lisburne: it is said to contain some very large trout. Before reaching it, a plantation bordering the road to our left, in some measure relieved the monotonous character of the scenery, and afforded protection from the fervid rays of the sun, which glared upon us with almost tropical brilliancy. After a short halt at Tregaron, which we have described in the previous chapter, we pursued our route to Llanddewi Brevi, where we arrived about five o'clock in the evening. We had now reached the confines of civilization, and were about to plunge into the wilds—*Cambria Deserta*, as it might properly be styled.

Here we abandoned the turnpike road, and struck across the hills towards Ystrad Ffyn, and the sources of the Towy. On leaving the village, we ascended a precipitous path to some bare elevated table-land, which is literally, not only almost pathless, but, as we were informed, utterly destitute of the semblance of a human habitation for miles. We therefore deemed it prudent to secure the services of a guide, to accompany us across the wildest part of the route. The guide proved to be the village tailor; and he engaged to lead us as far as the confines of the "gorges," where the tributary streams running into the Towy derive their source.

Fancy yourself alone on this trackless waste on a winter's evening, the snow falling thickly upon you, and darkness coming on : how cheering on such a perilous occasion would the distant baying of a shepherd's dog fall on the ear of the wayfarer! A friend of ours was once actually in a similar predicament to the one we have sketched. He had occasion to walk across these wastes on a cold winter's day, from Llandovery to Ystrad Meiric, and narrowly escaped being lost, owing to a violent snow-storm having suddenly arisen whilst on the wildest part of the route. We, however, had no "moving accidents" of this kind to fear. The evening was lovely in the extreme, and at that delightful period of the year when Nature in some degree smiles upon you, even in a desolate wilderness, and which, on the uplands of Wales, adds such an additional charm to the pleasures of a mountain excursion.

Cardiganshire is the "lake country of South Wales;" and nowhere in the Principality is better sport to be met with than in the lakes and rivers which lie amongst the sequestered *cwms* and hills of this portion of the county. After we had proceeded for several miles, we became aware that the path, or sheep-track, for it was little else, had become gradually more and more indistinct, until at last not a vestige of a path was to be seen. We therefore had to rely wholly on the knowledge of our guide, who appeared to thread his way across the country without the least hesitation or difficulty. The locality we were now traversing is one of the most untamed and desolate in either Division of the Principality; it has indeed with perfect truth been called the "great desert of Wales." Vast sweeping ranges of hills with rounded tops, add to the dreary aspect of this nearly unpeopled region; and the cottages or "shielings" you very rarely fall in with, are wretched and primitive in the extreme, scarcely affording shelter to the rude but hardy peasantry from the inclemency of the weather. If human habitations are scarce, churches are few and far between, the parishes being of considerable extent; and it is, we believe, a fact that in some parts the inhabitants have to travel from eight to ten miles to church or chapel.

The portentous stillness that prevailed around was unbroken by the slightest sound; not a living creature was visible, except a few scared sheep, which, unused to the sight of the stranger, scampered off, uttering that peculiar shrill bleat or whistle which *Welsh* sheep always emit when suddenly disturbed. It is the signal of danger amongst them; and it is amusing to observe when the note is sounded by some patriarch of the flock, how they start, and dart away at the top of their speed. Our guide, after proceeding apparently almost at random for several miles, brought us at last to the edge of a hill, at the foot of which we observed a thin blue column of peat smoke proceeding from the rude chimney of a solitary farmhouse; and we at once joyfully hastened to make acquaintance with its interior, for by this time the heat and fatigue we had endured during the day rendered it necessary to obtain, if possible, some refreshment. The exterior of the dwelling was miserable and primitive enough, but quite in keeping with the desolate appearance of the surrounding scenery. Amidst the barking and yelping of curs, that evinced a great desire to be more familiar than agreeable, we entered a dark smoky apartment with a great turf fire blazing on the rude hearth, over which a huge iron cauldron was suspended, the contents of which were to form the evening supper for the family. It consisted of what appeared to be a mess of flour and milk, resembling what is called "furmenty." The farmer rose at our appearance, and, in the language of the country, bade us welcome. He was a tall, hard-featured man, with the true Celtic cast of countenance, clad in a threadbare, blue, homespun coat, corduroy continuations, and dark blue woollen hose—the usual costume of the Welsh peasantry. Our stock of Welsh being limited, we were obliged to have recourse to the "Saxon" dialect, which we found our host understood sufficiently well to comprehend our wants. *Bara a caws*, bread and cheese, *ymenyn*, butter of excellent quality, and some home-brewed *cwrw*, were speedily produced; and the appetizing effect of a long walk through the "incense-breathing" air of the mountains added not a little to the zest of the repast. Our wants being satisfied, we produced a case of cigars, and handing one to the farmer, we were highly amused at his awkward attempts to smoke it; after which we asked him the news of the country. "Deed to goodness," said he, "these be strange times; yes, indeed, we have lately had several 'Rebecca' riots; and it was only this morning that a large party of 'Rebecca's' men had been chased from the vicinity of Llandovery by a troop of dragoons hastily sent for from Brecon. The soldiers did not arrive, however, until one of the toll-gates had been destroyed." We had before heard of the exploits of "Rebecca" and her followers; but we were not aware at the time that the insurrection had extended so far to the eastward. This news, therefore, rather damped our ardour, as a rencontre with a band of these lawless desperadoes would be far from agreeable; and there was every reason to believe, from the farmer's account, that several of these bands were outlying in this neighbourhood. When, therefore, we expressed our intention of proceeding to Llandovery that evening, our host earnestly endeavoured to dissuade us, as several travellers, he said, had recently been attacked, robbed, and in some cases ill-treated. However, we determined to proceed at all hazards; and trusted to get to our quarters at the "Castle Hotel" without molestation. It was also probable that the reports which had reached the farmer's ears might have been much exaggerated.

Before we proceed with our narrative, perhaps it may not be

considered out of place if we give a brief account of "Rebecca" and her proceedings.

THE REBECCA INSURRECTION—as it was called—originated in Caermarthenshire, in 1843, and was at its height in 1844. The rebellion afterwards extended into the neighbouring counties of Pembroke, Cardigan, and Glamorgan; and at one time assumed a rather formidable aspect. At the commencement of these lawless proceedings, the rioters confined themselves to the destruction of toll-gates, but encouraged by the success and impunity which attended their nightly forays, they commenced a series of still graver outrages, including even murder, highway robberies, attacks on private dwellings, incendiarism, and organised attempts on union workhouses. In spite of soldiers, and rewards offered by the authorities for the apprehension of the ringleaders, "Rebecca" continued for many months her lawless career unchecked; the whole rural population of the disturbed districts appeared to be either sworn to secrecy, or connived at the acts of the rioters. Who "Rebecca," the leader, was, has never yet been satisfactorily explained. He has been described as a tall personage, dressed in woman's clothes, generally on horseback, and ever foremost in the fray. It is probable, that latterly there were many leaders, as the conspiracy at length became too extensive to be under the guidance of one chief. St. Clears, near Caermarthen, was at one time what may be termed their headquarters; and almost nightly they assembled to the number of 600 and upwards, nearly all mounted on horseback, and proceeded on their crusade against the toll houses, most of which were in a very short period completely demolished. It was not until one of the Divisions of the Metropolitan police arrived at the scene of war, to assist the troops, that headway was made against the rioters. Several important prisoners were captured, and some of them transported; and from their confessions, many farmers and others, moving in a respectable condition of life, were implicated. There is little doubt that the origin of the insurrection may be traced to a movement amongst the small tenant farmers and others, who felt aggrieved by the excessive tollage levied for the repair of the roads, and which pressed with extreme severity upon the occupiers of small holdings.

Such are the leading features of the celebrated " Rebecca Rebellion," which has been justly termed one of the most "romantic. incidents in modern history." In some of its phases, it was closely allied to the secret and lawless proceedings of " Captain Rock," and the Ribbon Conspiracy, in Ireland, although not attended with such numerous instances of atrocity.

We must now resume the narrative of our subsequent adventures. After partaking of a parting glass with our host, and dispensing with the further services of the guide, we prepare to resume our journey. The evening was exceedingly fine and serene, although from the heat of the day,

"The far-folded mist"

began to envelope the mountain-tops, and as it might possibly descend and spread over the lowlands, we deemed it a matter of precaution to obtain the services of one of the farmer's sons to guide us to the head of the dingle, which we understood led down to the river Towy : once there, there would be no further difficulty in finding our way, as the path runs through the gorge until it reaches the Llandovery road.

After heartily shaking hands with the farmer, and wishing him " *Nos da i chwi*," *Anglicè*, "good night to you," with many thanks for his kindness and hospitality, as we were passing out of the house, one of the sons came to us and made a demand of " one shilling and a half," in Welsh, " *un swllt a chwe cheiniog*," in payment of the bill. The charge was moderate enough, but we felt hurt and surprised at the demand, so contrary to the time-honoured observance of Cambrian hospitality; however, we pocketed the affront without any observation. The name of this solitary habitation is Blaen-Twrch-Uchaf ; it stands in one of the most naked, desolate situations we had ever seen. With the assistance of the farmer's son, we now made tolerable progress across a wild bog, which in winter must be almost impassable. It was nearly eight P. M., and the twilight was rapidly approaching. Our companion, a raw, ignorant lad, was shy and taciturn, partly arising, perhaps, from his entire ignorance of English, and all attempts to draw him into conversation were of course useless. Before our departure, we had foolishly paid his father in advance for his services, and the young rascal, aware of this, after proceeding for about two miles, suddenly left us in the lurch, pointing in "dumb show" with his hand—something after the fashion of the countryman and the fox—the direction we were to take. Although we shouted and hallooed to urge him to return, he was deaf to entreaty, and bounded away with the speed of a roebuck. We were now left in a pretty "fix;" the more so, as the fog was rapidly increasing in density, and began to enfold us in its chilly embrace. There was now no time to be lost, every minute was of consequence, as the increasing gloom would soon prevent any trace of the route from being seen. The moon, we knew, would rise in an hour or two, and, at the worst, we must endure for a time exposure to the raw chilly fog, which increased in density every moment. Thanks, however, to the invigorating effects of the *cwrw*, we felt tolerably fresh, and pushed on at our best pace. After walking for nearly an hour, we at length perceived, to our great delight, the opening of what appeared a woody dingle or gorge, this we were certain must be the one we were in search of. Previously, we had certainly felt rather nervous at the prospect of a night's lodging on the wild hilly waste—a not very enviable position to be placed in. We now hastened on, and soon came to the head of the gorge, and got into a precipitous path leading down it, well clothed with coppice-wood. Presently we heard the rippling of water, at the bottom of the dingle, and we knew we were safe: soon afterwards, the distant barking of a dog assured us we were again in the vicinity of a human dwelling. How cheering is such a sound to the solitary wayfarer! It absolutely revels in his ears like distant music, and dispels in a moment the gloom and depression which had previously come over him. As near as we could guess, we had still six or seven miles to walk before we could reach our destination. The stream we were following, we had reason to believe, was the Dothie, one of the tributaries to the Towy. To the left of us lay Capel Ystrad Ffyn, and we were in the immediate vicinity of "Twm Sion Cattis Cave." The wild country we had left behind is called the "Forest of Esgob," and on referring to a map, it will be seen there is not the name of a place laid down for eight or nine miles. This region, from its name, was probably covered with wood in ancient times.

Soon after we resumed our march, we got clear of the mist; the moon had risen, and by the light of her silvery rays we were now enabled to follow the path with ease and safety. We were much impressed with the magnificent scene before us, and the fragrant odour of the honeysuckle and sweetbriar, covered with bright dewdrops, sweetly perfumed the air, as we leisurely surveyed the exquisitely beautiful glen through which we were silently wandering. Well may the "land of the gorges" be called one of the *gems* of Wales. At length we got into a road, and commenced anew to accelerate our progress. We had proceeded for about two miles, when we suddenly heard what seemed to be the sound of human voices; but a sharp turn in the road prevented us from seeing very far ahead. "Rebecca" now suddenly flashed across our mind, and for an instant we were undecided whether to advance or retreat. With as much self-possession as we could muster, we paused for a short time to deliberate as to the best course to adopt. We were unarmed, but to retreat at that hour of the night appeared simply impossible. Should the sounds proceed from an outlying band of Rebeccaites, it was highly probable we should be stopped; as it was reported they had on several occasions lately, levied "black mail" on such unlucky individuals as had fallen in their way. They had also recently, we had reason to believe, had a skirmish with the soldiery, and it was likely that their "Welsh blood was up." Such and similar ideas flashed across us, and we now fervently wished we had taken the farmer's advice and remained at Blaen-Twrch-Uchaf for the night. We blamed ourselves for undertaking such a rash freak as to walk at night unarmed and alone, whilst the country was in such a disturbed state. However, it was now too late to repent or indulge in vain regrets, and we at length determined to brave the encounter, if to such it came, in the best way we could. Our plan was to walk quietly on until we could, unobserved, reconnoitre the enemy, and then to rush past them at the top of our speed. We had now nearly reached the turn of the road, and halted for a moment to listen again for the sounds that had so lately arrested our attention. We could

hear nothing, however; all appeared as still as death, save the
gentle murmuring of the neighbouring river. As soon as we
had cautiously reached the turn, a scene presented itself which
required all the nerve we could muster, and for a moment had
nearly upset our self-possession. We found ourselves in the
immediate presence of the dreaded "Rebecca." Within less
than twenty paces, at least twenty tall dark-looking figures lay
basking in the moonlight on the road-side, prepared, as we supposed, to dispute the road with every passer-by. We had come
upon these men so silently, that we must have taken them by
surprise as we rushed past with headlong speed. We were
tolerably agile then, and being in good training, we managed to
get over the ground with marvellous celerity. At first we fancied
we heard the sounds of pursuit, but we soon discovered that it
proceeded from an over-excited imagination; and by the time we
had reached the bridge leading over the river, we discovered no
signs of "Rebecca." Here, as well as we can remember, the
mountain road joins the regular turnpike road to Llandovery. To
our great relief, we soon afterwards heard the sound of horses'
feet rapidly approaching, and presently an orderly and two other
mounted dragoons came up. They halted as soon as they perceived us, and we then gave them information of what we had
seen. We found, from their account, that it was quite true there
had been a toll-gate riot on the previous day, and several parties
of Rebeccaites were supposed to be still lurking in the neighbourhood. These men were out on patrol. Having thanked us
for the information we had given, they trotted off towards the
scene of our encounter. What were their subsequent adventures
we never heard. The sequel is soon told. We arrived safely at
our quarters about half-past twelve A.M., mentally resolving hence-
forth to avoid the perils of a lonely walk at night amongst Welsh
wilds, and more particularly, to be careful in avoiding for the
future another interview with "Rebecca."

CHAPTER XVIII.

THE LAKES OF CARDIGANSHIRE—THE TEIFI POOLS—LELAND'S
DESCRIPTION — SPORT ON THE LAKES—LLYN HIR — LLYN
EGNANT — LLYN GORLAN — LLYN GYNON — LLYN GORAST—
LLYNNIAU FYRDDIN VAWR AND VACH—LLYN CRUGNANT—
LLYN DU—LEGENDS.

> " Here the bleak mount,
> The bare bleak mountain speckled thin with sheep ;
> Grey clouds, that shadowing spot the sunny fields ;
> And river, now with bushy rocks o'er-browed,
> Now winding bright and full, with naked banks ;
> * * *   the abbey and the wood,
> And cots and hamlets : God, methought,
> Had built Him here a temple !"—COLERIDGE.

THE lakes of South Wales are chiefly to be found amongst the
desolate mountain wastes of Cardiganshire, and present as wild
an aspect, although destitute of scenic grandeur, as some of
the llyns of North Wales. The county of Cardigan does not
contain any pools of considerable extent; the largest is Llyn
Gynon, which is an extensive sheet of water. The exact number
of lakes in the county we cannot particularize with any degree of
certainty ; but probably they do not exceed five-and-twenty, or at
most, thirty. Of these, the celebrated Teifi group, called "the
Teifi Pools," including Llyn Gynon, claim the pre-eminence, some
of them being the largest in the county.

We have never visited these pools, and must therefore be content to borrow such information as we can collect from oral and
other sources ; but as it has occurred to us that our rambles in
Cardiganshire might appear incomplete without some account of
these lakes, we have in this instance departed from a rule we

Q

have invariably observed—never to describe any portion of the Principality that we have not seen and minutely examined.

The Teifi Lakes.

On the "lofty mountains of Moruge, which in Welsh are called Ellennith," or more correctly, Maelienydd, says *Giraldus*, are a group of five lakes, the largest of which are Llyns Egnant and Teifi.* According to popular belief these pools are unfathomable; at any rate, they are of great depth. Roscoe states that Llyn Teifi is supposed by some authors to rest on the bed of an extinct volcano, "but the stones around bear no marks of volcanic action." These five pools are in such immediate contiguity, that from the summit of a hill above Llyn Teifi you can command a view of all the others. Llyn Gynon, another pool, and the largest on these hills, lies rather more than a mile from the southern extremity of Llyn Egnant. Llyn Teifi is the nearest to Pontrhydvendigaid, and is distant from thence about four miles and a half; Llyn Egnant is nearly six miles.

Leland, in his description of the possessions of the abbey of Strata Florida, which at one period were of immense extent, expressly alludes to the Teifi lakes. He saw them from the mountains above "Strateflere," at a place he calls the "Cragnaulin Stone." He says, "These iiii Pooles be in the Lordship of Pennarth, the chefe towne of this Lordship being in Cardiganshire is Tregaron. But the Abbate of Strateflere hath much landes in the same Lordship, and thes iiii Pooles long to the Abbate of Strateflere." One of the lakes he calls Llinynigin Velin, the "lake of the yellow quaking bog," which we suppose means Llyn Teifi. "There is in it veri good troutes and elys, and no other fishch."

The names of the Teifi group, properly speaking, are Llyn Teifi, Llyn Hir, "the long pool," Llyn Egnant, and two smaller lakes, Llyn Gorlan and Llyn Gron: the latter is said to be destitute of fish. These llyns are partly crown property; Colonel Powell, of Nantcos, and Lord Lisburne, of Crosswood, are the other proprietors. The right of fishing is exercised by the latter,

---

* Moruge is a corruption from moors.

but we believe the lakes are not strictly preserved; and gentlemen staying at the inn at Pontrhydvendigaid may angle there without the necessity of applying for permission. There is, we understand, a boat, or boats, on Llyn Teifi, belonging to Lord Lisburne, but they are not available to anglers.

From their bleak, exposed situation, these pools are subject to violent gusts of wind, which at times lash their waters with considerable fury. The Teifi lakes are situate on some of the most elevated ground in the county; and the country on every side, for a considerable distance, is desolate in the extreme. The lofty summits of Cader Idris and Plinlumon may be seen to the north, and there is a fine view of the sea-coast stretching away to the west and south, with Cardigan and its bay looming in the distance. Altogether, the panoramic view from these naked, lofty uplands is grand and imposing.

The sport on these lakes is very uncertain; sometimes you may visit the whole of them in succession without moving a fish. They are not *early* lakes; the best month to fish them is, we believe, July. Llyn Teifi is said to contain the largest trout; but unless the weather is lowering, accompanied with a very strong breeze, little is to be done. The trout are described to be "sometimes free;" but several friends of ours who have visited this lake have found it otherwise. Captain Medwin says, that with the exception of killing two small fish in Llyn Egnant, he could not obtain even "a rise" on any of these pools. Possibly the weather was unpropitious, although he had plenty of breeze. Such anglers as can safely manage a *coracle* would find it of great advantage in fishing these lakes, as the larger trout generally lie away from the shore. The fish in the Teifi pools, from the dark, peaty water they inhabit, are of a disagreeable colour, and, early in the season, are generally thin, lanky, and in very poor condition; not to be compared to their congeners in many of the Caernarvonshire and Merionethshire lakes. Possibly a lack of food is the cause of this, as is the case in other mountain lakes where the bottom is stony and free from grass or weeds. Some of these lakes are, however, full of weeds. The insect tribe are also later in making their appearance on water lying on cold, high, exposed situations.

LLYN HIR, which lies nearly two furlongs to the north-east of

Llyn Teifi—from which it is divided by a narrow ridge—is a long narrow pool, as its name implies, and is nearly half a mile in length, in a direction north and south. It is hardly a furlong broad in the widest part. The trout are described as "large, but rather shy." To obtain sport, it must blow hard: large, dark flies, with tinsel on the bodies, are most successful here.

LLYN EGNANT is the largest of this group. It lies one furlong due east from Llyn Hir, and is connected with the latter by a small brook. The north part of the lake is the broadest, about one furlong and a half. The southern portion is very narrow, and connected with the broader part by a very narrow channel, scarcely a quarter of a furlong in width. Its extreme length from north to south is nearly half a mile. At its southern extremity a small brook issues from it, which, after flowing through Nant Egnant for about two miles and a half, joins the Teifi, one mile above Strata Florida Abbey. Llyn Egnant is described as "an excellent lake;" the fish are generally "free," and although there *are* large trout, the average size is much smaller than in the lakes previously described.

LLYN GORLAN, a very small pool, nearly half a furlong to the south of Llyn Hir, and a short distance due west of Llyn Egnant, contains some very large trout, which are, however, *extremely shy*. A small stream issues from its southern extremity, and after flowing about three-quarters of a mile, empties itself into the Egnant brook. This pool is two furlongs in length, but very narrow; in shape it resembles Llyn Hir. LLYN GRON is the smallest of these five lakes, and lies about half a furlong from the south end of Egnant, which is connected with it by a very small streamlet from the former. This lake is said to be entirely destitute of fish, which is surprising, as you would suppose that Llyn Egnant, which swarms with trout, would supply it. It is probable that its waters are impregnated with some poisonous mineral.

LLYN GYNON.—This fine sheet of water is about three miles in circumference, and its extreme breadth is fully three furlongs. Four or five brooks empty themselves into this lake, and a rather large stream issues from it at the north-east corner, and flows in an easterly direction. The distance to Llyn

Gynon — pronounced   Gunnon — from   Pontrhydvendigaid, *via*
Strata Florida, is about five or five and a half miles to the east.
After leaving the abbey, you follow for a short way the road to
the Teifi pools, you then turn up Nant Egnant, and follow the road
for a mile; on leaving the valley, you turn up a road to the right.
You can here cross the moorlands in a south-easterly direction—
this course will bring you to the lake—or you can proceed by the
road, which rather lengthens the distance.   The road runs within
a furlong to the south of the pool.

Llyn Gynon is said to swarm with trout, some of which are
large, but the average size is small, especially near the shore; a
boat here is essential, as it would enable you to throw over the
larger fish.   The trout are very "free," as small fish usually are,
and are reported of excellent quality.

There is a very small tarn, lying about one mile to the south
of Gynon, called LLYN GORAST.   We have been informed that the
trout here are *very large*, and of fine quality, but *shy*.   This pool
is, we believe, preserved.

LLYNNIAU FYRDDIN VAWR AND VACH.—The former of these
lakes is of some extent, at least three miles in circumference.
Its length from north to south is nearly half a mile, but it is
narrow in proportion, being scarcely one furlong and a half wide.
Its sister lake lies a short distance to the south-west, and is connected with it by a small stream.   These lakes lie farther from
Pontrhydvendigaid than the others we have enumerated.   The
road to them is the same as for Llyn Teifi.   You must then cross
the trackless moors in a north-easterly direction, until you arrive
at the smaller lake.   The distance is about one mile and a half.
The fish are reported "*very free*," but small.

We have now enumerated all, or nearly all, of the pools belonging to the "Teifi group."

Llyn Berwyn, which lies about six miles, as the "crow flies,"
from Gynon, we have minutely described in chapter xvi.   There
are two other small llyns, about three miles to the south of Strata
Florida, Llyn Crugnant and Llyn Dù.   Of these we can afford no
reliable information; the former, we have heard, sometimes gives
good sport, but these pools are scarcely larger than Llyn Gron.

The hills surrounding these lakes are clothed with heather,

which affords shelter to grouse, plover, and snipe. The sportsman, however, will find little or no shelter on the hills of Cardigan, and they are perhaps the most scantily populated of any portion of Wales. We are not aware that even a shepherd's hut is within miles of one of these lakes, and to provide against the effects of wet, stormy weather, waterproof garments are absolutely essential; without which you may often "come to grief," as the rain in Wales, when it drives along from the sea over these desolate uplands, comes down in a deluge, and, aided by the fury of the wind, will find its way through almost any kind of macintosh, unless you can manage to keep yourself well wrapped up.

Although we have endeavoured to describe as accurately as we can the position and bearings of all these lakes, it must be obvious that the angler, if he is a stranger to the locality, unless he carries with him a pocket-compass and the Ordnance map, will find the services of a guide exceedingly useful. Some years ago, there were one or two excellent guides and fishermen resident at Pontrhydvendigaid, who were well acquainted with the neighbouring lakes, and the proper flies to use on them; no doubt they, or others, are still to be met with. During a sojourn at Tregaron, a few years since, we met with a man named Williams, formerly gamekeeper to Colonel Powell of Nanteos, who was not only a good fisherman, but made most excellent flies; and to this man we were indebted for the sport we enjoyed there. He was also well acquainted, not only with the Cardigan lakes, but also with those in Montgomeryshire. To obtain sport in Wales, you must look out for a good local fisherman, who can give accurate information as to the flies suitable for the district you purpose to visit; without taking this step, you will obtain little or no success. In almost every locality different flies, both in size and colour, are required; and Welsh trout, like their English congeners, require their appetites to be *tickled*. This applies more particularly to the lake than the stream.

LEGENDS.—There are several curious traditions in Wales, relative to the existence of ruined cities lying beneath the waters of some of the lakes. Thus it is affirmed that the ancient "City of Tregaron" lies buried, or rather ingulfed, in the waters of a small lake—Llyn Cringlas—in the neighbourhood of Pontrhydvendigaid.

The ancient Roman station of Loventium, it is affirmed by some credulous writers, exists under the waters of Llyn Savaddon, commonly called Llangorse Pool, in Brecknockshire. This assertion, however, rests upon a legend possessing no substantial foundation. It is generally supposed by the best authorities, that Llanio Isau, near the banks of the Teifi, in Cardiganshire, is the Roman Loventium. We refer those of our readers who may wish for further information on this subject, to the late Sir S. R. Meyrick's "History of Cardiganshire," a work replete with erudite information upon the antiquities of the county. At Bala, also, there is a similar legend. It is affirmed by some old chronicler, that beneath the waters of Llyn Tegid a ruined city of considerable extent exists, and that it was swallowed up in a single night by a miraculous visitation, through the wickedness of one of its rulers. There is not, however, any reason to believe that a Welsh Sodom or Gomorrah exists under the waters of any lake in the Principality.

CHAPTER XIX.

> " If thou art worn and hard beset
> With sorrows that thou wouldst forget—
> If thou wouldst read a lesson that will keep
> Thy heart from fainting and thy soul from sleep—
> Go to the LAKES and HILLS !   No tears
> Dim the sweet look that Nature wears."

Bala.

THE situation of Bala is pleasing and picturesque ; one of those charming localities, which are nowhere in Wales altogether so attractive to the admirer of Nature, as in the county of Merioneth. Surrounded by lofty mountains which tower into the clouds on both sides of the vale, and lying near the shore of the largest, and, in some of its features, the most beautiful lake in Wales, it is not surprising that this pleasant little town is such a favourite resort during the summer months.

Bala has become an excellent angling station within the last few years, and so numerous are the votaries of the rod during the summer and autumn, that it is frequently difficult to procure accommodation.   There are two excellent old-fashioned but comfortable inns here, the " White Lion," and " Bull's Head."   We can speak favourably of the former from personal experience, and we have always met with every comfort and attention.   There are several lodging-houses in the town.   Bala signifies " the Outlet of the Lake " — an appropriate designation, as the celebrated river Dee, famed for its picturesque beauty—its salmon and trout fishing—runs out from the north-east extremity of the lake, about three-quarters of a mile from the town.

Many charming excursions can be made in this romantic locality; and the angler, especially if he is conversant with the neighbourhood, need be at no loss for sport in the various streams and lakes, especially if he comes *early* in the season. There is excellent lake and river fishing, as it were, on the spot; and if he can "rough" it, and bear the fatigue of a long day's ramble amongst the wild mountain solitudes around, we can promise to lead him where he will find some exciting sport.

Bala is a place of considerable antiquity, and, from the traces that remain, was probably a Roman station. Close to the town, on the south-east, is an artificial mound called Tomen-y-Bala, which is supposed to have been a Roman earthwork. There are also several other fortified camps in the vicinity, believed to be of Roman origin. The chief attractions here to visitors, however, are the Dee and the lake. Several ancient Roman roads passed near the town, amongst others, one from Uriconium—Wroxeter, near Shrewsbury, which is now creating such an interest in the antiquarian world, from the recent excavations made, and which are still going on. This buried Roman city has been appropriately styled the "English Pompeii."

We have previously, in chapter III., given a general enumeration of the lakes in Merionethshire: many of them we have visited, some we have minutely described. We have now, therefore, to particularise such only as belong to the Bala district, all of which, except Llyn Tegid, not only lie at some distance off, but are difficult to reach, from the altitude of their situations and the rough country to be traversed. Of these llyns, first in size and importance is

Llyn Tegid,

or Pimblemere, better known as Bala Pool. This lake is of considerable extent, and by far the largest in the Principality. Its extreme length is three miles five furlongs; its greatest breadth is opposite Llan-y-cil, on the north-west shore near the lower extremity, where it exceeds half a mile. Its average width throughout its entire length is about half a mile, except at a point of land jutting into the lake opposite Gwern Hefin, where it becomes much narrower for a short distance. Llyn Tegid lies in a direction from north-east to south-west, and is comparatively narrow according to its length. In some parts it is of great depth, particularly opposite Bryn Goleu, where it is said to be twenty-three fathoms, or 138 feet, with several yards of mud. There are, however, at least two lakes in Wales, Llyn Peris and Llyn Cwellyn, the known depth of which far exceeds this; and there are probably others. During the summer, Llyn Tegid generally wears a smiling, placid aspect; but in the winter the lake is subject to furious gales of wind, which create a tremendous swell, and frequently, accompanied with rain, raise the lake considerably above its ordinary level. On such occasions, its waters being driven along with the impetuosity of the wind, it overflows its boundaries, and sometimes causes considerable damage in the vale below. It is seldom or never entirely frozen over, even in the severest winters, probably owing to the presence of springs.

Sixty years ago, Llyn Tegid was considered the finest lake in Wales for trout; but the late Sir Watkin W. Wynn, of Wynnstay, from some whim or other, introduced pike, which, of course, speedily destroyed the trout; and for many years few, if any, were caught, except those of large size. When we were at Bala, a few years ago, we were informed that, from some cause, not known, the pike had considerably decreased, and trout were becoming more abundant. If this continues, Bala Pool may, in the course of time, again afford good trout-fishing. Trout of six or eight pounds are occasionally caught by trolling tackle, and we saw a stuffed specimen of one of at least six pounds weight in the window of Mr. Jones' shop, in Bala. Large trout are sometimes taken with the artificial fly, but of course rarely. The lake contains several other species of fish, especially perch, which are exceedingly plentiful. There is also an Alpine fish called Gwynniad, remarkable for the whiteness of its scales, hence its Welsh name. We are not aware that these fish exist in any other Welsh lake. There are not any char, as far as we are aware, which is surprising, as they are generally found in all very deep waters. Capital perch-fishing is sometimes obtained from a boat, either with worm or by trolling; by the latter method, large trout are occasionally captured. Sir Watkin W. Wynn liberally allows anglers free permission to fish in all parts of the lake, but the use of the net is reserved.

During the season a great many anglers amuse themselves on the lake, perch-fishing, and frequently obtain excellent sport. The average size of these fish is from a quarter to half a pound. Shore-fishing is not much pursued, the banks of the pool being in many places fringed with wood; and besides, in a large llyn like this, it is impossible for the stranger to find out the haunts of the fish. In all lakes, trout swim in shoals; and when your boat drifts over one of these, you are almost certain, for a short time, if the fish are feeding, to have numerous "rises." This circumstance accounts for that irregularity in the "rise" which occurs even on the most favourable day.

The pike in Bala Pool attain to a great size; and, some years ago, many noble fish were captured. Eels and roach also abound. Sir Watkin W. Wynn has a very neat fishing box, called Glan Llyn, on the west shore of the lake, for the accommodation of his friends; it is about two miles from Bala.

Previous to the Reformation, the exclusive right of fishing in this lake belonged to the Abbey of Basingwerk, in Flintshire. Afterwards it came into the possession of the Wynn family.

The scenery around Llyn Tegid is very lovely; the western shore, for nearly the whole of its extent, is adorned with wood; and on a fine summer's day the lake is frequently without a ripple on its surface. The view of the Arans, especially Aran Benllyn, which towers majestically to the south, and from whence the Dee has its source, and the highest peak of Cader Idris appearing in the extreme distance, forms one of the finest mountain vistas in the Principality. Perhaps the best view of the lake and the scenery generally is from the road leading to Mallwyd, on the eastern shore; but on all sides this beautiful sheet of water is captivating in the extreme.

> " Lake Leman woos me with its crystal face,
> The mirror where the stars and mountains view
> The stillness of their aspect in each trace
> Its clear depth yields of their far height and hue."—BYRON.

Llyn Arenig Vawr.

Under the steeps of the lofty Arenig Vawr, which looms up in majestic grandeur to the left, as you proceed on the road from Bala to Ffestiniog, lies a fine pool, called Llyn Arenig Vawr. It is at least half a mile in length, by nearly the same distance in breadth; of an oval form, and of immense depth. This lake contains some very large trout, many of them from three to six pounds weight; but they are amongst the *most shy*, wary fish in the Principality. Nothing can be done on the lake, during the spring and summer, with the artificial fly, but in autumn, previous to the spawning season, some heavy fish are occasionally caught, especially by those anglers who are acquainted with the lake. These trout are said to be exceedingly strong, and fight well when on the hook. It is singular they are so shy during the other seasons of the year; but we have been informed, by a good local authority, that it is supposed to arise from the abundance of tiny fish, probably minnows, which are to be found in the lake, and which these trout are supposed to feed upon. It is certain that where there is abundance of small bait, large trout seldom rise well at the fly.

Our first view of Llyn Arenig was near the close of one of those lovely summer evenings, the brightness of which casts such a charm even over the wildest and most desolate mountain solitudes. The day had been exceedingly hot, hotter, in fact, than we had ever before experienced amongst the mountains of Wales. After skirting the north-east shoulder of the stupendous mountain above, we suddenly came in sight of the lake, which appeared to our vision—probably owing to the peculiarly rarified state of the atmosphere—of more than twice the magnitude that it really is. Not a breath of air disturbed its surface; there lay its blue pellucid waters in calmness and repose, reflecting with the accuracy of the photograph the savage crags and deep hollows of the sublime mountain above, the outlines of which were as crisp and defined, from the perfect absence of cloud or vapour, as imagination can conceive. It was, indeed, a magnificent picture, and one we have often since remembered with feelings of delight.

Not a whisper disturbed the intense stillness and solitude of this
mountain retreat, nor was there a living creature to be seen.
The untamed majesty of nature, in all its wildness and beauty,
was here depicted with startling effect.

> "Who hath not felt the softness of the hour
>   Sink on the heart, as dew along the flower?
> Who hath not shared that calm, so still and deep,
>   The voiceless thought, that would not wake but weep?"

Arenig Vawr

is one of the loftiest mountains in Wales; grand and sublime in
appearance. Its height, according to the Ordnance survey, is
2,809 feet; about 105 feet lower than Cader Idris. A visit to
the summit would form a most delightful excursion from Bala.

ROUTE TO THE LAKE.—There is a wild, rough mountain road
between Bala and Pont Rhyd-y-Fen, on the Ffestiniog road,
which passes within half a mile of the pool. Leave the road at
Bryn Evan, cross a turbary, and proceed over a ridge called Garth,
on the far side of which lies the lake; the distance from Bala is
about six miles and a half. Before you reach the foot of the
ridge you cross a small brook, the Derfil, which flows through
Aber Derfil in its course to the river Tryweryn. This brook has
its source near one of the eastern arms of the Arenig; a small
feeder, which issues from the south-east side of the lake, joins it
after flowing a short distance to the south-east.

There is another stream which runs from the north-east corner
of the pool into the Tryweryn, through Nant-y-Llyn—"the vale
of the lake"—its length is about a mile due north. This description is sufficiently minute to enable the pedestrian to find his
way *without* a guide. If he has the Ordnance map in his pocket,
not the smallest difficulty can occur.

Llyn Arenig Vach

is a wild secluded pool, on elevated ground, lying under the precipices of Arenig Vach, to the right of the road leading to
Ffestiniog. On leaving Bala, you proceed along the road which

runs near the banks of the Tryweryn for the entire distance, about six miles. This river is a rapid, rocky mountain torrent flowing from a small llyn of that name in a solitary mountain district near the vicinity of Castell Prysor and Trawsfynydd. Here you leave the road after crossing Pont-Ar-Gelyn, and strike up the lower ranges of Arenig Vach in a north-west direction. After a stiff walk of about one mile and a half, you are at length rewarded with a view of the lake, which presents a more dreary, solemn aspect than the sister pool. Nevertheless, from the hollow it lies in, being encompassed by hills on both sides, it has a romantic appearance. Its extreme length from north to south does not much exceed two furlongs and a half. At the southern extremity it is about one furlong and a half broad, but it gradually gets narrower towards the north, which gives it a triangular form. At its extreme or lower end its waters are dammed up by an artificial embankment, and a small brook runs from the lake which joins the Gelyn about a mile off. The Gelyn rises in a wild, desolate mountain range called Bryn Cerbyd, a few miles to the southeast of Yspytty Evan.

On the east shore, the walking is tolerably easy for the entire length of the lake, but on the west side the shore is for the most part rocky and precipitous, and in some places it is impossible to approach the pool, as the water washes the bases of the perpendicular rocks which lie above it. The distance from Bala to this lake is at least eight miles. Llyn Arenig Vach contains some fine trout, which are sometimes tolerably "free" when there is a good breeze, and excellent sport is to be had. Some trout of four pounds weight have been taken here with the fly. Williams, the guide and fisherman at Tregaron, informed us that he had several times caught here some very large trout, which afforded splendid sport; they were very strong, and difficult to kill.

We once made an excursion from Bala to this llyn, during some very hot, bright weather in June. We followed the route previously indicated, and were disappointed to find on our arrival at the pool, that it was a dead calm; not a breath of wind ruffled its surface. Of course, angling was out of the question, at least with any prospect of success. Nevertheless, we made a few "casts" as we proceeded along the east shore, and saw some very

large fish lazily rolling about near the surface, apparently on the
feed. During "a cat's paw" of wind, we at length succeeded in
rising a noble trout of at least three pounds; but he rose so
"fine," that, to our extreme mortification, after holding him on
for nearly a minute, the hook broke from its hold, and away went
our fish. We are satisfied, with a good breeze, we should have
had some exciting sport. The lake is situate in a hollow, and so
sheltered from the wind in every quarter except the north, that
it is very often quite calm in the summer.

After trying in vain for upwards of two hours, we made a circuit of the lake, and proceeded from the upper end towards the
Ffestiniog road, distant about a mile and a half. After descending
from these uplands into the road, we wended our way to a solitary
public house, and were really glad to get under shelter, as the
rays of the sun were quite overpowering in the vale. The name
of this place is Rhyd-y-Fen; it is about seven miles from Bala.
The distance between Bala and Ffestiniog is nineteen miles, over
one of the most wild and lonely roads we ever traversed; not a
house or a human being to be met with for miles. Upon one
occasion, during the exceedingly dry summer of 1844, whilst
travelling on foot through these wilds, we had some difficulty to
procure even a cup of water, as nearly all the mountain rills and
springs were dried up, and it was not until we arrived at Rhyd-
y-Fen that we could procure any refreshment whatever. As far as
we can recollect, this is the only tavern to be met with throughout
the entire distance. The *cwrw* here is excellent, almost equal to
any we have ever met with in the by-ways of Wales.

We afterwards proceeded to visit Llyn Arenig Vawr, crossing
a wet spongy morass, intersected by a small brook, with no little
difficulty, as several drains in the turbary were wide and deep.
We were afterwards entangled for some time among the rocks
and boulders, which strew the sides and bottom of the mountain,
and from the roughness of the way it was very fatiguing. We
have previously described this lake. The distance between these
pools is probably about two miles and a half by "crow flight;"
but if you take Rhyd-y-Fen in your way, it is at least a mile and
a half more. These lakes are seldom visited by anglers; they lie
at too great a distance from Bala; but, notwithstanding, we

strongly recommend an excursion to the lesser pool. You must choose a day when there is a brisk wind, and not too bright. Mr. Jones, saddler, of Bala, who is very obliging, and an experienced fisherman, will, if you require it, procure you a guide, and give you every information. His flies are very neatly tied, equal, if not superior, to any we have met with elsewhere in Wales. It is no use to attempt to fish these lakes without being supplied with a stock of flies suitable for the water.

The Dee.

> " We wind the zigzag path, and pause to hear
> The river's deepening echoes—oh ! how clear,
> How lovely, in the morn's white light appear
> Those tufted rocks, those crags, whose shadows wear
> Magic varieties."

" Deva's wizard stream " is one of the most picturesque and beautiful of Welsh rivers. Its name is said to be derived from a Welsh word—Dwfr Dwy—which signifies " the water of two rivers." A sister stream—the Twrch—joins the Dee about half a mile before it enters into Llyn Tegid, in the flat, marshy meadow lands, which might with propriety be called the *delta* of the river, and which in winter are sometimes under water. The sources of the Dee are about two miles to the west of the summit of Aran Benllyn, near the left of the road leading to Dolgelley, and consist of two small brooks, which, springing from a lower range of the mountain, called y-Gorls-Wyd, unite together, and form the river called Dwfr Dwy, hence the name. These brooks rise about nine miles from Bala.

The Twrch, a considerable stream, also consists of two branches, one of which rises near the head of Cwm Croes; the main branch springs in Cwm Cwnllwd, a lonely recess in one of the spurs of the mighty Aran Mowddwy, and flows for some distance near the road leading through Bwlch-y-Groes, "the Pass of the Cross." This pass was formerly so dangerous as to be a terror to travellers. A cross was erected at the head of the pass, in order that the pious might offer up their thanksgivings at its foot for safe deliverance from the dangers of the way. The waters of all these rivers, unless swollen by rain, are beautifully clear and pellucid, so much so, that one of the old chroniclers, *Giraldus Cambrensis,* gravely informs us, in his "Itinerary of Wales," that the course of the Dee might be traced through Bala Lake for the whole of its course. We need hardly add, that this assertion is entirely fabulous. The fact is, the water in Llyn Tegid is mainly derived from the Dee and its tributaries, so that its water is equally as clear as the river. Our jaunty heroine, after its confluence with the lake, passes from it under a stone bridge at the north-east lower extremity, about half a mile from Bala, and flows in a rather rapid silvery stream through the "sweet vale of Edeirnion," on its course to Corwen and Llangollen. Along its entire course to these towns, its banks present on either side, a succession of varied and most enchanting scenery; the stream is embowered in some parts with trees and coppice, which, although it adds greatly to its adornment and beauty, interferes with the free use of the rod; and to fish the river properly, an India-rubber boat or coracle is absolutely indispensable to such anglers as can safely use them.

Trout fishing in the Dee, under judicious conservation, has much improved of late years; and in spring, during the month of April, when the river is in good order, capital sport is obtained by such anglers as know the river well. Salmon abound also at the proper season.

The Dee, in its course to Chester, receives several tributaries, amongst the most important of which are the Alwen, flowing from a Llyn of that name in Denbighshire, the Ceiriog, the Clywedog, and the Alyn: the latter rises in the mountains near Llandegla.

The Tryweryn joins the Dee about three-quarters of a mile from Bala; this river is full of small trout, which in the spring and summer are a source of profit to the local fishermen. The length of the Tryweryn is about twelve miles; it flows out of

Llyn Tryweryn,

a small pool, the north shore of which is bounded by the solitary road leading to Castell Prysor and Trawsfynydd. This road

branches to the right, out of the Ffestiniog turnpike-road, near
Pont Rhyd-y-Fen. The river, soon after it leaves the lake, is
joined by several small streams, the chief of which rises in the
hills to the north-west, and at Pont Rhyd-y-Fen its size is considerably augmented.

Llyn Tryweryn—" the transparent lake "—is of small dimensions; it scarcely exceeds three furlongs in length, and lies in a
direction from north-west to south-east. In breadth, it is hardly
one furlong and a half in its broadest part. It is full of small
trout, which sometimes rise freely; but they have not a very inviting appearance, being dark coloured; and those we have caught
were in poor condition. This lake, therefore, does not hold out
any very great attraction to the angler. The pool can hardly be
said to belong to the Bala district, as its distance from that town
—twelve or thirteen miles—is rather too far to tempt even the
most ardent fisherman. The chief pleasure to be derived from a
visit to some of these sequestered tarns, is the love of wild adventure, and a desire to explore the hidden works of Nature; in
short, to make acquaintance with its scenic attractions, which
often present to the eye of the inquirer features the most sublime
and romantic; and there is a charm, an excitement, in the pursuit
of novel scenery, to feast the eye, to expand the taste, and to
elevate the mind.

There are several other lakes in this vicinity, chiefly the property
of Sir W. W. Wynn; they are, we believe, preserved, but none
of them afford good sport: in one or two perch are to be found.
All these pools properly belong to the Trawsfynydd district, in
the neighbourhood of which they lie.

In thus concluding this brief and imperfect sketch of Bala, its
lakes and rivers, we bring our Wanderings to a close.

Those who travel through Wales in search of health, or for the
enjoyment of fine scenery, will find throughout the country, not
only very comfortable accommodation at most of the respectable
inns and hotels, but into the bargain, the greatest attention and
civility. Anglers, in pursuit of sport, can generally make themselves "at home" in any wild sequestered nook. The sportsman
may fearlessly roam at all hours, amongst the wildest mountain
retreats, the most secluded lakes and streams, without molesta-

tion or interruption; and we have frequently met with genuine hospitality and kindness, when in "out of the world" places, from the humblest peasants.

To such as delight to inhale pure invigorating mountain air, or "to revel in the varied delights that are to be found in the wild and wonderful of Nature," who feel a pleasurable excitement of mind and body, as they trace the flashing stream to its source in a wild hill solitude, or view the sun rise from the summit of some lofty mountain, we strongly recommend—if leisure permits—an exploration of the "treasures of Cambria." Some of these scenes we have endeavoured, perhaps faintly, but at least truthfully, to depict; and may the votaries of the "gentle arte" derive as much pleasure and gratification as we have experienced, amongst the hills and dales of Wales.

APPENDIX.

The Angler's Entomology.

ARTIFICIAL FLIES.—In some of the previous chapters of this work, we have pointed out a few of the flies that we have found most successful on the Welsh lakes; but as the best lake fishing occurs in June and part of July, the flies mentioned are chiefly useful during those months *only*. It may therefore be useful to anglers in Wales, if we furnish a more complete list of both lake and river flies for every month during the season, from March to the end of August.

FLIES FOR MARCH.—As we have already remarked, many of the Welsh rivers are early, and the angler will, on some of them, have the best sport during this month, if the water is suitable. The most successful fly we have ever used during March, is the Cob Fly, as it is termed in Wales; but better known as the March Brown. During the flights of this fly on some of the rivers—we may especially instance the Usk and the Teifi—the trout seize upon this insect with great avidity, and during its continuance on the water, it is perfectly useless to fish with any other fly. The great Red Spinner, called also the light Mackerel, is also an excellent fly; and with these two flies, weather and water suitable, first rate sport may be obtained. The Cow Dung fly is chiefly serviceable during windy weather. We have used it on the lakes in May and June, during a gale, accompanied with rain, and often with success. This fly may occasionally be observed on the water throughout the season, particularly during rough weather. The Red Spinner, which is the Blue Dun, after it has cast its coat, is a good general fly for the river, either in March, or later in the

season. The Blue Dun is an excellent fly, especially during March
and April. With a good stock of these flies, the requirements of
the angler will be amply provided for during this month.

FLIES FOR APRIL.—This month, if mild, and free from frosty
nights, is one of the best months for river fishing in the year. In
most rivers, trout rise well during the whole of this month, and
many of the flies that appear on the water may be successfully
used in May. One of these, the Sand fly, is a good general stream
fly from April to September. In May it is the best fly you can
use on the Teifi, indeed, it is absolutely *indispensable* to ensure
success. The Stone fly, Yellow Dun, Iron Blue Dun, and Haw-
thorn fly, complete our list for April.

FLIES FOR MAY.—River fishing for trout during this month,
may virtually be said to be nearly over in Wales. If the weather
is fine and dry, which is frequently the case, especially from the
middle to the end of the month, the rivers and brooks become low
and clear; and as the trees at this season have put on their summer
livery, trout fishing with the artificial fly becomes an unprofitable
pursuit. We must leave it to naturalists to account for the fact
of trout ceasing to rise when the leaves are out; the only reason
we can assign is, that it may probably arise from the fish preferring to prey on the larvæ of the insect tribe, which lie at the
bottom of the water, and which only spring into life when they
reach the surface. Of course these remarks apply only to large
trout; "tittlebats" will at times rise freely throughout the whole
of the summer. We shall now indicate a few flies, some of which
will be found equally useful on the lake or stream. The Oak fly,
Black Gnat, Yellow Sally—useless on a lake—Alder fly, one of
the most killing flies on a lake we ever tried in May or June—
the Fern fly, Sky Blue, and Little Dark Spinner, should also be
found in the angler's book.

FLIES FOR JUNE.—This is the very best month in the year for
the lakes, if not too hot and bright. The angler may discard the
whole of the Drake tribe from his collection. They are alike
useless for the river or lake in Wales, as far as our experience
goes. One of the most successful flies during this month, especially during a moderately calm, warm, sunny day, is the Coch-a-
Bonddu, called in England the Marlow Buzz, or Shorn fly. Indeed,

with this and the Alder fly, we have killed more good trout on the lakes during June, than with almost any other fly. The dark Mackerel is also a capital fly, especially on Llyn Cwellyn. There are several other flies which we have found very successful in June on the Caernarvonshire lakes. These are what are locally called the Peahen, the Pale-yellow Dun, the March Brown, with pale-yellow silk body—excellent during rain—the Cinnamon, the Governor—John Shaw, of Shrewsbury, makes a capital fly of this name—and the Wrentail. The angler, however, on his arrival at a Fishing Station, will do well to consult a local fisherman, who will always be able to afford a "wrinkle" or two, as well as supply him with flies adapted for the locality.

FLIES FOR JULY.—Several of the flies previously enumerated, · we have found equally good during the present month, particularly the Peahen, dark Mackerel, Wrentail, and Coch-a-Bonddu. The Silver-horns is well spoken of by some anglers; but we never tried it. The Red Ant and July Dun we have occasionally used. Avoid all the Palmer species, which we never found of much account on the lakes. These flies, so much in vogue with anglers on English rivers, do not seem to suit the palates of Welsh trout.

FLIES FOR AUGUST.—Lake fishing in Wales we consider to be nearly over by the end of July. You may now and then have tolerably good sport on some of the pools—especially Llyn Cwellyn; but, as a general rule, angling in most of the lakes is an unprofitable pursuit. On some of the best lakes in Merioneth-shire, you will hardly be able to stir a fish during this month. We need hardly specify any flies. On Llyn Cwellyn, we have found the dark Mackerel and the Peahen the most successful flies, especially the former. The August Dun, Cinnamon, and Grouse Hackle, with bright orange body, are perhaps amongst the best flies.

FISHING TACKLE.—It is perhaps necessary to observe, that although you may procure good flies, you seldom or never meet with good gut in Wales. The angler therefore will act wisely to take with him a hank or two of the best London gut, round, but not too thick, as the finer the tackle employed, the better is the chance of sport. A supply of fish-hooks is also a *desideratum*, as the hooks in Wales are frequently very indifferent. There are several sorts of hooks, but, on the whole, we prefer the " Kirby bend" to any other. Numbers 9 to 12 are the best sizes. Generally speaking, small flies on number 11 hooks kill the most fish : of course, the Alder fly, the Peahen, and some others, require larger ones. As the water on some of the lakes is of a dark peaty colour, it is desirable to stain your gut, to assimilate it to the colour of the water. This can be accomplished by infusing it in some strong coffee, which gives it the requisite hue. Some use a weak solution of copperas, but coffee is far preferable. With these precautions, you can have your flies tied—if you are not a proficient in the art—by some experienced local fly-dresser; and at several of the angling stations, Beddgelert, Bala, Dolgelley, and other places, there are professed artificial fly-dressers, who tie flies extremely well. A line of silk and hair mixed, not too fine, about thirty-five yards long, some "gut-bottoms," and a skein or two of orange-coloured silk, will nearly complete the angler's wants. Be careful, on your return home from fishing, to unwind your line from the winch round the back of a chair, and thoroughly dry it before you wind it on again. If you leave the line wet on the winch, it is soon apt to get rotten, and frequently leads to disappointment and annoyance. In pp. 116, 117, and 118, *ante,* the reader will find some instructions as to lake fishing, choice of rods, &c., and other essential particulars.

𝔑otes.

NOTE 1, *page* 20.—(PRESERVATION OF THE DYFI.)—Since the first sheets of this work passed through the hands of the printer, we have received a communication from an esteemed friend in North Wales, relative to the " Dyfi Angling Club," and the prospects of the incoming season.   We are informed that the Dyfi fishing is now better preserved than ever ; a "strong aristocratic club having been formed," withnew and revised rules.

Last year (1859) was a very bad fishing season on the Dyfi, and on all the rivers in Wales, owing to the long *drought.*   The lake fishing was also very indifferent ; at Tal-y-Llyn there was bad sport throughout the summer.'   This year, from present appearances, there is every prospect of a successful season, both for salmon and trout.

Anglers will be glad to learn that a railway, now in course of construction between Oswestry, Shrewsbury, and Newtown, Montgomeryshire, will be open for traffic next autumn ; which will bring the rail to within thirty miles of Machynlleth.

NOTE 2, *page* 201.—(CORACLES.)—These primitive boats, which are doubtless ;as old as the time of the ancient Britons, are only to be met with, as far as we know, on the rivers in Wales.   They are common on the Wye, the Usk, the Teifi, and the Dyfi ; and are employed by the native fishermen either for the purposes of netting salmon or angling for trout or grayling.   The word *coracle,* or coriacle, is derived from the Latin word *coria,* a skin ; and from this, it has been conjectured that the Britons were indebted to their Roman conquerors for the introduction of the *coracle.*   Be this as it may, there can be no doubt of the high antiquity of these boats.   The coracle is about four feet wide, and two feet in depth : the framework is constructed of wicker-work, which is generally covered with a skin, well tarred and pitched ; but some we have seen were covered with stout canvas, of course well anointed with the same materials, and rendered perfectly water-tight.   These fragile barks are so light, that the fishermen can carry them on their heads, or over their shoulders, with ease.   It is surprising with what skill they can manage these ticklish boats, which to the uninitiated are exceedingly dangerous ; for they are so "crank," that a slight oscillation is sufficient to upset them.   The coracle is navigated by means of two short paddles, the blades of which are broad.   In experienced hands, there is little or no danger of being "capsized ;" we have known several old fishermen on the Wye, at Monmouth, who had been engaged in fishing all their lives without ever meeting with an accident.   Several of these men could not even swim. The chief art in the navigation of the *coracle* is to preserve a steady *equilibrium,* and to sit in the centre perfectly *quiet;* if you have sufficient nerve to do this, you may safely descend the rapids of rivers without danger, as these boats ride like a cork on the water.

NOTE 3, *page* 213.—(DAVYDD-AP-GWILYM.)—In our brief sketch of the history of the Abbey of Strata Florida, we alluded to the traditionary assertion that this celebrated bard lies interred under one of the aged yew-trees in the Abbey cemetery. Davydd-ap-Gwilym flourished in the thirteenth century, and his poetry has always been considered by Welsh scholars as being of a high standard of excellence. The following beautiful ode " To the Sky-lark" is, as Captain Medwin observes, "steeped in inspirntion," and we are indebted to that author for a version of it from the original Welsh. The opening line, " Hail, thou ! who singest at Heaven's gate !" has, however, a marvellous affinity to Shakspere.

"I'R EHEDYDD."

"TO THE SKY-LARK."

" HAIL, thou ! who singest at Heaven's gate !
    Blest chorister of May !
Before the throne of God elate,
    Who lov'st on joyous wings to soar and play
    With homeless clouds and winds ; forerunner of the day !

" Would I, as thou, up yon steep height
    Could climb, as blithe and free ;
View the first blush of morning light,
    Make the pale westering moon my love, and be,
    ˙. 'Twixt darkness and the dawn—a link of melody.

" No lover of the woods thou art,
    Thou dread'st no archer's war ;
Thou dwell'st as Seraphs do, apart ;
    Fill with thy warblings earth and sea, and air,
    And float, the stars among, a spirit and a star."

Index.

THE END.